IF YOU COULD SEE ME NOW

Before embarking on her writing career, Cecelia Ahern completed a degree in Journalism and Media Communications. At twenty-one years old, she wrote her first novel, *PS I Love You* which instantly became an international bestseller and was adapted into a major motion picture starring Hilary Swank. Her successive novels, *Where Rainbows End*, *If You Could See Me Now*, *A Place Called Here*, *Thanks for the Memories* and *The Gift* were also bestsellers. Her books are published in forty-six countries and have collectively sold over nine million copies. Cecelia has also co-created the hit ABC Network comedy series *Samantha Who?* which stars Christina Applegate. Cecelia lives in Dublin, Ireland.

To sign up for the   as newsletter and disc   s interviews, photo   www.cecelia-ahern.c

Praise for *If You Could See Me Now*:

'A beautifully written love story.'   *Closer*

'A contemporary fairytale.'   *Irish Times*

'An enchanting blend of magic and whimsy.'   *Daily Mail*

CECELIA AHERN

If You Could See Me Now

HARPER

Harper
HarperCollinsPublishers
77–85 Fulham Palace Road,
Hammersmith, London W6 8JB

www.harpercollins.co.uk

This paperback edition 2009
1

First published in Great Britain by
HarperCollinsPublishers 2005

A catalogue record for this book is
available from the British Library

ISBN: 978 0 00 785020 4

Set in Sabon by Palimpsest Book Production Limited,
Grangemouth, Stirlingshire

Printed and bound in Great Britain by
Clays Limited, St Ives plc

Mixed Sources
Product group from well-managed
forests and other controlled sources
www.fsc.org Cert no. SW-COC-1806
© 1996 Forest Stewardship Council

FSC is a non-profit international organisation established to promote the
responsible management of the world's forests. Products carrying the FSC
label are independently certified to assure consumers that they come
from forests that are managed to meet the social, economic
and ecological needs of present and future generations.

Find out more about HarperCollins and the environment at
www.harpercollins.co.uk/green

For Georgina, who believes …

Infinite thank yous to my family, Mimmie, Dad, Georgina and Nicky for everything – I couldn't narrow that down if I tried. To David, the best coffee-maker around – thanks for checking on me every few hours and for believing so passionately in this book. Huge thanks to the endlessly encouraging you-know-what agent Marianne for the buns, tea and advice, and thank you Pat and Vicki at the you-know-what agency for taking care of you-know-what.

Thank you Lynne and Maxine and all at HarperCollins for your faith in me and for all your hard work.

To my readers, old and new, I hope this is as good for you as it was for me – an absolute joy to work on.

Most importantly thanks to Ivan for keeping me company in my office until all hours. Do you think they will ever believe our story?

Chapter 1

It was a Friday morning in June when I first became best friends with Luke. It was 9.15 a.m., to be precise and I happen to know exactly what time it was because I looked at my watch. I don't know why I did, because I didn't need to be anywhere by any specific time. But I believe there's a reason for everything so perhaps I checked my watch at that time just so I could tell you my story properly. Details are important in storytelling, aren't they?

I was glad I met Luke that morning because I was a bit down after having to leave my old best friend, Barry. He couldn't see me any more. But it doesn't really matter because he's happier now and that's what's important, I suppose. Having to leave my best friends is all part of my job. It's not a very nice part, but I believe in finding a positive side in everything, so the way I see it is, if I didn't have to leave my best friends then I wouldn't be able to make new ones. And making new friends is my favourite part by far. That's probably why I was offered the job.

We'll get on to what my job is in just a moment but first I want to tell you about the morning I first met my best friend Luke.

I closed the gate to Barry's front garden behind me and I started walking, and for absolutely no reason at all I took the first left, then a right, then a left, went straight on for a while, took another right and I ended up beside a housing estate called Fuchsia Lane. It must have been called that because of the fuchsias growing all around the place. They grow wild here. Sorry, when I say 'here' I mean a town called Baile na gCroíthe which is in County Kerry. That's in Ireland.

Baile na gCroíthe somewhere along the line ended up being known in English as Hartstown, but as a direct translation from Irish it means the Town of Hearts. Which I think sounds nicer.

I was glad I ended up back here again; I had done a few jobs here when I was starting out but hadn't returned for years. My work takes me all over the country, sometimes even overseas when my friends take me away on holidays which just goes to show, no matter where you are, you always need a best friend.

Fuchsia Lane had twelve houses, six on each side, and all were different. The cul-de-sac was really busy with lots of people buzzing about. It was a Friday morning, remember, and June too, so it was really sunny and bright and everyone was in a good mood. Well, not *everyone*.

There were lots of children playing on the road, cycling, chasing, enjoying hopscotch, tip the can and loads of other stuff. You could hear the sounds of delighted screams and laughter coming from them. I suppose they were happy to be on their school holidays too. As much as they seemed really nice and all, I just wasn't drawn to them. You see, I can't just make friends with anyone. That's not what my job is about.

A man was cutting the grass in his front garden, and a woman tending to the flowerbed with big mucky gloves on her hands. There was a lovely smell of freshly cut grass and the sound of the lady snipping, clipping, cropping and pruning was like music in the air. In the next garden a man whistled a tune I wasn't familiar with while he pointed the garden hose towards his car and watched as the soapy suds slithered down the side, revealing a new sparkle. Every now and again he whipped round and sprayed water on two little girls who were dressed in yellow and black striped swimsuits. They looked like big bumble bees. I loved hearing them giggling so much.

In the next driveway a boy and girl were playing hopscotch. I observed them for a spell but none of them responded to my interest so I kept on moving. I walked by children playing in every garden yet none of them saw me or invited me to play. People on bicycles and skateboards, and remote controlled cars were whizzing by, oblivious to me. I was beginning to think that coming to Fuchsia Lane was a bit of a mistake, which was rather confusing because usually I was so good at choosing places and there were so many children here. I sat down on the garden wall of the last house and began to think about where I could have taken a wrong turn.

After a few minutes, I came to the conclusion that I was in the right area after all. I very rarely take wrong turns. I spun on my backside to face the house behind the garden wall. There was no action in this garden so I sat and studied the house. It had two storeys and a garage with an expensive car parked outside that glistened in the sun. A plaque on the garden wall beneath me said 'Fuchsia House', and the house had blooming fuchsia climbing up the wall, clinging to the brown bricks over the front door and reaching all the way up to the roof. It looked pretty. Fractions of the house had brown bricks and other sections had been painted a honey colour. Some of the windows were square and others were circles. It was really unusual. It had a fuchsia-coloured front door with two long windows with frosted glass in the top two panels, a huge brass knocker and letter box beneath; it looked like two eyes, a nose and a mouth smiling at me. I waved and smiled back just in case. Well, you can never be too sure these days.

Just as I was studying the face of the front door, it opened and was slammed shut rather loudly and angrily by a boy who came running outside. He had a big red fire engine in his right hand and a police car in his left hand. I love red fire engines; they're my favourite. The boy jumped off the front step of the porch and ran to the grass where he skidded to his knees. He got grass stains all down his black tracksuit bottoms, which made me laugh. Grass stains are so much fun because they never come out. My old friend Barry and I used to slide all of the time. Anyway, the little boy started crashing his fire engine against his police car and making all these noises with his mouth. He was good at the noises. Barry and I always used to do that too. It's fun pretending to do things that don't usually happen in real life.

The boy rammed the police car into the red fire engine and the head fireman, who was clinging to the ladder at the side of the truck, slid off. I laughed out loud and the boy looked up.

He actually looked at me. Right into my eyes.

'Hi,' I said, nervously clearing my throat and shifting from one foot to the other. I was wearing my favourite blue Converse runners and they still had grass stains on the white rubber tips from when Barry and I went sliding. I started to run the rubber tip against the brick garden wall to try to scrape it off and thought about what to say next. As much as making friends is my favourite thing to do I still get a bit nervous about it. There's always that scary chance that people won't like me and it gives me the collywobbles. I've been lucky so far but it would be silly to presume that the same thing will happen every time.

'Hi,' the boy replied, fixing the fireman back onto the ladder.

'What's your name?' I asked, kicking my foot against the wall on front of me and scraping the rubber tip. The grass stains still wouldn't come off.

The boy studied me for a while, looked me up and down as though trying to decide whether to tell me his name or not. This is the part of my job I absolutely loathe. It's tough wanting to be friends with someone and them not wanting the same back. That happens sometimes but in the end they always come round because, whether they know it or not, they want me to be there.

The boy had white-blond hair and big blue eyes. I knew his face from somewhere but couldn't quite think where.

Finally he spoke. 'My name's Luke. What's yours?'

I shoved my hands deep into my pockets and concentrated on kicking my right foot against the garden wall. I was making parts of the bricks crumble and fall to the ground. Without looking at him I said, 'Ivan.'

'Hi, Ivan,' he smiled. He had no front teeth.

'Hi, Luke,' I smiled back.

I have all mine.

'I like your fire engine. My bes— my old best friend Barry used to have one just like it and we used to play with it all the time. It's got a stupid name, though, because it can't drive through fire because it melts,' I explained, still keeping my hands shoved into my pockets, causing my shoulders to hunch up past my ears. It made things a little quieter so I took my hands out of my pocket just so I could hear what Luke was saying.

Luke rolled on the grass laughing. 'You put your fire engine through *fire*?' he screeched.

'Well, it is called a *fire* engine, isn't it?' I replied defensively.

Luke rolled onto his back, kicked his feet in the air and hooted. 'No, you dummy! Fire engines are for putting *out* fires!'

I thought about that one for a while. 'Hmm. Well, I'll tell you what puts out fire engines, Luke,' I explained matter-of-factly. 'Water does.'

Luke hit himself lightly on the side of the head, screamed 'Doh!', made his eyes go cockeyed and then fell over on the grass.

I started laughing. Luke was really funny.

'Do you want to come and play?' He raised his eyebrows questioningly.

I grinned. 'Of course, Luke. Playing is my favourite!' and I jumped over the garden wall and joined him on the grass.

'What age are you?' He looked at me suspiciously. 'You look like you're the same age as my aunt,' he frowned, 'and my aunt doesn't like to play with my fire engine.'

I shrugged. 'Well, then your aunt is a boring old gnirob!'

'A *gnirob*!' Luke screamed with mirth. 'What's a gnirob?'

'Someone who's *boring*,' I said, scrunching my nose up and saying the word like it was a disease. I liked saying words backwards; it was like inventing my own language.

'Boring,' Luke repeated after me and scrunched up his nose, 'uugh.'

'What age are you anyway?' I asked Luke as I crashed the police car into the fire engine. The fireman fell off the ladder again. 'You look like *my* aunt,' I accused him, and Luke fell about the place. He had a loud laugh.

'I'm only six, Ivan! And I'm not a *girl*!'

'Oh.' I don't really have an aunt but I just said it to make him laugh. 'Well, there's nothing *only* about being six.'

Just as I was about to ask him what his favourite cartoon was, the front door opened and I heard screaming. Luke went white and I looked up to where he was faced.

'SAOIRSE, GIVE ME BACK MY KEYS!' a voice yelled desperately. A flustered-looking woman, red in the cheeks, frantic eyes, with long unwashed red hair swinging in strands around her face, came running out of the house alone. Another shriek from the voice in the house behind caused her to stumble in her platforms on the step of the front porch. She cursed loudly and reached out to the wall of the house for balance. Looking up, she stared in the direction of where Luke and I were sitting at the end of the garden. Her mouth widened into a smile to reveal a set of crooked yellow teeth. I crawled back a few more inches. I noticed Luke did too. She gave Luke the thumbs-up and croaked, 'See ya, kiddo.' She let go of the wall, wavered slightly and walked quickly to the car parked in the driveway.

'SAOIRSE!' The voice of the person inside the house screamed again. 'I'M CALLING THE GARDAÍ IF YOU SET ONE FOOT IN THAT CAR!'

The red-haired woman snorted, pressed the car keys and the lights flashed and beeped. She opened the door, climbed in, banged her head on the side, cursed loudly again and slammed the door shut behind her. I could hear the doors locking from where I was at the end of the garden. A few kids on the road stopped playing and stared at the scene unfolding before them.

Finally the owner of the mystery voice came running outside with a phone in her hand. She looked very different from the other lady. Her hair was tied back neatly and tightly at the back of her head. She wore a smart grey trouser suit, which didn't match the high-pitched, un-controlled voice she currently had. She too was red in the face and out of breath. Her chest heaved up and down rapidly as she tried to run as quickly as she could in her high heels to the car. She danced around beside the car, first trying the door handle and, when finding it locked, threatened to dial 999.

'I'm calling the gardaí, Saoirse,' she warned, waving the phone at the window on the driver's side.

Saoirse just grinned from inside the car and started up the engine. The lady with the phone's voice cracked as she pleaded with her to get out of the car. Jumping from foot to foot, she looked like there was somebody else bubbling under her own flesh, trying to get out, like the Incredible Hulk.

Saoirse sped off down the long cobble-stoned driveway. Halfway down, she slowed the car. The woman with the phone relaxed her shoulders and looked relieved. Instead of stopping completely, the car crawled along as the window of the driver's side was lowered and two fingers appeared out of it, held up proud and high for all to see.

'Ah, she'll be back in two minutes, so,' I said to Luke, and he looked at me oddly.

The woman with the phone watched in fright as the car sped off again down the road, narrowly missing hitting a child on the road. A few hairs escaped from the tight bun on her head, as though attempting to chase the car themselves.

Luke lowered his head and quietly put the fireman back on his ladder. The woman let out an exasperated screech, threw her hands in the air and turned on her heel. There was a crack as the heel of her shoe became lodged between the cobbles of the drive. The woman shook her leg wildly, growing more frustrated by the second, and eventually the shoe flew out, but the heel remained lodged between the crack.

'FUUUUCCCK!' she yelled. Hobbling on one high heel and what was now one flat pump, she made her way back up the front porch. The fuchsia door was slammed shut and she was swallowed back up by the house. The windows, door knob and the letter box smiled at me again and I smiled back.

'Who are you smiling at?' Luke asked with a frown on his face.

'The door,' I replied, thinking it an obvious answer.

He just stared at me with the same frown, his mind evidently lost in the thoughts of what he had just seen, and the oddity of smiling at a door.

We could see the woman with the phone through the glass of the front door, pacing the hall.

'Who is she?' I asked, turning to Luke.

He was clearly shaken.

'That's my aunt,' he almost whispered. 'She looks after me.'

'Oh,' I said. 'Who was the one in the car?'

Luke slowly pushed the fire engine through the grass, flattening the blades as he went along. 'Oh, her. That's Saoirse,' he said quietly. 'She's my mom.'

'Oh.' There was a silence and I could tell he was sad. 'Seer-sha,' I repeated the name, liking how it felt when I said it; like the wind blowing out of my mouth in one big gust or how the trees sounded when they talked to one another on windy days. 'Seeeeer-ssshaaaa . . .' I eventually stopped when Luke looked at me oddly.

I picked a buttercup out of the ground and held it under Luke's chin. A yellow glow appeared on his pale skin. 'You like butter,' I stated. 'So Saoirse's not your girlfriend then?'

Luke's face immediately lit up and he giggled. Not as much as before, though.

'Who's your friend Barry that you mentioned?' Luke asked, smashing into my car much harder than before.

'Barry McDonald is his name,' I smiled, remembering the games me and Barry used to play.

Luke's eyes lit up. 'Barry McDonald is in my class in school!'

Then it clicked. 'I knew I knew your face from somewhere, Luke. I used to see you everyday when I went to school with Barry.'

'You went to school with Barry?' he said, surprised.

'Yeah, school was fun with Barry,' I laughed.

Luke narrowed his eyes, 'Well, I didn't see you there.'

I started laughing. 'Well, *of course* you didn't *see* me, you silly sod,' I said matter-of-factly.

Chapter 2

Elizabeth's heart hammered loudly against her chest, as, having slipped on another pair of shoes, she paced the long maple-floored hall of her home. With the phone pressed hard between her ear and shoulder, her mind was a blizzard of thoughts as she listened to the shrill ring tone in her ear.

She stopped pacing long enough to stare at her reflection in the mirror. Her brown eyes widened with horror. Rarely did she allow herself to look so bedraggled. *So out of control.* Strands of her chocolate-brown hair were fleeing from the tight French pleat, causing her to appear as though she had placed her fingers in an electric socket. Mascara nestled in the lines under her eyes; her lipstick had faded, leaving only her plum-coloured lipliner as a frame, and her foundation clung to the dry patches of her olive skin. Gone was the usual pristine look. This caused her heart to beat faster, the panic to accelerate.

Breathe, Elizabeth, just breathe, she told herself. She ran a trembling hand over her tousled hair, forcing the wild hairs back down. She wiped the mascara away with a wet finger, pursed her lips together, smoothed down her suit jacket and cleared her throat. It was simply a momentary lapse of concentration on her part, that was all. Not to happen again. She transferred the phone to her left ear and noticed the impression of her Claddagh earring against her neck. Such was the pressure of her shoulder's grip on the phone against her skin.

Finally someone answered and Elizabeth turned her back on the mirror to stand to attention. Back to business.

'Hello, Baile na gCroíthe Garda Station.'

Elizabeth winced as she recognised the voice on the phone. 'Hi, Marie, Elizabeth here . . . again. Saoirse's gone off with the car,' she paused, 'again.'

There was a gentle sigh on the other end of the phone. 'How long ago, Elizabeth?'

Elizabeth sat down on the bottom stair and settled in for the usual line of questioning. She closed her eyes, only meaning to rest them briefly, but at the relief of blocking everything out she kept them closed. 'Just five minutes ago.'

'Right. Did she say where she was going?'

'The moon,' she replied matter-of-factly.

'Excuse me?' Marie asked.

'You heard me. She said she was going to the moon,' Elizabeth said firmly. 'Apparently people will understand her there.'

'The moon,' Marie repeated.

'Yes,' Elizabeth replied, feeling irritated. 'You could perhaps start looking for her on the motorway. I would imagine that if you were heading to the moon that would be the quickest way to get there, wouldn't you? Although I'm not entirely sure which exit she would take. Whichever is more northerly, I suppose. She could be headed north-east to Dublin, or, who knows, she could be making her way to Cork; perhaps they've a plane that can take her off this planet. Either way, I'd check the motor—'

'Relax, Elizabeth; you know I have to ask.'

'I know,' Elizabeth tried to calm herself again. She was missing an important meeting right now. Important for her, important for her interior design business. Luke's babysitter was standing in as a replacement for his nanny, Edith. Edith had left a few weeks ago for the three months of travelling the world she had threatened Elizabeth with for the past six years, leaving the young babysitter inexperienced to the ways of Saoirse. She had rung her at work in a panic . . . again . . . and Elizabeth had to drop everything . . . again . . . and rush home . . . again. But she shouldn't be surprised that this had happened . . . again. She was, however, surprised that Edith, apart from the current trip to Australia, was still turning up to work every day. Six years she had been helping Elizabeth with Luke, six years of drama, and still after all her years of loyalty, Elizabeth expected a phone call or her letter of resignation practically every day. Being Luke's nanny came with a lot of baggage. Then again, so did being Luke's adoptive parent.

'Elizabeth, are you still there?'

'Yes.' Her eyes shot open. She was losing concentration. 'Sorry, what did you say?'

'I asked you what car she took.'

Elizabeth rolled her eyes and made a face at the phone. 'The same one, Marie. The same bloody car as last week, and the week before and the week before that,' she snapped.

Marie remained firm, 'Which is the—'

'BMW,' she interrupted. 'The same damn black BMW 330 Cabriolet. Four wheels, two doors, one steering wheel, two wing mirrors, lights and—'

'A partridge in a pear tree,' Marie interrupted. 'What condition was she in?'

'Very shiny. I'd just washed her,' Elizabeth replied cheekily.

'Great, and what condition was Saoirse in?'

'The usual one.'

'Intoxicated.'

'That's the one.' Elizabeth stood up and walked down the hall to the kitchen. Her sun trap. Her heels against the marble floor echoed loudly in the empty high-ceilinged room. Everything was in its place. The room was hot from the sun's glare through the glass of the conservatory. Elizabeth's tired eyes squinted in the brightness. The spotless kitchen gleamed, the black granite counter tops sparkled, the chrome fittings mirrored the bright day. A stainless steel and walnut heaven. She headed straight to the espresso machine. Her saviour. Needing an injection of life into her exhausted body, she opened the kitchen cabinet and took out a small beige coffee cup. Before closing the press she turned a cup round so that the handle was on the right side like all the others. She slid open the long steel cutlery drawer, noticed a knife in the fork's compartment, put it back in its rightful place, retrieved a spoon and slid it shut.

From the corner of her eye she saw the hand towel messily strewn over the handle of the cooker. She threw the crumpled cloth into the utility room, retrieved a fresh towel from the neat pile in the press, folded it exactly in half and draped it over the cooker handle. Everything had its place.

'Well, I haven't changed my licence plate in the past week so yes, it's still the same,' she replied with boredom to another of Marie's pointless questions. She placed the steaming espresso cup on a marble coaster to protect the glass kitchen table. She smoothed out her trousers, removed a piece of fluff from her jacket, sat down in the conservatory and looked out at her long garden and the rolling green hills beyond that seemed to stretch on for ever. Forty shades of green, golds and browns.

She breathed in the rich aroma of her steaming espresso and immediately felt revived. She pictured her sister racing over the hills with the top down on Elizabeth's convertible, arms in the air, eyes closed, flame-red hair blowing in the wind, believing she was free. Saoirse meant freedom in Irish. The name had been chosen by their mother in her last desperate attempt to make the duties of motherhood she despised so much seem less like a punishment. Her wish was for her second daughter to bring her freedom from the shackles of marriage, motherhood, responsibility . . . reality.

Her mother had met her father when she was sixteen. She was travelling through the town with a group of poets, musicians and dreamers, and got talking to Brendan Egan, a farmer in the local pub. He was twelve years her senior and was enthralled by her mysterious wild ways and carefree nature. She was flattered. And so they married. At eighteen they had their first child, Elizabeth. As it turned out, her mother couldn't be tamed and found it increasingly frustrating being held in the sleepy town nestled in the hills she had only ever intended to pass through. A crying baby and sleepless nights drove her further and further away in her head. Dreams of her own personal freedom became confused with her reality and she started to go missing for days at a time. She went exploring, discovering places and other people.

Elizabeth, at twelve years of age, looked after herself and her silent, brooding father and didn't ask when her mother would be home because she knew in her heart that she would eventually return, cheeks flushed, eyes bright, and speaking breathlessly of the world and all it had to offer. She would waft into their lives like a fresh summer breeze, bringing excitement and hope. The feel of their bungalow farmhouse always changed when she returned; the four walls absorbed her enthusiasm. Elizabeth would sit at the end of her mother's bed, listening to stories, giddy with delight. This ambience would last for only a few days until her mother quickly tired of sharing stories rather than making new ones.

Often she brought back mementoes such as shells, stones, leaves. Elizabeth could recall a vase of long fresh grasses that sat in the centre of the dining-room table as though they were the most exotic plants ever created. When asked about the field they were pulled from, her mother just winked and tipped her nose, promising Elizabeth that she would understand some day. Her father would sit silently in his chair by the fireplace, reading his paper but never turning the page. He was as lost in her world of words as she was.

When Elizabeth was twelve years old her mother became pregnant again and, despite the new-born baby being named Saoirse, this child didn't offer the freedom her mother craved, and so she set off on another expedition. And didn't return. Her father, Brendan, had no interest in the young life that had driven his wife away so he waited in silence for her in his chair by the fire. Reading his paper but never turning the page. For years. For ever. Soon Elizabeth's heart grew weary of awaiting her mother's return and Saoirse became Elizabeth's responsibility.

Saoirse had inherited her father's Celtic looks of strawberry-blonde hair and fair skin, while Elizabeth was the image of her mother. Olive skin, chocolate hair, almost black eyes; in their blood from the Spanish influence thousands of years before. Elizabeth resembled her mother more and more with every passing day and she knew her father found that difficult. She grew to hate herself for it, and along with making the effort of trying to have conversations with her father, she tried even harder to prove to her father and to herself that she was nothing like her mother – that she was capable of loyalty.

When Elizabeth finished school at eighteen she was faced with the dilemma of having to move to Cork to attend university. A decision that took all her courage to make. Her father regarded her acceptance of the course as abandonment; he saw any friendship she created with anyone as abandonment. He craved attention, always demanding to be the only person in his daughters' lives, as though that would prevent them from moving away from him. Well, he almost succeeded and certainly was part of the reason for Elizabeth's lack of a social life or circle of friends. She had been conditioned to walk away when polite conversation was started, knowing she would pay for any unnecessary time spent away from the farm with sullen words and disapproving glares. In any case, looking after Saoirse as well as going to school was a full-time job. Brendan accused her of being like her mother, of thinking she was above him and superior to Baile na gCroíthe. She found the small town claustrophobic and felt the dull farmhouse was dipped in darkness, with no sense of time. It was as though even the grandfather clock in the hall was waiting for her mother to return.

'And, Luke, where is he?' Marie asked over the phone, bringing Elizabeth swiftly back to the present.

Elizabeth replied bitterly. 'Do you really think Saoirse would take him with her?'

Silence.

Elizabeth sighed. 'He's here.'

The name Saoirse had brought more than something to call Elizabeth's sister by. It had given her an identity, a way of life. Everything the name represented was passed into her blood. She was fiery, independent, wild and free. She followed the pattern of the mother she could not remember, so much that Elizabeth almost felt as though she were watching her mother. But she kept losing sight of her. Saoirse became pregnant at sixteen and no one knew who the father was, not least Saoirse. Once she had the baby she didn't care much for naming him but eventually took to calling him Lucky. Another wish. So Elizabeth named him Luke. And once again, at the age of twenty-eight, Elizabeth took responsibility for a child.

There was never as much as a flicker of recognition in Saoirse's eyes when she looked at Luke. It startled Elizabeth to see that there was no bond, no connection at all. Elizabeth had never planned on having children – in fact she had made a pact with herself *never* to have children. She had raised herself and raised her sister; she had no desires to raise anybody else. It was time to look after herself. But at twenty-eight years old, after having slaved away at school and college, she had been successful in starting up her own interior design business. Her hard work meant that she was the only member of the family capable of providing a good life for Luke. She had reached her goals by being in control, maintaining order, not losing sight of herself, always being realistic, believing in fact and not dreams, and above all applying herself and working hard. Her mother and sister had taught her that she wouldn't get anywhere by following wistful dreams and having unrealistic hopes.

So now she was thirty-four years old and living alone with Luke in a house that she loved. A house she had bought, and was paying for, all by herself. A house she had made her haven, the place she could retreat to and feel safe. Alone because love was one of those feelings that you could never control. And she needed to be in control. She had loved before, had been loved, had tasted what it was to dream and had felt what it was to dance on air. She had also learned what it was to land back on the earth with a cruel thud. Having to take care of her sister's child had sent her love away and there had been no one since. She had learned not to lose control of her feelings again.

The front door banged shut and she heard the patter of little feet running down the hall.

'Luke!' she called, putting her hand over the receiver.

'Yeah?' he asked innocently, blue eyes and blond hair appearing round the doorpost.

'*Yes*, not yeah,' Elizabeth corrected him sternly. Her voice was full of the authority she had become a pro at over the years.

'*Yes*,' he repeated.

'What are you doing?'

Luke stepped into the hall and Elizabeth's eyes immediately went to his grass-stained knees.

'Me and Ivan are just playing the computer,' he explained.

'Ivan and I,' she corrected him, and continued listening to Marie at the other end of the phone arranging to send a garda car out. Luke looked at his aunt and returned to the playroom.

'Hold on a minute,' Elizabeth shouted down the phone, finally registering what Luke had just told her. She jumped up from her chair, bumping the table leg and spilling her espresso onto the glass. She swore. The black wrought-iron legs of the chair screeched against the marble. Holding the phone to her chest, she raced down the long hall to the playroom. She tucked her head round the corner and saw Luke sitting on the floor, eyes glued to the TV screen. Here and his bedroom were the only rooms in the house she allowed his toys. Taking care of a child had not succeeded in changing her as many thought it would; he hadn't softened her views in any way. She had visited many of Luke's friends' houses, picking him up or dropping him off, so full of toys lying around, they tripped up everyone who dared walk in their path. She reluctantly had cups of coffee with the mothers while sitting on teddies, surrounded by bottles, formula and nappies. But not in her home. Edith had been told the rules at the beginning of their working relationship and she had followed them. As Luke grew up and understood his aunt's ways, he obediently respected her wishes and contained his playing to the one room she had dedicated to his needs.

'Luke, who's Ivan?' Elizabeth asked, eyes darting around the room. 'You know you can't be bringing strangers home,' she said, worried.

'He's my new friend,' he replied, zombie-like, not moving his eyes from the beefed-up wrestler body-slamming his opponent on the screen.

'You know I insist on meeting your friends first before you bring them home. Where is he?' Elizabeth questioned, pushing open the door and stepping into Luke's space. She hoped to God that this friend would be better than the last little terror who had decided to draw a picture of his happy family in magic marker on her wall, which had since been painted over.

'Over there.' Luke nodded his head in the direction of the window, still not budging his eyes.

Elizabeth walked towards the window and looked out at the front garden. She crossed her arms. 'Is he hiding?'

Luke pressed Pause on his computer keypad and finally moved his eyes away from the two wrestlers on the screen. His face crinkled in confusion. 'He's right there!' He pointed at the beanbag at Elizabeth's feet.

Elizabeth's eyes widened as she stared at the beanbag. 'Where?'

'Right there,' he repeated.

Elizabeth blinked back at him. She raised her arms questioningly.

'Beside you, on the beanbag.' Luke's voice became louder with anxiety. He stared at the yellow corduroy beanbag as though willing his friend to appear.

Elizabeth followed his gaze.

'See him?' He dropped the control pad and stood up quickly.

This was followed by a tense silence in which Elizabeth could feel Luke's hatred for her emanating from his body. She could tell what he was thinking: why couldn't she just see him, why couldn't she just play along just this once, why couldn't she ever pretend? She swallowed the lump in her throat and looked around the room to see if she really was missing his friend in some way. Nothing.

She leaned down to be on an even level with him and her knees cracked. 'There's no one else but you and me in this room,' she whispered softly. Somehow saying it quietly made it easier. Easier for herself or Luke, she didn't know.

Luke's cheeks flushed and his chest heaved faster. He stood in the centre of the room, surrounded by computer keypad wires, with his little hands down by his side, looking helpless. Elizabeth's heart hammered in her chest as she silently begged, *please do not be like your mother, please do not be like your mother.* She knew only too well how the world of fantasy could steal you away.

Finally Luke exploded and, staring into space, demanded, 'Ivan, say something to her!'

There was a silence as he looked into space and then giggled hysterically. He looked back at Elizabeth and his smile quickly faded when he noticed her lack of response. 'Do you not see him?' he squealed nervously. Then, more angrily, repeated, 'Why don't you see him?'

'OK, OK!' Elizabeth tried not to panic. She stood back up to her own level. A level where she had control. She couldn't see him and her brain refused to let her pretend. She wanted to get out of the room quickly. She lifted her leg to step over the beanbag and stopped herself, instead choosing to walk round it. Once at the door, she glanced around one last time to see if she could spot the mystery Ivan. No sign.

Luke shrugged, sat down and continued playing his wrestling game.

'I'm putting some pizza on now, Luke.'

Silence. What else should she say? It was at moments like this she realised that reading all the parenting manuals in the world never helped. Good parenting came from the heart, was instinctive, and not for the first time she worried she was letting Luke down.

'It will be ready in twenty minutes,' she finished awkwardly.

'What?' Luke pressed Pause again and faced the window.

'I said it will be ready in twen—'

'No, not you,' Luke said, once again being sucked into the world of video games. 'Ivan would like some too. He said pizza is his favourite.'

'Oh.' Elizabeth swallowed helplessly.

'With olives,' Luke continued.

'But, Luke, you hate olives.'

'Yeah, but Ivan loves them. He says they're his favourite.'

'Oh . . .'

'Thanks,' Luke said to his aunt, looked to the beanbag, gave the thumbs-up, smiled, then looked away again.

Elizabeth slowly backed out of the playroom. She realised she was still holding the phone to her chest. 'Marie, are you still there?' She chewed on her nail and stared at the closed playroom door, wondering what to do.

'I thought you'd gone off to the moon as well. I was about to send a car over to your house too,' Marie chuckled.

Marie mistook Elizabeth's silence for anger and apologised quickly. 'Anyway, you were right, Saoirse *was* headed to the moon but luckily she decided to stop off on the way to refuel. Refuelling herself, more like. Your car was found blocking the main street with the engine still running and the driver's door wide open. You're lucky Paddy found it when he did before someone took off with it.'

'Let me guess. The car was outside the pub.'

'Correct.' Marie paused. 'Do you want to press charges?'

Elizabeth sighed. 'No. Thanks, Marie.'

'Not a problem. We'll have someone bring the car home to you.'

'What about Saoirse?' Elizabeth paced the hall. 'Where is she?'

'We'll just keep her here for a while, Elizabeth.'

'I'll come get her,' Elizabeth said quickly.

'No,' Marie insisted. 'Let me get back to you about that. She needs to calm down before she goes anywhere yet.'

From inside the playroom Elizabeth heard Luke laughing and talking away to himself.

'Actually, Marie,' she added with a weak smile, 'while we're on the phone, tell whoever's bringing the car to bring a shrink with them. It seems Luke is imagining friends now . . .'

Inside the playroom Ivan rolled his eyes and wiggled his body down further into the beanbag. He had heard her on the phone. Ever since he had started this job, parents had been calling him that and it was really beginning to bother him. There was nothing imaginary about him whatsoever.

They just couldn't see him.

Chapter 3

It was really nice of Luke to invite me to lunch that day. When I said that pizza was my favourite I hadn't actually intended being asked to stay to eat it. But how can you say no to the treat of *pizza* on a *Friday*? That's a cause for double celebration. However, I got the impression from the incident in the playroom that his aunt didn't like me very much, but I'm not at all surprised because that's usually the way it goes. The parents always think that making food for me is a waste because they always just end up throwing it out. But it's tricky for me – I mean, you try eating your dinner squashed in a tiny place at the table while everyone looks at you and wonders whether the food is going to disappear or not. I eventually get so paranoid that I can't eat and just have to leave the food on the plate.

Not that I'm complaining – being invited to dinner is nice but the grown-ups never quite put the same amount of food on my plate as everyone else's. It's never even half as much food as the rest and they always say things like, 'Oh, I'm sure Ivan's not that hungry today anyway.' I mean, how would they know? They never even ask. I'm usually sandwiched between whoever my best friend is at the time and some annoying older brother or sister who steals my food when no one's looking.

They forget to give me things like serviettes, cutlery, and they sure aren't generous with the wine. (Sometimes they just give me an empty plate and tell my best friends that invisible people eat invisible food. I mean, *please*, does the invisible wind blow invisible trees?) I usually get a glass of water and that's only when I ask my friends politely. The grown-ups think it's weird that I need a glass of water with my food, but they make an even bigger deal about it when I want ice. I mean, the ice is free anyway and who doesn't like a cool drink on a hot day?

It's usually the moms who have conversations with me. Only they ask questions and don't listen to the answers, or pretend to everyone else that I've said something else just to make them all laugh. They even look at my chest when they're talking to me as if they expect me to be three feet tall. It's such a stereotype. For the record, I'm six foot tall and we don't really do the 'age' thing where I'm from; we come into existence as we are and grow spiritually rather than physically. It's our brains that do the growing. Let's just say my brain is pretty big by now, but there's always room for more growth. I've been doing this job for a long, long time and I'm good at it. I've never failed a friend.

The dads always say things under their breath to me when they think no one else is listening. For example, me and Barry went to Waterford on our summer holidays and we were lying on the beach on Brittas Bay and a lady walked by in a bikini. Barry's dad said under his breath, 'Getta loada that, Ivan.' The dads always think that I agree with them. They always tell my best friends that I told them things like, 'It's good to eat vegetables. Ivan told me to tell you to eat your broccoli,' and stupid things like that. My best friends know full well that's not what I would say.

But that's grown-ups for you.

Nineteen minutes and thirty-eight seconds later, Elizabeth called Luke for dinner. My tummy was grumbling and I was really looking forward to the pizza. I followed Luke down the long hall to the kitchen, looking in every room as we passed. The house was really quiet and our footsteps echoed. Every room was all white or beige, and so spotless that I began to get nervous about eating my pizza because I didn't want to make a mess. As far as I could see, not only was there no sign of a child living in the house, there was no sign of *anyone* living in the house. It didn't have what you'd call a homely feel.

I liked the kitchen, though. It was warm from the sun and because it was surrounded by glass, it felt like we were sitting in the garden. Kind of like a picnic. I noticed the table was set for two people so I waited until told where to sit. The plates were big, black and shiny, the sun through the window made the cutlery sparkle and the two crystal glasses reflect rainbow colours on the table. There was a bowl of salad and a glass jug of water with ice and lemon in the centre of the table. Everything was resting on black marble place mats. Looking at how everything glistened, I was afraid even to get the napkins dirty.

Elizabeth's chair legs squeaked against the tiles as she sat down. She put her serviette on her lap. I noticed she'd changed into a chocolate-brown tracksuit to match her hair and complement her skin. Luke's chair squeaked and he sat down. Elizabeth picked up the giant salad fork and spoon and began to gather leaves and baby tomatoes onto her plate. Luke watched her and frowned. Luke had a slice of margherita pizza on his plate. No olives. I shoved my hands deep into my pockets and shuffled nervously from foot to foot.

'Is something wrong, Luke?' Elizabeth asked, pouring dressing over her lettuce.

'Where's Ivan's place?'

Elizabeth paused, screwed the lid on tightly and put the jar back in the centre of the table. 'Now, Luke, let's not be silly,' she said light-heartedly, not looking at him. I knew she was afraid to look.

'I'm not being silly,' Luke frowned. 'You said Ivan could stay for dinner.'

'Yes, but where *is* Ivan?' She tried to keep the soft tone in her voice while sprinkling grated cheese over her salad. I could tell she didn't want this to become an issue. She would knock it on the head straight away and there would be no more talk of invisible friends.

'He's standing right beside you.'

Elizabeth slammed her knife and fork down and Luke jumped in his seat. She opened her mouth to silence him but was interrupted by the doorbell ringing. As soon as she left the room, Luke got up from his chair and took out a plate from the kitchen press. A big black one just the same as the other two. He placed a slice of pizza on the plate, took out the cutlery and a napkin and placed it on a third place mat beside him.

'That's your seat, Ivan,' he said happily, and took a bite out of his pizza. A piece of melted cheese dribbled down his chin, looking like yellow string.

To be truthful I wouldn't have sat down at the table if it wasn't for my grumbling stomach shouting at me to eat. I knew Elizabeth would be mad, but if I gobbled the food up real fast before she returned to the kitchen then she wouldn't even know.

'Want some olives on that?' Luke asked, wiping his tomatoey face on his sleeve.

I laughed and nodded. My mouth was watering.

Elizabeth hurried back into the kitchen just as Luke was reaching up to the shelf.

'What are you doing?' she asked, rummaging through a drawer for something.

'Getting the olives for Ivan,' Luke explained. 'He likes olives on his pizza, remember?'

She looked across to the kitchen table and saw that it had been set for three. She rubbed her eyes tiredly. 'Look, Luke, don't you think it's a waste of food, putting the olives on the pizza? You hate them and I'll only have to throw it out.'

'Well, it won't be a waste because Ivan will eat them, won't you, Ivan?'

'I sure will,' I said, licking my lips and rubbing my aching tummy.

'Well?' Elizabeth cocked an eyebrow. 'What did he say?'

Luke frowned. 'You mean you can't *hear* him either?' He looked at me and circled his forefinger around his temple, signalling to me that his aunt was crazy. 'He said he sure will eat them all.'

'How polite of him,' Elizabeth mumbled, continuing to rummage through the drawer. 'But you better make sure every last crumb is gone because it'll be the last time Ivan eats with us if not.'

'Don't worry, Elizabeth, I'll gobble it all right up,' I told her, taking a bite. I couldn't face not being able to eat with Luke and his aunt again. She had sad eyes, sad brown eyes, and I was convinced that I was going to make her happy by eating every last crumb. I ate quickly.

'Thanks, Colm,' Elizabeth said tiredly, taking the car keys from the garda. She circled the car slowly, inspecting the paintwork closely.

'There's no damage done,' Colm said, watching her.

'Not to the car, anyway,' she attempted a joke, patting the bonnet. She always felt embarrassed. At least once a week there was some sort of incident involving the gardaí and although they were never anything but professional and polite about the situation, she couldn't help feeling ashamed. She would work even harder in their presence to appear 'normal' just to prove that it wasn't her fault, and that it wasn't the *entire* family that was nuts. She wiped down the splashes of dried mud with a tissue.

Colm smiled at her sadly. 'She was arrested, Elizabeth.'

Elizabeth's head shot up, now fully alert. 'Colm,' she said, shocked, 'why?' They had never done that before. They had always just warned Saoirse off and then dropped her back to wherever she was staying. Unprofessional, Elizabeth knew, but in such a small town where everyone knew everyone, they had always just kept their eye on Saoirse, stopping her before she did anything incredibly stupid. But Elizabeth feared Saoirse had been warned once too often.

Colm fidgeted with the navy-blue cap in his hands. 'She was drink driving, Elizabeth, in a stolen car, and she doesn't even have a licence.'

Hearing those words, Elizabeth shivered. Saoirse was a danger. Why did she keep protecting her sister? When would the words finally sink in and she'd accept that they were right: that her sister would never be the angel she wished her to be?

'But the car wasn't stolen,' Elizabeth stammered, 'I told her that she c—'

'Don't, Elizabeth.' Colm's voice was firm.

She had to hold her hand across her mouth to stop herself. She took a deep breath and tried to regain control. 'She has to go to court?' Her voice was a whisper.

Colm looked down at the ground and moved a stone with his foot. 'Yes. It's not just about her harming herself now. She's a danger to others.'

Elizabeth swallowed hard and nodded. 'One more chance, Colm,' she gulped, feeling her pride disintegrating. 'Just give her one more chance . . . please.' The last word pained her to have to say. Every bone in her body pleaded with him. Elizabeth never asked for help. 'I'll keep an eye on her. I promise she won't be out of my sight for a minute. She's going to get better, you know. She just needs time to work things out.' Elizabeth could feel her voice shaking. Her knees trembled as she begged on behalf of her sister.

There was a sad tone in Colm's voice. 'It's already been done. We can't change it now.'

'What will the punishment be?' She felt sick.

'It depends on the judge on the day. It's her first offence – well, her first *known* offence. He may go lightly on her, then again he may not.' He shrugged then looked at his hands. 'And it also depends on what the garda who arrested her says.'

'Why?'

'Because if she was co-operative and gave no trouble it could make a difference, but then again . . .'

'It might not,' Elizabeth said worriedly. 'Well? Did she co-operate?'

Colm laughed lightly. 'Took two people to hold her down.'

'Damn it!' Elizabeth swore. 'Who arrested her?' She nibbled on her nails.

There was a silence before Colm spoke. 'I did.'

Her mouth dropped open. Colm had always had a soft spot for Saoirse. He was the one who was always on her side so the fact that he had arrested her rendered Elizabeth speechless. She chewed nervously on the inside of her mouth and the taste of blood slid down her throat. She didn't want people to start giving up on Saoirse.

'I'll do the best I can for her,' he said softly. 'Just try and keep her out of trouble until the hearing in a few weeks.'

Elizabeth, who realised she hadn't been breathing for the last few seconds, suddenly let her breath out. 'Thank you.' She couldn't say any more. Although she felt huge relief, she knew it was no victory. No one could protect her sister this time; she would have to face the consequences of her actions. But how was she expected to keep her eye on Saoirse when she didn't know where to begin looking for her? Saoirse couldn't stay with her and Luke – she was far too out of control to be around him – and her father had long since told her to move out and stay out.

'I'd better leave you at it so,' Colm said gently, fixed his cap back on his head, and he made his way down the cobbled drive.

Elizabeth sat on the porch, trying to rest her knocking knees, and looked at her mud-stained car. Why did Saoirse have to taint every-thing? Why was everything . . . every*one* Elizabeth loved chased away by her younger sister? She felt the clouds above push all that was between them and her onto her shoulders and she worried about what her father was going to do when they would undoubtedly bring Saoirse to his farm. She would give him five minutes before he rang Elizabeth complaining.

Inside the house, the phone started ringing and Elizabeth's heart sank even deeper. She rose from the porch, turned slowly on her heel and headed inside. When she got to the door the ringing had stopped and she spotted Luke sitting on the stairs with the phone pressed to his ear. She leaned against the wooden doorframe, arms folded, and watched him. A small smile crept onto her face. He was growing up so fast and she felt such a disconnection from the whole process, as though he was doing everything without her help, without the nurturing she knew she should be providing but that she felt awkward summoning. She knew she lacked that emotion – sometimes lacked emotion full stop – and everyday she wished the maternal instincts had come with the paperwork she signed. When Luke fell and cut his knee, her immediate response was to clean it and plaster his cut. To her that felt like enough, not dancing him around the room to stop his tears and slapping the ground like she'd watched Edith do.

'Hi, Granddad,' Luke was saying politely.

He paused to listen to his granddad on the other end.

'I'm just having lunch with Elizabeth and my new best friend, Ivan.'

Pause.

'A cheese and tomato pizza but Ivan likes olives on his.'

Pause.

'Olives, Granddad.'

Pause.

'No, I don't think you can grow them on the farm.'

Pause.

'O-L-I-V-E-S.' He spelled it out slowly.

Pause.

'Hold on, Granddad, my friend Ivan is telling me something.' Luke held the phone to his chest and looked into thin air, concentrating hard. Finally he lifted the phone back to his ear. 'Ivan said that the olive is a small, oily fruit that contains a pit. It's grown for its fruit and oil in subtropical zones.' He looked away and appeared to be listening. 'There are lots of types of olives.' He stopped talking, looked into the distance and then back to the phone. 'Underripe olives are always green but ripe olives are either green or black.' He looked away and listened to the silence again. 'Most tree-ripened olives are used for oil, the rest are brine- or salt-cured and are packed in olive oil or a brine or vinegar solution.' He looked into the distance. 'Ivan, what's brine?' There was silence then he nodded. 'Oh.'

Elizabeth raised her eyebrows and laughed nervously to herself. Since when had Luke become an expert on olives? He must have learned about them at school; he had a good memory for things like that. Luke paused and listened to the other end. 'Well, Ivan can't wait to meet you too.'

Elizabeth rolled her eyes and dashed towards Luke for the phone in case he said any more. Her father was confused enough as it was, at times, without having to explain the existence, or lack thereof, of an invisible boy.

'Hello,' Elizabeth said, grabbing the phone. Luke dragged his feet back to the kitchen. Irritation at the noise reared itself within Elizabeth again.

'Elizabeth,' said the stern formal voice, thick with a Kerry lilt, 'I just returned to find your sister lying on my kitchen floor. I gave her a boot but I can't figure out whether she's dead or not.'

Elizabeth sighed. 'That's not funny, and my sister is *your* daughter, you know.'

'Oh, don't give me that,' he said dismissively. 'I want to know what you're going to do about her. She can't stay here. The last time she did, she released the chickens from the coop and I spent all day getting them back in. And with my back and my hip, I can't be doing that any more.'

'I know, but she can't stay here either. She upsets Luke.'

'That child doesn't know enough about her to be upset. Half the time she forgets she's given birth to him. You can't have him all to yourself, you know.'

Elizabeth bit her tongue in rage. 'Half the time' was being overly generous. 'She can't come here,' she said more patiently than she felt. 'She was around earlier and took the car again. Colm just brought it back a few minutes ago. It's really serious this time.' She took a deep breath. 'They arrested her.'

Her father was silent for a moment and then he tutted. 'And rightly so. The experience will do her the world of good.' He quickly changed subject. 'Why weren't you at work today? Our Lord only intended us to rest on a Sunday.'

'That's the whole point. Today was a really important day for me at wor—'

'Well, your sister's come back to the land of the living and is outside trying to push the cows over again. Tell young Luke to come around with this new friend on Monday. We'll show him the farm.'

There was a click and the line went dead. Hello and goodbye were not her father's speciality; he still thought that mobile phones were some sort of futuristic alien-like technology designed to confuse the human race.

Elizabeth hung up the phone and made her way back to the kitchen. Luke sat alone at the table, holding his stomach and laughing hysterically. She took her seat and continued eating her salad. She wasn't one of those people who was interested in eating food; she only did it because she had to. Evenings spent over long dinners bored her and she never had much of an appetite – she was always too busy worrying about something or too hyper to be able to sit still and eat. She glanced at the plate directly ahead of her and to her surprise saw that it was empty.

'Luke?'

Luke stopped talking to himself and faced her. 'Yeah?'

'Yes,' she corrected him. 'What happened to the slice of pizza that was on that plate?'

Luke looked at the empty plate, looked back at Elizabeth like she was crazy and took a bite of his own pizza. 'Ivan ate it.'

'Don't speak with your mouth full,' she admonished him.

He spat the food out onto the plate. 'Ivan ate it.' He began laughing hysterically again at the mush on his plate that had been in his mouth.

Elizabeth's head began to ache. What had gotten into him? 'What about the olives?'

Sensing her anger, he waited until he swallowed the rest of his food before speaking. 'He ate them too. I told you olives were his favourite. Granddad wanted to know if he could grow olives on the farm,' Luke smiled and revealed his gums.

Elizabeth smiled back. Her father wouldn't even know what an olive was if it walked up to him and introduced itself. He wasn't into any of those 'fancy' foods; rice was about as exotic as he would get and even then he complained that the pieces were too small and that he'd be better off eating 'a crumblin' spud'.

Elizabeth sighed as she scraped the remainder of her food from her plate into the bin but not before checking through the rubbish to see if Luke had thrown the pizza and olives in. No sign. Luke usually had such a small appetite and would struggle to finish one large slice of pizza, never mind two. She presumed she would find it weeks later, mouldy and hiding at the back of a cabinet somewhere. But if he had eaten the entire thing, he would be sick all night and Elizabeth would have to clean up the mess. Again.

'Thank you, Elizabeth.'

'You're very welcome, Luke.'

'Huh?' Luke said, poking his head around the corner of the kitchen.

'Luke, I told you before, it's pardon, not huh.'

'Pardon?'

'I said you're very welcome.'

'But I haven't said thank you yet.'

Elizabeth slid the dishes into the dishwasher and stretched her back. She rubbed the base of her aching spine. 'Yes you did. You said, "Thank you, Elizabeth."'

'No I didn't,' Luke frowned.

Elizabeth felt her temper rising. 'Luke, stop playing games now, OK? We've had our fun at lunchtime, now you can stop pretending. OK?'

'No. That was Ivan who said thank you,' he said angrily.

A shiver ran through her body. She didn't think this was funny. She banged the dishwasher door shut, too fed up even to reply to her nephew. Why couldn't he, just this once, not give her a hard time?

Elizabeth rushed by Ivan with a cup of espresso in her hand, and the smell of perfume and coffee beans filled his nostrils. She sat down at the kitchen table, her shoulders sagged and she held her head in her hands.

'Ivan, come on!' Luke called impatiently from the playroom. 'I'll let you be The Rock this time!'

Elizabeth groaned quietly to herself.

But Ivan couldn't move. His blue Converse runners were rooted to the marble kitchen floor.

Elizabeth had heard him say thank you. He knew it.

He circled her slowly for a few minutes, studying her for signs of a reaction to his presence. He snapped his fingers next to her eardrums, jumped back and watched her. Nothing. He clapped his hands and stamped his feet. The sound echoed loudly in the large kitchen but Elizabeth remained at the table with her head in her hands. No reaction at all.

But she had said, 'You're very welcome.' After all his efforts of making noise around her, he was confused to discover his deep disappointment that she couldn't sense him. After all, she was a parent and who cared what parents thought? He stood behind her and stared down at the top of her head, wondering what noise he could make next. He sighed loudly, exhaling a deep breath.

Suddenly Elizabeth sat up straight, shuddered and pulled the zip on her tracksuit top higher.

And then he *knew* she had felt his breath.

Chapter 4

Elizabeth pulled her dressing gown tighter around her body and secured it at the waist. She tucked her long legs up underneath her body and snuggled down into the oversized armchair in the living room. Her wet hair sat tower-like on the top of her head, twisted in a towel; her skin smelled fruity from her passion fruit bubble bath. She cradled a fresh cup of coffee, complete with dollop of cream, in her hands and stared at the television. She was literally watching paint dry. Her favourite house makeover show was on and she loved to see how they could transform the most run-down rooms into sophisticated, elegant homes.

Ever since she was a child she had loved giving everything she touched a makeover. She had passed the time, spent waiting for her mother to return, by decorating the kitchen table with scattered daisies, sprinkling glitter on the welcome mat by the door, causing a trail of glitter to garnish the dull stone floors of the bungalow, decorating the photo frames with fresh flowers and sprinkling the bed linen with petals. She supposed it was her fix-it nature, always wanting something better than she had, never settling, never satisfied.

She also supposed it was her own childish way of trying to convince her mother to stay. She remembered thinking that perhaps the prettier the house, the longer her mother would remain home. But the daisies on the table were celebrated for no more than five minutes, the glitter on the doormat quickly trampled on, the flowers by the photo frames could not survive without water and the petals on the bed would be tossed and float to the floor during her mother's fitful night's sleep. As soon as these were tired of, Elizabeth would immediately start thinking of something that would really grab and take hold of her mother's attention, something that she would be drawn to for longer than five minutes, something that she would love so much she would be unable to leave it. Elizabeth never considered that as her mother's daughter, she should have been that something.

As she got older she grew to love bringing the beauty out in things. She had had much practice with that at her father's old farmhouse. Now she loved the days at work when she could restore old fireplaces and rip up ancient carpets to reveal beautiful original floors. Even in her own home she was always changing things, rearranging and trying to improve. She strived for perfection. She loved setting herself tasks, sometimes impossible ones, to prove to her heart that underneath every seemingly ugly thing there was something beautiful inside.

She loved her job, loved the satisfaction it brought, and with all the new housing developments in Baile na gCroíthe and the surrounding nearby towns, she had made a very good living out of it. If anything new was happening, Elizabeth's company was the one the developers all called. She was a firm believer that good design enhanced life. Beautiful, comfortable and functional spaces were what she endorsed.

Her own living room was about soft colours and textures. Suede cushions and fluffy carpets; she loved to touch and feel everything. There were light colours of coffees and creams and just like the mug in her hand they helped clear her mind. In a world where most things were a clutter, having a peaceful home was vital to her sanity. It was her hide-away, her nest, where she could hide from the problems outside her door. At least in her home she was in control. Unlike the rest of her life, she could allow whoever she wanted in, she could decide how long they should stay and where in her home they could be. Not like a heart that invites people in without permission, holds them in a special place she never had any say in and then yearns for them to remain there longer than they plan. No, the guests in Elizabeth's home could come and go on her command. And she chose for them to stay away.

Friday's meeting had been vital. She had spent weeks planning for it, updating her portfolio, creating a slide show, gathering magazine cuttings and newspaper write-ups of the places she had designed. Her whole life's work had been condensed into a folder book in order to convince these people to hire her. An old tower standing high on the mountainside overlooking Baile na gCroíthe was to be knocked down to make space for a hotel. It had once protected the small town from approaching attackers during the Viking times, but Elizabeth couldn't see the point of it remaining there today as it was neither pretty nor of any historical interest. When the tour buses, packed full with eager eyes from all over the world, passed through Baile na gCroíthe, the tower wasn't even mentioned. No one was proud of it nor interested in it. It was an ugly pile of stones that had been allowed to crumble and decay, that by day housed the village teenagers and by night housed the village drunks, Saoirse having been among both groups.

But many of the townspeople had put up a fight to prevent the hotel from being built, claiming the tower had some sort of mythical and romantic story behind it. A story began to circulate that if the building was knocked down, all love would be lost. It grabbed the attention of the tabloids and soft news programmes, and eventually the developers saw the opportunity for an even bigger goldmine than expected. They decided to restore the tower to a version of its former glory and build around it, leaving the tower as a historical piece for their courtyard, that way keeping the love alive in the Town of Hearts. There was suddenly a huge rush of interest from believers all around the country wanting to stay in the hotel to be near the tower blessed by love.

Elizabeth would have driven the JCB through it herself. She thought it was a ridiculous story, one created by a town afraid of change and intent on keeping the tower on the mountain. It was a story kept alive for tourists and dreamers, but she couldn't deny that the job of designing the hotel's interiors would be perfect for her. It would be a small place, but one that would provide employment for the people of Hartstown. Better yet, it was only a few minutes from her home and she wouldn't have to worry about being away from Luke for long periods of time while working on the project.

Before Luke was born Elizabeth used to travel all the time. She would never spend more than a few weeks in Baile na gCroíthe and loved having the freedom to move around and work in different counties on various projects. Her last big project took her to New York, but as soon as Luke was born that had all ended. When Luke was younger, Elizabeth couldn't continue with her work around the country, never mind around the world. It had been a very difficult time, trying to set up her business in Baile na gCroíthe and trying to get used to raising a child again. She had no other choice but to hire Edith, as her father wouldn't help out and Saoirse certainly hadn't any interest. Now Luke was older and settled at school, Elizabeth was discovering that finding work within commuting distance was becoming increasingly difficult. The development boom in Baile na gCroíthe would eventually settle and she constantly worried whether the work would then dry up completely.

Her walking out of the meeting on Friday should not have happened. Nobody in her office could sell her abilities as an interior decorator better than she could. Her employees consisted of receptionist Becca, and Poppy. Becca was a timid and extremely shy seventeen-year-old, who had joined Elizabeth in her transition year while on work experience and decided not to go back to school. She was a hard worker who kept to herself, and was quiet around the office, which Elizabeth liked. Elizabeth had hired her quickly after Saoirse, who had been hired by Elizabeth to work there part time, had let her down. She had *more* than let her down and Elizabeth had been desperate to get someone in quickly. To tidy up the mess. Again. Keeping Saoirse near her during the day as an attempt to help her on her feet had only succeeded in driving her further away and knocking her right back down.

Then there was twenty-five-year-old Poppy, a recent graduate from art college, full of lots of wonderfully impossible creative ideas and ready to paint the world a colour she had yet to invent. There were just the three of them in the office but Elizabeth often called on the services of Mrs Bracken, a sixty-eight-year-old genius with a needle and thread, who ran her own upholstery shop in the town. She was also an incredible grump and insisted on being called *Mrs Bracken* and not Gwen, out of respect for her dearly departed *Mr Bracken*, whom Elizabeth didn't think had been born with a first name. And finally there was Harry, fifty-two years old and an all-round handyman, who could do anything from hanging paintings to rewiring buildings but who couldn't understand the concept of an unmarried woman with a career, not to say an unmarried woman with a career and a child not her own. Depending on people's budgets, Elizabeth would do anything from instructing painters and decorators to doing it all herself, but mostly she liked to be hands-on. She liked to see the transformation before her very eyes and it was part of her nature to want to fix everything herself.

It wasn't unusual for Saoirse to have shown up at Elizabeth's house that morning. She would often arrive drunk and abusive, and willing to take anything that she could get her hands on – anything worth selling, of course, which automatically excluded Luke. Elizabeth didn't even know if it was just the drink she was addicted to any more; it was a long time since she'd had a conversation with her sister. She had been trying to help her since she was fourteen. It was as if a switch had been flicked in her head and they had lost her to another world. She tried sending her to counselling, rehab, doctors, she gave her money, found her jobs, hired her herself, allowed her to move in with her, rented her flats. She had tried being her friend, had tried being her enemy, had laughed with her and shouted at her, but nothing would work. Saoirse was lost to her, lost in a world where nobody else mattered.

Elizabeth couldn't help thinking of the irony of her name. Saoirse wasn't free. She may have felt that she was, coming and going as she pleased, not being tied down to anyone, anything, any place, but she was a slave to her addictions. She couldn't see it, though, and Elizabeth couldn't help her see it. She couldn't turn her back completely on her sister but she had run out of energy, ideas and faith in ever believing Saoirse could be changed, and had lost lovers and friends with her persistence. Their frustration would grow as they stood by and watched Elizabeth being taken advantage of time and time again till they could no longer be in her life. But contrary to their beliefs, Elizabeth didn't feel like the victim. She was always in control. She knew what and why she was doing what she was doing, and she refused to desert a family member. She would not be like her mother. She had worked too hard all her life at trying not to be.

Elizabeth suddenly pressed Mute on the television remote control and the room was silenced. She cocked her head to one side. She thought she'd heard something again. After looking around the room and seeing that everything was as it should be, she turned the volume back up again.

There it was again.

She silenced the TV once more and stood up from the armchair.

It was 10.15 and not yet fully dark. She looked out to the back garden and in the dusk she could only see black shadows and shapes. She pulled the curtains closed quickly and immediately felt safer in her cream and beige cocoon. She tightened her dressing gown again and sat back down in her armchair, tucking her legs even closer to her body and wrapping her arms protectively around her knees. The vacant cream leather couch stared back at her. She shuddered again, turned the volume up even higher than before and took a gulp of coffee. The velvety liquid slid down her throat and warmed her insides and she tried once again to be sucked back into the world of television.

All day she had felt odd. Her father always said that when you got a chill up your spine it meant that someone was walking over your grave. Elizabeth didn't believe that but as she stared at the television, she turned her head away from the three-seater leather couch and tried to shake off the feeling that a pair of eyes was watching her.

Ivan watched her mute the television once again, quickly put her coffee cup on the table next to her and jump out of her chair as though she had been sitting on pins. Here she goes again, he thought. Her eyes were wide and terrified as they darted around the room. Once again Ivan prepared himself and pushed his body to the edge of the couch. The denim of his jeans squeaked against the leather.

Elizabeth jumped to face the couch.

She grabbed a black iron poker from the large marble fireplace and spun round on her heels. Her knuckles turned white as they tightened around it. She slowly tiptoed about the room, eyes wild with fear. The leather squeaked again underneath him and Elizabeth charged towards the couch. Ivan leaped from his seat and dived into the corner.

He hid behind the curtains for protection and watched as she pulled the cushions out of the chair while grumbling to herself about mice. After ten minutes of searching through the couch, Elizabeth put all the cushions back in place to restore its immaculate form.

She picked up her coffee cup self-consciously and made her way into the kitchen. Ivan followed closely on her heel; he was so close that strands of her soft hair tickled his face. Her hair smelled of coconut and her skin of rich fruits.

He couldn't understand his fascination with her. He had been watching her since after lunch on Friday. Luke had kept calling him to play game after game and all Ivan had wanted was to be around Elizabeth. At first it was just to see if she could hear him or sense him again, but then after a few hours he found her compelling. She was obsessively neat. He noticed she couldn't leave the room to answer the phone or front door until everything had been tidied away and wiped clean. She drank a lot of coffee, stared out to her garden, picked imaginary pieces of fluff from almost everything. And she thought. He could see it in her face. Her brow would furrow in concentration and she would make facial expressions as though she was having conversations with people in her head. They seemed to turn into debates more often than not, judging by the activity on her forehead.

He noticed she was always surrounded by silence. There was never any music or sounds in the background like most people had, a radio blaring, the window open to allow in the sounds of summer – the birdsong and the lawn mowers. Luke and she spoke little and when they did it was mostly her giving him orders, him asking permission, nothing fun. The phone rarely rang, nobody called by. It was almost as if the conversations in her head were loud enough to fill her silence.

He spent most of Friday and Saturday following her around, sitting on the cream leather couch in the evenings and watching her watching the only programme she seemed to like on TV. They both laughed in the same places, groaned in the same places and they seemed to be completely in sync, yet she didn't know he was there. He had watched her sleeping the previous night. She was restless – she slept only three hours at the most; the rest of the time she spent reading a book, putting it down after five minutes, staring into space, picking the book up again, reading a few pages, reading back over the same pages, putting it down again, closing her eyes, opening them again, turning the light on, doodling sketches of furniture and rooms, playing with colours and shades and scraps of material, turning the light off again.

She had made Ivan tired just watching her from the straw chair in the corner of the room. The trips to the kitchen for coffee couldn't have helped her either. On Sunday morning she was up early, tidying, vacuuming, polishing and cleaning an already spotless home. She spent all morning at it while Ivan played chasing with Luke out in the back garden. He recalled Elizabeth being particularly upset by the sight of

Luke running around the garden laughing and screaming to himself. She had joined them at the kitchen table and watched Luke playing cards, shaking her head and looking worried when he explained the rules of patience in extreme detail to thin air.

But when Luke went to bed at nine o'clock, Ivan read him the story of Tom Thumb quicker than he usually would, and then hurried to continue watching Elizabeth. But he could sense her getting jitterier as the days wore on.

She washed her coffee cup out, ensuring it was already spotless before putting it in the dishwasher. She dried the wet sink with a cloth and put the cloth in the wash basket in the utility room. She picked imaginary fluff from a few items in her path, picked crumbs from the floor, switched off all the lights and began the same process in the living room. She had done the exact same thing the last two nights.

But before leaving the living room this time, she stopped abruptly, almost sending Ivan into the back of her. His heart beat wildly. Had she sensed him?

She turned round slowly.

He fixed his shirt to look presentable.

Once facing him he smiled. 'Hi,' he said, feeling very self-conscious.

She rubbed her eyes tiredly and opened them again. 'Oh, Elizabeth, you are going mad,' she whispered. She bit her lip and charged towards Ivan.

Chapter 5

Elizabeth knew she was losing her mind right at that moment. It had happened to her sister and mother, and now it was her turn. For the last few days she had felt incredibly insecure, as if someone was watching her. She had locked all the doors, drawn all the curtains, set the alarm. That probably should have been enough but now she was going to go that one step further.

She charged through the living room straight towards the fireplace, grabbed the iron poker, marched out of the room, locked the door and made her way upstairs. She looked at the poker lying on her bedside locker, rolled her eyes and turned her lamp off. She *was* losing her mind.

Ivan emerged from behind the couch and looked around. He had dived behind it thinking Elizabeth was charging towards him. He had heard the door lock after she stormed out. He slumped with a dis-appointment he had never experienced before. She still hadn't seen him.

I'm not magic, you know. I can't cross my arms, nod my head, blink and disappear and reappear on the top of a bookshelf or anything. I don't live in a lamp, don't have funny little ears, big hairy feet or wings. I don't replace loose teeth with money, leave presents under a tree or hide chocolate eggs. I can't fly, climb up the walls of buildings or run faster than the speed of light.

And I can't open doors.

That has to be done for me. The grown-ups find that part the funniest but also the most embarrassing when their children do it in public. I don't laugh at grown-ups when they can't climb trees or can't say the alphabet backwards because it's just not physically possible for them. It doesn't make them freaks of nature.

So Elizabeth needn't have locked the living-room door when she went to bed that night because I couldn't turn the handle anyway. Like I said, I'm not a superhero; my special power is friendship. I listen to people and I hear what they say. I hear their tones, the words they use to express themselves and, most importantly, I hear what they *don't* say.

So all I could do that night was think about my new friend, Luke. I need to do that occasionally. I make notes in my head so that I can file a report for admin. They like to keep it all on record for training purposes. We've new people joining up all the time. In fact, when I'm between friends, I lecture.

I needed to think about why I was here. What made Luke want to see me? How could he benefit from my friendship? The business is run extremely professionally and we must always provide the company with a brief history of our friends and then list our aims and objectives. I could always identify the problem straight away but this scenario was slightly baffling. You see, I'd never been friends with an adult before. Anyone who has ever met one would understand why. There's no sense of fun with them. They stick rigidly to schedules and times, they focus on the most unimportant things imaginable, like mortgages and bank statements, when everyone knows that the majority of the time it's the people around them that put the smiles on their faces. It's all work and no play, and I work hard, I really do, but playing is by far my favourite.

Take, for example, Elizabeth; she lies in bed worrying about car tax and phone bills, babysitters and paint colours. If you can't put magnolia on a wall then there are always a million other colours you can use; if you can't pay your phone bill then just write letters telling them. People forget they have options. And they forget that those things really don't matter. They should concentrate on what they have and not what they don't have. But I'm veering away from the story again.

I worried about my job a little the night I was locked in the living room. It's the first time that had ever happened. I worried because I couldn't figure out why I was there. Luke had a difficult family scenario but that was normal and I could tell he felt loved. He was happy and loved playing, he slept well at night, ate all his food, had a nice friend called Sam and when he spoke I listened and listened and tried to hear the words he wasn't saying but there was nothing. He liked living with his aunt, was scared of his mom and liked talking about vegetables with his granddad. But Luke seeing me every day and wanting to play with me every day meant that I definitely needed to be here for him.

On the other hand, his aunt never slept, ate very little, was constantly surrounded by silence so loud that it was deafening, she had nobody close to her to talk to, that I had seen yet anyway, and she *didn't* say *far more* than she did actually say. She had heard me say thank you once, felt my breath a few times, heard me squeak on the leather couch but yet she couldn't see me nor could stand me being in her house.

Elizabeth did not want to play.

Plus she was a grown-up, she gave me butterflies and wouldn't know fun if it hit her in the face, and believe me I'd tried to throw it at her plenty of times over the weekend. So I couldn't possibly be here to help her. It was unheard of.

People refer to me as an invisible or an imaginary friend. Like there's some big mystery surrounding me. I've read the books that grown-ups have written asking why kids see me, why do they believe in me so much for so long and then suddenly stop and go back to being the way they were before? I've seen the television shows that try to debate why it is that children invent people like me.

So just for the record for all you people, I'm not invisible or imaginary. I'm always here walking around just like you all are. And people like Luke don't *choose* to see me, they just see me. It's people like you and Elizabeth that choose not to.

Chapter 6

Elizabeth was woken up at 6.08 a.m. by the sun streaming through the bedroom window and onto her face. She always slept with the curtains open. It had stemmed from growing up on a farm. Lying in her bed she could see through the bungalow window, down the garden path and out of the front gate. Beyond that was a country road that led straight from the farm, stretching on for a mile. Elizabeth could see her mother returning from her adventures, walking down the road for at least twenty minutes before she reached home. She could recognise the half-hop, half-skip from miles away. Those twenty minutes always felt like an eternity to Elizabeth. The long road had its own way of building up Elizabeth's excitement, almost teasing her.

And finally she would hear that familiar sound, the squeak of the front gate. The rusting hinges acted as a welcoming band to the free spirit. Elizabeth had a love/hate relationship with that gate. Like the long stretch of road, it would tease her, and some days on hearing the creak she would run to see who was at the door and her heart would sink that it was only the postman.

Elizabeth had annoyed college room-mates and lovers with her insistence on keeping the curtains open. She didn't know why she remained firm on this; it certainly wasn't as though she was still waiting. But now in her adulthood, the open curtains acted as her alarm clock; with them open she knew the light would never allow her to fall back into a deep sleep. Even in her sleep she felt alert, and in control. She went to bed to rest, not to dream.

She squinted in the bright room and her head throbbed. She needed coffee, fast. Outside the window a bird's song echoed loudly in the quiet of the countryside. Somewhere far away a cow answered its call. But despite the idyllic morning, there was nothing about this Monday that Elizabeth was looking forward to. She had to try to reschedule a meeting with the hotel developers, which was going to prove difficult because after the little stunt in the press about the new love nest at the top of the mountain, they had people flying in from all parts of the world willing to share their design ideas. This annoyed Elizabeth; this was her territory. But that wasn't her only problem.

Luke had been invited to spend the day with his grandfather on the farm. That bit, Elizabeth was happy with. It was the part about him expecting another six-year-old by the name of Ivan that worried her. She would have to have a discussion with Luke this morning about it because she dreaded to think of what would happen if there was a mention of an imaginary friend to her father.

Brendan was sixty-five years old, big, broad, silent and brooding. Age had not mellowed him; instead it had brought bitterness, resentment, and even more confusion. He was small-minded and unwilling to open up or change. Elizabeth could at least try to understand his difficult nature if being that way made him happy, but as far as she could see, his views frustrated him and only made his life more miserable. He was stern, rarely spoke except to the cows or vegetables, never laughed, and whenever he did decide someone was worthy of his words, he lectured. There was no need to respond to him. He didn't speak for conversation. He spoke to make statements. He rarely spent time with Luke as he didn't have time for the airy-fairy ways of children, for their silly games and nonsense. The only thing that Elizabeth could see that her father liked about Luke was that he was an empty book, ready to be filled with information and not enough knowledge to question or criticise. Fairy tales and fantasy stories had no place with her father. She supposed that was the only belief they actually shared.

She yawned and stretched and, still unable to open her eyes against the bright light, she felt around her bedside locker for her alarm clock. Although she woke up every morning at the same time, she never forgot to set her alarm. Her arm knocked against something cold and hard and it fell with a loud bang to the floor. Her sleepy heart jumped with fright.

Hanging her head over the side of the bed she caught sight of the iron poker lying on her white carpet. Her 'weapon' also reminded her that she had to call Rentokil to get rid of the mice. She had sensed them in the house all weekend and she had felt so paranoid that they were in her bedroom the past few nights she could hardly sleep, although that wasn't particularly unusual for her.

Washed and dressed, after waking Luke she made her way downstairs to the kitchen. Minutes later, with espresso in hand, she dialled the number of Rentokil. Luke wandered into the kitchen sleepily, blond hair tossed, dressed in an orange T-shirt half tucked into red shorts. The outfit was completed with odd socks and a pair of runners that lit up with every step he took.

'Where's Ivan?' he asked groggily, looking around the kitchen as though he'd never been in the room before in his life. He was like that every morning; it took him at least an hour to wake up even once he was up and dressed. During the dark winter mornings it took even longer. Elizabeth supposed that at some point in his morning classes as school he finally realised what he was doing.

'Where's Ivan?' he repeated.

Elizabeth silenced him by holding her finger to her lips, and giving him the glare, as she listened to the lady from Rentokil. He knew not to interrupt her when she was on the phone. 'Well, I only noticed it this weekend. Since Friday lunchtime actually, so I was wond—'

'IVAN?' Luke yelled, and began looking under the kitchen table, behind the curtains, behind the doors. Elizabeth rolled her eyes. This carry-on again.

'No, I haven't actually seen . . .'

'IVAAAAN?'

'. . . one yet but I definitely feel that they're here.' Elizabeth finished, and tried to catch Luke's eye so that she could give him the glare again.

'IVAN, WHERE ARE YOOOUUU?' Luke called.

'Droppings? No, no droppings,' Elizabeth said, getting frustrated.

Luke stopped shouting and his ears perked up. 'WHAT? I CAN'T HEAR YOU PROPERLY.'

'No, I don't have any mousetraps. Look, I'm very busy, I don't have time for twenty questions. Can't someone just come out and check for themselves?' Elizabeth snapped.

Luke suddenly ran from the kitchen and out into the hall. She heard him banging at the living-room door. 'WHAT ARE YOU DOING IN THERE, IVAN?' He pulled at the handle.

Finally Elizabeth's conversation ended and she slammed down the phone. Luke was shouting through the living-room door at full volume. Her blood boiled.

'LUKE! GET IN HERE NOW!'

The banging at the living-room door stopped immediately. He shuffled slowly into the kitchen.

'DON'T DRAG YOUR FEET!' she yelled.

He lifted his feet and the lights on the soles of his runners flashed with every step. He stood before her and spoke quietly and as innocently as he possibly could in his high-pitched voice. 'Why did you lock Ivan in the living room last night?'

Silence.

She had to put an end to this now. She would choose this moment to sit down and discuss the issue with Luke and by the end of it he would respect her wishes. She would help him see sense and there would be no more talk of invisible friends.

'And Ivan wants to know why you brought the fire poker to bed with you?' he added, feeling more confident by her failure to scream at him again.

Elizabeth exploded. 'There will be no more talk of this Ivan, do you hear me?'

Luke's face went white.

'DO YOU HEAR ME?' she shouted. She didn't even give him a chance to answer. 'You know as well as I do that there is *no such thing* as Ivan. He does *not* play chasing, he does *not* eat pizza, he is *not* in the living room and he is *not* your friend because he *does not exist.*'

Luke's face crumpled up as though he were about to cry.

Elizabeth continued, 'Today you are going to your granddad's and if I hear from him that there was one mention of Ivan, you will be in *big trouble.* Do you understand?'

Luke began to cry softly.

'Do you understand?' she repeated.

He nodded his head slowly as tears rushed down his face.

Elizabeth's blood stopped boiling and her throat began to ache from shouting. 'Now sit at the table and I'll bring you your cereal,' she said softly. She fetched the Coco Pops. Usually she didn't allow him to eat such sugary breakfasts but she hadn't exactly discussed the Ivan situation with him as planned. She knew she had a problem keeping her temper. She sat at the table and watched him pour Coco Pops into his cereal bowl and then his little hands wobbled with the weight of the milk carton. Milk splashed onto the table. She held back from shouting at him again although she had cleaned that only yesterday evening until it sparkled. Something Luke had said was bothering her and she couldn't quite remember what it was. She rested her chin on her hand and watched him eating.

He munched slowly. Sadly. There was silence apart from his crunching. Finally, after a few minutes, he spoke. 'Where's the key to the living room?' he asked, refusing to catch her eye.

'Luke, not with your mouth full,' she said softly. She took the key to the living room out of her pocket, went to the doorway in the hall and twisted the key. 'There now, Ivan is free to *leave* the house,' she joked, and immediately regretted saying it.

'He's not,' Luke said sadly from the kitchen table. 'He can't open doors himself.'

Silence.

'He can't?' Elizabeth repeated.

Luke shook his head as if what he had said was the most normal thing in the world. It was the most ridiculous thing Elizabeth had ever heard. What kind of an imaginary friend was he if he couldn't walk through walls and doors? Well, she wasn't opening the door, she had unlocked it and that was silly enough. She went back to the kitchen to gather her belongings for work. Luke finished his cereal, placed the bowl in the dishwasher, washed his hands, dried them and made his way to the living-room door. He turned the handle, pushed open the door, stepped out of the way, smiled broadly at nothing, placed a finger over his lips, pointed at Elizabeth with his other hand and giggled quietly to himself. Elizabeth watched with horror. She walked down the hall and stood beside Luke at the doorway. She looked into the living room.

Empty.

The girl from Rentokil had said that it would be unusual for mice to be in the house in June and as Elizabeth eyed the living room suspiciously, she wondered what on earth could be making all those noises.

Luke's giggling snapped her out of her trance and, glancing down the hall, she spotted him sitting at the table, swinging his legs happily and making faces into thin air. There was an extra place set and a freshly poured bowl of Coco Pops across from him.

'Boy, is she strict,' I whispered to Luke at the table, trying to grab spoonfuls of Coco Pops without her noticing. I wouldn't usually whisper around parents but as she had heard me a couple of times already over the past few days, I wasn't about to take any risks.

Luke giggled and nodded.

'Is she like this all the time?'

He nodded again.

'Does she never play games and give you hugs?' I asked, watching as Elizabeth cleaned every inch of the already sparkling kitchen countertops, moving things half an inch to the right and a half an inch to the left.

Luke thought for a while and then shrugged. 'Not much.'

'But that's horrible! Don't you mind?'

'Edith says that there are some people in the world that don't hug you all the time or play games but they still love you. They just don't know how to say it,' he whispered back.

Elizabeth eyed him nervously.

'Who's Edith?'

'My nanny.'

'Where is she?'

'On her holidays.'

'So who's going to mind you while she's on her holidays?'

'You,' Luke smiled.

'Let's shake on it,' I said, holding out my hand. Luke grabbed it. 'We do it like this,' I explained, shaking my head and my whole body, like I was having a convulsion. Luke started laughing and copied me. We laughed even harder when Elizabeth stopped cleaning to stare. Her eyes widened.

'You ask a lot of questions,' Luke whispered.

'You answer a lot,' I fired back, and we both laughed again.

Elizabeth's BMW rattled along the bumpy track leading to her father's farm. She clenched her hands around the steering wheel in exasperation as the dust flew up from the ground and clung to the side of her newly washed car. How she had lived on this farm for eighteen years was beyond her. Nothing could be kept clean. The wild fuchsias danced in the light breeze, waving their welcome from the side of the road. They lined the mile-long road like landing lights and rubbed against the windows of the car, pressing their faces to see who was inside. Luke lowered his window and allowed his hand to be tickled by their kisses.

She prayed that no traffic would come towards her as the road just about allowed her car through, leaving no room for two-way traffic. In order to let someone pass she would have to reverse half a mile back the way she'd come just to make room. At times it felt like the longest road in the world. She could see where she was trying to get to yet she would have to keep reversing in order to get there.

Two steps forward and one step back.

It was like when she was a child seeing her mother from a mile away but being forced to wait the twenty minutes it took her to dance down the road, till Elizabeth heard the familiar sound of the gate creak.

But thankfully, because they were already delayed as it was, no traffic came this time. Elizabeth's words had obviously fallen on deaf ears because Luke refused to leave the house until Ivan had finished his cereal. He then insisted on pushing forward the passenger seat in the car in order to let Ivan into the back seat.

She glanced quickly at Luke. He sat buckled up in the front seat, arm out the window, humming the same song he had been singing all weekend. He looked happy. She hoped he wouldn't keep his play-acting up for much longer, at least while he was at his granddad's.

She could see her father at the gate, waiting. A familiar sight. A familiar action. Waiting was his forte. He wore the same brown cords Elizabeth could have sworn he was wearing when she was a child. They were tucked into muddy green Wellington boots that he wore in the house. His grey cotton jumper was stitched with a faded green and blue diamond pattern, there was a hole in the centre, and the green of his polo shirt peeked through from underneath. A tweed cap sat firmly on his head, a blackthorn cane in his right hand kept him steady, and silver grey stubble decorated his face and chin. His eyebrows were grey and wild, and when he frowned they seemed to cover his grey eyes completely. His nose commanded his face with large nostrils filled with grey hairs. Deep wrinkles cracked his face, his hands as big as shovels, shoulders as wide as the Gap of Dungloe. He dwarfed the bungalow that stood behind him.

Luke stopped humming as soon as he saw his grandfather and brought his arm back into the car. Elizabeth pulled up, turned the engine off and jumped out. She had a plan. As soon as Luke climbed out of the car she shut the door and locked it before he had a chance to push the seat forward and make way for Ivan. Luke's face crumpled again as he looked from Elizabeth and back to the car.

The gate outside the bungalow creaked.

Elizabeth's stomach churned.

'Morning,' a deep voice boomed. It wasn't a greeting. It was a statement.

Luke's lower lip trembled and he pressed his face and hands up against the glass of the back seat of the car. Elizabeth hoped he wouldn't throw a tantrum now.

'Aren't you going to say good morning to your granddad, Luke?' Elizabeth asked sternly, fully aware that she herself had yet to acknowledge him.

'Hi, Granddad.' Luke's voice wobbled. His face remained pressed against the glass.

Elizabeth contemplated opening the car door for him just to avoid a scene but thought better of it. He needed to get over this phase.

'Where's th'other one?' Brendan's voice boomed.

'The other what?' She took Luke's hand and tried to turn him away from the car. His blue eyes looked pleadingly into hers. Her heart sank. He knew better than to cause a scene.

'The young lad who knew about them foreign veg.'

'Ivan,' Luke said sadly, tears welling up.

Elizabeth jumped in, 'Ivan couldn't come today, isn't that right, Luke? Maybe another day,' she said quickly, and before it could be discussed any further, 'Right, I'd better go to work or I'll be late. Luke, have a good day with your granddad, OK?'

Luke looked at her uncertainly and nodded.

Elizabeth hated herself but she knew she was right to control this ludicrous behaviour.

'Off you go so.' Brendan swung his blackthorn cane at her as if to dismiss her and he turned his back to face the bungalow. The last thing she heard was the gate creaking before she slammed her car door shut. She had to reverse twice down the road in order to let two tractors pass. From her mirror she could see Luke and her father in the front garden, her father towering over him. She couldn't get away from the house fast enough; it was as though the flow of traffic kept pulling her back to it, like the tide.

Elizabeth remembered the moment when she was eighteen when she thrived on the freedom of such a view. For the first time in her life, she was leaving the bungalow with her bags packed and with the intention of not coming back until Christmas. She was going to Cork University, after winning the battle with her father but in turn losing all respect he had ever had for her. Instead of sharing in her excitement, he had refused to see her off on her big day. The only figure standing outside the bungalow Elizabeth could see that bright August morning as they drove away was that of six-year-old Saoirse, her red hair in messy pigtails, her smile toothless in places yet broad and wide, with her arm waving frantically goodbye, full of pride for her big sister.

Instead of the relief and excitement she always dreamed of feeling when the taxi finally pulled away from her home, breaking the umbilical cord that held her there, she felt dread and worry. Not for what lay ahead but for what she was leaving behind. She couldn't mother Saoirse for ever, she was a young woman who needed to be set free, who needed to find her own place in the world. Her father needed to step into his rightful place of fatherhood, a title he had discarded many years ago and refused to recognise. She only hoped now that as the two of them were alone, he would realise his duties and show as much love as he could for what he had left.

But what if he didn't? She continued watching her sister out the back window, feeling as if she was never going to see her again, waving as fast and as furiously as she could as tears filled her eyes for the little life and bundle of energy she was leaving behind. The red hair jumping up and down was visible from a mile away and so they both kept on waving. What would her little sister do now that the fun of waving her off had ended and the realisation set in that she was alone with the man who never spoke, never helped and never loved. Elizabeth almost asked the driver to stop the car right there and then, but quickly told herself to stay strong. She needed to live.

You do the same as me someday, little Saoirse, her eyes kept telling the little figure as they drove away. Promise me you'll do the same. Fly away from there.

*   *   *

With eyes full of tears, Elizabeth watched as the bungalow got smaller and smaller in her mirror until finally it disappeared when she reached the end of the mile-long road. At once her shoulders relaxed and she realised she had been holding her breath the entire time.

'Right, Ivan,' she said, looking in the mirror at the empty back seat, 'I guess you're coming to work with me so.' Then she did a funny thing. She giggled childishly.

Chapter 7

Baile na gCroíthe was stirring as Elizabeth drove over the grey-stone bridge that served as its gateway. Two huge coaches full of tourists were currently trying to inch past each other on the narrow street. Inside, Elizabeth could see faces pressed against the windows, oohing and aahing, smiling and pointing, cameras being held up to the glass to snap the doll-like town on film. The coach driver facing Elizabeth licked his lips in concentration and she could see the sweat glistening on his brow as he slowly manoeuvred the oversized vehicle along the narrow road originally designed for horses and carts. The sides of the coaches were almost touching. Beside him, the tour guide, with microphone in hand, did his best to entertain his one-hundred-strong audience so early in the morning.

Elizabeth lifted the handbrake and sighed loudly. This wasn't a rare occurrence in the town and she knew it could take a while. She doubted the coaches would stop. They rarely did unless it was for a toilet break. Traffic always seemed to be moving through Baile na gCroíthe but never stopping. She didn't blame them; it was a great place to help you get to where you're going but not one for sticking around in. Traffic would slow down and visitors would take a good look alright, but then the drivers would put a foot down and accelerate off out the other end.

It's not that Baile na gCroíthe wasn't beautiful – it was certainly that. Its proudest moment was winning the Tidy Town competition for the third year running, and as you entered the village, over the bridge, a display of bright blooming flowers spelled out a welcome. The flower display continued through the town. Window boxes adorned the shop fronts, hanging baskets hung from black lampposts, trees grew tall along the main street. Each building was painted a different colour, and the main street, the only street, was a rainbow of pastels and bold colours of mint greens, salmon pinks, lilacs, lemons and blues. The pavements were litter free and gleaming, and as soon as you averted your gaze above the grey slate roofs you found yourself surrounded by majestic green mountains. It was as though Baile na gCroíthe was cocooned, safely nestled in the bosom of Mother Nature.

Cosy or suffocating.

Elizabeth's office was located beside a green post office and a yellow supermarket. Her building was a pale blue, and sat above Mrs Bracken's curtain, fabric and upholstery shop. The shop had previously been a hardware shop run by Mr Bracken, but when he died ten years ago, Gwen had decided to turn it into her own store. She seemed to make decisions based purely on what her deceased husband would think. She opened the shop 'because it's what Mr Bracken would have wanted'. However, Gwen refused to go out at the weekends or involve herself in any social outings as 'it's not what Mr Bracken would have wanted'. As far as Elizabeth could see, what made Mr Bracken happy or unhappy seemed to tie in nicely with Gwen's philosophy on life.

The coaches moved past each other inch by inch. Baile na gCroíthe in rush-hour traffic; the result of two oversized buses trying to share the narrow road. Finally they were successful in their passing and Elizabeth looked on, not amused as the tour guide jumped from his seat in excitement, microphone in hand, succeeding in turning what was essentially a boring halt into an eventful bus journey on Ireland's country roads. Cue clapping and cheering on board the bus. A nation in celebration. More flashes out the window and the occupants on both buses waved goodbye to each other after sharing the morning's excitement.

Elizabeth drove on, looked in her rear-view mirror to see the excitement on the celebrating coach die down as they came face to face with another on the small bridge that led out of the town. Arms slowly went down and the flashes died as the tourists settled down for another lengthy struggle to continue.

The town had a tendency to do that. Almost as if it did it purposely. It welcomed you into its heart with open arms, showed you all it had to offer with its gleaming multicoloured florally decorated shop fronts. It was like bringing a child into a sweet shop and showing them the shelves of luminous sugar-coated, mouth-watering delights. And then while they stand there looking around with wide eyes and a racing pulse, the lids were put back on the jars and sealed tightly. Once its beauty was realised, so was the fact that it had nothing else to offer.

The bridge, oddly, was easier to drive over from outside the town. It curved in an unusual shape, making driving out of the village difficult. It disturbed Elizabeth every time.

It was just like the road leading from Elizabeth's childhood home; she found it impossible to leave in a hurry. But something about the town kept dragging her back and she had spent years trying to fight it. She had successfully moved to New York at one time. She had followed her boyfriend, and the opportunity to design a nightclub, over. She had loved it there. Loved that no one knew her name, her face or family history. She could buy a coffee, a thousand different types of coffee, and not receive a look of sympathy for whatever recent family drama had occurred. Nobody knew that her mother had left her when she was a child, that her sister was wildly out of control and that her father barely spoke to her. She had loved being in love there. In New York she could be whoever she wanted to be. In Baile na gCroíthe she couldn't hide from who she was.

She realised she had been humming to herself the entire time, that silly song that Luke was trying to convince her that 'Ivan' had made up. Luke called it 'the humming song', and it was annoyingly catchy, chirpy and repetitive. She stopped herself singing and spun her car into the empty space along the road. She pushed back the driver's seat and reached in to grab her briefcase from the back seat of the car. First things first: coffee. Baile na gCroíthe had yet to be educated on the wonders of Starbucks – in fact, it was only last month Joe's had finally allowed Elizabeth to take away her coffee, but the owner was growing increasingly tired of having to ask for his mugs back.

Sometimes Elizabeth thought that the entire town needed an injection of caffeine; it was as though some winter days the place still had its eyes closed and was sleepwalking. It needed a good shake. But summer days like today were always busy with people passing through. She entered the purple painted Joe's, which was virtually empty all the same. The concept of eating breakfast outside their own homes had yet to be grasped by the townspeople.

'Ah, there she is, the very woman herself,' boomed the singsong voice of Joe. 'No doubt spittin' feathers for her coffee.'

'Morning, Joe.'

He made a show of checking his watch and tapping the clock face. 'Bit behind time this morning, aren't we?' He raised his eyebrows at her. 'Thought maybe you were in bed sick with a bout of the summer flu. Seems like everyone's got it this week.' He tried to lower his voice but only succeeded in lowering his head and raising his voice. 'Sure didn't Sandy O'Flynn come down with it right after disappearing the other night from the pub with P. J. Flanagan, who had it the other week. She's been in bed all weekend.' He snorted. 'Walking her home me arse. I've never heard such nonsense before in my life.'

Irritation rose within Elizabeth. She didn't care for tittle-tattle about people she didn't know, especially as she was aware for so many years that her own family had been the root of all the gossip.

'A coffee, please, Joe,' Elizabeth said crisply, ignoring his rambling. 'To take away. Cream not milk,' she said sternly, even though she had the same every day, while rooting in her bag for her wallet, trying to hint to Joe that she hadn't time for yapping.

He moved slowly towards the coffee pot. To Elizabeth's utter annoyance Joe's sold only one kind of coffee. And that was the instant kind. Elizabeth missed the variety of flavours that she used to get in other towns; she missed the smooth, sweet-tasting French vanilla in a Paris café, the creamy full-bodied flavour of hazelnut cream in a bustling café in New York, the rich velvety masterpiece of the macadamia nut in Milan and her favourite, the Coco Mocha-Nut, the mixture of chocolate and coconut that transported her from a Central Park bench to a sunbed in the Caribbean. Here in Baile na gCroíthe, Joe filled the kettle with water and flicked the switch. One measly little kettle in a café and he hadn't even boiled the water. Elizabeth rolled her eyes.

Joe stared at her. He looked like he was going to say –

'So what has you so late then?'

– that.

'I'm *five minutes* later than usual, Joe,' Elizabeth said incredulously.

'I know, I know, and five minutes could be five hours for you. Sure don't the bears plan their hibernation on your time?'

That made Elizabeth smile, despite herself.

Joe chuckled and winked. 'That's better.' The kettle clicked as it boiled and he turned his back to make the coffee.

'The coaches delayed me,' Elizabeth said softly, taking the warm mug from Joe's hands.

'Ah, I saw that.' He nodded towards the window. 'Jaimsie did well to get himself out of that one.'

'Jaimsie?' Elizabeth frowned, adding a dollop of cream. It quickly melted and filled the cup to the top. Joe looked on with disgust.

'Jaimsie O'Connor. Jack's son,' he explained. 'Jack, whose other daughter, Mary, just got engaged to the Dublin boy last weekend. Lives down in Mayfair. Five kids. The youngest was arrested there last week for throwing a wine bottle at Joseph.'

Elizabeth froze and stared back at him blankly.

'Joseph McCann,' he repeated, as though she were crazy for not knowing. 'Son of Paddy. Lives up in Newtown. Wife died last year when she drowned in the bog. His daughter Maggie said it was an accident but sure weren't the family suspicious on account of the row they'd being having about not letting her run off with that troublemaker from Cahirciveen.'

Elizabeth placed her money on the counter and smiled, no longer wanting to be a part of his bizarre conversations. 'Thanks, Joe,' she said as she made her way to the door.

'Well, anyway,' he concluded his rambling, 'Jaimsie was the one driving the coach. Don't forget to bring that mug back,' he called to her, and grumbled to himself, 'Takeaway coffee, have you ever heard something so ludicrous in your life?'

Before Elizabeth stepped outside she called from the door, 'Joe, would you not think of getting a coffee machine? So you can make lattes and cappuccinos and espressos instead of all this instant stuff?' She held up her mug.

Joe crossed his arms, leaned against the counter and replied in a bored voice, 'Elizabeth, you don't like my coffee, you don't drink it. I drink tea. There's only one kind of tea I like. It's called Tea. No fancy names for it.'

Elizabeth smiled. 'Actually, there are lots of different types of tea. The Chinese—'

'Ah, be off with you.' He waved his hand at her dismissively. 'We'd all be drinking tea with chopsticks and putting chocolate and cream in our coffees like they're desserts, if you have your way. But, if you're at it, why don't I make a suggestion too then: how's about you buy yourself a kettle over there for your office and put me out of my misery?'

'And out of business,' Elizabeth smiled, and stepped outside.

The village had taken a big stretch and a yawn and was wandering sleepily from its bed to the bathroom. Soon it would be showered, dressed and wide awake. As usual she was one step ahead of it, even if she was running late today.

Elizabeth was always the first in; she loved the silence, the stillness that her office brought at that time of day. It helped her focus on what lay ahead before her noisy colleagues rattled around and before the major traffic hit the road. Elizabeth wasn't the chatty giggly type. Just as she ate to keep herself alive, she spoke to say only what she had to say. She wasn't the type of woman that she overheard in restaurants and cafés, chuckling and gossiping over what someone said someday about something. Conversations about nothing just didn't interest her.

She didn't break down or analyse conversations, glares, looks or situations. There were no double meanings with her; she meant what she said at all times. She didn't enjoy debates or heated discussions. But sitting in the silence of her small office she supposed that was why she didn't have a group of friends. She had tried to be involved before, especially during her college days with her attempts to settle in, but, just as she did then, she would quickly tune out of the mindless nattering.

Since childhood she hadn't pined for friendship. She liked her own company and liked her own thoughts, and then later, in her teens, she had Saoirse as a distraction. She liked the orderly way in which she could depend on herself and manage her time more effectively without friends. When she returned from New York she had tried to host a dinner party in her new home with the neighbours. She thought she would try a fresh beginning, try to make friendships, like most people did, but Saoirse as usual burst into the house and in one fell swoop managed to offend every single person at the table. She accused Ray Collins of having an affair, Bernie Conway of having a boob job and sixty-year-old Kevin Smith of looking at her in a sexual way. The result of Saoirse's ranting and raving was a crying nine-month-old Luke, a few red faces at the table and a burned rack of lamb.

Of course her neighbours wouldn't be as close-minded as to think that Elizabeth was responsible for her family's behaviour, but she gave up after that. She didn't desire company enough to be able to cope with the embarrassment of having to explain and apologise all the time.

Her silence was worth more to her than a thousand words. In that silence she had peace and clarity. Apart from during the night, when her own jumbled thoughts would keep her awake, sounding like a thousand voices jumping in, out and interrupting each other so much that she could barely close her eyes.

She was worried about Luke's behaviour right now. This Ivan character had been hanging around her nephew's head for too long. She had watched Luke all weekend walking, talking and playing games by himself. Laughing and giggling as though he were having the time of his life. Maybe there was something she should be doing. And Edith wasn't there to witness his odd behaviour and deal with it in the wonderful way she always succeeded in doing. Perhaps Elizabeth was supposed to know automatically what to do. Once again the mysteries of motherhood reared their ugly head and she had no one to ask for advice. Nor had she any example to learn from. Well, that wasn't strictly true – she had learned what *not* to do, a lesson just as good as any. So far she had followed her gut instinct, had made a few mistakes along the way, but overall thought Luke had turned out to be a polite and stable child. Or maybe she was doing it all wrong. What if Luke ended up like Saoirse? What had she done so wrong with Saoirse as a child that had caused her to turn out the way she was? Elizabeth groaned with frustration and rested her head on her desk.

She turned on her computer and sipped on her coffee while it loaded. Then she went to Google, typed in the words 'imaginary friend', and hit Search. Hundreds of sites came up on her screen. Thirty minutes later she felt much better about the Ivan situation.

To her surprise she learned that imaginary friends were very common and not a problem as long as they didn't interfere with normal life. Although the very fact that having an imaginary friend was a direct interference with normal life, it didn't seem to be an issue with the online doctors. Site after site told her to ask Luke what Ivan was thinking and doing as it would be a positive way of giving Elizabeth an understanding into what Luke was thinking. They encouraged Elizabeth actually to set a place for their phantom dinner guest and that there was no need to point out that Luke's 'friend' existed only in his imagination. She was relieved to learn that imaginary friends were a sign of creativity and not of loneliness or stress.

But even so, this was going to be difficult for Elizabeth to grasp. It went against everything she believed. Her world and the land of make-believe existed on two very different plains and she found it difficult to play-act. She couldn't make baby noises to an infant, she couldn't pretend to hide behind her hands or give life or a voice to a teddy, she couldn't even role-play at college. She had grown up knowing not to do that, not to sound like her mother for fear of her father getting mad. It was instilled in her from an early age but now the experts were telling her to change all that.

She finished the last of her cold coffee and read the final line on the screen.

Imaginary friends disappear within three months, whether or not you encourage them.

After three months she would be more than glad to see the back of Ivan and return to normal life again. She flicked through her calendar and circled August with a red marker. If Ivan wasn't out of her house by then, she'd open the door and show him the way herself.

Chapter 8

Ivan laughed as he spun around in the black leather chair at the reception desk outside Elizabeth's office. He could hear her in the other room on the phone, organising a meeting using her boring grown-up voice. But as soon as she hung up the phone he heard her humming his song again. He laughed to himself. It definitely was addictive; once you got the tune in your head there was very little you could do to stop.

He swirled himself round in the chair faster and faster, doing pirouettes on wheels until his stomach danced and his head began to throb. He decided that chair spinning was his absolute favourite. Ivan knew that Luke would have loved to play the spin-the-chair game and, on picturing his sad little face pressed up against the car window from earlier that morning, his mind drifted and the chair slowed. Ivan wanted so much to visit the farm, and Luke's granddad looked like he could do with a bit of fun. He was similar to Elizabeth in that way. Two boring old gnirobs.

Anyway, at least this separation gave Ivan time to monitor Elizabeth so he could write a report on her. He had a meeting in a few days and would have to give a presentation to the rest of the team about who he was working with at the moment. They did it all the time. A few more days with her to prove that she couldn't see him would be enough and then he could get back to concentrating on Luke. Maybe there was something he was missing with him, despite his years of experience.

As Ivan's head began to get dizzy he put his foot down on the floor to stop. He decided to leap from the whirling chair so he could pretend he was jumping from a moving car. He rolled dramatically across the floor just like they did in the movies and looked up from where he was crouched in a ball to see a teenage girl standing before him open-mouthed, watching her office chair spin out of control.

Ivan saw her look around the office to see if anyone else was present. She frowned, approached the desk as if she were walking on landmines and placed her bag on the desk ever so quietly as if afraid to disturb the chair. She looked to see if anyone was watching and then tiptoed over to study it. She held out her hands as though trying to tame a wild horse.

Ivan chuckled.

Seeing that nothing was wrong Becca scratched her head in wonder. Perhaps Elizabeth had been sitting in the chair before she came in. She smirked at the thought of Elizabeth swinging around like a child, hair tied back tightly, dressed in one of her sharp black suits with her sensible shoes dangling in the air. No, the picture didn't fit. In Elizabeth's world chairs were made to be sat on. So that's exactly what Becca did and got to work immediately.

'Good morning, everyone,' a high-pitched voice sang from the door later that morning. A plum-haired Poppy danced into the room, dressed in denim flares embroidered with flowers, platform shoes and a tie-dyed T-shirt. As usual, every inch of her body was splashed with paint. 'Everyone have a nice weekend?' She was always singing her sentences and dancing about the room, flinging her arms around with all the grace of an elephant.

Becca nodded.

'Great.' Poppy stood in front of Becca with her hands on her hips. 'What did you do, Becca, join a debating team? Go out on a date and talk the ear off some bloke? Huh?'

Becca turned the page of the book she was reading and ignored her.

'Wow, that's fabulous, sounds like a blast. You know, I really do love the banter we have in this office.'

Becca turned a page.

'Oh, really? Well, that's enough information for now, if you don't mind. What the . . . ?' She whipped her body away from Becca's desk and was silent.

Becca didn't look up from the book she was reading. 'It's been doing that all morning,' she said in a quiet bored tone.

It was Poppy's turn to remain quiet.

There was silence in the office for a few minutes while Becca read her book and Poppy stared at the sight ahead of her. In her office, Elizabeth heard the long silence between the two and stuck her head out of her door.

'Everything alright, girls?' she asked.

A mystery squeaking sound was all the reply.

'Poppy?'

She didn't move her head as she spoke. 'The chair.'

Elizabeth stepped out of her office. She turned her head in the same direction. The paint-splattered chair behind Poppy's desk, which Elizabeth had been trying to convince Poppy to get rid of for months, was flying around all by itself, the screws squeaking loudly. Poppy let out a nervous laugh. They both moved closer to examine it. Becca was still reading her book in silence as if it was the most normal thing in the world.

'Becca,' Elizabeth half laughed, 'have you seen this?'

Becca still didn't lift her eyes from the page. 'It's been doing that for the past hour,' she said softly. 'It just stops and starts all the time.'

Elizabeth frowned. 'Is it some sort of new artistic creation of yours, Poppy?'

'I wish it was,' Poppy replied, still in awe.

They all watched it spin in silence. Squeak, squeak, squeak.

'Maybe I should call Harry. It's probably something to do with the screws,' Elizabeth reasoned.

Poppy raised her eyebrows uncertainly. 'Yeah, I'm sure the *screws* are making it spin out of control,' she said sarcastically, gazing in wonder at the whirling multicoloured chair.

Elizabeth picked an imaginary piece of fluff from her jacket and cleared her throat. 'You know, Poppy, you really need to get your chair reupholstered; it's not a very positive sight for when customers come to see us. I'm sure Gwen will do it quickly for you.'

Poppy's eyes widened. 'But it's supposed to be like that. It's an expression of personality, an extension of myself. It's the only item I can project myself onto in this room.' She looked around in disgust. 'This fucking *beige* room.' She said the word like it was a disease. 'And *Mrs Bracken* spends more time gossiping with those pals of hers that have nothing else to do but drop by everyday, than actual work.'

'You know that's not true, and remember that not everyone appreciates your taste. Besides, as an interior design company we should be reflecting less . . . alternative designs and more of what people can apply to their own homes.' She studied the chair some more. 'It looks like a bird with a very bad stomach has gone to the toilet on it.'

Poppy looked at her proudly. 'I'm glad *someone* got the idea.'

'Anyway, I've already allowed you to put up that screen,' Elizabeth nodded her head at the partition Poppy had decorated with every colour and material known to man, to act as a dividing wall between Becca and herself.

'Yes, and people *love* that screen,' Poppy said. 'I've already had three requests from customers.'

'Requesting what? To take it down?' Elizabeth smiled.

They both studied the divider thoughtfully, arms folded, heads cocked to one side as though studying a piece of art in a museum, while the chair continued to spin in front of them.

Suddenly the chair leaped and the screen beside Poppy's desk went crashing to the floor. The three women jumped and each took a step back. The chair began to slow down and came to a stop.

Poppy held her hand over her mouth. 'It's a sign.' Her voice was muffled.

On the other side of the room the usually silent Becca began laughing loudly.

Elizabeth and Poppy looked at each other, stunned.

'Hmm,' was all Elizabeth could say before she turned slowly and returned to her office.

Lying on the floor of the office from where he had leaped from the chair to on top of he couldn't tell what, Ivan held his head in his hands until the room stopped spinning. He had a headache and had come to the conclusion that maybe chair spinning wasn't his favourite any more. He watched groggily as Elizabeth entered her office and pushed the door closed behind her with her foot. He leaped from the floor and dived towards it, managing to squeeze his body between the gap before it shut. She wouldn't be locking any doors on him today.

He sat in the (non-swivel) chair on front of Elizabeth's desk and looked around the room. He felt like he was in a principal's office waiting to be given out to. It had the atmosphere of a principal's office, quiet and tense, and it smelled like one too, apart from the scent of Elizabeth's perfume, which he loved so much. Ivan had been in a few headmasters' offices with previous best friends so he knew well what that feeling was like. In training they were generally taught not to go to school with their best friends. There was really no need for them to be there and the rule was introduced because children were getting into trouble and parents were being called in. Instead they hung around outside and waited in the yard until break time. And even if the children chose not to play with them in the yard, they knew they were around, which gave them more confidence to play with the other kids. This was all a result of years of research but Ivan tended to ignore all those facts and statistics. If his best friend needed him at school, he'd be there and he sure wasn't afraid of breaking any rules.

Elizabeth sat behind a large glass desk in an oversized black leather chair, dressed in a severe black suit. As far as he could see, that was all she seemed to wear. Black, brown and grey. So restrained and so very boring, boring, boring. The desk was immaculate, glistening and sparkling as though it had just been polished. All that was on it was a computer and keypad, a thick black diary and the work Elizabeth was huddled over, which looked to Ivan like some boring pieces of material cut into small squares. Everything else had been tidied away in black cabinets. There was absolutely nothing on display apart from framed photographs of rooms that Elizabeth had obviously decorated. As with the house there was no sign of a personality in the room. Just black, white and glass. He felt like he was in a space- ship. The principal's office of a space ship.

Ivan yawned. She definitely was a gnirob. There were no photographs of family or friends, no cuddly toys sitting on the computer, and Ivan couldn't see any sign of the picture Luke had drawn for her over the weekend. She had told him she would put it in her office. The only thing of interest was a collection of coffee mugs from Joe's sitting on the windowsill. He bet Joe wouldn't be happy about that.

He leaned forward in his chair, rested his elbows on the desk and stuck his face near hers. Her face was fixed in pure concentration, her forehead was smooth and no frown lines creased her skin like they usually did. Her glossy lips, which smelled to Ivan like strawberries, pursed and unpursed themselves gently. She hummed quietly to herself.

His opinion of her changed once again right then. She was no longer the headmistress he saw her as when she was among others; she had become peaceful, calm and untroubled, and unlike the way she normally was when she was thinking alone. He guessed it was because for once she wasn't worrying. After watching her for a while, Ivan's eyes drifted down to the piece of paper she was working on. Between her fingers she held a brown colouring pencil and was shading in a drawing of a bedroom.

Ivan's eyes lit up. Colouring was by far his favourite. He stood up from the chair and made his way behind her so he could get a better look at what she was doing and to see if she was any good at staying between the lines. She was left-handed. He leaned over her shoulder and placed his arm on the desk beside her to steady himself. He was so close he could smell the coconut from her hair. He breathed in deeply and felt her hair tickle his nose.

Elizabeth stopped shading for a moment, closed her eyes, leaned her head back, relaxed her shoulders, took a deep breath and smiled softly to herself. Ivan did the same and felt her skin brush against his cheek. His body tingled. For a moment he felt odd, a nice kind of odd. Like the feeling he got when embraced in a warm hug and that was good because hugging was by far his favourite. He felt light-headed and a bit dizzy but nothing like the chair-spinning dizzy. This feeling was so much better. He held onto the feeling for a few minutes until eventually they opened their eyes at the same time and stared down at her drawing of a bedroom. Her hand moved over to the brown pencil as she decided whether or not to pick it up.

Ivan groaned softly. 'Elizabeth, not brown again. Come on, go for some colour, like that lime green,' he whispered into her ear, fully aware she couldn't hear him.

Her fingers hovered over the pencil as though a magnetic force was stopping her from touching it. She moved slowly away from the chocolate-brown pencil and moved to the lime green. She smiled slightly as though amused by her choice and gingerly held the implement between her fingers as if it was for the first time. She moved it around in her fingers as though holding it felt alien to her. Slowly she began to shade in the scatter cushions on the bed, and the tassels on the curtain tiebacks, moving on to bigger pieces like the throw at the end of the bed and eventually the lounger in the corner of the room.

'Much better,' Ivan whispered, feeling proud.

Elizabeth smiled and closed her eyes again, breathing slowly and deeply.

There was suddenly a knock at the door. 'Can I come in?' Poppy sang.

Elizabeth's eyes sprang open and dropped the offending pencil from her hand as though it were a dangerous weapon. 'Yes,' she called out, sitting back in the chair, her shoulder briefly brushing off Ivan's chest. Elizabeth looked around behind her, touched her shoulder lightly with her hand and turned back to face Poppy, who was skipping into the room, eyes glistening with excitement.

'OK, so Becca just told me you've got another meeting with the love hotel people.' Her words skipped together as though she were singing a song.

Ivan sat down on the windowsill behind Elizabeth's desk and stretched out his legs. They both folded their arms across their chests at the same time. Ivan smiled.

'Poppy, please do *not* call it "the love hotel",' Elizabeth rubbed her eyes wearily. Ivan was disappointed. That gnirob voice was back.

'OK, so the "hotel", then,' Poppy exaggerated the word. 'I have some ideas. I'm thinking waterbeds in the shape of hearts, hot tubs, champagne flutes that rise from the bedside lockers.' She lowered her voice to an excited whisper. 'I'm thinking the *Romantic era* meets *art deco*. *Caspar David Friedrich* meets *Jean Dunand*. It will be an *explosion* of rich reds, burgundys and wines that make you feel like you're being embraced in a velvet-lined *womb*. Candles *everywhere*. French boudoir meets—'

'Las Vegas,' Elizabeth finished drily.

Poppy snapped out of her trance and her face fell in disappointment.

'Poppy,' Elizabeth sighed, 'we've been through this before. I really think you should stick to the profile for this one.'

'Ah,' she fell back as though she'd been shot in the chest, 'but the profile is so *boring*.'

'Hear, hear!' Ivan stood and applauded. 'Gnirob,' he said loudly into Elizabeth's ear.

Elizabeth flinched and scratched at her ear. 'I'm sorry you feel that way, Poppy, but unfortunately what you consider boring is how other people choose to decorate their homes. In liveable, comfortable, and calming environments. People don't want to return home after a hard day's work to a house that shouts dramatic statements from every beam or colours that give them a headache. With work environments so full of stress, people just want manageable, relaxing and peaceful homes.' It was a speech she delivered to all of her customers. 'And this is a *hotel*, Poppy. We need to appeal to all kinds of people and not just the few, the *very* few, in fact, that would like to reside in a velvet-lined womb,' she added, deadpan.

'Well, I don't know many people that *haven't* once resided in velvet-lined wombs, do you? I don't think it rules out anyone, on *this* planet at least.' She kept trying. 'It might spark off some comforting memories for people.'

Elizabeth looked disgusted.

'Elizabeth.' Poppy groaned her name and dissolved dramatically into the chair in front of her. 'There has to be something that you will let me put my stamp on. I just feel so constrained here, like my creative juices aren't being allowed to flow and – oooh, that's nice,' she said chirpily, leaning over to look at the page in front of Elizabeth. 'Chocolate and lime are really gorgeous together. What made *you* of all people go for that?'

Ivan returned to Elizabeth's side and crouched down beside her, studying her face. Elizabeth stared at the sketch before her as if seeing it for the first time. She frowned but then her face softened. 'I don't know, actually. It just,' she closed her eyes briefly, breathed deeply and remembered the feeling, 'it just kind of . . . floated into my head suddenly.'

Poppy smiled and nodded excitedly. 'You see, now you understand how it is for me. I can't suppress my creativeness, you know? I know *exactly* what you mean. It's such a natural instinctive thing,' her eyes glistened and her voice lowered to a whisper, 'like *love*.'

'Hear, hear!' Ivan repeated, watching Elizabeth, so close to her now his nose was almost touching her cheek, but this time it was a light whisper that blew Elizabeth's loose hair softly around her ear.

Chapter 9

'Poppy, did you call me?' Elizabeth asked from under the mound of carpet samples piled on her desk later that day.

'No, *again*,' came the dull, bored reply. 'And please refrain from disturbing me as I'm about to order two thousand pots of magnolia paint for our future projects. May as well be organised and plan ahead for the next twenty years,' she muttered, then grumbled loud enough for Elizabeth to hear, 'because it's not as if we're about to change our ideas any time soon.'

'Oh, OK,' Elizabeth smiled, giving in. 'You can order another colour in too.'

Poppy almost fell off her chair with excitement.

'Order a few hundred pots of beige as well, while you're at it. "Barley" it's called.'

'Ha ha,' Poppy said drily.

Ivan raised his eyebrows at Elizabeth. 'Elizabeth, Elizabeth,' he sang, 'did you just make a funny? I think you did.' He stared directly at her, elbows on the desk. He sighed, blowing the loose strands of her hair as he did so.

Elizabeth froze, moved her eye sockets from left to right suspiciously and then continued working.

'Oh, see how she treats me?' Ivan said dramatically, holding his hand to his forehead and pretending to faint onto a black leather chaise longue in the corner of the room. 'It's like I'm not even here,' he declared. He put his feet up and stared at the ceiling. 'Forget about being at a principal's office, this is like being at a shrink's.' He stared at the cracks in the ceiling and put an American accent on. 'You see, Doc, it all started when Elizabeth kept ignoring me,' he said loudly in the room. 'It just made me feel so *unloved*, so *alone*, so *very, very alone*. It's like I don't exist. Like I'm *nothing*,' he exaggerated. 'My life is a mess.' He pretended to cry. 'It's all Elizabeth's fault.' He stopped and watched her for a while, matching carpets with fabrics and paint charts, and when he spoke again, his voice had returned to normal and he said softly, 'But it is her fault that she can't see me because she's just too afraid to believe. Isn't that right, Elizabeth?'

'What?' Elizabeth shouted again.

'What do you mean, "what"?' shouted back an irritated Poppy. 'I didn't say anything!'

'You called me.'

'No I didn't, you're hearing voices again, and please stop humming that bloody song!' Poppy shrieked.

'What song?' Elizabeth frowned.

'Whatever that *thing* is that you've been humming all morning. It's driving me *insane*.'

'Thank you very much!' Ivan announced, standing up and taking a dramatic bow before plonking his body back down on the chaise longue. 'I *invented* that song. Andrew Lloyd Webber, eat your heart out.'

Elizabeth continued working. She started humming again, then immediately stopped herself.

'You see, Poppy,' Ivan called into the other room, 'I think Elizabeth can hear me.' He crossed his hands over his chest and twiddled his thumbs. 'I think she can hear me very well. Isn't that right, Elizabeth?'

'Christ Almighty.' Elizabeth dropped the samples onto her desk. 'Becca, is that you saying my name?'

'No.' Becca's voice was barely audible.

Elizabeth's face turned red and flustered-looking, embarrassed at appearing a fool in front of her employees. Trying to assert control again, she called out sternly, 'Becca, can you get me a coffee from Joe's?'

'Oh, by the way,' Ivan sang, enjoying himself, 'don't forget to tell her to take one of the mugs over with her. Joe will be pleased.'

'Oh,' Elizabeth snapped her fingers as though she'd just remembered something, 'you might as well bring one of these with you.' She handed Becca a coffee mug. 'Joe will be,' she paused and looked confused, 'pleased.'

'Oh, she can hear me alright,' laughed Ivan. 'She just won't admit it to herself. That self-commanding mind of hers just won't allow her to. Everything is black and white to her,' then he added, 'and beige. But I'm going to shake things up a bit around here and we are going to have some *fun*. Ever done that before, Elizabeth? Had fun?' His eyes danced with mischief.

He swung his legs off the chaise longue and jumped upright. He sat on the edge of Elizabeth's desk and glanced at the printouts of the online information about imaginary friends. He tutted and shook his head. 'No, you don't believe all that gobbledegook, do you, Lizzie? Can I call you Lizzie?'

Elizabeth's face flinched.

'Oh,' Ivan said gently, 'you don't like being called Lizzie, do you?'

Elizabeth swallowed softly.

He lay across the desk on top of all the carpet samples and rested his head on his hand. 'Well, I've got news for you,' he lowered his voice to a whisper, 'I'm real. And I'm not going anywhere until you open those eyes properly and see me.'

Elizabeth stopped fiddling with the paint charts and raised her eyes slowly. She looked around her office and then settled on staring straight ahead of her. For some reason she felt calm, calmer than she had felt in a very long time. She was stuck in a trance, staring at nothing but unable to blink or look away, feeling surrounded by warmth and security.

Suddenly the door to her office sprung open, so quickly and forcefully that the handle crashed against the wall. Elizabeth and Ivan jolted in fright.

'Oooh, well excuse me for interrupting the lovebirds,' Saoirse cackled from the door.

Ivan jumped off the desk.

Elizabeth, mystified, immediately started to tidy her desk, a natural panicked reflex to her at the unannounced arrival of her younger sister. She smoothed down her jacket and pushed her palms over her hair.

'Oh, don't tidy up on my account.' Saoirse waved her hand dismissively, chewing quickly on a piece of gum. 'You're such a fusspot, you know. Just *chill*.' Her eyes moved up and down as she examined the area beside Elizabeth's desk suspiciously. 'So aren't you going to introduce me?'

Elizabeth examined her sister through narrow eyes. Saoirse made her nervous with her neurotic behaviour and sporadic tantrums. Alcohol or no alcohol, Saoirse had always been the same – difficult. In fact Elizabeth could hardly tell when she was drunk or sober. Saoirse had never found herself; she had never grown into a personality or learned about who she was, what she wanted, what made her happy or where she wanted to go in life. She still didn't know. She was a concoction of personalities never allowed to develop. Elizabeth wondered who her sister could be if she ever managed to stop drinking. She feared it would only be one problem less on a list of many.

It was so rare that Elizabeth could get Saoirse on her own in a room to talk to her – like, as a child alone in the fields, trying to catch a butterfly in a jar. They were so beautiful to look at, brightened up a room but never settled on anything for long enough to be caught. Elizabeth was forever chasing and when she did manage to catch her sister, Saoirse would all the time be fluttering her wings in panic, wanting to get away.

When she did have Saoirse's company she tried so hard to be under-standing, to treat Saoirse with the sympathy and empathy she deserved. She had learned all about it when she had sought professional help. She wanted advice from as many places as possible in order to help her sister. She needed to know the elusive magical words to say to Saoirse on the rare times that she visited. So even when Saoirse mistreated Elizabeth, she remained supportive and kind because she was afraid to lose her for good, afraid of how much further out of control Saoirse might spiral. Besides, she felt she had a duty to look out for her. But mostly it was because she was tired of seeing all the beautiful butterflies in her life fly away.

'Introduce you to whom?' Elizabeth replied gently.

'Oh, stop with that patronising tone. If you don't want to introduce me then that's fine.' She turned to the empty seat. 'She's ashamed of me, you see. She thinks I let her "good name" down. You know how the neighbours like to talk,' she laughed bitterly. 'Or maybe she's afraid I'll chase you away. Happened to the other one, you see. He—'

'OK, OK, Saoirse,' Elizabeth interrupted her play-acting. 'Look, I'm glad you dropped by because there's something I wanted to talk to you about.'

Saoirse's knee bounced up and down. Her jaw chomped on the gum.

'Colm brought the car back to me on Friday and he told me they'd arrested you. This is serious, Saoirse. You have to be really careful between now and the hearing. It's on in a few weeks and if you do anything . . . else, well, it will effect your punishment.'

Saoirse rolled her eyes, 'Elizabeth, *relax*! What are they going to do? Lock me up for years for driving two minutes down the road in my own sister's car? They can't take away my licence because I don't have one and if they prevent me from ever getting one I don't care because I don't want one. All they'll do is give me a few weeks of some commu-nity service bullshit, probably helping a few old ladies cross the road or something. It'll be fine.' She blew a bubble and it smacked against her chapped lips.

Elizabeth's eyes widened with disbelief. 'Saoirse, you didn't *borrow* my car. You took it without my permission and you don't have a licence. Come on,' her voice cracked, 'you're not stupid, you know well that's wrong.'

Elizabeth paused and tried to compose herself. This time she would succeed in talking her round. But even though it was the same situa-tion every time, Saoirse continued to be in denial. She swallowed hard.

'Look,' Saoirse said, getting angry, 'I'm twenty-two years old and I'm doing exactly the same thing that everyone else my age is doing – going out and having fun.' Her tone turned nasty. 'Well, just because you had no life at my age it doesn't mean that I can't have one.' Her wings were fluttering wildly as if she was trapped in a jar and was running out of air.

That's because I was busy raising you, Elizabeth thought angrily. And obviously doing a terrible job of it too.

'Are you going to sit here and listen to our entire conversation or what?' Saoirse said rudely to the chaise longue.

Elizabeth frowned and cleared her throat. 'But what about what Paddy said? Whether *you* think you did nothing wrong is not important. The gardaí think that you have.'

Saoirse chewed her gum and her cold blue eyes stared back. 'Paddy couldn't organise a piss-up in a brewery. He has no reason to charge me for *anything*. Unless having fun is suddenly illegal.' Flutter, flutter.

'Please, Saoirse,' Elizabeth said softly, 'please listen to me. They really mean it this time. Just . . . just relax a bit with the, eh,' she paused, 'with the drinking, OK?'

'Oh, shut up about that,' Saoirse's face twisted. 'Shut up, shut up, shut up, I'm fed up listening to you.' She stood up. 'My drinking's fine. It's you who's got the problem, thinking you're fucking perfect.' She opened the door and shouted so that everyone could hear, 'Oh, and you,' she nodded at the chaise longue, 'I don't think you'll be hanging around for long. They all leave eventually, isn't that right, *Lizzie*?' She spat out the name.

Elizabeth's eyes glistened with angry tears.

Saoirse banged the door loudly behind her. She had forced the jar lid open and was free to fly away once again. The noise of the bang shuddered through Elizabeth's body. The office was so silent even the fly that had been buzzing around stopped to settle on the light fitting. A moment later there was a feeble knock on the door.

'What?' she snapped.

'It's, eh, Becca,' came the quiet reply, 'with your coffee?'

Elizabeth smoothed back her hair and dabbed her eyes. 'Come in.'

As Becca was leaving the room, Elizabeth spotted Saoirse marching back through the reception area.

'Oh, by the way, I forgot to ask you for a loan of a few euros.' Her voice was gentler. It always was when she wanted something.

Elizabeth's heart sank. 'How much?'

Saoirse shrugged her shoulders. 'Fifty.'

Elizabeth rooted in her bag. 'You still staying at the B&B?'

Saoirse nodded.

She pulled out fifty euro and paused before handing it over. 'What's it for?'

'Drugs, Elizabeth, lots and lots of drugs,' Saoirse said smartly.

Elizabeth's shoulders dropped, 'I just meant—'

'Groceries – you know, bread, milk, toilet paper. That kind of thing.' She swiped the crisp note out of Elizabeth's hand. 'Not all of us wipe our arses on silk, you know.' She lifted a swatch of material from the desk and tossed it at her.

The door banged shut behind her as Elizabeth stood alone in the centre of her office and watched the black piece of silk effortlessly drift to the white carpet.

She knew what it felt like to fall.

Chapter 10

A few hours later, Elizabeth shut down her computer, tidied her desk for the twentieth time and left her office for the day. Becca and Poppy stood together staring into space. Elizabeth turned to see what kept their attention.

'It's doing it again,' Poppy sang nervously.

They all watched the chair spinning around unaided.

'You think it's Mr Bracken?' Becca asked quietly.

Poppy imitated Mrs Bracken's voice. 'Chair-spinning isn't what Mr Bracken would have wanted.'

'Don't worry, girls,' Elizabeth said, trying not to laugh. 'I'll get Harry in tomorrow to fix it. You two head off home.'

After saying their goodbyes Elizabeth continued to stare at the chair spinning in silence. She neared it slowly, inch by inch. As she got very close to it, it stopped spinning.

'Chicken,' Elizabeth muttered.

She looked about to ensure she was alone and slowly she grabbed the handles of the chair and lowered herself into it. Nothing happened. She bounced up and down a few times, looked to the sides and under the seat and still nothing happened. Just as she was about to get up and leave, the chair began to move. Slowly at first, then gradually it began to pick up speed. Feeling nervous, she contemplated leaping off but as it spun faster and faster she began to giggle. Louder and louder she laughed, the faster it went. Her sides ached. She couldn't remember the last time she had felt so young, legs up, feet out, hair blowing in the breeze. Eventually, after a few moments, it slowed to a stop and Elizabeth caught her breath.

Her smile slowly faded and the childish laughing in her head began to die down. All she was left with was complete silence in the abandoned office. She began to hum and her eye scanned across Poppy's disorganised desk of books of material, paint sample tubs, sketches and house interior magazines. Her eye fell upon a gold photo frame. In it was a photograph of Poppy, her two sisters, three brothers and parents, all squeezed together on a couch like a football team. The resemblance between them was obvious. They had little button noses and green eyes that narrowed to slits when they laughed. In the corner of the frame was a strip of passport photos of Poppy and her boyfriend, both of them making faces to the camera in the first three of them. But the fourth was of them staring lovingly into each other's eyes. A moment between them eternally caught on camera.

Elizabeth stopped humming and swallowed. She had known that look once.

She continued to stare at the frame, trying not to remember those times but, again, she lost the battle, drowning in the sea of memories that flooded her mind.

She began to sob. Quiet whimpers at first that soon exited her mouth as pain-filled wails from the depths of her heart. She could hear her own hurt. Each tear was a call for help that had never been answered before, and that she didn't expect to be answered now. And that made her cry even more.

Elizabeth marked off another day on her calendar with a red pen. Her mother had been gone for exactly three weeks this time. Not the longest amount of time so far but long enough for Elizabeth. She hid the calendar under her bed and got into bed. She had been sent to her room by her father three hours ago as he had grown tired of her excited pacing in front of the living-room window. Since then she had been battling to keep her eyes open. She needed to fight sleep so that she wouldn't miss her mother returning. Those were the best times because her mother would be in one of her happy moods, delighted to be home, telling Elizabeth how much she'd missed her, smothering her with hugs and kisses so much that Elizabeth couldn't remember ever feeling sad.

Her mother would float through the rooms of the house almost as if her feet weren't touching the ground. Her words were big whispers of excitement, her voice so hushed making Elizabeth feel that every word her mother breathed was their big secret. Her eyes glistened and danced with delight as she told her daughter of her adventures and who she'd met along the way. Elizabeth certainly did not want to miss all that while she was sleeping.

Elizabeth jumped out of bed again and splashed ice-cold water over her face from the sink in her room. Stay awake, Elizabeth, stay awake, she told herself. She propped her pillows up against the wall and sat up straight on her bed, staring out through the open curtains and out to the dark road that led into blackness. She had no doubt that her mother would be back tonight because she had promised her. And she just had to keep that promise because it was Elizabeth's tenth birthday the next day and she wouldn't miss that. Only weeks ago she had promised her that they would eat cakes, buns and all the sweets they wanted. And they'd have balloons of all Elizabeth's favourite colours that they'd bring out into the field, let them go and watch fly away up to the clouds. Elizabeth hadn't stopped thinking of it since her mother had left. Her mouth watered for fairy cakes with pretty pink icing, and she dreamed of pink balloons attached to white ribbons floating up to the blue sky above. And the day was almost here, no more waiting!

She picked up *Charlotte's Web*, a book she had been reading at night to keep herself awake and she turned on her torch as her father wouldn't let her keep the lights on past eight. A few pages in and her eyelids grew heavy and started to droop. She slowly closed her eyes, only intending to rest them for a little while. Every night she fought sleep because it was always sleep that allowed her mother to slip away into the night and it was sleep that missed her big arrivals. Even when her mother was home she fought it, instead choosing to stay outside her door, sometimes watching her sleep, other times protecting her and guarding her from leaving. Even the rare times that she did sleep, her dreams shouted at her to wake up as though she was doing wrong. People were always commenting to her father that she was too young for the dark circles under her eyes.

The book fell away from Elizabeth's hands and she was lost to the world of sleep.

The front gate creaked.

Elizabeth's eyes shot open to the brightness of the early morning and her heart beat wildly. She heard the crunching of footsteps over gravel as they approached the front door. Elizabeth's heart did cartwheels across her chest with delight. Her mother hadn't forgotten her; she knew she wouldn't have missed her birthday.

She leaped out of bed and did a little dance around her room, not knowing whether or not to open the door for her mother or to allow her to make the grand entrance she loved doing so much. She ran out into the hall in her nightdress. She could see the blurry image of a body through the rippled glass of the front door. She hopped from foot to foot with nervousness and excitement.

Elizabeth's father's bedroom door opened. She turned to face him with a grin. He gave her a small smile and leaned against the doorframe, watching the door. Elizabeth turned her head back to the door, twisting her hem of her nightdress in her little hands. The letter box opened. Two white envelopes slid through and landed on the stone floor. The figure at the door began to fade again. The gate creaked and closed.

Elizabeth dropped the hem of her nightdress from her hands and stopped hopping. She suddenly felt the cold of the stone floor.

She slowly picked up the envelopes. Both were addressed to her and her heart quickened again. Maybe her mother hadn't forgotten, after all. Maybe she had got so caught up in one of her adventures that she couldn't make it home in time and had to explain it all in a letter. She opened the envelopes, careful not to rip the paper that could contain precious words from her mother.

Both were birthday cards from distant, dutiful relatives.

Her shoulders slumped and her heart fell. She turned to face her father and shook her head slowly. His face darkened and he stared angrily into the distance. They caught eyes again and for a moment, a rare moment, Elizabeth and he shared the same knowing feeling and Elizabeth didn't feel so alone any more. She took a step forward to give him a hug.

But he turned away and closed his door behind him.

Elizabeth's bottom lip trembled. There were no fairy cakes or buns that day. The pink balloons floating up towards the clouds remained nothing but dreams. And Elizabeth learned that imagining and fantasising did nothing but break her heart.

Chapter 11

The hissing of the water boiling over onto the cooker brought Elizabeth sharply back to the present. She raced across the kitchen to lift the pot off the hob and lowered the heat. She poked at the steamed chicken and vegetables, wondering where her head was today.

'Luke, dinner,' she called.

She had collected Luke from her father's after work, although she had been in absolutely no mood to drive down that road after sobbing in her office. She hadn't cried in years. She didn't know what was happening to her over the last few days. Her mind just kept drifting, and she never drifted. She always stayed the same, had stable, controlled thoughts and was always constant, never stopped. Nothing at all like her behaviour today at the office.

Luke shuffled into the kitchen, already dressed in his Spiderman pyjamas. He stared sadly at the table. 'You didn't set a place for Ivan again.'

Elizabeth opened her mouth to protest but stopped herself in time, remembering the advice the websites had given. 'Oh, didn't I?'

Luke looked at her in surprise.

'Sorry, Ivan,' she said, taking out a third plate. What a waste of food, she thought spooning broccoli, cauliflower and potatoes onto his plate. 'I'm sure he doesn't like chicken so this will have to do.' She placed the plate of leftover vegetables down opposite her.

Luke shook his head. 'No, he said he really does like chicken.'

'Let me guess,' Elizabeth said, cutting a corner off her own, 'chicken's his favourite.'

Luke smiled. 'He says it's his favourite kind of *poultry*.'

'Right.' Elizabeth rolled her eyes. She watched Ivan's plate, wondering how on earth Luke was going to manage to eat a second plate of vegetables. It was difficult enough trying to get him to eat his own.

'Ivan said he had fun in your office today,' Luke said, forking broccoli into his mouth, chewing quickly and making a face in disgust. He swallowed quickly and gulped back some milk.

'Did he?' Elizabeth smiled. 'What was so fun about my office?'

'He liked the chair-spinning,' he replied as he speared a baby potato. Elizabeth stopped chewing and stared at Luke. 'What do you mean?'

Luke popped the potato into his mouth and munched. 'He says spinning around in Poppy's chair is his favourite.'

Elizabeth for once ignored the fact that he was speaking with his mouth full. 'Did you speak to Poppy today?' Luke loved Poppy and sometimes chatted to her when Edith called the office to check a detail with Elizabeth. He knew Elizabeth's office number by heart – she had insisted he learn it as soon as he learned his numbers – so it was quite possible he might have called, missing his little chats with her while Edith was away. That must have been it, she thought, relieved.

'Nope.'

'Did you speak to Becca?'

'Nope.'

The chicken suddenly tasted like cardboard in her mouth. She swallowed it quickly and put down her knife and fork. She watched Luke eat, lost in thought. Ivan's plate went untouched unsurprisingly.

'Did you speak to Saoirse today?' She studied his face. She wondered if Saoirse's little role-play in her office earlier had anything to do with Luke's new obsession with Ivan. Knowing her sister as well as she did, she would have continued to taunt her had she found out about an invisible friend.

'Nope.'

Perhaps it was just a coincidence. Perhaps Luke was just guessing about the chair-spinning. Perhaps, perhaps, perhaps. Where had all her certainties suddenly gone?

'Don't play with your vegetables, Luke. Ivan told me to tell you that they are good for you.' She may as well use the Ivan situation to her advantage.

Luke started laughing.

'What's so funny?'

'Ivan says that all mums use him to make their kids eat vegetables.'

Elizabeth raised her eyebrows and smiled. 'Well, you can tell Ivan that's because mums know best.' Her smile faded – well, *some* mums, at least.

'Tell him yourself,' Luke giggled.

'Right then.' Elizabeth faced the empty chair ahead of her. 'Where do you come from Ivan?' She leaned forward and spoke as if addressing a child.

Luke started laughing at her and she felt silly. 'He's from Ekam Eveileb.'

It was Elizabeth's turn to laugh. 'Oh, really? And where's that?'

'Far, far away,' Luke said.

'How far? Like Donegal-far?' she smiled.

Luke shrugged, already bored with the conversation.

'Hey,' Elizabeth looked at Luke and laughed, 'how did you do that?'

'Do what?'

'Take a potato from Ivan's plate?'

'I didn't,' Luke frowned. 'Ivan ate it.'

'Don't be sil—' she stopped herself.

Later that evening Luke lay on the floor of the living room, humming *that* song, while Elizabeth drank a cup of coffee and stared at the television. It was a long time since they had done that. Usually they went their own separate ways after dinner. Usually they didn't talk so much during the meal, but then *usually* Elizabeth didn't humour Luke by playing silly games. She began to regret what she had done. She watched Luke colouring with his crayons on the floor. She had put down a mat so that he wouldn't dirty the carpet and although she hated when he played with his toys outside the playroom, she was glad that he was playing with some toys that she could at least see. Every cloud and all that. She turned her attention back to her house makeover show.

'Elizabeth.' She felt the tap of a little finger on her shoulder.

'Yes, Luke?'

'Drew this for you.' He handed her a brightly coloured picture. 'It's of me and Ivan playing in the garden.'

Elizabeth smiled and studied the drawing. Luke had written their names over two matchstick men but what came to her as a surprise was the height of Ivan. He was over twice the size of Luke and was dressed in a blue T-shirt, blue jeans, blue shoes and had black hair and great big blue eyes. What looked like black stubble lined his jawline, and he held hands with Ivan with a big smile on his face. She froze, not quite knowing what to say. Shouldn't his imaginary friend be the same age as he?

'Eh, Ivan is very tall for only being six, isn't he?' Maybe he had drawn him larger than life because he was so important to him, she reasoned.

Luke rolled around the floor giggling. 'Ivan always says there's nothing *only* about being six and, anyway, *he's* not six.' He laughed loudly again. 'He's old like you!'

Elizabeth's eyes widened in horror. *Old like her?* What kind of imaginary friend had her nephew created?

Chapter 12

Friends come in all different shapes and sizes, we all know that, so why should 'imaginary' friends be any different? Elizabeth had it all wrong. In fact Elizabeth had it *completely* wrong because as far as I could see she didn't have *any* friends. Maybe it's because she was only looking for thirty-four-year-old women that looked, dressed and acted like her. You could tell by the look on her face, she thought Luke should have found someone exactly like himself when she looked at Luke's picture of me and him. And that's no way to make friends.

The important thing is not what we *look* like but the role we play in our best friend's life. Friends choose certain friends because that's the kind of company they are looking for at that specific time, not because they're the correct height, age or have the right hair colour. It's not always the case but often there's a reason why, for example, Luke will see me and not my colleague Tommy, who looks six years old and constantly has a runny nose. I mean, I don't see any other older males interacting with Luke, do you? Just because you see 'imaginary' friends, it doesn't mean you see them all. You have the *ability* to see them all but as humans only use ten per cent of the brain, you wouldn't believe the other abilities there are. There are so many other wonderful things that eyes could see if they really focused. Life's kind of like a painting. A really bizarre abstract painting. You could look at it and think that all it is is a blur. And you can continue living your life thinking that all it is is a blur. But if you really look at it, really see it, focus on it and use your imagination, life can become so much more. That painting could be of the sea, the sky, people, buildings, a butterfly on a flower or *anything* except the blur you were once convinced it was.

After the events in Elizabeth's office I needed to call an emergency 'What IF' meeting. I've been in this job for years and I thought I'd seen it all but I obviously hadn't. Saoirse seeing me and talking to me had really stumped me. I mean, that's completely unheard of. OK, so Luke could see me – that was normal. Elizabeth had some sort of a sense of me, which was weird enough, but I was beginning to get used to it. But Saoirse seeing me? Of course it's common to be seen by more than one person on a job, but never by an *adult*, and never by *two* adults. The only friend in the company who dealt with adults was Olivia and it wasn't any kind of a rule, just what seemed to be happening all the time. I was confused, I can tell you that, so I got 'the boss' to round up all the usual suspects for an unscheduled 'What IF' meeting.

Our 'What IF' meetings were set up to discuss everyone's current situations and to knock around some ideas and suggestions for people who are slightly stuck. I've never had to call one on my behalf, so I could tell the boss was shocked when I did. The name of the meeting has a double meaning. We were all tired of being labelled as 'imaginary friends' among people and the media, so we decided to call the meeting the What Imaginary Friends meeting. I thought up that idea myself.

The six people that meet are the most senior people in the company. I arrived at the What IF room to the sound of everyone laughing and playing. I greeted them all and we sat and waited for the boss. We don't meet around long conference tables with smelly leather chairs in a board-room with no windows. We have a more relaxed approach to it and it really has a much more positive effect because the more comfortable we all feel, the more we can contribute. We sit in a circle on comfort-able seats. Mine's a beanbag. Olivia's is a rocking chair. She says it's easier for her to do her knitting that way.

The boss's not really bossy, we just call her that. She's really one of the nicest people you'll ever meet in your whole entire life. Now she's *really* seen it all: she knows everything there is to know about being a best friend. She's patient and caring, listens and hears what people don't say more than anyone I know. Opal is her name and she's beautiful. She floated into the room just then in a purple robe, her dreadlocks tied back in a half-ponytail away from her face, and they hung down past her shoulders. She had tiny sparkling beads throughout that glistened when she moved. She had daisies nestled into her dreadlocks like a tiara, a daisy chain around her neck and around her wrists. Round purple-tinted glasses sat on her nose, and when she smiled the beam was enough to guide ships into shore on a black night.

'Nice daisies, Opal,' Calendula said softly from beside me.

'Thank you, Calendula,' she smiled. 'Me and little Tara made them today in her garden. You're looking very dressed up today. What a lovely colour.'

Calendula beamed. She's been a best friend for absolute donkey's years, like me, but she only looks the same age as Luke. She is small with blonde hair that was today styled into bouncing curls, softly spoken, with big blue eyes, and was dressed in a yellow summer dress with matching yellow ribbons in her hair. She had gleaming new white shoes that swung from her hand-crafted wooden chair. The chair always reminded me of a Hansel and Gretel chair, yellow with painted hearts and candy sticks.

'Thank you, Opal.' Calendula's cheeks turned rosy. 'I'm going to a tea party after this meeting with my new best friend.'

'Oh?' Opal raised her eyebrows, impressed. 'Very nice. Where is it?'

'In the back garden. She got a new tea set for her birthday yesterday,' she replied.

'Well, that's lovely. How are things with little Maeve?'

'Well, thank you.' Calendula looked down in her lap.

The noise from the others in the room died down and all the focus was on Opal and Calendula. Opal wasn't the type of person to ask everyone to be quiet in order to start the meeting. She always began it quietly herself, knowing that the others would soon finish their conversations and settle down in their own time. She always said that all people needed was time and then they could figure most things out for themselves.

Opal was still watching Calendula fidgeting with a ribbon on her dress.

'Is Maeve still bossing you around, Calendula?'

Calendula nodded and looked sad. 'She's still telling me what to do all the time and when she breaks things and her parents get mad, she blames it on me.'

Olivia, an old-looking best friend, who was rocking in her chair while knitting, tutted loudly.

'You know why Maeve is doing that, don't you, Calendula?' Opal said softly.

Calendula nodded. 'I know that me being around provides her with the opportunity to be in charge and she is mirroring the behaviour of her parents. I understand why she is doing it and the importance of her doing it, but that kind of treatment day in day out becomes a little disheartening at times.'

Everybody nodded in agreement. We had all been in her shoes at some stage. Most young children liked to boss us around as it was their only chance to do it without getting into trouble.

'Well, you know she won't be doing it for very much longer, Calendula,' Opal said encouragingly, and Calendula nodded, her curls bouncing up and down.

'Bobby.' Opal turned to face a little boy sitting on a skateboard with his cap turned backwards. He had been rolling back and forth while listening to the conversation. On hearing his name he stopped rolling. 'You must stop playing computer games with little Anthony. You know why, don't you?'

The little boy with the face of an angel nodded and when he spoke his voice sounded much older than his apparent six years. 'Well, because

Anthony is only three and he shouldn't be forced to conform to gender roles. He needs to play with toys that allow him to take control, that are flexible and that do more than one thing. Too many of the other toys will stunt his early development.'

'What kind of things do you think you should be playing with?' Opal asked.

'Well, I'm going to concentrate on playing with, well, mostly nothing, actually, so we can do role-playing, or else use boxes, cooking utensils or empty toilet paper rolls.'

We all laughed at the last one. Toilet paper rolls are my absolute favourite. You can do so many things with them.

'Very good, Bobby. Just try to keep it in mind when Anthony tries to get you to play the computer again. Like Tommy does . . .' She trailed off, looking around. 'Actually, where is Tommy?'

'Sorry I'm late,' a loud voice called from the door. Tommy charged in with his shoulders back and arms swinging like a man fifty years older than he. There was muck all over his face, grass stains all down his knees and shins, cuts, scabs and mud on his elbows. He dived onto the beanbag, making a crashing noise with his mouth.

Opal laughed. 'Welcome, Tommy. Busy, were you?'

'Yeah,' Tommy replied cockily. 'Me and Johnno were down in the park, digging up grubs.' He wiped his snotty nose across his bare arm.

'Uugh!' Calendula wrinkled her nose in disgust and moved her chair closer to Ivan.

'Alright, princess.' Tommy winked at Calendula, resting his feet on the table in front of him. The table had been laid out with fizzy drinks and chocolate biscuits.

Calendula looked away from him with wide eyes and concentrated on Opal.

'So John is the same as usual,' Opal stated with amusement.

'Yep, still sees me,' he replied as though that were some kind of victory. 'He's got a problem with bullies at the moment, Opal, and as he's been intimidated into secrecy, he won't tell his parents.' He shook his head sadly. 'He's afraid they'll criticise him or intervene, which will make it worse, and he's also ashamed that he allowed it to happen. All the typical emotions that goes with bullying.' He popped a sweet into his mouth.

'So what are you doing about it?' Opal asked with concern.

'Unfortunately what was happening before I came along is that John was experiencing chronic intimidation. He developed a pattern of compliance with the unfair demands of those he perceived as stronger and he was beginning to identify with the bully and become one himself. But I wouldn't let him push me around,' Tommy said toughly.

'We've been working on his posture, voice and eye contact – as you know, these communicate a lot about whether you're vulnerable. I'm teaching him to be vigilant for suspicious individuals and everyday we run over a list of possible attributes.' He sat back and rested his arms behind his head. 'We're working on him developing a mature sense of justice.'

'And you've been digging for grubs,' Opal added with a smile.

'There's always time for grub-digging, isn't there, Ivan?' Tommy winked at me.

'Jamie-Lynn.' Opal turned to a little girl in denim dungarees and dirty runners. Her hair was cut short and she balanced her behind on a football. 'How's little Samantha getting along? I hope you're both not still digging up her mother's flower garden.'

Jamie-Lynn was a tomboy and kept getting her friends into trouble, whereas Calendula mostly went to tea-parties in pretty dresses and played with Barbie and My Little Pony. Jamie-Lynn opened her mouth and began blabbering away in a mystery language.

Opal raised her eyebrows. 'So I see you and Samantha are still speaking your own language.'

Jamie-Lynn nodded.

'OK, but be careful. It's not a good idea to keep speaking like that for much longer.'

'Don't worry, I know Samantha is learning to talk in sentences and develop her memory so I won't keep it up,' Jamie-Lynn said, returning to normal language. Her voice saddened. 'Samantha didn't see me this morning when she woke up. But then she did again at lunchtime today.'

Everyone felt sad for Jamie-Lynn and we gave her our condolences because we all knew how that felt. It was the beginning of the end.

'Olivia, how's Mrs Cromwell?' Opal's voice was gentler.

Olivia stopped knitting and rocking and shook her head sadly. 'Not long for her to go now. We had a great chat last night about a day trip she had with her family seventy years ago to Sandymount beach. That put her in a great mood. But as soon as she told her family this morning that she'd been talking to me about it they all left. They think she's talking about her great-aunt Olivia that died forty years ago and are convinced she's going mad. Anyway, I'll stay with her till the end. Like I said, there isn't long for her to go and the family have only visited twice in the past month. She's not hanging on for anyone.'

Olivia always made friends in hospitals, hospices and homes for the elderly. She was good at that kind of thing, helping people reminisce to fill the time if they couldn't sleep.

'Thanks, Olivia,' Opal smiled, and then she turned to me. 'So, Ivan, how's it all going in Fuchsia Lane? What's the big emergency? Little Luke seems to be doing OK.'

I made myself comfortable on the beanbag. 'Yeah, he is OK. There are a few things we need to work on, like how he feels about his family set-up, but nothing earth-shattering.'

'Good.' Opal looked pleased.

'But that's not what the problem is.' I looked around the circle at everyone. 'His *aunt*, who adopted him, is *thirty-four* and sometimes she can feel my *presence.*'

Everyone gasped and looked at each other in horror. I knew they'd react like that.

'But that's not even the half of it,' I continued, trying not to enjoy the drama too much because, after all, it was my problem. 'Luke's *mom*, who's *twenty-two*, came into Elizabeth's office today and *saw* me and *spoke* to me!'

Double gasp – apart from Opal, whose eyes twinkled back at me knowingly. I felt better when I saw that because I knew that Opal would know what to do. She always did and I wouldn't have to feel so confused any more.

'Where was Luke when you were in Elizabeth's office?' Opal asked, a smile forming at the corner of her lips.

'On his granddad's farm,' I explained. 'Elizabeth wouldn't let me out of the car to go with him because she was afraid her dad would get mad that Luke had a friend that he couldn't see.' I was out of breath after that.

'So why didn't you walk back to Luke when you got to the office?' Tommy asked, sprawled across the beanbag with his arms behind his head.

Opal's eyes glinted again. What was up with her?

'Because,' I replied.

'Because why?' Calendula asked.

Not her too, I thought.

'How far is the farm from the office?' Bobby asked.

Why were they asking all these questions? Shouldn't the important thing be why on earth all these people were sensing me?

'It's about a two-minute drive but twenty minutes' walking,' I explained, confused. 'What's with all the questions?'

'Ivan,' Olivia laughed, 'don't act the fool. You know that when you get separated from a friend you find them. A twenty-minute walk is nothing compared to what you did to get to that last friend of yours.' She chuckled.

'Ah, come on, everyone.' I threw my hands up helplessly. 'I was trying to figure out whether Elizabeth could see me or not. I was confused, you know. This has never happened before.'

'Don't worry, Ivan,' Opal smiled, and when she spoke again her voice was like honey. 'It's rare. But it's happened before.'

Everyone gasped once more.

Opal stood up, gathered her files together and prepared to leave the meeting.

'Where are you going?' I asked in surprise. 'You haven't told me what to do yet.'

Opal took off her purple-tinted shades and her chocolate-brown eyes gazed at me. 'This is not an emergency at all, Ivan. There is no advice that I can give you. You will just have to trust yourself that when the time comes, you'll make the right decision.'

'What decision? About what?' I asked, feeling even more confused now.

Opal grinned at me. 'When the time comes, you will know. Good luck.' And with that she left the meeting, with everyone staring at me in confusion. The blank faces were enough to prevent me from asking any of them for advice.

'Sorry, Ivan, I would be just as confused as you are,' Calendula said, standing up and smoothing out the wrinkles in her summer dress. She gave me a big hug and a kiss on the cheek. 'I'd better go now too or I'll be late.'

I watched her skipping towards the door, her blonde curls bouncing with every step. 'Enjoy your tea party!' I called.

'Make the right decision,' I grumbled to myself, thinking about what Opal had said. 'The right decision about what?' And then a chilling thought occurred to me. What if I didn't make the right decision? Would someone get hurt?

Chapter 13

Elizabeth pushed herself forward gently on the swinging bench in her back garden. She cradled a warm coffee cup in her hands, wrapping her slender fingers round the limestone-coloured mug. The sun was slowly setting and a slight chill was creeping out from hiding to take its place. She stared up into the sky, a perfect vision of candy-floss clouds, pink, red and orange, like an oil painting. An amber glow rose from behind a mountain before her, like the kind of secret glow that rose from Luke's bedcovers when he was reading with a torch. She breathed in the cooling air deeply.

Red sky at night, she heard a voice inside her head say.

'Shepherd's delight,' she whispered softly.

A soft breeze blew, as if the air, like her, was sighing. She had been sitting outside now for the past hour. Luke was upstairs playing with his friend Sam, after spending the day at his grandfather's. She was awaiting the arrival of Sam's father, whom she'd never met before, to come and collect him. Usually Edith dealt with the friends' parents and so Elizabeth wasn't at all looking forward to children chitchat.

It was 9.45 p.m. and light, it seemed, was calling it a day. She had been rocking herself back and forth, fighting the tears that threatened to fall, swallowing the lump that threatened to rise in her throat, forcing back the thoughts that threatened to drown her mind. She felt that she was fighting the world that threatened to jeopardise her plans. She fought the people that invited themselves into her world without her permission; she fought Luke and his head of childish ways, her sister and her problems, Poppy and her ideas at work, Joe and his coffee shop, competitors in her business. She felt she was always fighting, fighting, fighting. And now here she sat fighting her very own emotions.

She felt as if she'd been through a hundred rounds in the ring, as if she'd taken every punch, thump and kick her opponents could throw at her. Now she was tired. Her muscles ached, her defence was falling and her wounds weren't healing so quickly. A cat leaped from the high wall that separated Elizabeth from her neighbours and landed in her garden. It glanced at Elizabeth; chin held high, eyes glowing in the darkness. It walked slowly across the grass without a care in the world. So sure of itself, so confident, so full of its own self-importance. It jumped onto the opposite wall and disappeared into the night. She envied its ability to come and go as it pleased without owing anybody anything, not even those closest, who loved and cared for it.

Elizabeth used her foot to push herself back again. The swing squeaked slightly. In the distance the mountain appeared to be burning as the sun slipped down and out of sight. On the other side the full moon awaited its final call to centre stage. The crickets continued to chatter loudly to each other, the last of the children ran to their homes for the night. Car engines stopped, car doors slammed, front doors closed, windows shut and curtains were drawn. And then there was silence and Elizabeth was once again alone, feeling like a visitor in her own back garden that had taken on a new life in the falling darkness.

Her mind began to rewind over the events of the day. It stopped and played Saoirse's visit. Played it over and over again, the volume rising at every repetition. *They all leave eventually, isn't that right, Lizzie?* The sentence repeated itself like a broken record. It kept on at her like a finger prodding her chest. Harder and harder, first grazing the skin, then breaking it, prodding and prodding until eventually it tore right through and reached her heart. The place where it hurt most. The breeze blew and stung her open flesh wound.

She shut her eyes tightly. For the second time that day Elizabeth cried. *They all leave eventually, isn't that right, Lizzie?*

It played continuously, waiting for an answer from her. Her mind exploded. *YES!* it shouted. Yes, they all eventually leave. Every single one of them, every single time. Every person that ever succeeded in brightening her day and cheering her heart disappeared as quickly as a cat in the night. As though happiness was only supposed to be some kind of weekend treat, like ice cream. Her mother had done, just as this evening's sun had done: had left her, had taken away the light and warmth and replaced it with a chill and dark.

Uncles and aunts that visited and helped moved or passed on. Friendly school teachers could only care for a school year; school friends developed and tried to find themselves too. It was always the good people that left, the people that weren't afraid to smile or to love.

Elizabeth hugged her knees and cried and cried, like a little girl who had fallen and cut her knee. She wished for her mother to come and pick her up, to carry her and rest her on the kitchen counter while she applied a plaster to her cut. And then just like she always did, she would carry her around the room, dancing and singing until the pain was forgotten and her tears had dried.

She wished for Mark, her only love, to take her in his arms, in arms so big she was dwarfed in his embrace. She wished to be surrounded by his love while he rocked her slowly and softly as he used to do, whispering hushes of assurance in her ears and running his fingers through her hair. She believed him when he said them. He made her believe that everything would be OK and, lying in his arms, she knew that it would, *felt* that it would.

And the more she wished the more she cried because she realised she was surrounded by a father who could barely look her in the eye for fear of remembering his wife, a sister who had forgotten her own son, and a nephew who looked to her everyday with big hopeful blue eyes, just *asking* to be loved and cuddled. Emotions that she felt she was never given enough of to be able to share.

And as Elizabeth sat there crying and rocking, shivering in the breeze, she wondered why it was that she allowed one sentence that had passed the lips of a girl who had never received enough kisses of love, felt warm embraces or who had never herself allowed words of love to drift over her own lips to be the one whose thump and kick sent her falling to the ground. Just as she had done with the piece of black silk in her office.

Damn Saoirse. Damn her and her hatred of life, damn her for her disregard for others and disrespect for her sister. Damn her for not trying when all Elizabeth did was try with her whole heart. What gave her the power to speak with such churlishness? How could she be so flippant with her insults? And the voice inside Elizabeth's head reminded her that it wasn't the drink talking, it was never the drink talking. It was the hurt.

Elizabeth's hurt was screaming at her tonight. 'Oh, help,' she cried softly, covering her face in her hands. 'Help, help, help . . .' she whispered through her sobs.

A light creaking at the sliding door of the kitchen caused her head to jerk up from where it was cradled in her knees. At the door stood a man, lit like an angel by the kitchen light behind him.

'Oh.' Elizabeth swallowed hard, her heart pounding at being caught. She wiped her eyes roughly and smoothed down her wild hair. She rose to her feet. 'You must be Sam's dad.' Her voice still shook from the emotion bubbling inside her. 'I'm Elizabeth.'

There was a silence. He was probably wondering what on earth he was thinking of to let his six-year-old son be minded by this woman, a woman who let her young nephew open the front door by himself at ten o'clock at night.

'I'm sorry, I didn't hear the doorbell ring.' She pulled her cardigan tighter round her waist and crossed her arms. She didn't want to step into the light. She didn't want him to see that she had been crying. 'I'm sure Luke has told Sam you're here but . . .' *But what, Elizabeth?* '. . . but I'll just give him a quick call anyway,' she mumbled. She walked across the grass towards the house with her head down, rubbing her forehead with her hand to hide her eyes.

When she reached the kitchen door, she squinted against the bright light but kept her head lowered, not wanting to make eye contact with the man. All she could see of him were a pair of blue Converse runners at the end of faded blue jeans.

Chapter 14

'Sam, your dad is here to collect you!' Elizabeth called weakly upstairs. There was no answer, just the sound of a pair of little feet running along the landing. She sighed and looked at her reflection in the mirror. She didn't recognise the woman she saw. Her face was swollen and puffy, her hair messed from being blown in the breeze and damp from rubbing her teary hands through it.

Luke appeared at the top of the stairs, sleepy-eyed and dressed in his Spiderman pyjamas that he refused to allow her to wash, instead hiding them behind his favourite teddy, George, for protection. He rubbed his eyes tiredly with his fists and looked at her confused.

'Huh?'

'Luke, it's pardon, not huh,' Elizabeth corrected him, then wondered in her current mood why the hell it mattered. 'Sam's father is still waiting so could you please tell him to hurry down?'

Luke scratched his head in a daze. 'But,' he stopped and rubbed his face tiredly.

'But what?'

'Sam's dad collected him when you were in the gar—' He stopped as his gaze was averted to over Elizabeth's shoulder.

Luke's face broke into a toothless smile. 'Oh, hello Sam's dad.' He giggled uncontrollably. 'Sam will be down in a minute,' he laughed, and ran off back down the landing.

Elizabeth had no choice but to turn slowly and face Sam's father. She couldn't continue to avoid him while he waited in her home for his son. On first glance she noticed he had a look of bewilderment as he watched Luke run back down the landing, giggling. He turned to face her, evidently worried. He was leaning against the doorframe, hands tucked into the back pockets of a pair of faded blue jeans below a blue T-shirt, and wisps of jet-black hair escaped from under his blue cap. Despite his youthful attire she presumed he was her age.

'Don't worry about Luke,' Elizabeth said, slightly embarrassed at her nephew's behaviour. 'He's just a little hyper tonight and,' she rushed her words, 'I'm sorry you caught me at a bad time in the garden.' She wrapped her arms around her body protectively. 'I'm not usually like this.' She wiped her eyes with a trembling hand and quickly clasped her hands together to hide her shaking. Her overflow of emotion had disoriented her.

'That's OK,' the soft deep voice replied. 'We all have our bad days.'

Elizabeth chewed on the inside of her mouth and tried in vain to remember her last good one. 'Edith is away at the moment. I'm sure you've had dealings with her, which is why we've never met.'

'Oh, Edith—' he smiled – 'Luke's mentioned her lots of times. He's very fond of her.'

'Yes,' she smiled weakly and wondered if Luke had ever mentioned her. 'Would you like to sit down?' She motioned towards the living room. After offering him a drink she returned from the kitchen with a glass of milk for him and an espresso for herself. She paused at the door of the living room in surprise to catch him spinning around in the leather swivel chair. The sight of him made her smile.

On seeing her at the door he smiled back, stopped spinning, took the glass from her and then moved to the leather couch. Elizabeth sat in her usual chair, so oversized it almost swallowed her up, and hated herself for hoping his runners wouldn't dirty her cream carpet.

'I'm sorry, I don't know your name,' she said, trying to brighten up the dull tone in her voice.

'My name's Ivan.'

She spluttered coffee down her top as it caught in her throat.

Ivan rushed over to pat her on the back. His concerned eyes stared right into hers. His forehead creased with worry.

Elizabeth coughed, feeling stupid, quickly broke eye contact and cleared her throat. 'Don't worry, I'm fine,' she murmured. 'It's just funny that your name is Ivan because—' She stopped. What was she going to say? Tell a stranger that her nephew was delusional? Regardless of the internet advice she still wasn't sure his behaviour could be considered normal. 'Oh, it's a long story.' She waved her hand dismissively and looked away to take another sip. 'So what is it that you do, Ivan, if you don't mind me asking?' The warm coffee ran through her body, filling her with a familiar, comfortable feeling. She felt herself coming back, slipping out of the coma of sadness.

'I guess you could say I'm in the business of making friends, Elizabeth.'

She nodded understandingly. 'Aren't we all, Ivan.'

He contemplated that idea.

'So what's your company called?'

His eyes lit up. 'It's a good company. I really love my job.'

'Good Company?' she frowned. 'I'm not familiar with it. Is it based here in Kerry?'

Ivan blinked. 'It's based everywhere, Elizabeth.'

Elizabeth raised her eyebrows. 'It's international?'

Ivan nodded and gulped down some milk.

'What is the company involved in?'

'Children,' he said quickly. 'Apart from Olivia, who works with the elderly, but I work with children. I help them, you see. Well, it used to be children but now it seems we're branching out . . . I think . . .' He trailed off, tapped his glass with his fingernail and frowned into the distance.

'Ah, that's nice,' Elizabeth smiled. That explained the youthful clothes and playful nature. 'I suppose if you see room in another market you need to get in there, don't you? Expand the company, increase the profit. I'm always looking at ways to do that.'

'What market?'

'The elderly.'

'They have a market? Great, I wonder when it's on. Sundays, I suppose? You can always pick up a few good knick-knacks here and there, can't you? My old friend Barry's dad used to get second-hand cars and fix them up. His mom used to buy curtains and make them into clothes. She looked like something from *The Sound of Music*, good thing she lives here too because every Sunday she wanted to "climb every mountain", and because Barry was my best friend I had to do it, you see. When is it on, do you think? Not the film, I mean the market.'

Elizabeth barely heard him; her mind had slipped back into thinking mode. She couldn't stop herself.

'Are you alright?' the kind voice asked.

She stopped staring into the bottom of her coffee cup to face him. Why did he look like he cared so much? Who was this softly spoken stranger who made her feel so comfortable in his presence? Each twinkle in his blue eyes added another goose bump to her skin, his gaze was hypnotic and the tone of his voice was like a favourite song she wanted to blare and put on repeat. Who was this man who came into her house and asked her a question not even her own family could ask? *Are you alright?* Well? Was she alright? She swirled the coffee around in the cup and watched it hitting the sides and spraying up like the sea against the cliffs of Slea Head. She thought about it and came to the conclusion that if the last time she had heard those words uttered by anyone was more than a few years ago then she supposed the answer was no. She was not alright.

She was tired of hugging pillows, counting on blankets for warmth and of reliving romantic moments only in her dreams. She was tired of hoping that every day would hurry so she could get on to the next.

Hoping that it would be a better day, an easier day. But it never was. Worked, paid the bills and went to bed but never slept. Each morning the weight on her shoulders got heavier and heavier and each morning she wished for night to fall quickly so she could return to her bed to hug her pillows and wrap herself in the warmth of her blankets.

She looked at the kind stranger with the blue eyes watching her and saw more care in those eyes than she had in anyone she knew. She wanted to tell him how she felt, she wanted to hear him say it would be OK, that she wasn't alone and that they would all live happily ever after and that— She stopped herself. Dreams, wishes and hopes were not realistic. She needed to stop her mind from wandering onto those paths. She had a good job and she and Luke were healthy. That was all she needed. She looked up at Ivan and thought about how to respond to his question. Was she alright?

He took a sip of his milk.

Her face broke into a smile and she started laughing, for above his lip was a milk moustache so big it reached the end of his nostrils. 'Yes, thank you, Ivan, I'm alright.'

He looked unsure as he wiped his mouth and, after a while of studying her, spoke. 'So, you're an interior designer?'

Elizabeth frowned. 'Yes, how do you know?'

Ivan's eyes danced. 'I know everything.'

Elizabeth smiled. 'Don't all men?' She looked at her watch. 'I don't know what Sam's up to. Your wife will probably think I've abducted the two of you.'

'Oh, I'm not married,' Ivan replied quickly. 'Girls, uugh!' He made a face.

Elizabeth laughed. 'I'm sorry, I didn't realise you and Fiona weren't together.'

'Fiona?' Ivan looked confused.

'Sam's mother?' Elizabeth asked, feeling foolish.

'Oh, her?' Ivan made another face. 'No way.' He leaned forward on the leather couch and it squeaked beneath his jeans. A familiar sound to Elizabeth. 'You know she makes this awful chicken dish. Sauce really ruins the chicken.'

Elizabeth found herself laughing again. 'That's an unusual reason not to like someone,' but funnily enough Luke had complained about it to her also, after eating dinner at Sam's over the weekend.

'Not if you like chicken, it's not,' Ivan replied honestly. 'Chicken is by far my favourite,' he smiled.

Elizabeth nodded, trying to suppress a giggle.

'Well, my favourite kind of poultry really.'

That did it. She started laughing again. Luke must have picked up some of his phrases.

'What?' Ivan smiled widely, revealing a set of sparkling white teeth.

'You,' Elizabeth said, trying to calm herself and control her laughter. She couldn't believe she was acting like this with a total stranger.

'What about me?'

'You're funny,' she smiled.

'You're beautiful,' he said calmly and she looked up at him in surprise.

Her face flushed. What kind of a thing was that to say? There was another silence, uncomfortable on her part as she wondered whether to be insulted or not. Rarely did people make such comments to Elizabeth. She didn't know how she was supposed to feel.

On sneaking a peak at Ivan she was intrigued to see he didn't look at all perplexed or embarrassed. As though he said it all the time. A man like him probably did, she thought cynically. A charmer, that's all he was. Although, as much as she stared at him with forced disdain, she couldn't really bring herself to believe that. This man did not know her, had met her less than ten minutes ago, had told her she was beautiful and yet remained seated in her living room as if he were her best friend, looking around the room as if it were the most interesting place he had ever seen. He had such a friendly nature, was easy to talk to, easy to listen to, and despite telling her she was beautiful while she sat in old tattered clothes with red-rimmed eyes and greasy hair, he didn't make her feel uncomfortable. The more they sat in silence the more she realised he had simply paid her a compliment.

'Thank you, Ivan,' she said politely.

'And thank you too.'

'For what?'

'You said I was funny.'

'Oh, yes. Well, em . . . you're welcome.'

'You don't get many compliments, do you?'

Elizabeth should have stood up right there and then, and ordered him out of her living room for being so intrusive, but she didn't, because as much as she thought she should *technically*, according to her own rules, be bothered by this, she wasn't. She sighed, 'No, Ivan, I don't.'

He smiled at her. 'Well, let that be the first of many.'

He stared at her and her face began to twitch from holding his stare for so long. 'Is Sam staying with you tonight?'

Ivan rolled his eyes. 'I hope not. For a boy of only six years of age, he snores awfully loud.'

Elizabeth smiled. 'There's nothing *only* about being si—' She stopped herself and gulped back some coffee.

He raised his eyebrows. 'What was that?'

'Nothing,' she mumbled. While Ivan was looking around the room Elizabeth stole another glance at him. She couldn't figure out how old he was. He was tall and muscular, manly but yet had a boyish charm. He confused her. She decided to cut to the chase.

'Ivan, I'm confused about something.' She took a breath to ask her question.

'Don't be. Never be confused.'

Elizabeth felt herself frown and smile at the same time. Even her face was confused by his statement. 'OK,' she said slowly, 'do you mind me asking what age you are?'

'No,' he said happily. 'I don't mind at all.'

Silence.

'Well?'

'Well what?'

'What age are you?'

Ivan smiled. 'Let's just say I've been told by one person in particular that I'm old like you.'

Elizabeth laughed. She had thought as much. Obviously Ivan hadn't been spared any of Luke's unsubtle comments.

'Children keep you young, though, Elizabeth.' His voice turned serious, his eyes deep and thoughtful. 'My job is to care for children, help them along and just be there for them.'

'You're a care worker?' Elizabeth asked.

Ivan thought about that. 'You could call me a care worker, professional best friend, guide . . .' He held out his hands and shrugged. 'Children are the ones that know exactly what's going on in the world, you know. They *see* more than adults, *believe* in more, are honest and will always, *always* let you know where you stand.'

Elizabeth nodded along with him. He obviously loved his job – as a father and as a care worker.

'You know, it's interesting,' he leaned forward again, 'children learn much more, far more quickly than adults. Do you know why that is?'

Elizabeth assumed there was some scientific explanation for it but shook her head.

'Because they're open-minded. Because they *want* to know and they *want* to learn. Adults,' he shook his head sadly, 'think they know it all. They grow up and forget so easily and instead of opening their minds and developing it they *choose* what to believe and what not to believe. You can't make a choice on things like that: you either believe or you don't. That's why their learning is slower. They are more cynical, they lose faith and they only demand to know things that will help them get by day by day.

They've no interest in the extras. But, Elizabeth,' he said, his voice a loud whisper, eyes wide and sparkling, and Elizabeth shivered as goose pimples rose on her arms. She felt as if he was sharing the world's greatest secret with her. She moved her head closer. 'It's the *extras* that make life.'

'That make life what?' she whispered.

He smiled. 'That make *life.*'

Elizabeth swallowed the lump in her throat. 'That's it?'

Ivan smiled. 'What do you mean, that's it? How much more can you get than life, how much more can you ask for than life? That's the gift. Life is *everything*, and you haven't lived it properly until you believe.'

'Believe in what?'

Ivan rolled his eyes and smiled. 'Oh, Elizabeth, you'll figure it out.'

Elizabeth wanted the extras he spoke about. She wanted the sparkle and the excitement of life, she wanted to release balloons in a barley field and fill a room with pink fairy cakes. Her eyes filled again and her heart thudded in her chest at the thought of crying in front of him. She needn't have worried because he stood up slowly.

'Elizabeth,' he said gently, 'on that note, I shall leave you. It was my pleasure to spend this time with you.' He held out his hand.

When Elizabeth held out her own to touch his soft skin, he grasped it gently and pumped it hypnotically. She couldn't speak for the lump in her throat that had taken over.

'Good luck with your meeting tomorrow,' he smiled encouragingly, and with that he exited the living room. The door was closed behind him by Luke who shouted, 'Bye, Sam!' at the top of his voice, laughed loudly, and then pounded up the stairs.

Later that night Elizabeth lay in bed, her head hot, her nose blocked and her eyes sore from crying. She hugged her pillow and snuggled down into her duvet. The open curtains allowed the moon to shine a path of silver-blue light across her room. She gazed out the window at the same moon she had watched as a child, at the same stars she had wished upon, and a thought struck her.

She hadn't mentioned anything at all to Ivan about her meeting tomorrow.

Chapter 15

Elizabeth hauled her luggage out of the boot of the taxi and trailed it along behind her into the departure and arrival area of Farranfore Airport. She breathed a sigh of relief. Now she really felt that she was going home. After spending only a month living in New York she felt she fitted in there more than she ever had in Baile na gCroíthe. She was beginning to make friends; more importantly, she was beginning to *want* to make friends.

'The plane is on time at least,' Mark said, joining the small check-in queue.

Elizabeth smiled at him and rested her forehead against his chest. 'I'll need another holiday to recover from this one,' she joked wearily.

Mark chuckled, kissed the top of her head and ran his hands through her dark hair. 'You call coming home to visit our families a holiday?' he laughed. 'Let's go to Hawaii when we get back.'

Elizabeth lifted her head and raised an eyebrow, 'Of course, Mark, I'll just let you tell my boss that. You know I need to get back to that project urgently.'

Mark studied her determined face. 'You should go it alone.'

Elizabeth rolled her eyes and leaned her forehead against his chest again. 'Not this again.' Her voice was muffled in his duffel coat.

'Just listen.' He lifted her chin with his forefinger. 'You work all the hours under the sun, rarely take time off and stress yourself out. For what?'

She opened her mouth to reply.

'For what?' he repeated, stopping her.

Again she opened her mouth to answer and he jumped in. 'Well, seeing as you're so reluctant to answer,' he smiled, 'I'll tell you what for. For *other people*. So that they get all the glory. *You* do all the work, *they* get all the glory.'

'Excuse me,' Elizabeth half laughed, 'that job pays me extremely well as you *well* know, and at the rate I'm going, by this time next year – if we decide to stay in New York, that is – I'll be able to afford that house we saw—'

'My dear Elizabeth,' Mark interrupted, 'the rate you're going, this time next year that house will be *sold* and in its place will be a skyscraper or terribly trendy bar that doesn't sell alcohol or a restaurant that doesn't serve food "*just to be different*"; he made quotation marks with his fingers, making Elizabeth laugh, 'which you will no doubt paint white, put fluorescent lights in the floors and refuse to purchase furniture for, in case it clutters the place,' he teased. 'And other people will get the credit for that.' He looked at her in pretend disgust. 'Imagine. That's *your* blank canvas, nobody else's, and they shouldn't take that away from you. I want to be able to bring our friends in there and say, "Look, everyone, Elizabeth did this. Took her three months to do, all it is is white walls and no chairs but I'm proud of her. Didn't she do well?"'

Elizabeth held her stomach from laughing so hard. 'I would *never* let them knock down that house. Anyway, this job pays me *lots* of money,' she explained.

'That's the second time you've mentioned money. We're doing fine. What do you need all this money for?' Mark asked.

'A rainy day,' Elizabeth said, her laughter dying down and her smile fading as her thoughts drifted to Saoirse and her father. A very rainy day, indeed.

'Just as well we're not living here any more then,' Mark said, not noticing her face and looking out the window, 'or you'd be broke.'

Elizabeth looked out the window to the wet day and couldn't help feeling that the week had been a complete waste of time. She hadn't exactly been expecting a welcoming committee and bunting to be hung from the shops but neither Saoirse nor her father seemed to be in the least bit interested in whether she was home or not, and what she has been up to in her time away. But she hadn't returned to share stories about her new life in New York; she had returned to check up on them.

Her father still wasn't talking to her on account of her leaving home and deserting him. Working for a few months at a time in different counties had seemed at the time the ultimate sin, but leaving the country altogether was now the mightiest sin of all. Before Elizabeth had left she had made arrangements to ensure they would both be looked after. Much to her great disappointment, Saoirse had dropped out of school the previous year and Elizabeth had had to set her up with her eighth job in two months, stocking shelves in the local supermarket. She had also arranged with a neighbour to drive her into Killarney twice a month to see her counsellor. To Elizabeth, that part was far more important than the job and she knew that Saoirse had only agreed to it as it gave her the opportunity to escape from her cage twice a month. In the unlikely event that Saoirse ever decided to talk about how she was feeling, at least there would be someone there to listen.

There had been no sign of the housekeeper Elizabeth had organised for her father, though. The farmhouse was a dusty, smelly, damp mess and after spending two days scrubbing the place Elizabeth gave up, realising there was no amount of cleaning products that would bring back the shine to the farmhouse. When her mother left, she had taken the sparkle with her.

Saoirse had moved out of the bungalow and into a house with a group of strangers she had met while camping out at a music festival. All they seemed to do was sit in a circle by the old tower near the town, lying on the grass, with long hair and beards, strumming on a guitar and singing songs about suicide.

Elizabeth had only managed to catch her sister twice during her stay. The first meeting was very brief. On the day of Elizabeth's arrival she received a phone call from the only ladies' clothes store in Baile na gCroíthe. They were holding Saoirse as they had caught her shoplifting some T-shirts. Elizabeth had gone down, apologised profusely, paid the women for the T-shirts and as soon as they had stepped outside Saoirse had headed for the hills. The second time they met was only long enough for Elizabeth to loan Saoirse some money and then organise to meet for lunch the next day, a lunch Elizabeth ended up eating alone. At least she was glad to see Saoirse had put on some weight at last. Her face was fuller and her clothes didn't seem to hang off her as they once had. Perhaps living alone was good for her.

November in Baile na gCroíthe was lonely. The young population was away at school and college, the tourists were at home or visiting hotter countries, businesses were quiet and empty, some closed, the others struggling. The village was drab, cold and dreary, the flowers not yet out to brighten the streets. It was like a ghost town. But Elizabeth was glad she had returned. Her small family may not have given two flutes whether she was home or not, but she knew with a certainty now that she couldn't live her life worrying about them.

Mark and Elizabeth moved up the queue. There was only one person ahead of them and then they would be free. Free to catch their flight to Dublin so they could go on to New York from there.

Elizabeth's phone rang and her stomach lurched instinctively.

Mark whipped around. 'Don't answer that.'

Elizabeth took the phone out of her bag and looked at the number.

'Don't answer it, Elizabeth.' His voice was steady and stern.

'It's an Irish number.' Elizabeth bit down on her lip.

'Don't,' he said gently.

'But something could be wro—' The ringing stopped.

Mark smiled, looked relieved. 'Well done.'

Elizabeth smiled weakly and Mark turned back to face the check-in desk. He took a step forward to approach the desk and as he did so her phone began ringing again.

It was the same number.

Mark was talking to the woman behind the desk, laughing and as charming as usual. Elizabeth clutched the phone tightly in her hand and stared at the number on her screen until it disappeared and the ringing stopped again.

It beeped, signalling a voicemail.

'Elizabeth, she needs your passport.' Mark swirled round. His face fell.

'I'm just checking my messages,' Elizabeth said quickly, and began rooting in her bag for her passport, phone pressed to her ear.

'Hello, Elizabeth, this is Mary Flaherty calling from the maternity ward in Killarney Hospital. Your sister, Saoirse, has been taken in with labour pains. It's a month earlier than expected, as you know, so Saoirse wanted us to call you to let you know in case you wanted to be here with her . . .' Elizabeth didn't hear the rest. She stood frozen to the spot. Labour pains? Saoirse? She wasn't even pregnant. She replayed the message, thinking maybe it was the wrong number, ignoring Mark's pleas for her to hand over her passport.

'Elizabeth,' Mark said loudly, interrupting her thoughts, 'your passport. You're holding everyone up.'

Elizabeth turned round and was greeted by a line of angry faces.

'Sorry,' she whispered, her whole body shaking, feeling stunned.

'What's wrong?' Mark said, his anger fading and concern spreading across his face.

'Excuse me,' the check-in assistant called. 'Are you getting on this flight?' she asked as politely as she could.

'Em,' Elizabeth rubbed her eyes in confusion, looked from Mark's issued ticket on the counter, to his face and back again. 'No, no, I can't.' She stepped backwards out of the queue. 'Sorry.' She turned to the few people in the queue who looked at her with softened faces. 'So sorry.' She looked at Mark standing in the queue, looking so . . . so disappointed. Not disappointed she wasn't coming but disappointed *in* her.

'Sir,' the lady called, handing him his ticket.

He took it distractedly and slowly stepped out of the queue. 'What happened?'

'It's Saoirse,' Elizabeth said weakly, a lump forming in her throat. 'She's been taken into hospital.'

'Did she drink too much again?' The concern had instantly disappeared from Mark's voice.

Elizabeth thought about that answer long and hard, and the shame and embarrassment of not having known about Saoirse's pregnancy took charge and shouted at her to lie. 'Yes, I think so. I'm not too sure.' She shook her head – trying to shake her thoughts away.

Mark's shoulders relaxed. 'Look, she probably just has to get her stomach pumped again. It's nothing new, Elizabeth. Let's just get you checked in and we can talk about it in the café.'

Elizabeth shook her head. 'No, no, Mark, I have to go.' Her voice trembled.

'Elizabeth, it's probably *nothing*,' he smiled. 'How many of these phone calls do you get a year and it's always the same thing.'

'It could be *something*, Mark.' Something that a sister in her right mind should have known, should have spotted.

Mark's hands dropped from her face. 'Don't let her do this to you.'

'Do what?'

'Don't let her make you choose her life over your own.'

'Don't be so ludicrous, Mark, she's my sister, she *is* my life. I have to look out for her.'

'Even though she never looks out for you. Even though she couldn't care less whether you were here for her or not.'

It was like a thump in the stomach.

'No, I've got you to look out for me.' She tried to lighten the mood, tried to make everyone happy as usual.

'But I can't if you won't let me.' His eyes were dark with hurt and anger.

'Mark,' Elizabeth tried to laugh but failed, 'I promise I'll be on the earliest flight possible. I just need to find out what's happened. Think about it. If this was your sister you'd be out of this airport long before now, you'd be by her side as we speak and you wouldn't have given a bit of thought to having this stupid conversation.'

'Then what are you still standing here for?' he said coldly.

Anger and tears welled in Elizabeth all at once. She lifted her case and walked away from him. Walked out of the airport and rushed to the hospital.

She did return to New York, just as she promised him. She flew over two days after him, collected her belongings from their apartment, handed in her notice at work and returned to Baile na gCroíthe with a pain in her heart so sore she almost couldn't breathe.

Chapter 16

Elizabeth was thirteen years old and had settled into her first few weeks of secondary school. This meant she had to travel further out of town to go to school so she was up and out earlier than everyone else in the morning and, because classes finished later, she returned home in the dark in the evening. She was spending very little time with eleven-month-old Saoirse. Unlike her primary school bus, the school bus dropped her at the end of the long road that led from the bungalow, leaving her to her lonely walk to the front door where nobody stood to greet her. It was winter and the dark mornings and evenings draped black velvet over the country. Elizabeth, for the third time that week, had walked down the road in the harsh wind and rain, her school skirt lifting and dancing around her legs while her school bag, laden with books, stooped her back.

Now she sat by the fire, in her pyjamas, trying to warm her body, with one eye on her homework, the other eye on Saoirse, who was crawling along the floor, putting everything she could lay her chubby hands on in her drooling mouth. Her father was in the kitchen heating up his homemade vegetable stew again. It's what they ate everyday. Porridge for breakfast, stew for dinner. Occasionally they would have a thick piece of beef or some fresh fish her father had caught that day. Elizabeth loved those days.

Saoirse gurgled and dribbled to herself, waving her hands around and watching Elizabeth, happy to see her big sister home. Elizabeth smiled at her and made encouraging noises before turning back to her homework. Using the couch as security, Saoirse pulled herself up onto her feet as she had been doing for the past few weeks. She slowly stepped sideways, going back and forth, back and forth before turning round to Elizabeth.

'Come on, Saoirse, you can do it.' Elizabeth put down her pencil and fixed her attention on her little sister. Every day now, Saoirse had attempted the walk across the room to her sister, but had ended on her padded behind. Elizabeth was determined to be there when she finally made that leap. She wanted to make a song and dance about it like her mother would if she'd been still here.

Saoirse blew air out of her mouth, bubbles forming on her lips, and spoke in her own mysterious language.

'Yes,' Elizabeth nodded, 'come to Elizabeth.' She held her arms out.

Slowly Saoirse let go and with a determined look on her face she began to take those steps. Further and further she walked while Elizabeth held her breath, trying not to shout in excitement for fear of throwing her off. Saoirse held Elizabeth's stare all the way. Elizabeth would never forget that look in her baby sister's eyes, such determination. Finally she reached Elizabeth and she took her in her arms and danced her around, smothering her in kisses while Saoirse giggled and blew more bubbles.

'Dad, Dad!' Elizabeth called out.

'What?' he shouted crankily.

'Come here, quick!' Elizabeth called, helping Saoirse applaud herself.

Brendan appeared at the door, concern written across his face.

'Saoirse walked, Dad! Look, do it again, Saoirse; walk for Daddy!' She placed her sister on the floor and encouraged her to repeat the feat.

Brendan huffed, 'Jaysus, I thought it was something important. I thought there was somethin' wrong with ya. Don't be botherin' me like that.' He turned his back and returned to the kitchen.

When Saoirse looked up in her second attempt to show her family how clever she was and saw that her daddy was gone, her face fell, and so did she, landing on her bum again.

Elizabeth had been at work the day Luke learned to walk. Edith had called her in the middle of a meeting and she couldn't talk so had heard about it when she got home. Thinking about it now, she realised she had reacted very similarly to her dad and, once again, she hated herself for it. As an adult she could now understand her father's reaction. It wasn't that he wasn't proud or that he didn't care, it was just that he cared too much. First they walk, then they fly away.

The encouraging thought was, if Elizabeth had managed to help her sister to walk once, surely she could help her back on her feet a second time.

Elizabeth awoke with a jump, feeling cold and frozen in fear after a nightmare. The moon had finished its shift on her side of the world and had moved on, making way for the sun. The sun kept a paternal gaze on Elizabeth, keeping a close eye on her as she slept. The silver-blue light thrown across her bedclothes had been replaced by a yellow trail. It was 4.35 a.m., and Elizabeth immediately felt awake. She propped herself up on her elbows. Her duvet lay half on the floor, the other half caught up in her legs. She'd had a fitful sleep where dreams began and were unfinished before jumping into new ones, overlapping into each other to create a bizarre blur of faces, places and random words. She felt exhausted.

Looking around the room, she felt irritation seeping into her body. Although she had cleaned the house from top to bottom till it glistened two days ago, she felt the urge to do it all over again. Items were out of place and kept catching the corner of her eye. She rubbed her nose, which was beginning to itch out of frustration, and she threw off the bedclothes.

Immediately she began tidying. She had a total of twelve pillows to display on her bed, six rows of two consisting of regular pillows, with oblong-shaped and circular at the front. All had different textures, ranging from rabbit fur to suede, and were various shades of cream, beige and coffee. Once satisfied with the bed, she ensured her clothes were hanging in the correct order, from dark colours on the left to bright, although she had very little colour in her wardrobe. Wearing the slightest bit of colour felt to her as though she were walking down the street in flashing neon. She vacuumed the floor, dusted and polished the mirrors, straightened the three small hand towels in the bathroom, taking a few minutes to perfectly align the stripes through them. The taps glistened and she kept on scrubbing furiously until she could see her reflection in the tiles. By 6.30 she had completed the living room and kitchen and, feeling less restless, she sat outside in the garden with a cup of coffee while looking over her designs in preparation for that morning's meeting. She had had a total of three hours sleep that night.

Benjamin West rolled his eyes and ground his teeth in frustration while his boss paced the floor of the Portakabin and ranted in his thick New York accent.

'You see, Benji, I'm just—'

'Benjamin,' he interrupted.

'– sick and tired,' he continued, not acknowledging him, 'of hearing all the same shit from everyone. All these designers are the same. They want contemporary this, minimalist that. Well, art deco my balls, Benji!'

'It's—'

'I mean, how many of these companies have we met with over here so far?' He stopped pacing and looked at Benjamin.

Benjamin flicked through his diary, 'Em, eight, not including the woman who had to leave early on Friday, Elizabeth—'

'It doesn't matter,' he cut him off, 'she's the same as the rest.' He waved his hand dismissively and spun round to look out the window at the construction site. His thin grey plait swung with his head.

'Well, we have another meeting with her in a half-hour,' Benjamin said, checking his watch.

'Cancel it. Whatever she has to say I don't care. She's as strait-laced as they come. How many hotels have you and I worked on together, Benji?'

Benjamin sighed. 'It's Benjamin and we've worked together a lot, Vincent.'

'A lot.' He nodded to himself. 'That's what I thought. And how many of them have had as good a view as this?' He held out his hand to display the scenery out the window. Benjamin spun round in his chair, uninterested, and could barely bring himself to look past the noise and mess of the site. They were behind time. Sure it was pretty, but he'd prefer to look out that window and see a hotel standing there, not rolling hills and lakes. He'd been in Ireland for two months now and the hotel was scheduled to be finished by August, three months away. Born in Haxton, Colorado but living in New York, he thought he'd long escaped the claustrophobic feeling that only a small town could bring. Apparently not.

'Well?' Vincent had lit a cigar and was sucking on the end.

'It's a great view,' Benjamin said in a bored tone.

'It's a fucking fantastic view and I'm not gonna let some fancy shmancy interior designer come in here and make it look like some city hotel we've done a million times before.'

'What have you got in mind, Vincent?' All Benjamin had been hearing for the past two months was what he didn't want.

Vincent, dressed in a shiny grey suit, marched towards his briefcase, took out a folder and slid it down the table to Benjamin. 'Look at those newspaper articles. The place is a goddamn goldmine. I want what they want. People don't want some average hotel – it needs to be romantic, fun, artistic, none of all this clinical modern stuff. If the next person walks in here with the same shitty ideas I'll design the damn thing myself.' He turned his reddening face to the window and puffed on his cigar.

Benjamin rolled his eyes at Vincent's dramatics.

'I want a real artist,' he continued, 'a raving damn lunatic. Someone creative with a bit of flair. I'm sick of these corporate suits talking about paint colours like they're pie charts, who've never picked up a paint brush in their life. I want the Van Gogh of interior design—'

A knock on the door interrupted him.

'Who's that?' Vincent said gruffly, still red in the face from his rant.

'It's probably Elizabeth Egan, here for the meeting.'

'I thought I told you to cancel that.'

Benjamin ignored him and walked over to the door to let Elizabeth in.

'Hello,' she said, entering the room, followed by a plum-haired Poppy, spattered with paint and weighed down with folders spilling with carpet samples and fabrics.

'Hi, I'm Benjamin West, project manager. We met on Friday.' He shook Elizabeth's hand.

'Yes, I'm sorry about having to leave early,' she replied crisply, not looking him in the eye. 'It's not a regular occurrence, I can assure you.' She turned to face the struggling lady behind her. 'This is Poppy, my assistant. I hope you don't mind her sitting in with us,' she said curtly.

Poppy battled with the folders in order to shake Benjamin's hand, resulting in a few folders crashing to the ground.

'Oh shit,' she said loudly, and Elizabeth spun round with a face like thunder.

Benjamin laughed. 'That's OK. Let me help you.'

'Mr Taylor,' Elizabeth said loudly, walking across the room with an extended hand, 'good to meet you again. Sorry about the last meeting.'

Vincent turned from the window, looked her black suit up and down and puffed on his cigar. He didn't shake her hand, but instead turned to face out the window again.

Benjamin helped Poppy carry the folders to the table and spoke to clear the awkwardness from the room. 'Why don't we all take a seat?'

Elizabeth, flushed in the face, slowly lowered her hand and turned to face the table. Her voice went up an octave. 'Ivan!'

Poppy's face crumpled into a frown and she looked about the room.

'It's OK,' Benjamin said to her, 'people get my name wrong all the time. The name's Benjamin, Ms Egan.'

'Oh, not you,' Elizabeth laughed. 'I'm talking about the man in the chair beside you.' She walked towards the table. 'What are you doing here? I didn't know you were involved in the hotel. I thought you worked with children.'

Vincent raised his eyebrows and watched her nodding and smiling politely in the silence. He began to laugh, a hearty guffaw that ended in hacking coughs.

'Are you OK, Mr Taylor?' Elizabeth asked with concern.

'Yes, Ms Egan, I'm fine. Absolutely fine. It's a pleasure to meet you.' He held out his hand.

While Poppy and Elizabeth were arranging their files, Vincent spoke under his breath to Benjamin. 'This one mightn't be too far from cutting her ear off after all.'

The door to the cabin opened and in walked the receptionist with a tray of coffee cups.

'Well, it was lovely to meet you again. Bye, Ivan,' Elizabeth called out as the door closed behind the woman.

'Gone now, is he?' Poppy asked drily.

'Don't worry,' Benjamin laughed under his breath to Poppy while watching Elizabeth in admiration, 'she's fitting the profile perfectly. You guys were listening outside the door, right?'

Poppy looked at him confused.

'Don't worry, you're not gonna get into trouble or anything,' he laughed. 'But you heard us talking, right?'

Poppy thought for a while then nodded her head slowly up and down, still looking rather confused.

Benjamin chuckled and looked away. 'I knew it. Clever woman,' he thought aloud, watching Elizabeth engrossed in conversation with Vincent.

They both tuned into the conversation.

'I like you, Elizabeth, I really do,' Vincent was saying genuinely. 'I like your eccentricity.'

Elizabeth frowned.

'You know, your quirkiness. That's when you know someone's a genius and I like geniuses on my team.'

Elizabeth nodded slowly, utterly bewildered at what he was going on about.

'But,' Vincent continued, 'I'm not too convinced on your ideas. In fact, I'm not convinced at all. I don't like 'em.'

There was silence.

Elizabeth moved uncomfortably in her seat. 'OK,' she tried to remain businesslike, 'what is it exactly that you have in mind?'

'Love.'

'Love,' Elizabeth repeated dully.

'Yes. Love.' He leaned back in the chair, fingers interlocked across his stomach.

'You have love in mind,' Elizabeth said stonily, looking at Benjamin for assurance.

Benjamin rolled his eyes and shrugged.

'Hey, *I* don't give a shit about love,' Vincent said. 'I've been married twenty-five years,' he added by way of explanation. 'It's the Irish public that wants it. Where is that thing?' He looked around the table, then slid the folder of newspaper articles towards Elizabeth.

After a moment of flicking through the pages, Elizabeth spoke. In her voice Benjamin sensed disappointment. 'Ah, I see. You want a *themed* hotel.'

'You make it sound tacky when you say that.' He waved his hand dismissively.

'I believe themed hotels *are* tacky,' Elizabeth said firmly. She couldn't forsake her principles, even for a plum job like this.

Benjamin and Poppy looked to Vincent for his response. It was like watching a tennis match.

'Elizabeth,' Vincent said with a smile twitching at the corner of his lips, 'you're a beautiful young woman, surely you should know this. Love is not a theme. It's an atmosphere, a mood.'

'I see,' Elizabeth said, sounding and looking as if she didn't see at all. 'You want to create a feeling of love in a hotel.'

'Exactly!' Vincent said, looking pleased. 'But it's not what I want, it's what *they* want.' He stabbed the newspaper with his finger.

Elizabeth cleared her throat and spoke as if addressing a child. 'Mr Taylor, it's June, what we call silly season, when there's nothing else to write about. The media simply represents a distorted image of the public's opinion – it's not accurate, you know. It doesn't represent the hopes and wishes of the Irish people. To strive for something to meet the needs of the media would be to make a huge mistake.'

Vincent looked unimpressed.

'Look, the hotel is in a wonderful location with stunning views, bordering a beautiful town with an endless amount of outdoor amenities available. My designs are about bringing the outside in, making the landscapes part of the interior. With the use of natural earthy tones like the dark greens, browns and with the use of stone we can—'

'I've heard all this before,' Vincent puffed. 'I don't want the hotel to blend in with the mountains, I want it to stand out. I don't want the guests to feel like damn hobbits sleeping in a mound of grass and mud.' He stabbed his cigar out angrily in the ashtray.

She's lost him, Benjamin thought. Too bad: this one really tried. He watched her face melt as the job slipped away from her.

'Mr Taylor,' she said quickly, 'you haven't heard *all* my ideas yet.' She was grasping at straws.

Vincent grunted and looked at his diamond-studded Rolex. 'You've thirty seconds.'

She froze for twenty of them and eventually her face fell and she looked to be in a great deal of pain as she spoke her next few words. 'Poppy,' she sighed, 'tell him your ideas.'

'Yes!' Poppy jumped up in excitement and danced around the other side of the table to Vincent. 'OK, so I'm thinking waterbeds in the shape of hearts, hot tubs, champagne flutes that rise from the bedside lockers. I'm thinking the *Romantic era* meets *art deco*. An *explosion*,' she made explosion signs with her hands, 'of rich reds, burgundy and wine that make you feel like you're being embraced in a velvet-lined *womb*. Candles *everywhere*. French boudoir meets . . .'

As Poppy rambled on and Vincent nodded his head animatedly while hanging on her every word, Benjamin turned to look at Elizabeth, who in turn had her head in her hand, wincing at every one of Poppy's ideas. Their eyes met and they both shared an exasperated look over their respective colleagues.

Then they shared a smile.

Chapter 17

'Oh, my goodness, oh, my goodness,' Poppy squealed with delight, dancing towards Elizabeth's car. 'I'd like to thank Damien Hirst for inspiring me, Egon Schiele,' she wiped an imaginary tear from her eye, 'Banksy and Robert Rauschenberg for providing me with such incredible art that helped my creative mind develop, opening delicately like a bud and for—'

'Stop it,' Elizabeth hissed through gritted teeth. 'They're still watching us.'

'Oh, they are not, don't be so paranoid.' Poppy's tune changed from elation to frustration. She turned to face the cabin on the site.

'Don't turn round, Poppy!' Elizabeth spoke as if giving out to a child.

'Oh, why not? They're not watchi— Oh, they are. BYEEE! THA-ANKSSS,' she waved her hands wildly.

'Do you *want* to lose your job?' Elizabeth threatened, refusing to turn round. Her words had the same effect as they would on Luke when she threatened to take away his PlayStation. Poppy stopped skipping immediately and they both walked in silence back to the car, Elizabeth feeling two pairs of eyes burning into her back.

'I can't believe we got the job,' Poppy said breathily once inside, hand on her heart.

'Nor can I,' Elizabeth grumbled, securing her seat belt around her body and starting up the engine.

'What's wrong with you, grumpy? You'd swear we didn't *get* this job or something,' Poppy accused, settling down in the passenger seat and drifting off to her own world.

Elizabeth thought about that. In fact she *hadn't* got the job, Poppy had. It was the kind of victory that didn't feel like a victory at all. And why had Ivan been there? He had told Elizabeth he worked with children – what had the hotel got to do with children? He hadn't even stuck around long enough for her to find out, instead leaving the room as soon as the drinks were brought without a goodbye to anyone apart from Elizabeth. She pondered this. Perhaps he was involved in business with Vincent and she'd walked in during an important meeting, which would make sense as to why Vincent had seemed so rudely preoccupied. Well, whatever it was, she needed to be informed and she was angry that Ivan hadn't mentioned it last night. She had plans to make and despised disruptions.

Separating from an overexcited Poppy, she headed over to Joe's for a coffee and to think.

'Good afternoon, Elizabeth,' Joe shouted. The three other customers jumped in their seats at his sudden outburst.

'Coffee, please, Joe.'

'For a change?'

She smiled tightly. She chose a table by the window looking onto the main street. She sat with her back to the window. She wasn't a gazer, she needed to think.

'Excuse me, Ms Egan.' The male American voice startled her.

'Mr West,' she said, looking up in surprise.

'Please call me Benjamin.' He smiled and indicated to the chair beside her. 'Mind if I join you?'

Elizabeth moved her papers out of his way. 'Would you like a drink?'

'Coffee would be great.'

Elizabeth took her mug and held it out towards Joe, 'Joe, two tall slim mango Frappaccinos, please.'

Benjamin's eyes lit up. 'You're kidding, I thought they didn't sell that he—' He was cut short by Joe dumping two mugs of milky coffee on the table. It spilled over the sides of the mugs. 'Oh,' he finished, looking disappointed.

She turned her attention to the extremely dishevelled-looking Benjamin. His thick black hair was in wavy curls around his head, and he had jet-black stubble growing from the top of his hairy chest to his cheekbones. He wore scruffy jeans streaked with muck, an identically soiled denim jacket, turf-clad sandy Caterpillar boots that had left a trail from the front door to the table, under which a small mountain of dry mud was gathering. A line of black dirt collected underneath his finger-nails and as he rested his hands on the table on front of Elizabeth, she felt herself having to look away.

'Congratulations on today,' Benjamin said, seeming genuinely happy. 'It was a very successful meeting for you. You really pulled it off. You guys say *sláinte*, right?' He held up his coffee mug.

'Excuse me?' Elizabeth asked coldly.

'*Sláinte*? Isn't that right?' He looked worried.

'No,' she said with frustration, 'I mean yes, but I'm not talking about that.' She shook her head. 'I didn't "pull it off", as you say, Mr West. Getting this contract was no stroke of luck.'

Benjamin's sun-kissed skin pinked slightly. 'Oh, that's not what I meant at all and please call me Benjamin. Mr West seems so formal.'

He moved uncomfortably in his chair. 'Your assistant, Poppy . . .' he looked away, trying to find the words, 'she's very talented, has lots of "out there" ideas and Vincent pretty much has the same philosophy but sometimes he gets carried away and it's up to us to talk him down from the window ledge. Look, it's my job to make sure we get this thing built on time and under budget so I plan to do what I usually do and just convince Vincent that we haven't the money to put Poppy's ideas from paper to practice.'

Elizabeth's heart quickened. 'Then he'll want a designer he can afford. Mr West, have you come here to try to talk me out of this job?' she asked coldly.

'No,' Benjamin sighed. 'It's *Benjamin*,' he stressed, 'and no, I'm not trying to talk you out of this job.' He said it in a way that made her feel foolish. 'Look, I'm trying to help you out here. I can see that you're not happy with the whole idea and truthfully I don't think the locals would be too delighted by it either.' He gestured around at the people in the room and Elizabeth tried to picture Joe going for Sunday lunch in a 'velvet womb'. No, it definitely wouldn't work, definitely not in this town.

Benjamin continued, 'I care about the projects I work on, and I think this hotel has a huge amount of potential. I don't want it to end up looking like a Las Vegas shrine to Moulin Rouge.'

Elizabeth had slid down ever so slightly in her seat.

'Now,' he said assertively, 'I came here to meet you because I like your ideas. They're sophisticated yet comfortable, modern without being too modern, and the look will appeal to a broad range of people. Vincent and Poppy's idea is too themed and will alienate three-quarters of the country immediately. However, maybe you could punch them with a bit more colour? I do agree with Vincent that your whole concept needs to look less like The Shire and more like a hotel. We don't want people feeling like they have to travel barefoot to Macgillycuddy's Reeks to drop a ring down the centre.'

Feeling offended, Elizabeth dropped her mouth open.

'Do you think,' he continued, ignoring her reaction, 'that you could work with Poppy? You know, water down her ideas . . . a lot?'

Elizabeth had been prepared once again for a stealth attack but he was here to help her. She cleared her throat that didn't need clearing and pulled at the end of her suit jacket, feeling awkward. Once she had composed herself she said, 'Well, I'm glad we're on the same page here, but.' She signalled to Joe for another coffee and thought about fusing her natural colours with Poppy's rich tones.

Benjamin shook his head wildly to Joe's offer of another coffee, still with a full untouched mug in front of him. 'You drink a lot of coffee,' he commented as Joe placed her third mug on the table before her.

'It helps me think,' she said, taking a sip.

There was a silence for a moment.

Elizabeth snapped out of her trance. 'OK, I've an idea.'

'Wow, that worked fast,' Benjamin smiled.

'What?' Elizabeth frowned.

'I said it—'

'OK,' Elizabeth interrupted, not hearing him in her rush of ideas. 'Let's say Mr Taylor is right and the legend lives on and people see this place as a place of love, blah dee blah.' She made a face, clearly not impressed by that belief. 'So there's a market there we need to cater for, which is where Poppy's ideas will work, but we'll keep them just to a minimum. Maybe a honeymoon suite and a snug thrown in here and there, the rest can be my designs,' she said happily. 'With a bit more colour,' she added with less enthusiasm.

Benjamin smiled when she'd finished. 'I'll run it by Vincent. Look, when I said earlier about you pulling it off in the meeting I didn't mean you hadn't the talent to back it up. I meant doing that whole *crazy* thing.' He circled his dirty fingers beside his temples.

Elizabeth's good mood vanished. 'Excuse me?'

'You know,' Benjamin smiled broadly, 'the whole I-see-dead-people-thing.'

Elizabeth stared at him blankly.

'You know, the *guy* at the table. The one you were talking to? Is this ringing any bells with you?'

'Ivan?' Elizabeth asked uncertainly.

'That's the name!' Benjamin snapped his fingers and bounced back in his chair, laughing. 'That's it, Ivan the very, very silent partner,' he laughed.

Elizabeth's eyebrows almost lifted off her forehead. 'Partner?'

Benjamin laughed even harder. 'Yeah, that's it, but don't tell him I said so, will you? I'd be so embarrassed if he ever found out.'

'Don't worry,' Elizabeth said drily, shocked by this information. 'I'll be seeing him later and I won't mention a word.'

'Neither will he,' Benjamin chuckled.

'Well, we'll see about that,' Elizabeth huffed. 'Although I was with him last night and he didn't say a word then either.'

Benjamin looked shocked by her. 'I don't think that kind of thing is allowed in Taylor Constructions. Office dating is strictly frowned upon. I mean, you never know, Ivan could be the reason you got the job in the first place.' He wiped his eyes wearily and his laughter calmed. 'When you think about it, isn't it amazing what we do to get jobs these days?'

Her mouth dropped.

'But it shows how much you love your job to be able to do a thing like that.' He looked at her in admiration. 'I don't think I could.' His shoulders shook again.

Elizabeth's mouth gaped even wider. Was he accusing her of sleeping with Ivan to get the job? She was rendered speechless.

'Anyway,' Benjamin said, standing up, 'it's been great meeting you. I'm glad we got the Moulin Rouge thing fixed up. I'll run it by Vincent and give you a call as soon as I know more. Do you have my number?' he asked, padding down his pockets. He reached into his front breast pocket and pulled out a leaking biro that had left a blob of ink at the bottom of his pocket. He grabbed a napkin from the dispenser and messily scrawled his name and number across the tissue.

'That's my cell number and the office number.' He handed it to her and pushed forward his leaking pen and a ripped napkin damp from his spilled coffee. 'Can I have yours? Saves me having to go through the files.'

Elizabeth was still angry and offended but reached into her bag, retrieved her leather-bound card holder and held out one of her gold-trimmed business cards. She would refrain from hitting him just this once; she needed this job. For Luke and her business's sakes, she would hold her tongue.

Benjamin flushed slightly. 'Oh right,' he retracted his torn napkin and leaking biro and took her card. 'That's a better idea, I guess.' He held out his hand to her.

She took one look at his hand stained with blue ink and with dirty fingernails, and she instantly sat on her hands.

After he had left, Elizabeth looked around in confusion, wondering if anyone else had witnessed what she had. Joe met her eyes, winked and tapped his nose as though they were sharing some sort of secret. After work she planned to collect Luke from Sam's house and although she knew Ivan and Sam's mother were no longer together she was hoping among all hopes that she would see him there.

To give him a piece of her mind, naturally.

Chapter 18

Mistake number one: going to Elizabeth's meeting. I shouldn't have done it. It's the same rule as not being allowed to go into school with our younger friends, and I should have had the sense to realise that Luke's school is the equivalent to Elizabeth's workplace. I could have kicked myself. Actually I did, but Luke thought it looked so funny that he started doing it to himself and now both his shins are bruised. So I stopped.

After I left the meeting I walked back to Sam's house, where Luke was being minded. I sat on the grass in the back garden, keeping an eye on them wrestling each other, hoping it wouldn't end in tears and also doing my favourite mental sport. Thinking

It was constructive thinking too because I realised a few things. One of the things I learned was that I went to the meeting that morning because my gut feelings were telling me to. I couldn't figure out how my being there would possibly help Elizabeth but I had to go with my instincts and I just presumed she wouldn't see me. My meeting her the previous night had been so dreamlike and unexpected that I started the day feeling as if it was all in my imagination. And yes, I am aware of the irony there.

I was so happy she saw me. When I saw her swinging on that garden bench looking so lost, I knew that if she was ever going to see me that would be the time. I felt it in the air. I knew she needed to see me and I had prepared myself for the fact that one day she would, but I hadn't prepared myself for the shiver that ran up my spine when our eyes first locked together. It was odd because I'd been looking at Elizabeth for the past four days and I was used to her face, knew it inside out, could see it clearly even when I shut my eyes, knew that there was a tiny mole on her left temple, that one cheekbone was slightly higher than the other, that her bottom lip was larger than her top, that she had fine baby hair at the edge of her hairline. I knew it so well, but isn't it strange how different people can look when you actually look them in the eyes? They suddenly appear to be someone else. If you ask me, it's true what they say about eyes being the windows to your soul.

I had never felt that feeling before, but I put that down to not having been in the position before. I had never had a friendship with someone of Elizabeth's age and I supposed it was nerves. It was all a new experience for me but one I was immediately willing and able to take on.

There are two things that I am rarely. The first is confused and the second is worried, but while I waited in Sam's back garden on that sunny day, I was worried. And that confused me and because I was confused, that worried me even more. I was hoping I hadn't caused trouble for Elizabeth at work, but later that evening, as the sun and I were playing hide and seek, I soon found out.

The sun was trying to hide behind Sam's house, covering me in a blanket of shadow. I was moving around the garden, sitting in the very last patches of sun before they disappeared completely. Sam's mom was having a bath after doing a dance work-out video in her back room, which had been hugely entertaining, so when the doorbell rang Sam answered it. He was under strict instructions not to answer to anyone except Elizabeth.

'Hello, Sam,' I heard her say, stepping into the hall. 'Is your dad here?'

'No,' Sam replied, 'He's at work. Me and Luke are playing in the garden.'

I heard footsteps coming down the hall, the sound of heels on wood and then an angry voice as she stepped out into the garden.

'Oh, he's at work, is he?' Elizabeth said standing at the top of the garden with her hands on her hips looking down at me.

'Yeah, he is,' Sam said, confused, and ran off to play with Luke.

There was something so endearing about the sight of Elizabeth looking so bossy that it made me smile.

'Is something funny, Ivan?'

'Lots of things are,' I replied, sitting down on the only part of the grass that still had sun on it. I guess I won the hide-and-seek game. 'People getting splashed with puddles by passing cars, being tickled right here,' I gestured to my side, 'Chris Rock, Eddie Murphy in the second *Beverly Hills Cop* an—'

'What are you talking about?' She frowned, moving closer.

'Things that are funny.'

'What are you doing?' She stepped closer still.

'Trying to remember how to make a daisy chain. Opal's looked nice,' I looked up at her. 'Opal's my boss and she had them in her hair,' I explained. 'The grass is dry if you want to sit down.' I continued pulling daisies from the ground.

It took Elizabeth a moment to settle herself on the grass. She looked uncomfortable and made faces as though she was sitting on pins. After brushing invisible dirt off her slacks and attempting to sit on her hands so her bum wouldn't get grass stains, she resumed glaring at me.

'Is something the matter, Elizabeth? I sense that there is.'

'How acutely aware of you.'

'Thank you. It's part of my job but nice of you to compliment me.'
I sensed her sarcasm.

'I've a bone to pick with you, Ivan.'

'A funny one, I hope.' I threaded one stalk through the other. 'There's
another thing that's funny – funny bones. They hurt but they also make
you laugh. Like lots of things in life, I suppose, or even life itself. Life
is like a funny bone. Hmm.'

She looked at me in confusion. 'Ivan, I've come to give you a piece
of my mind. I spoke to Benjamin today after you left and he told me
you were a partner in the company. He also accused me of something
else but I won't even get into that,' she fumed.

'You've come to give me a piece of your mind,' I repeated, looking
at her. 'That phrase is really beautiful. The mind is the most powerful
thing in the body, you know. Whatever the mind believes, the body can
achieve. So to give someone a piece of it . . . well, thank you, Elizabeth.
Funny how people are always intent on giving it to the people they
dislike when it really should be for the ones they love. There's another
funny thing. But a piece of your mind . . . what a gift that would be.' I
looped the last stalk and formed a chain. 'I'll give you a daisy chain in
return for a piece of your mind.' I slid the bracelet onto her arm.

She sat on the grass. Didn't move, didn't say anything, just looked
at her daisy chain. Then she smiled and when she spoke her voice was
soft. 'Has anyone ever been mad at you for more than five minutes?'

I looked at my watch, 'Yes. You, from ten o'clock this morning until
now.'

She laughed. 'Why didn't you tell me that you work with Vincent
Taylor?'

'Because I don't.'

'But Benjamin said that you did.'

'Who's Benjamin?'

'The project manager. He said you were a silent partner.'

I smiled. 'I suppose I am. He was being ironic, Elizabeth. I've nothing
to do with the company. I'm so silent that I don't say anything at all.'

'Well, that's one side of you I've never met,' she smiled. 'So you're
not actively involved with this project?'

'My work is with people, Elizabeth, not buildings.'

'Well then, what on earth was Benjamin talking about?' She was
confused. 'He's an odd one, that Benjamin West. What business were
you talking to Vincent about? What have children got to do with the
hotel?'

'You're very nosy,' I laughed. 'Vincent Taylor and I weren't talking about any business.' Anyway, that's a good question – what do you think children *should* have to do with the hotel?'

'Absolutely nothing,' Elizabeth laughed, and then stopped abruptly, afraid she had offended me. 'You think the hotel should be child-friendly.'

I smiled. 'Don't you think everything and every*one* should be child-friendly?'

'I can think of a few exceptions,' Elizabeth said smartly, looking out to Luke.

I knew she was thinking of Saoirse and her father, possibly even herself.

'I'll talk to Vincent tomorrow about a playroom/play area kind of thing . . .' She trailed off. 'I've never designed a children's room before. What the hell do children want?'

'It will come easily to you, Elizabeth. You were a child once – what did you want?'

Her brown eyes darkened and she looked away. 'It's different now. Children don't want what I wanted then. Times have changed.'

'Not that much they haven't. Children always want the same things because they all need the same basic things.'

'Like what?'

'Well, why don't you tell me what you wanted and I'll let you know if they're the same things?'

Elizabeth laughed lightly. 'Do you always play games, Ivan?'

'Always,' I smiled. 'Tell me.'

She studied my eyes, battling with herself about whether to speak or not and after a few moments she took a deep breath. 'When I was a child, my mother and I would sit down at the kitchen table every Saturday night with our crayons and fancy paper and we'd write out a full plan of what we were going to do the next day.' Her eyes shone with the fondness of remembering. 'Every Saturday night I got so excited about how we were going to spend the next day, I'd pin the schedule up on the wall of my bedroom and force myself to go to sleep so that morning would come.' Her smile faded and she snapped out of her trance. 'But you can't incorporate those things into a playroom; children want PlayStations and Xboxes and that kind of thing.'

'Why don't you tell me what sorts of things were on the Sunday schedule?'

She looked away into the distance, 'They were collections of hopelessly impossible dreams. My mother promised me we would lie on our backs in the field at night, catch as many falling stars as we could and then make all the wishes our hearts desired. We talked about lying in great big baths filled up to our chins with cherry blossoms, tasting sun showers, twirling around in the village sprinklers that watered the grass in the summer, having a moon-lit dinner on the beach and then doing the soft-shoe shuffle in the sand.' Elizabeth laughed at the memory. 'It's all so silly, really when I say it aloud, but that's the way she was. She was playful and adventurous, wild and carefree, if not a bit eccentric. She always wanted to think of new things to see, taste and discover.'

'All those things must have been so much fun,' I said, in awe of her mother. Tasting sun showers beat a toilet roll telescope any day.

'Oh, I don't know.' Elizabeth looked away and swallowed hard. 'We never actually did any of them.'

'But I bet you did them all a million times in your head,' I said.

'Well, there was one thing we did together. Just after she had Saoirse, she brought me out to the field, lay down a blanket and set down a picnic basket. We ate freshly-baked brown bread, still piping hot from the oven, with homemade strawberry jam.' Elizabeth closed her eyes and breathed in. 'I can still remember the smell and the taste.' She shook her head in wonder. 'But she chose to have the picnic in our cow field. There we were, in the middle of the field, having a picnic surrounded by curious cows.'

We both laughed.

'But that's when she told me she was going away. She was too big a person for this small town. It's not what she said but I know it must have been how she felt.' Elizabeth's voice trembled and she stopped talking. She watched Luke and Sam chasing each other around the garden but didn't see them, listened to their childish squeals of joy but didn't hear them. She shut it all out.

'Anyway,' her voice became serious again and she cleared her throat, 'that's irrelevant. It's got nothing to do with the hotel; I don't even know why I brought it up.'

She was embarrassed. I bet Elizabeth had never said all that aloud, ever in her life, and so I let the long silence sit between us as she worked it all out in her head.

'Do you and Fiona have a good relationship?' she asked, still not looking me in the eye after what she told me.

'Fiona?'

'Yes, the woman you're not married to.' She smiled for the first time and seemed to settle.

'Fiona doesn't talk to me,' I replied, still confused as to why she thought I was Sam's dad. I would have to have a chat with Luke about that one. I wasn't comfortable with this case of mistaken identity.

'Did things end badly between you both?'

'They never began to be able to end,' I answered honestly.

'I know that feeling.' She rolled her eyes and laughed. 'At least one good thing came out of it, though.' She looked away and watched Sam and Luke playing. She had been referring to Sam but I got the feeling she was looking at Luke and I was pleased at that.

Before we left Sam's house, Elizabeth turned to me. 'Ivan, I've never spoken to anyone about what I said before,' she swallowed, 'ever. I don't know what made me blurt it out.'

'I know,' I smiled, 'so thank you for giving me a very big piece of your mind. I think that deserves another daisy chain,' I held out another bracelet I'd made.

Mistake number two: when sliding it onto her wrist, I felt myself give her a little piece of my heart.

Chapter 19

After the day I gave Elizabeth the daisy chains . . . and my heart, I learned far more about her than just what she and her mother did on Saturday evenings. I realised she's like one of those cockles that you see clinging to the rocks down on Fermoy beach. You know by looking at it that it's loose but as soon as you touch it or get close to it, it seizes up and clings onto the rock's surface for life. That's what Elizabeth was like: open until someone came near and then she'd tense up, and cling on for dear life. Sure, she opened up to me on that day in the back garden, but then the next day when I dropped by it was as though she was mad at me because she'd talked about it. But that was Elizabeth all round – mad at everyone including herself – and she was probably embarrassed. It wasn't often Elizabeth told anybody anything about herself unless she was talking to customers about her company.

It was difficult to spend time with Luke now that Elizabeth could see me and, frankly she would have been worried if I'd knocked on her fuchsia door to ask her if Luke was coming out to play. She has a thing about friends being a certain age. The important thing, though, was that Luke didn't seem to mind. He was always so busy playing with Sam and whenever Luke decided to include me, it would make Sam frustrated because he couldn't see me, of course. I think I was getting in Luke's way of playing with Sam and I don't think Luke was bothered if I showed up or not because it wasn't him I was there for, you see, and I think he knew it. I told you kids always know what's going on, even before you know yourself sometimes.

As for Elizabeth, I think she'd go crazy if I just strolled into her living room at twelve o'clock at night. A new kind of friendship meant that there had to be new boundaries. I had to be subtle, call round less yet still be there for her at the right moments. Like an adult friendship.

One thing I definitely didn't like was the fact that Elizabeth thought that I was Sam's dad. I don't know how that started and without me even saying anything it just kept going. I never lie to my friends, ever, so I tried many times to tell her that I wasn't Sam's dad. One of the times, the conversation went like this.

'So where are you from, Ivan?'

It was one evening after Elizabeth had been at work. She had just finished a meeting with Vincent Taylor about the hotel and apparently, according to her, she just walked right up to him and told him she had been speaking with Ivan and we both felt the hotel needed a children's area to give the parents even more relaxing romantic time together. Well, Vincent laughed so much that he just gave in and agreed. She's still confused as to why he thought it was so funny. I told her it was because Vincent hadn't a clue who I was and she just rolled her eyes at me and accused me of being secretive. Anyway, because of that, she was in a good mood so she was ready to talk, for a change. I was wondering when she'd start asking me questions (other than the ones about my job, how many staff we had, what was the turnover every year. She bored me to tears with all that kind of stuff).

But she'd finally asked me where I was from so happily I answered, 'Ekam Eveileb.'

She frowned. 'That name is familiar; I've heard of it somewhere before. Where is it?'

'A million miles from here.'

'Baile na gCroíthe is a million miles from everywhere. Ekam Eveileb . . ' she allowed the words to roll off her tongue, 'what does that mean? That's not Irish *or* English, is it?'

'It's draw kcab-ish.'

'Draw Cab?' she repeated, raising an eyebrow. 'Honestly, Ivan, sometimes you're as bad as Luke. I think he gets most of his sayings from you.'

I chuckled.

'In fact,' Elizabeth leaned forward, 'I didn't want to say this to you before but I think he looks up to you.'

'Really?' I was flattered.

'Well, yes, because . . . well,' she searched for the correct words, 'please don't think my nephew is insane or anything but last week he invented this friend.' She laughed nervously. 'We had him over in the house for dinner for a few days, they chased each other around outside, played everything from football, to the computer to *cards*, can you believe it? But the funny thing is that his name was *Ivan*.'

My blank reaction started her back-tracking and she blushed wildly. 'Well, actually it's not funny at all, it's completely preposterous, *of course*, but I thought that maybe it meant that he looked up to you and saw you as some sort of male role model . . ' she trailed off. 'Anyway, Ivan's gone now. He left us. All alone. It was devastating as you can imagine. I was told that they could stay around for as long as *three* months.' She made a face. 'Thank God he left. I had the date marked off on the calendar and everything,' she said, her face still red. 'Actually, funnily

enough, he left when you arrived. I think you scared Ivan off . . . Ivan.'
She laughed but my blank face caused her to stop and sigh. 'Ivan, why
am I the only one talking?'

'Because I'm listening.'

'Well, I'm finished now so you can say something,' she snapped.

I laughed. She always got mad when she felt stupid. 'I have a theory.'

'Good, share it with me for once. Unless it's to put me and my nephew
in a grey concrete building run by nuns with bars on the windows.'

I looked at her in horror.

'Go on,' she laughed.

'Well, who's to say that Ivan disappeared?'

Elizabeth looked horrified. 'No one says he disappeared because he
never appeared in the first place.'

'He did to Luke.'

'Luke made him up.'

'Maybe he didn't.'

'Well, I didn't see him.'

'You see me.'

'What have you got to do with Luke's *invisible* friend?'

'Maybe I *am* Luke's friend, only I don't like being called invisible.
It's not very PC.'

'But I can see you.'

'Exactly, so I don't know why people insist on saying "invisible". If
someone can see me then surely that's visible. Think about it – has Ivan,
Luke's friend, and me ever been in the same room at the same time?'

'Well, he could be here right now, for all we know, eating olives or
something,' she laughed, then suddenly stopped, realising Ivan was no
longer smiling. 'What are you talking about, Ivan?'

'It's very simple, Elizabeth. You said that Ivan disappeared when I
arrived.'

'Yes.'

'Don't you think that means that I'm Ivan and you just suddenly
started seeing me?'

Elizabeth looked angry. 'No, because you are a real person with a
real life and you have a wife and a child and you—'

'I'm not married to Fiona, Elizabeth.'

'Ex-wife then, it's not the point.'

'I was never married to her.'

'Well, far be it for me to judge.'

'No, I mean Sam isn't my son.' My voice sounded more forceful than
I intended. Children understand these things far better. Adults always
make things so complicated.

Elizabeth's face softened and she reached out to put her hand on mine. Her hands were delicate, with baby-soft skin and long slender fingers.

'Ivan,' she spoke gently, 'we have something in common. Luke isn't my son either,' she smiled. 'But I think it's great that you still want to see Sam.'

'No, no, you don't understand, Elizabeth. I'm *nothing* to Fiona, and I'm *nothing* to Sam. They don't see me like you do, they don't even *know* me, that's what I'm trying to tell you. I'm invisible to them. I'm invisible to everybody else but you and Luke.'

Elizabeth's eyes filled with tears and her grip tightened. 'I understand,' her voice shook. She placed her other hand on mine and clung to it tightly. She struggled with her thoughts. I could tell she wanted to say something but couldn't. Her brown eyes searched mine and after a moment's silence, looking as though she had found what she was looking for, her face finally softened. 'Ivan, you have no idea how similar you and I are, and it's such a *relief* to hear you talking like this because I sometimes feel invisible to everybody too, you know?' Her voice sounded lonely. 'I feel like nobody knows me, that nobody sees me how I really am . . . except you.'

She looked so upset that I put my arms around her. Still I couldn't help feeling so disappointed that she'd completely misunderstood me, which was odd, because my friendships aren't supposed to be about me, or what I want. And it had never been about me before.

But as I lay down alone that night and processed all the information of the day, I realised that for the first time in my life, Elizabeth was the only friend I had ever met who had completely understood me after all.

And for anyone who's ever had that connection with someone, even if it only lasted for five minutes, it's important. For once I didn't feel that I was living in a different world from everyone else, but that, in fact, there was a person, a person I *liked* and *respected*, who had a piece of my heart, who felt the same way.

You all know exactly how I was feeling that night.

I didn't feel so alone. Even better than that, I felt as if I was floating on air.

Chapter 20

The weather had changed overnight. The past week of June sunshine had burned the grass, dried the soil and brought wasps in their thousands to swarm around and annoy everyone. Saturday evening it all changed. The sky darkened and the clouds had moved in. But that was typical Irish weather: one moment a heat wave and the next, gale-force winds. It was predictably unpredictable.

Elizabeth shivered in her bed and pulled her duvet up to her chin. She didn't have the heating on and even though she needed it she refused to put it on during the summer months as a principle. Outside the trees shivered, their leaves tossed in the wind. They cast wild shadows across her bedroom walls. The fierce gusts blowing sounded like giant waves crashing against the cliffs. Inside, the doors rattled and shuddered. The bench in the garden swung back and forth, squeaking. Everything moved violently and sporadically; there was no rhythm and no sense of consistency.

Elizabeth wondered about Ivan. She wondered why she was feeling a pull towards him, and why every time she opened her mouth the world's best-kept secrets flowed out. She wondered why she welcomed him into her home and into her head. Elizabeth loved to be alone – she didn't crave companionship – but she craved Ivan's companionship. She wondered if she should take a few steps back because of Fiona living only down the road. Wouldn't her closeness to Ivan, albeit only a friendship, be disturbing for Sam *and* Fiona? She relied so much on Fiona to mind Luke at last-minute notice.

As usual, Elizabeth tried to ignore such thoughts. She tried to pretend that everything was the same as always, that there hadn't been a shift within her, that her walls weren't crumbling down and allowing in unwelcome guests. She didn't want that to happen, she couldn't deal with change.

Eventually she focused on the only thing that remained constant and unmoving in the determined gusts. And in return, the moon kept its watchful eye on her as she eventually fell into an uneasy sleep.

'Cock-a-doodle-doo!'

Elizabeth opened one eye, confused at the sound. The room was bright. She slowly opened the other eye and saw that the sun had returned and was perched low in the cloudless blue sky, yet the trees were still dancing wildly, having a disco in the back garden.

'Cock-a-doodle-doo!'

There it was again. Feeling groggy from her sleep, she dragged herself out of bed and to the window. Out on the grass in the garden stood Ivan, hands cupped to his mouth shouting, 'Cock-a-doodle-doo!'

Elizabeth covered her mouth, laughing, and pushed open the window. The wind rushed in.

'Ivan, what are you doing?'

'This is your wake-up call!' he shouted, the wind stealing the end of his words and taking them north.

'You are crazy!' she yelled.

Luke appeared at her bedroom door, looking afraid. 'What's happening?'

Elizabeth motioned for Luke to come to the window and he relaxed as he saw Ivan standing outside.

'Hi, Ivan!' Luke yelled.

Ivan looked up and smiled, removed his hand from holding down his cap to wave at Luke. His cap disappeared from his head as a sudden great big gust of wind lifted it off. They laughed as they watched him chase it across the garden, dashing to and fro as the wind's direction changed. Eventually he used a fallen branch to knock it down from a tree where it was caught.

'Ivan, what are you doing out there?' Luke yelled.

'It's Jinny Joe day!' Ivan announced, holding his arms out to display his surroundings.

'What's that?' Luke looked at Elizabeth, confused.

'I have no idea,' she shrugged.

'What's Jinny Joe day, Ivan?' Luke yelled.

'Come on down and I'll show you both!' Ivan replied, his loose clothes flapping around his body.

'We're not dressed, we're in our pyjamas!' Luke giggled.

'Well then, get dressed! Just throw anything on, it's six a.m., no one's going to see us!'

'Come on!' Luke said excitedly to Elizabeth, clambering off the windowsill, running out of her room and returning minutes later with one leg in his tracksuit bottoms, an inside-out sweater on and his runners on the wrong feet.

Elizabeth laughed.

'Come on, hurry!' he said, gasping for breath.

'Calm down, Luke.'

'No.' Luke threw open Elizabeth's wardrobe. 'Get dressed, IT'S JINNY JOE DAY!' he shouted with a toothless grin.

'But, Luke,' Elizabeth said uneasily, 'where are we supposed to be going?' She was looking for reassurance from a six-year-old.

Luke shrugged. 'Somewhere fun?'

Elizabeth thought about it, saw the excitement in Luke's eyes, felt the curiosity welling within her, went against her better judgement, threw on a tracksuit and ran outside with Luke.

The warm wind hit her as she stepped outside, taking her breath away.

'To the Bat Mobile!' Ivan announced, meeting them at the front door.

Luke giggled with excitement.

Elizabeth froze. 'Where?'

'The car,' Luke explained.

'Where are we going?'

'Just drive and I'll tell you when to stop. It's a surprise.'

'No,' Elizabeth said as if it were the most ridiculous thing she had ever heard. 'I never get into the car unless I know exactly where I'm going,' she huffed.

'You do it every morning,' Ivan said softly.

She ignored him.

Luke held the door open for Ivan and once they were all in, Elizabeth very uncomfortably set out on her journey with an unknown destination, feeling that she wanted to turn the car round at every turn and then wondering why she wasn't.

After driving for twenty minutes through winding roads, an agitated Elizabeth followed Ivan's directions for the last time and pulled up outside a field that, to her, looked the same as all the others they had passed. Except this one had a view over the glistening Atlantic Ocean. She ignored the scenery and fumed in her wing mirror at the mud splashed along the side of her shining car.

'Wow, what are they?' Luke leaped forward between the two front seats and pointed out the front window.

'Luke, my friend,' Ivan announced happily, 'they are what you call Jinny Joes.'

Elizabeth looked up. Ahead of her were hundreds of dandelion seeds, blowing in the wind, catching the light of the sun with their white fluffy threads and floating towards the three in the car like dreams.

'They look like fairies,' Luke said in amazement.

Elizabeth rolled her eyes. 'Fairies,' she tutted. 'What books have you been reading? They're dandelion seeds, Luke.'

Ivan looked at her in frustration. 'How did I know you'd say that? Well, I got you here, at least. I suppose *that's* something.'

Elizabeth looked at him in surprise. He had never snapped at her like that before.

'Luke,' Ivan turned to him, 'they're also known as the Irish Daisy but they're not only dandelion seeds, they are what most *normal* people,' he threw Elizabeth a nasty look, 'call Jinny Joes. They carry wishes in the wind and you're supposed to catch them in your hand, make your wish and then let them go so they can deliver them.'

Elizabeth snorted.

'Wow,' Luke whispered. 'But why do people do that?'

Elizabeth laughed. 'That's my boy.'

Ivan ignored her. 'Hundreds of years ago people used to eat the green leaves of the dandelion plant because they are extremely high in vitamins,' he explained, 'which gave it its Latin name, which translates as the "official cure of all ills". So people see them as good luck and now make their wishes on the seeds.'

'Do the wishes come true?' he asked hopefully.

Elizabeth looked at Ivan angrily for filling her nephew's head with false hopes.

'Only the ones that are delivered properly, so who knows? Remember, even the post gets lost sometimes, Luke.'

Luke nodded his head, understanding. 'OK then, let's go catch them!'

'You two go on, I'll wait here in the car,' Elizabeth said, staring straight ahead.

Ivan sighed. 'Eliza—'

'I'll wait here,' she said firmly, turning on the radio and settling down to show them she wasn't budging.

Luke climbed out of the car and she turned to Ivan. 'I think it's ridiculous that you fill his head with these lies,' she fumed. 'What are you going to tell him when absolutely nothing he wishes for comes true?'

'How do you know it won't come true?'

'I have *common sense*. Something which you seem to be lacking.'

'You're right, I don't have common sense. I don't want to believe what every one else believes. I have my *own* thoughts, things that weren't taught to me or things that I didn't read in a book. I learn from experience – you, you are afraid to experience anything and so you will always have your common sense and only your common sense.'

Elizabeth looked out the window, counting to ten so that she wouldn't explode. She hated all this new-age crap; contrary to what he said, she believed it was *exactly* the kind of thing that could be learned only from books. Written and read by people who spent their life searching for something, *anything*, to take them away from the boredom that was their real life. People who had to believe that there was always more than the very obvious reason, for everything.

'You know, Elizabeth, a dandelion is also known as a love herb. Some say that to blow the seeds upon the winds will carry your love to your lover. If you blow the puff ball while making a wish and succeed in blowing off all the seeds, your wish will come true.'

Elizabeth frowned in confusion. 'Stop your gobbledy-gook, Ivan.'

'Very well. For today, Luke and I will settle for catching Jinny Joes. I thought you always wanted to catch a wish?' Ivan asked.

Elizabeth looked away. 'I know what you're doing, Ivan and it won't work. I told you about my childhood in the strictest of confidence. It took a lot for me to say the things I said. It wasn't so you could turn it into some game,' she hissed.

'This is not a game,' Ivan said quietly. He clambered out of the car.

'Everything is a game to you,' Elizabeth snapped. 'Tell me, how is it you know so much about dandelion seeds? What exactly is the point of all your silly information?'

Ivan leaned forward through the open door and spoke softly. 'Well, I think it's quite obvious that if you're going to rely on something to carry your wishes in the wind, you might as well know where exactly it has come from and where it intends on going.'

The door slammed shut.

Elizabeth watched them both run to the field. 'Then if that's so, where exactly are you from, Ivan?' she asked aloud. 'And where and when do you intend going?'

Chapter 21

Elizabeth watched as Ivan and Luke darted around the long grass in the field, jumping and diving to catch the dandelion seeds that floated in the air like balls of feathers.

'I got one!' she heard Luke yell.

'Make a wish,' Ivan whooped.

Luke pressed it between his hand and squeezed his eyes shut. 'I wish that Elizabeth would get out of the car and play Jinny Joes!' he roared. He lifted his podgy hand to the air, opened his tiny fingers slowly and released the ball to the wind, which carried it away.

Ivan raised his eyebrows at Elizabeth.

Luke watched the car to see if his wish came true.

As much as Elizabeth watched his hopeful little face she couldn't bring herself to do it – to get out of the car and make Luke believe in fairy tales, just a fancy word for lies. She wouldn't do it. But again she watched as Luke raced around the field, holding his arms out. He caught the seed, grasped it tightly and shouted the same wish.

Her chest tightened and her breathing quickened. They both watched her with such hope in their eyes and she felt the pressure of being relied upon. It was only a game, she tried to convince herself; all she had to do was get out of the car. But it meant more to her than that. It meant filling a child's head with thoughts and ideas that would never happen. It meant sacrificing a moment of fun for a lifetime of disappointment. She gripped the steering wheel so tightly her knuckles were white.

Again a joyful Luke jumped up and down, trying to catch another. He repeated his wish at the top of his lungs this time adding, 'Please, please, please, Jinny Joe!' Holding up his arm he looked like the Statue of Liberty and then he released the ball of seeds.

Ivan didn't do anything. He just stood still in the field observing it all with a look and presence Elizabeth felt so drawn to. She saw the frustration and disappointment growing in Luke's face as he caught another, squashed it angrily between his hands and let it go with an attempt to kick it into the air.

Already he was losing faith and she hated to be the one to be the cause of that. She took a deep breath and reached for the door handle.

Luke's face lit up and immediately began chasing more. As she walked onto the field, the fuchsias danced wildly, like spectators waving their red and purple flags to welcome a player on to the field.

Driving slowly by in his tractor, Brendan Egan almost drove into a ditch at the sight he saw in a faraway field. With the sparkling sea and the sun in the background he could see two dark figures dancing around in the field. One was a woman whose long black hair was being caught by the wind and wildly draped around her face and neck. She was whooping and hollering with joy as she leaped about with a young child, trying to catch the dandelion seeds that were parachuting in the wind.

Brendan stopped the tractor and stopped breathing in shock at the familiar sight. It was as though he was seeing a ghost. His body shook as he watched in wonder and fright until a beeping behind him startled him and urged him on.

Benjamin was driving back from Killarney at 6.30 on Sunday morning, enjoying the sea view, when a tractor in the middle of the road caused him to step on the brakes. Inside the cab was an old man with a face as white as a sheet, looking into the distance. Benjamin followed his gaze. His face broke into a smile as he spotted Elizabeth Egan dancing with a young boy in a field filled with dandelions. She was laughing and cheering, bounding about. She was dressed in a tracksuit, her hair was down, loose and blowing freely instead of being tied back severely. He hadn't thought she had a son but he watched her lifting him up into the air, helping him to reach something and swinging him back down again. The little blond boy giggled with delight and Benjamin smiled, enjoying the sight. He could have watched her all morning but a beeping from behind startled him and as the tractor's engine started up and moved on, they both crawled down the road slowly, still watching Elizabeth.

Inventing imaginary men and dancing around fields at 6.30 on a Sunday morning . . . Benjamin couldn't help but laugh and admire her for her fun and energy for life. She never seemed to be afraid of what anyone thought. As he continued down the winding road his view of her became clearer. On Elizabeth's face was an expression of pure happiness. She looked like a completely different woman.

Chapter 22

Elizabeth felt giddy with delight as she drove back to town with Luke and Ivan. They had spent the past two hours chasing and catching what Ivan insisted she called Jinny Joes. Then when they were tired and out of breath they had collapsed in a heap in the long grass, breathing in the fresh early morning sea air. Elizabeth couldn't remember the last time she had laughed so much. In fact, she didn't think she had *ever* laughed so much in her life.

Ivan seemed to have boundless energy, with an appetite for all things new and exciting. Elizabeth hadn't felt excited in a very long time; it wasn't a feeling she associated with her adult life. She hadn't felt the tingle of anticipation in her stomach since she was a child; she hadn't looked forward to anything so much she felt she would burst if it didn't happen right here, right now. But being with Ivan brought all those feelings back. Time went so fast when she was with him, whether they were leaping in fields or simply sitting in each other's company in silence, as they so often did. She always wished for time to slow down when he was there, and when he left her she always felt she wanted more. She had caught many dandelion seeds that morning and among her many wishes had been for their time spent together that day to be longer and for the wind to keep up so she could hold on to the moment, with Luke too.

She likened it to a childhood crush, such strong, almost obsessive, feelings – but *more*, it had depth. She felt attracted to everything about Ivan – the way he talked, the way he dressed, the words he used, his apparent innocence yet he was filled with a deep knowledge of wise insights. He always said the right things, even when she didn't want to hear them. The darkness lifted from the end of her tunnels and she could suddenly see *beyond*. When he breezed into the room he brought clarity and brightness with him. He was walking hope, and she could tell that things for her could be, not fantastic or wonderful or happily-ever-after, but that they could be OK. And that was enough for Elizabeth.

He filled her head every moment; she recounted conversations over and over. She asked him question after question and he was always so open and honest in his answers, but then later, while lying in bed, she would realise she knew no more about him than before, despite his replies to every question. But she sensed that they were very similar beings. Two solitary people blowing around in the breeze like dandelion seeds, carrying each other's wishes.

Of course she felt frightened by her feelings. Of course it went against the grain of her every belief, but as much as she tried, she couldn't stop her heartbeat from quickening when his skin brushed against hers, she couldn't stop herself from seeking him out when she thought he might be nearby. She couldn't prevent him from invading her thoughts. He was welcoming himself into her arms even when they weren't open; he was dropping by her home uninvited yet she couldn't stop herself from opening her door time and time again.

She was attracted to his presence, to how he made her feel, to his silences and his words. She was falling in love with him.

On Monday morning Elizabeth found herself walking into Joe's with a spring in her step, humming the same song she'd been humming for the last week and couldn't seem to get out of her head. It was 8.30 and the café was crowded with tourists who had stopped for their breakfast before heading back to their coach, which would take hours to deliver them to the next stopping place. The café was noisy with chatter in German. Joe was rushing around collecting used crockery, bringing it to the kitchen and returning with plates full of Irish breakfasts that his wife had prepared.

Elizabeth signalled to him for a coffee and he quickly nodded his head in acknowledgement, having no time for gossip today. She looked for a seat and her heart quickened at the sight of Ivan in the far corner of the room. She couldn't control the smile that broke over her face. She felt the excitement rushing around her body as she wound her way between the tables to get to him. Elizabeth was overwhelmed by the sight of him.

'Hello,' she breathed, noticing the change in her voice, and hating herself for it.

'Morning, Elizabeth,' he smiled. His voice was different too.

They both sensed it, sensed *something*, and just stared at one another.

'Kept you a table.'

'Thanks.'

Smiles.

'Can I take a breakfast order?' Joe asked her, pen and pad in hand.

Elizabeth usually didn't eat breakfast, but by the way Ivan was looking through the menu she thought she could just be a few minutes late to the office for a change.

'Can I have a second menu, please, Joe?'

Joe glared at her. 'Why do you want a second menu?'

'So I can read it,' she stated.

'What's wrong with the one on the table?' he said moodily.

'OK, OK,' she backed off, leaning closer to Ivan to share the menu. Joe eyed her suspiciously.

'I think I'll have the Irish breakfast,' Ivan said, licking his lips.

'I'll have the same,' Elizabeth said to Joe.

'The same as what?'

'The Irish breakfast.'

'OK, so one Irish breakfast and a coffee.'

'No,' Elizabeth's forehead wrinkled, '*two* Irish breakfasts and *two* coffees.'

'Eatin' for two, are ye?' Joe asked, looking her up and down.

'No!' Elizabeth exclaimed, and turned to Ivan with an apologetic look on her face when Joe had walked away. 'Sorry about him; he acts oddly sometimes.'

Joe placed the two coffees on the table, eyed her suspiciously and hurried off to serve another table.

'Busy in here today.' Elizabeth barely even looked away from him.

'Is it?' he asked, not moving his eyes from hers.

A tingle ran through Elizabeth's body. 'I like it when the town's like this. It brings it to life. I don't know what Ekam Eveileb is like, but here you get sick of seeing the same people all the time. Tourists change the scenery, give you something to hide behind.'

'Why would you want to hide?'

'Ivan, the whole town knows about me. They practically know more about my family history than I do.'

'I don't listen to the town, I listen to you.'

'I know. During the summer, the place is like a big tree, strong and beautiful,' she tried to explain, 'but in winter, it's robbed of its leaves, standing bare, with nothing to cover you or give you privacy. I always feel like I'm on display.'

'You don't like living here?'

'It's not that. It's just it needs some livening up sometimes, a real kick in the behind. I sit in here every morning and dream of pouring my coffee all over the streets, to give it the buzz it needs to waken the place up.'

'Well then, why don't you?'

'What do you mean?'

Ivan stood up. 'Elizabeth Egan, come with me and bring your coffee cup.'

'Bu—'

'No buts, just come.' With that he walked out of the café.

She followed him in confusion, carrying her cup outside.

'Well?' she asked, taking a sip.

'Well, I think it's high time you gave this town a caffeine high,' Ivan announced, looking up and down the empty street.

Elizabeth stared at him blankly.

'Go on.' He tapped her cup slightly and milky coffee sploshed over the side and onto the pavement. 'Oops,' he said drily.

Elizabeth laughed at him. 'You're so silly, Ivan.'

'Why am I silly? You're the one that suggested it.' He hit her cup again, harder this time, sending more coffee dripping to the ground. Elizabeth let out a shout and jumped back to avoid it staining her shoes.

She attracted a few stares from inside the café.

'Go on, Elizabeth!'

It was ludicrous, preposterous, ridiculous and completely juvenile. It didn't make sense to do it, but remembering the fun in the field yesterday, how she laughed and how she floated for the remainder of the day, she craved more of that feeling. She toppled the cup to the side, allowing the coffee to fall to the ground. It first formed a pool, then she watched it flow down the cracks in the slabs of stones and run slowly down the street.

'Come on, that won't even have woken the insects up,' Ivan teased.

'Well then, stand back.' She raised an eyebrow. Ivan stepped away as Elizabeth held out her arm and spun around on the spot. The coffee shot out as though in a fountain.

Joe stuck his head out the door. 'What are you upta, Elizabeth? Did I make a bad cuppa?' He looked worried. 'You're not making me look good in front of these folk.' He nodded towards the tourists gathered at the window, watching her.

Ivan laughed. 'I think this calls for another cup of coffee,' he announced.

'Another cup?' Elizabeth asked startled.

'OK so,' Joe said, slowly backing up.

'Excuse me, what is she doing?' a tourist asked Joe as he headed back inside.

'Ah, 'tis a, eh,' Joe floundered, ''tis a custom we have here in Baile na gCroíthe. Every Monday morning we just, eh,' he looked back at Elizabeth, standing alone, laughing and twirling as she splattered coffee on the pavement, 'we like to splatter the coffee around, you see. It's good for the, eh,' he watched as it splashed over his window boxes, 'flowers,' he gulped.

The man's eyebrows rose with interest and he smiled in amusement. 'In that case, five more cups of coffee for my dear friends.'

Joe looked uncertain, then his face broke into a great big smile as the money was thrust towards him. 'Five cups on the way.'

Moments later Elizabeth was joined by five strangers who danced around beside her, whooping and hollering as they spilled coffee down the pavement. This made her and Ivan laugh even more until eventually they escaped the crowd, who were giving each other secret looks of confusion over the silly Irish custom of spilling coffee on the ground, but who were finding amusement in it all the same.

Elizabeth looked around the village in astonishment. Shopkeepers stood at their front doors watching the commotion outside Joe's. Windows opened and heads peaked out. Cars slowed down to have a look, causing the traffic behind to beep in frustration. In a matter of moments a sleepy town had woken.

'What's wrong?' Ivan asked, wiping the tears of laughter from his eyes. 'Why have you stopped laughing?'

'Are there no such things as dreams to you, Ivan? Can't some things remain only in your head?' As far as she could see he could make everything happen. Well, almost everything. She looked up into his blue eyes and her heart beat wildly.

He gazed down at her and took a step closer. He looked so serious, and older than he had previously appeared, as if he had seen and learned something new in the last few seconds. He placed a soft hand on her cheek and moved his head slowly towards her face. 'No,' he whispered, and kissed her so gently on the lips her knees almost buckled beneath her, '*everything* must come true.'

Joe looked out the window and laughed at the tourists dancing and splattering coffee outside his shop. Catching a glimpse of Elizabeth across the road, Joe moved closer to the window to get a better look. She held her head high in the air with her eyes closed in perfect bliss. Her hair, which was usually tied back, was down and blowing in the light morning breeze and she looked to be revelling in the sun shining down on her face.

Joe could have sworn he saw her mother in that face.

Chapter 23

It took Ivan and Elizabeth's mouths a while to pull away from one another but when they finally did, with tingling lips Elizabeth half skipped, half walked along the path to her office. She felt if she lifted her feet any higher from the ground she would float away. Humming as she tried to control her non-flight, she bumped straight into Mrs Bracken, who stood in her doorway, eyeing up the tourists across the road.

'Jesus!' Elizabeth jumped back in fright.

'Is the son of God, who sacrificed his life and died on the cross to spread the Lord's word and to give you a better life, so don't take his name in vain,' Mrs Bracken rattled off. She nodded in the direction of the café. 'What are those foreigners up to at all, at all?'

Elizabeth bit her lip and tried not to laugh. 'I have no idea. Why don't you join them?'

'Mr Bracken wouldn't be pleased about that carry-on at all.' She must have sensed something in Elizabeth's voice because her head shot up, her eyes narrowed and she studied Elizabeth's face intently. 'You look different.'

Elizabeth ignored her and laughed as Joe guiltily mopped up the coffee on the pavement.

'You've been spending time up at that tower?' Mrs Bracken accused her.

'Of course I have Mrs Bracken. I'm designing the place, remember? And by the way, I've ordered the fabric; it should be arriving in three weeks, which gives us two months to get everything ready. Do you think you can get some extra help here?'

Mrs Bracken's eyes narrowed suspiciously. 'Your hair's down.'

'And?' Elizabeth asked, moving into the fabric shop to see if her order had arrived.

'And Mr Bracken used to say beware of a woman who drastically changes her hair.'

'I would hardly call letting my hair down a drastic change.'

'Elizabeth Egan, for you of all people, I would call letting your hair down a drastic change. By the way,' she moved on quickly, not allowing Elizabeth to get a word in, 'there's a problem with the order that came in today.'

'What's wrong with it?'

'It's *colourful.*' She said the word as if it were a disease and, widening her eyes, she emphasised it even more: '*Red.*'

Elizabeth smiled. 'It's raspberry, not red, and what's wrong with a bit of colour?'

'What's wrong with a bit of colour, she says.' Mrs Bracken raised her voice an octave. 'Up until last week your world was brown. It's the tower that's doing it to you. The American fella, isn't it?'

'Oh, don't you start with that tower talk as well,' Elizabeth dismissed her. 'I've been up there all week, and all it is is a crumbling wall.'

'A crumbling wall is right,' Mrs Bracken said, eyeing her, 'and it's the American fella that's knocking it.'

Elizabeth rolled her eyes. 'Goodbye, Mrs Bracken.' She ran upstairs to her office.

On her entry a pair of legs sticking out from underneath Poppy's desk greeted her. They were men's legs – brown cords with brown shoes moving and squiggling around.

'Is that you, Elizabeth?' a voice shouted out.

'Yes, Harry,' Elizabeth smiled. Oddly, she was finding the two people who usually irritated her on a daily basis strangely lovable. Ivan was certainly passing the silly smile test.

'I'm just tightening up this chair. Poppy told me it was acting up on ya last week.'

'It was, Harry, thanks.'

'No problem.' His legs slithered up under the desk and disappeared as he struggled to his feet. Banging his head against the desk he finally appeared, his bald head covered by spaghetti-strings of hair brushed over from one side to the other.

'Ah, there you are,' he said, popping his head up, spanner in hand. 'It shouldn't spin on its own any more. Funny that it did that.' He gave it one last check, then looked at Elizabeth with the same expression as the one he had when examining the chair. 'You look different.'

'No, I'm still the same,' she said, walking through to her office.

'It's the hair. The hair's down. I always say it's better for a woman's hair to be down and—'

'Thank you, Harry. Will that be all?' Elizabeth said firmly, ending the conversation.

'Oh, right so.' His cheeks flushed as he waved her off and made his way downstairs, no doubt to gossip to Mrs Bracken about Elizabeth's hair being down.

Elizabeth settled at her desk and tried to concentrate on her work but found herself gently placing her fingers on her lips, reliving the kiss with Ivan.

'OK,' Poppy said, entering Elizabeth's office and placing a money box on her desk. 'See this here?'

Elizabeth nodded at the little pig. Becca stood at the door in the background.

'Well, I've come up with a plan.' Poppy gritted her teeth. 'Every time you start to hum that bloody song of yours, you have to put money in the pig.'

Elizabeth raised her eyebrows in amusement. 'Poppy, did you *make* this pig?' she stared at the papier-mâché pig sitting on her desk.

Poppy tried to hide her smile. 'It was a quiet night last night. But, seriously, it's getting beyond irritating now, Elizabeth, you've got to believe me,' Poppy pleaded. 'Even Becca is sick of it.'

'Is that right, Becca?'

Becca's cheeks pinked and she walked away quickly, not wanting to be dragged into the conversation.

'Great backup,' Poppy grumbled.

'So who gets the money?' Elizabeth asked.

'The pig. He's raising funds for a new sty. Hum a song and support a pig,' she said, quickly thrusting the pig in Elizabeth's face.

Elizabeth tried not to laugh. 'Out.'

Moments later, after they had settled down and gone back to work, Becca came charging into the office, placed the pig on the table and said with wide eyes, 'Pay!'

'Was I humming it again?' Elizabeth asked in surprise.

'Yes,' she hissed, her patience frayed, and turned on her heel.

Later that afternoon Becca brought a visitor into Elizabeth's office.

'Hello, Mrs Collins,' Elizabeth said politely, nerves forming in the pit of her stomach. Mrs Collins ran the B&B Saoirse had been staying in for the past few weeks. 'Please, sit down.' She indicated the chair before her.

'Thank you.' Mrs Collins took a seat. 'And call me Margaret.' She looked around the room like a frightened child who had been called to the principal's office. She kept her hands clasped on her lap as though afraid to touch anything. Her blouse was buttoned up to her chin.

'I've come to you about Saoirse. I'm afraid I haven't been able to pass on any of your notes and phone messages to her over the past few days,' Margaret said uncomfortably, fiddling with the hem of her blouse. 'She hasn't been back to the B&B for three days now.'

'Oh,' Elizabeth said, feeling embarrassed. 'Thank you for informing me, Margaret, but there's no need to worry. I expect she'll be calling me soon.' She was tired of being the last to know everything, of being informed of her own family's activities by complete strangers. Despite being distracted by Ivan, Elizabeth had tried to keep her eye on Saoirse

as much as she could. Her hearing was on in a few weeks, but Elizabeth
hadn't been able to find her anywhere. Anywhere being the pub, her
dad's or the B&B.

'Well, actually it's not that. It's just that, well, it's a very busy period
for us. There are a lot of tourists coming through and looking for
boarding, and we need to use Saoirse's room.'

'Yes.' She sprang back in her chair, feeling foolish. *Of course.* 'That's
completely understandable,' Elizabeth said awkwardly. 'I can call round
after work to collect her things, if you like.'

'That won't be necessary,' Margaret smiled sweetly, then shouted,
'BOYS!'

In walked Margaret's two young teenage sons, each with a suitcase
in his hand.

'I took the liberty of gathering her things together,' Margaret
continued, her smile still plastered across her face. 'Now all I need is the
three days' rent and that will be everything settled.'

Elizabeth froze. 'Margaret, I'm sure you'll understand that Saoirse's
bills are her own. Just because I'm her sister it doesn't mean I can be
expected to pay. She will return soon, I'm sure.'

'Oh, I know that, Elizabeth,' Margaret smiled, revealing a pink lipstick
stain on her front tooth. 'But seeing as mine is currently the only B&B
that will allow Saoirse to stay I'm sure you'll make an allow—'

'How much?' Elizabeth snapped.

'Fifteen per night,' Margaret said sweetly.

Elizabeth rooted through her wallet. She sighed. 'Look, Margaret, I
don't seem to have any ca—'

'A cheque will do fine,' she sang.

After handing over the cheque to Margaret, for the first time in a
while Elizabeth stopped thinking about Ivan and started worrying about
Saoirse. Just like old times.

At 10 p.m. in downtown Manhattan, Elizabeth and Mark stared out
of the huge black windows of the hundred-and-fourteenth-floor bar
that Elizabeth had finished designing. Tonight was the opening night
of Club Zoo, an entire floor dedicated to animal prints, fur couches
and cushions with greenery and bamboo sporadically placed. It was
everything she loathed in a design, but she had been given a brief and
she had to stick to it. It was a huge success, everyone was enjoying the
night, and a live performance of drummers performing jungle beats
and the constant sound of happy conversation added to the party
atmosphere. Elizabeth and Mark clinked their champagne glasses
together and looked outside to the sea of skyscrapers, the random

lights dotting the buildings like chequers and the tide of yellow cabs below them.

'To another of your successes,' Mark toasted, sipping on the bubble-filled glass.

Elizabeth smiled, feeling proud. 'We're a long way from home now, aren't we?' she pondered, looking out at the view and seeing the reflection of the party going on behind her. She saw the owner, Henry Hakala, making his way through the crowd.

'Elizabeth, there you are.' He held out his arms and greeted her. 'What is the star of the night doing in the corner away from everyone?' he asked.

'Henry, this is Mark Leeson, my boyfriend; Mark, this is Henry Hakala, owner of Club Zoo,' she introduced the two.

'So you're the person that's kept my girlfriend out late every night,' Mark joked, taking Henry's hand.

Henry laughed. 'She's saved my life. Three weeks to do all this?' He motioned at the room decorated vibrantly in zebra print on the walls, bear skins draped on the couches, leopard print lying across the timber floors, enormous plants sitting in chrome pots and bamboo lining the bar area. 'It was a tough deadline and I knew she'd do it, but I didn't think she'd do it this well.' He looked grateful. 'Anyway, the speeches are about to begin. I just want to say a few words, mention a few investors' names,' he muttered under his breath, 'thank all you glorious people that worked so hard. So don't go anywhere, Elizabeth, because I'll have all eyes on you in a minute.'

'Oh,' Elizabeth blushed, 'please don't.'

'Believe me, you'll have a few hundred more offers after I do,' he said before he made his way towards the microphone, decorated with a vine of leaves.

'Excuse me, Ms Egan.' A member of the bar staff approached her. 'You have a phone call just outside at the main desk.'

Elizabeth frowned, 'Me? A phone call? Are you sure?'

'You are Ms Egan, yes?'

She nodded, confused. Who would be ringing her here?

'It's a young woman, says she's your sister?' he explained quietly.

'Oh.' Her heart beat wildly. 'Saoirse?' she asked, shocked.

'Yes, that's it,' the young man said, sounding relieved. 'I wasn't sure I'd remembered right.'

At that moment it felt as if the music got louder, the drumming beats were pounding her head, the fur prints were all coming together in a blur. Saoirse never called her; something had to be seriously wrong.

'Leave it, Elizabeth,' Mark said rather forcefully. 'Tell the woman on the phone that Ms Egan is busy at the moment,' Mark said to the barman. 'This is your night, enjoy it,' he added softly to Elizabeth.

'No, no, don't tell her that,' Elizabeth stammered. It must be 3 a.m. in Ireland – why was Saoirse calling so late? 'I'll take the call, thank you,' she said to the young man.

'Elizabeth, the speech is about to begin,' Mark warned her as the room began to quieten down and gather before the microphone. 'You can't miss it,' he hissed. 'This is *your* moment.'

'No, no, I can't,' she trembled, and she left him, heading in the direction of the phone.

'Hello?' she said a few moments later, the concern evident in her voice.

'Elizabeth?' Saoirse's voice sobbed.

'It's me, Saoirse. What's wrong?' Elizabeth's heart thudded in her chest. There was silence in the club as Henry made his speech.

'I just wanted to . . .' Saoirse trailed off and was silent.

'You wanted to what? Is everything OK?' Elizabeth asked hurriedly.

Henry's voice boomed, '. . . And last but not least I'd like to thank the wonderful Elizabeth Egan from Morgan Designs for designing this place so wonderfully in such a short time. She's created something that's completely different to what's out there right now, making Club Zoo the most popular, trendy and newest club on the scene, guaranteed to have people queuing down the block to get in. She's down the back there somewhere. Elizabeth, give us all a wave, let them know who you are so they can steal you away from me.'

Everyone turned around in silence, searching for the designer.

'Oh,' Henry's voice echoed, 'well, she was there a second ago. Maybe someone's snapped her up already to do a job.'

Everyone laughed.

Elizabeth looked inside and saw Mark standing alone with two champagne glasses in his hand, shrugging at everyone who had turned to him and laughing. Pretending to laugh.

'Saoirse,' Elizabeth's voice broke, 'please tell me if there's something wrong. Have you gotten into trouble again?'

Silence. Instead of the weak sobbing voice Elizabeth had heard previously, Saoirse's voice had become strong again. 'No,' she snapped. 'No, I'm fine. Everything's fine. Enjoy your party,' and she hung up.

Elizabeth sighed and slowly hung up the phone.

Inside the speech had finished and the drums had started up again; the conversation and drinks continued to flow.

Neither she nor Mark was in the mood to party.

*   *   *

Elizabeth could see a giant figure looming in the distance as she drove down the road that led to her father's bungalow. She had left work early and was searching for Saoirse. Nobody had seen her for days, not even the local publican, which made a change.

It had always been difficult to direct people to the bungalow as it was so cut off from the rest of the town. The road didn't even have a name, which Elizabeth thought was appropriate; it was the road that people forgot. Postmen and milkmen new to the job always took a few days to find the address, politicians never canvassed to their door, there were no trick-or-treaters. As a child Elizabeth had tried to convince herself that her mother had simply become lost and couldn't find her way home. She remembered sharing her theory with her father, who gave a smile so small it was hardly a smile at all and replied, 'You know, you're not far wrong there, Elizabeth.'

That was the only explanation, if you could even call it that, which she got. They never discussed her mother's disappearance; neighbours and visiting family hushed when Elizabeth was near. Nobody would tell her what had happened and she didn't ask. She didn't want that uncomfortable quiet to descend on them or for her father to storm out of the house when her mother's name was mentioned. If not mentioning her mother ensured that everyone was happy, then Elizabeth was happy to oblige, as usual.

She didn't think she really wanted to know, anyway. The mystery of not knowing was more enjoyable. She would create scenarios in her head, painting her mother in exotic and exciting worlds and she would fall asleep imagining her mother on a desert island, eating bananas and coconuts and sending messages in a bottle to Elizabeth. She would check the coastline every morning with her father's binoculars for sign of a bobbing bottle.

Another theory was that she had become a Hollywood movie star. Elizabeth sat with her nose almost up against the TV screen for every Sunday matinée, searching for her mother's grand debut. But she grew tired of searching, hoping, imagining, and not asking, and eventually she no longer even wondered.

The figure didn't move from the window of Elizabeth's old bedroom. Usually her father would be waiting in the garden for her. Elizabeth hadn't been inside the bungalow for years. She waited outside for a few minutes, and when there was no sign of her father or of Saoirse she got out of the car, slowly pushed open the gate, goose pimples rising on her skin from the noise of the gate's hinges, and wobbled up the uneven stone slabs in her high heels. Weeds popped up from the cracks to study the stranger trespassing on their territory.

Elizabeth knocked twice on the green paint-flecked door and

quickly pulled her fist away, cradling it as though it had been burned. There was no answer yet she knew there was someone in the bedroom to the right. She held out her hand and pushed open the door. There was a stillness inside and the familiar musty smell of what she once considered home hit her and stopped her in her tracks for a few moments. Once she had adjusted to the emotions the scent had woken inside her, she stepped inside.

She cleared her throat. 'Hello?'

No answer.

'Hello?' she called more loudly. Her grown-up voice sounded wrong in her childhood home.

She began to walk towards the kitchen, hoping her father would hear her and come out to her. She had no desire to revisit her old bedroom. Her high heels echoed on the stone floor, another sound unfamiliar to the house. She held her breath as she stepped into the kitchen and dining area. Everything and nothing was the same. The smells, the clock on the mantel, the lace tablecloth, the rug, the chair by the fireplace, the red teapot on the green Aga, the curtains. Everything still had its place, had aged and was faded with time, but still belonged. It was as though no one had lived there since Elizabeth had left. Maybe no one *had* truly lived there.

She stayed standing in the centre of the room for a while, eyeing the ornaments, reaching out to touch them but allowing her fingers only to linger. Nothing had been disturbed. She felt as though she were in a museum; even the sounds of tears, laughter, fights and love had been preserved and hung in the air like cigarette smoke.

Eventually she couldn't take it any more; she needed to talk to her father, to find out where Saoirse was, and in order to do that she needed to go to her bedroom. She slowly turned the brass door knob that was still hanging loose as it had been in her childhood. She pushed the door open, didn't step in, and didn't look around. She just looked straight at her father, who sat in an armchair in front of the window, not moving.

Chapter 24

She didn't move her eyes from the back of his head, couldn't move her eyes anywhere else. She tried not to breathe in the smell but it gathered in her throat, blocking her wind pipe.

'Hello?' she croaked.

He didn't move, just kept his head straight ahead.

Her heart skipped a beat. 'Hello?' She detected an air of panic in her voice.

Without thinking, she stepped into the room and rushed towards him. She fell to her knees and examined his face. He still didn't move and kept his eyes straight ahead. Her heart quickened. 'Daddy?' rushed out of her mouth in a panic, sounding childlike. It felt real to her then. The word meant something. She held out to touch him, placed one hand on his face and another on his shoulder. 'Dad, it's me – are you OK? Talk to me.' Her voice shook. His skin was warm.

He blinked and she breathed a sigh of relief.

He slowly turned to look at her. 'Ah, Elizabeth, I didn't hear you come in.' His voice sounded like it was coming from another room. It was gentle; gone were his gravelly tones.

'I was calling you,' she said softly. 'I drove down the road – didn't you see me?'

'No,' he said in surprise, turning back to face the window.

'Then what were you looking at?' She too turned to the window and the view took her breath away. The scene – the path, the garden gate and the long stretch of road – momentarily threw her into the same trance as her father. The same hopes and wishes of the past came back in that instant. On the windowsill sat a photograph of her mother, which had never been there before. In fact, Elizabeth thought her father had got rid of all the photographs after her mother left.

But the image of her silenced Elizabeth. It was so long since she had seen her mother; she no longer had a face in Elizabeth's mind. All she was was a fuzzy memory, more like a feeling than a picture. Seeing her was a shock. It was like looking at herself, a perfect mirror image. When she found her voice again she spoke quietly, shaken. 'What are you doing, Dad?'

He didn't move his head, didn't blink, just had a faraway look in his eye and an unfamiliar voice that came deep from within him. 'I saw her, Elizabeth.'

Palpitations. 'Saw who?' But she knew who.

'Gráinne, your mother. I saw her. At least I think I did. It's been so long since I've seen her that I wasn't sure. So I got the photo just so I can remember. So that when she walks down the road I'll remember.'

Elizabeth gulped. 'Where did you see her, Dad?'

His voice was higher pitched and slightly bewildered. 'In a field.'

'A field? What field?'

'A field of magic.' His eyes glistened, seeing it all over again. 'A field of dreams, as they say. She looked so happy, dancing and laughing just like she always did. She hasn't aged a day.' He looked confused. 'But she should have, shouldn't she? She should be older, like me.'

'Are you sure it was her, Dad?' Her whole body was shaking.

'Oh aye, 'twas her, moving in the wind like the dandelions, sun shining on her like she was an angel. 'Twas her, alright.' He was sitting upright in the chair, two hands lying on the armrests, looking more relaxed than ever.

'She had a child with her, though, and it wasn't Saoirse. No, Saoirse's grown up now,' he reminded himself. 'It was a boy, I think. Little blond fella, like Saoirse's boy . . .' His thick caterpillar-like eyebrows furrowed for the first time.

'When did you see her?' Elizabeth asked, dread and relief both filling her body, realising it was she her father had seen in the field.

'Yesterday,' he smiled, remembering. 'Yesterday morning. She'll be coming to me soon.'

Tears filled Elizabeth's eyes. 'Have you been sitting here since yesterday, Dad?'

'Aye, I don't mind. She'll be here soon but I need to remember her face. I sometimes don't remember, you see.'

'Dad,' Elizabeth's voice was a whisper, 'wasn't there someone else in the field with her?'

'No,' Brendan smiled, 'just her and the boy. He looked so happy too.'

'What I mean is,' Elizabeth held his hand; hers was childlike next to his tough-skinned fingers, 'I was in the field yesterday. It was me, Dad, catching dandelion seeds with Luke and a man.'

'No.' He shook his head and scowled. 'There was no man. Gráinne was with no man. She's coming home soon.'

'Dad, I promise you it was me, Luke and Ivan. Perhaps you were mistaken,' she said as gently as she could.

'No!' he yelled, causing Elizabeth to jump. He faced her with a look of disgust. 'She's coming home to me!' He glared at her. 'Get out!' he finally yelled, waving his hand and knocking her small hand off his.

'What?' Her heart beat wildly. 'Why, Dad?'

'You're a liar,' he spat. 'I saw no man in the field. You know she's here and you're keeping her from me,' he hissed. 'You wear suits and sit behind desks, you know nothing of dancing in fields. You're a liar, pollutin' the place. Get out,' he repeated quietly.

She looked at him in shock. 'I've met a man, Dad, a beautiful, wonderful man who's been teaching me of all these things,' she started to explain.

He moved his face in front of hers until they were almost touching nose to nose. 'GET OUT!' he yelled.

Tears spilled from her eyes and her body shook as she rushed to her feet. Her room became a whirl as she saw everything she didn't want to see in her disoriented state – old teddies, dolls, books, a writing desk, the same duvet cover. She charged for the door, not wanting to see any more, not being able to see any more. Her trembling hands fumbled with the latch as her father's yells for her to leave got louder and louder.

She pulled the door open and ran outside into the garden, breathing the fresh air into her lungs. A knocking on the window spun her round. She faced her father, waving angrily at her to get out of his garden. She gasped for breath, her tears raced down her face and she pulled open the gate and left it open, not wanting to hear the closing creak of its hinges.

She sped down the road in her car as fast as she could, not looking in the rear-view window, not wanting ever to see the place again, not wanting ever to have to drive down the road of disappointment again.

There would be no more looking back.

Chapter 25

'What's wrong?' a voice called from the back patio door. Elizabeth was sitting at the kitchen table, head in her hands, as still as Muckross Lake on a calm day.

'Jesus,' Elizabeth said under her breath, not looking up but wondering how it was that Ivan always managed to appear at the moments when she least expected him but needed him most.

'Jesus? Has he been giving you a hard time?' He stepped into the kitchen.

Elizabeth looked up from her hands. 'It's actually his father I'm having an issue with right now.'

Ivan took another step towards her; he had the ability to overstep the boundaries but never in a threatening or intrusive way. 'I hear that a lot.'

Elizabeth wiped her eyes with a mascara-stained and crumpled tissue. 'Don't you ever work?'

'I work all the time. May I?' He gestured to the chair opposite her.

She nodded. 'All the time? So is this work for you? Am I just another hopeless case for you to deal with today?' she asked sarcastically, catching a tear halfway down her cheek with the tissue.

'There's nothing hopeless about you, Elizabeth. However, you are a case; I've already told you that,' he said seriously.

She laughed. 'A headcase.'

Ivan looked sad. Misunderstood again.

'So is that your uniform?' She indicated his attire.

Ivan looked down at himself in surprise.

'You've been wearing that outfit everyday I've seen you,' she smiled, 'so it's either a uniform or you're completely unhygienic and lack imagination.'

Ivan's eyes widened. 'Oh, Elizabeth, I don't lack imagination at all.' Not realising what he had implied, Ivan continued, 'Do you want to talk about why you are so sad?'

'No, we're always talking about me and my problems,' Elizabeth replied. 'Let's talk about you for a change. What did you do today?' she asked, trying to perk herself up. It had seemed like such a long time ago since she had kissed Ivan on the main street that morning. She had thought about it all day and had worried about who had seen her, but amazingly, for a town that learned of everything quicker than Sky News, nobody had mentioned a thing to her about the mystery man.

She had longed to kiss Ivan again, had felt scared about that longing and tried to numb herself of feeling for him but she couldn't. There was something about him so pure and untarnished, yet he was powerful and well-versed in life. He was like the drug she knew she shouldn't take but which kept coming back to feed her addiction. As her weariness set in later in the day, the memory of the kiss had become a comfort to her and the uneasiness vanished. All she wanted now was a repeat of that moment where her troubles fizzled away.

'What did I do today?' Ivan twiddled his thumbs and thought aloud. 'Well, today I gave Baile na gCroíthe a big wake-up call, kissed a very beautiful woman and then spent the rest of the day being unable to do anything but think of her.'

Elizabeth's face brightened and his piercing blue eyes warmed her heart.

'And then I couldn't stop thinking,' Ivan continued, 'so I sat down and spent the day thinking.'

'About what?'

'Apart from the beautiful woman?'

'Apart from her,' Elizabeth grinned.

'You don't want to know.'

'I can take it.'

Ivan looked uncertain. 'OK, if you really want to know,' he took a deep breath, 'I thought about the Borrowers.'

Elizabeth frowned. 'What?'

'The Borrowers,' Ivan repeated, looking thoughtful.

'The television programme?' Elizabeth said, feeling irate. She had prepared herself for whispers of sweet nothing like they did in the movies, not this unscripted loveless conversation.

'Yes.' Ivan rolled his eyes, not noticing her tone, 'if you want to refer to *that* commercial side of them.' He sounded angry. 'But I thought long and hard about them and I've come to the conclusion that they didn't borrow. They *stole*. They downright stole and everybody knows it but nobody ever talks about it. To borrow means to take and use something belonging to someone else and then eventually return it. I mean, when did they ever give anything back? I don't recall Peagreen Clock ever giving anything back to the Lenders at all, do you? Especially the food – how can you borrow *food*? You eat it and it's gone; there's no giving it back. At least when I eat your dinner you know where it's going.' He sat back and folded his arms, looking cross. 'And they get a film made about them, a bunch of thieves, while us? We do nothing but good but we get labelled a figment of people's imaginations and are still,' he made a face and made inverted commas with his fingers, '*invisible*. Please . . .' He rolled his eyes.

Elizabeth stared at him open-mouthed.

There was a long silence as Ivan looked around the kitchen, shaking his head in anger, and then returned his attention to Elizabeth. 'What?'

Silence.

'Oh, it doesn't matter.' He waved his hand dismissively. 'I told you, you wouldn't want to know. So enough about my problems. Please tell me, what's happened?'

Elizabeth took a deep breath, the question of Saoirse distracting her from the confusing talk of the Borrowers. 'Saoirse has disappeared. Joe, the man with his finger on the pulse of Baile na gCroíthe, told me she headed off with the group of people she was hanging out with. He heard it from a family member of a guy from the group she's with but she's been gone for three days and no one seems to know where they've gone.'

'Oh,' Ivan said in surprise, 'and here I am rattling off my problems. Did you tell the gardaí?'

'I had to,' she said sadly. 'I felt like a snitch but they had to know she was gone just in case she didn't turn up for her hearing in a few weeks, which I'm almost sure she won't be at. I'll have to get a solicitor to go on her behalf, which won't look very good.' She rubbed her face tiredly.

He took her hands and cradled them in his own. 'She'll be back,' he said confidently. 'Maybe not for the hearing but she'll come back. Believe me. There's no need to worry.' His soft voice was firm.

Elizabeth stared deep into his eyes, searching for the truth. 'I believe you,' she said. But deep down Elizabeth was afraid. She was afraid of believing Ivan, afraid of believing full stop, because when that happened, her hopes were raised up the flagpole, waving and blowing in the breeze for all to see. There they would weather the storms and winds, only to be lowered, tattered and ruined.

And she didn't think she could spend any more years with her bedroom curtains open, with one eye on the road, waiting for a second person to return. She was weary and she needed to close her eyes.

Chapter 26

As soon as I left Elizabeth's house the next morning, I decided to head straight to Opal. Actually, I had decided I was going to do that long before I left Elizabeth's house. Something she said had hit a nerve – actually, everything she said hit a nerve with me. When I was with her I was like a hedgehog, all prickly and sensitive, as if all of my senses were alert. The funny thing is I thought all my senses had been alert already – as a professional best friend they should have been – but there was one emotion I hadn't experienced before and that was love. Sure, I loved all my friends but not in this way, not in the way that made my heart thud when I looked at Elizabeth, not in a way that made me want to be with her the whole time. And I didn't want to be with her for *her*, I realised it was for me. This love thing awakened a group of slumbering senses in my body that I never even knew existed.

I cleared my throat, checked my appearance and made my way into Opal's office. In Ekam Eveileb there were no doors, because nobody here could open them, but there was another reason: doors acted as barriers; they were thick, unwelcoming things that you could control to shut people in or out and we didn't agree with that. We chose open-plan offices for a more open and friendly atmosphere. Although that's what we were always taught, lately I had found Elizabeth's fuchsia front door with the smiling letter box to be the friendliest door I had ever seen, so that shot that particular theory to hell. She was making me question all sorts of things.

Without even looking up, Opal called out, 'Welcome, Ivan.' She was sitting behind a desk, dressed in purple, as usual, her dreadlocks were tied up and scattered in glitter so that with every movement she sparkled. On each of her walls were framed photos of hundreds of children, all smiling happily. They were even covering her shelves, coffee table, sideboard, mantelpiece and windowsill. Everywhere I looked were rows and rows of photographs of people Opal had worked with and become friends with in the past. Her desk was the only surface that was clear and on it sat one single photo frame. The frame had sat there for years facing Opal so that nobody ever really got a chance to see who or what was in it. We knew that if we asked she would tell us, but nobody was ever rude enough to ask. What we didn't need to know, we didn't need to ask. Some people just don't quite get the gist of that. You can have plenty of conversations with people, *meaningful* conversations without getting too personal. There's a line, you know, like an invisible field around people that you just know not to enter or cross, and I had never crossed it with Opal, or anyone else for that matter. Some people just can't even see that.

Elizabeth would have hated the room, I thought as I looked around. She would have removed everything in an instant, dusted it and polished it until it gleamed with the clinical glow of a hospital. Even at the coffee shop she had arranged the salt and pepper shakers and the bowl of sugar into an equilateral triangle in the centre of the table. She always moved things an inch to the left or an inch to the right, back and forward until it stopped nagging and she could concentrate again. Funny thing was, she sometimes ended up moving things back to exactly how they were in the first place and then convincing herself she was happy with them. That said a lot about Elizabeth.

But why did I start thinking of Elizabeth just then? I kept on doing that. In situations that were totally unrelated to her, I would think of her and she would become part of the scenario. I would suddenly wonder, what would she think, how would she feel, what would she do or say if she was with me? That was all part of giving someone a piece of your heart; they ended up taking a whole chunk of your mind and reserving it all for themselves.

Anyway, I realised I had been standing in front of the desk not saying anything since I walked in.

'How did you know it was me?' I finally spoke.

Opal looked up and smiled one of those smiles that made her look as if she knew it all. 'I was expecting you.' Her lips looked like two big cushions, and were purple to match her robe. I thought of what it felt like to kiss Elizabeth's lips.

'But I didn't make an appointment,' I protested. I knew I was intuitive but Opal was in a whole league of her own.

She just smiled again. 'What can I do for you?'

'I thought you'd know that without having to ask me,' I teased, sitting down in her spinning chair and thinking about the spinning chair in Elizabeth's office, then thinking of Elizabeth, what it was like to hold her, hug her, laugh with her and hear the little breaths she took while she slept last night.

'You know the dress Calendula was wearing at last week's meeting?'

'Yes.'

'Do you know how she got that?'

'Why, do you want one too?' Opal asked with a glint in her eyes.

'Yes,' I replied, fidgeting with my hands. 'I mean no,' I said quickly. I took a breath. 'What I mean is, I was wondering where I could get a change of clothes for myself.' There I'd done it.

'The wardrobe department, two floors down,' Opal explained.

'I didn't know there was a wardrobe department,' I said in surprise.

'It's always been there,' Opal said, narrowing her eyes. 'May I ask what you need it for?'

'I don't know.' I shrugged. 'It's just that, Elizabeth, you see, is, um, she's *different* from all my other friends. She notices these things, you know?'

She nodded slowly.

I felt I should explain a bit more. The silence was making me uncomfortable. 'You see, Elizabeth said to me today that the reason I wore these clothes was because it was either a uniform, I was unhygienic or because I lacked imagination.' I sighed, thinking about it. 'The last thing I am is lacking in imagination.'

Opal smiled.

'And I know I'm not unhygienic,' I continued. 'And then I was thinking about the uniform part,' I looked myself up and down, 'and maybe she was right, you know?'

Opal pursed her lips.

'One of the things about Elizabeth is that she too is dressed in uniform. She wears black – the same stuffy suits all the time – her make-up is a mask, her hair is always tied back, *nothing* is free. She works all the time and takes it so seriously,' I looked up at Opal in shock, just realising something. 'That's exactly like me, Opal.'

Opal was silent.

'All this time I was calling her a gnirob.'

Opal laughed lightly.

'I wanted to teach her to have fun, to change her clothes, stop wearing a mask, change her life so she can find happiness and how can I do that when I'm the very same as her?'

Opal nodded her head lightly. 'I understand, Ivan. You're learning a lot from Elizabeth too, I can see that. She is bringing something out in you and you are showing her a whole new way of life.'

'We caught Jinny Joes on Sunday,' I said softly, agreeing with her.

Opal opened a cabinet behind her and grinned. 'I know.'

'Oh, good, they arrived,' I said happily, watching the Jinny Joes floating in a jar in the cabinet.

'One of yours arrived too, Ivan,' Opal said seriously.

I felt my face redden. I changed the subject. 'You know she got six hours of undisturbed sleep last night. That's the first time that's ever happened.'

Opal's expression didn't soften. 'Did she tell you that, Ivan?'

'No, I saw her . . .' I trailed off. 'Look, Opal, I stayed the night, I only held her in my arms till she fell asleep, it's no big deal. She asked me to.' I tried to sound convincing. 'And when you think about it, I do it all the time with other friends. I read them bedtime stories, stay with them till they sleep and sometimes even sleep on their floor. This is no different.'

'Isn't it?'

I didn't answer.

Opal picked up her fountain pen with a great big purple feather on the top, looked down and continued with her calligraphy writing. 'How much longer do you think you'll need to work with her?'

That got me. My heart did a little dance. Opal had never asked me that before. It was never a matter of time for anyone, it was always a natural progression. Sometimes you only had to spend a day with someone, other times you could be there months. When our friends were ready, they were ready, and we had never before had to put a time on it. 'Why do you ask?'

'Oh,' she was nervous, fidgety, 'I'm just wondering. As a matter of interest . . . you're the best I have here, Ivan, and I just want you to remember that there are lots more people that need you.'

'I know that,' I said rather forcefully. Opal's voice had all sorts of tones I had never heard before, negative ones that sent blue and black colours into the air and I didn't like it one bit.

'Great,' she said, a bit too perky for her, and she knew it. 'Can you drop these by the analysis lab on your way to wardrobe?' She handed me the jar of Jinny Joes.

'Sure.' I took the jar from her. There were three Jinny Joes inside, one from Luke, one from Elizabeth and the third was mine. They sat on the floor of the jar, resting from their journey in the wind. 'Bye,' I said rather awkwardly to Opal, backing out of the office. I felt as though we'd just had an argument even though we hadn't.

I made my way down the hall to the analysis lab, holding the lid of the jar closed tightly so they wouldn't escape. Oscar was running around the lab with a look of panic on his face when I reached the entrance.

'Open the hatch!' he yelled to me while passing the door, arms out in front of him, white coat flapping like a cartoon character.

I placed the jar away from danger and hurried to the hatch. Oscar ran towards me and, at the last minute, jumped to the side, fooling what was chasing him so that it raced straight into the cage.

'Ha!' he exploded, turning the key and waving it at the cage. His forehead was glittered with perspiration.

'What on earth is that?' I asked, moving closer to the cage.

'Be careful!' Oscar shouted, and I jumped back. 'You are incorrect in asking what on earth it is because it's not.' He dabbed his forehead with a handkerchief.

'It's not what?'

'On earth,' he replied. 'Never seen a shooting star before, Ivan?'

'Of course I have.' I circled the cage. 'But not up close.'

'Of course,' he added, an overly sweet tone to his voice, 'you just see them from afar, looking so pretty and bright, dancing across the sky, and you make your wishes on them but,' his tone turned nasty, 'you forget about Oscar, who has to gather your wishes from the star.'

'I'm sorry, Oscar, I really did forget. I didn't think stars were so dangerous.'

'Why?' Oscar snapped, 'Did you think a burning asteroid millions of miles away, which is visible from earth, is going to shoot down to me and kiss me on the cheek? Anyway, it doesn't matter. What have you brought to me? Oh great, a Jinny Joe jar. Just what I needed after that ball of fire,' he shouted loudly at the cage, 'something with a bit of respect.'

The ball of fire bounced around angrily in response.

I stepped further away from the cage. 'What kind of wish was it carrying?' I found it hard to believe that this burning ball of light could be of any help to anyone.

'Funny you ask,' Oscar said, showing it wasn't funny at all. 'This particular one was carrying the wish to chase me around the lab.'

'Was that Tommy?' I tried not to laugh.

'I can only assume so,' he said angrily. 'But I can't really complain to him because that was twenty years ago when Tommy didn't know any better and was just starting out.'

'Twenty years ago?' I asked in surprise.

'It took that long to get here,' Oscar explained, opening the jar and lifting out a Jinny Joe with an odd-looking implement. 'It is, after all, millions of light years away. I thought twenty years was doing rather well.'

I left Oscar studying the Jinny Joes and made my way to wardrobe. Olivia was in there being measured.

'Hello, Ivan,' she said in surprise.

'Hi, Olivia, what are you doing?' I asked, watching as a woman measured her tiny waist.

'Being measured for a dress, Ivan. Poor Mrs Cromwell passed away last night,' she said sadly. 'The funeral's tomorrow. I've been to so many funerals my only black dress is worn out.'

'I'm sorry to hear that,' I said, knowing how fond Olivia was of Mrs Cromwell.

'Thank you, Ivan, but we must keep going. A lady arrived at the hospice this morning, who needs my help and now I must focus on her.'

I nodded, understanding.

'So what brings you here?'

'My new friend, Elizabeth, is a woman. She notices my clothes.'

Olivia chuckled.

'You want a T-shirt in another colour?' the woman who was measuring asked. She took a red T-shirt from a drawer.

'Em, no.' I shifted from foot to foot and looked around at the shelves reaching from floor to ceiling. Each of them was labelled with a name and I saw Calendula's name underneath a row of pretty dresses. 'I was looking for something a lot . . . smarter.'

Olivia raised her eyebrows. 'Well then, you'll have to be measured for a suit, Ivan.'

We agreed to make me a black suit to go with a blue shirt and tie because they were my favourite colours.

'Anything else, or will that be all?' Olivia asked me with a twinkle in her eye.

'Actually,' I lowered my voice and looked around to make sure the woman was out of earshot. Olivia moved her head closer to mine.

'I was wondering if you could teach me the soft-shoe shuffle.'

Chapter 27

Elizabeth stared at the sparse wall, dirty with dried and patchy plaster. She already felt at a loss. The wall wasn't saying anything to her. It was 9.00 a.m. on the building site, and it was already overrun by men in hard hats, drooping jeans, check shirts and Caterpillar boots. They looked like an army of ants as they rushed around carrying all sorts of materials on their backs. In the emptiness of the hotel their cheers, laughter, songs and whistling echoed around the cemented shell on top of the hill that had yet to be filled by the ideas in Elizabeth's head. Their sounds rolled down the corridors like thunder and into what was to be the children's playroom.

All it was now was a blanched and pallid canvas that would in a matter of only weeks have children frolicking in the recreation room, while outside would be a cocoon of calm. Perhaps she should have sound-proofed the walls. She had no idea what she could add to these walls to bring a smile to the children's little faces when they walked in feeling nervous and upset at being taken from their parents. She knew about chaise longues, plasma screens, marble floors and wood of every kind. She could do chic, funky, sophisticated and rooms of splendour and grandeur. But none of these things would excite a child, and she knew she could do better than a few building blocks, jigsaw puzzles and beanbags.

She knew it would be perfectly within her rights to hire a muralist, ask the on-site painters to do the job or even ask Poppy for some guidance, but Elizabeth liked to be hands-on. She liked to get lost in her work and she didn't want to have to ask for help. Handing the brush over to someone else would be a sign of defeat in her eyes.

She laid ten tubs of primary colours in a line on the floor, opened the lids and placed the brushes next to them. She spread a white sheet on the floor and, making sure her jeans, which she wore only as work wear, wouldn't touch the dirty floor in any way, she sat crosslegged in the centre of the room and stared at the wall. But all she could think of was the fact she couldn't think of anything but Saoirse. Saoirse, who was on her mind every second of every day.

In time she wondered how long she had been sitting there. She had a vague recollection of builders entering and exiting the room, collecting their tools, watching her in puzzlement as she stared at a blank wall.

She had a feeling she was suffering an interior designer's version of writer's block. No ideas would come, no pictures could be formed and, just as the ink would dry in a pen, the paint would not flow from her brush. Her head was filled with . . . nothing. It was as though her thoughts were being reflected onto that drab plastered wall and it was probably thinking the very same thing as her.

She felt someone's presence behind her and she turned round. Benjamin was standing at the door.

'I'm sorry, I would have knocked but,' he held his hands up, 'there's no door.'

Elizabeth gave him a welcoming grin.

'Admiring my handiwork?'

'You did this?' She turned back to face the wall.

'My best work, I think,' he replied, and they both looked at it in silence. Elizabeth sighed. 'It's not saying anything to me.'

'Ah.' He took a step into the room. 'You have no idea how difficult it is to create a piece of art that doesn't say anything at all. Someone always has some kind of interpretation but with this . . .' he shrugged, 'nothing. No statements.'

'A sign of a true genius, Mr West.'

'Benjamin,' he winced. 'I keep telling you, please call me Benjamin; you make me sound like my math teacher.'

'OK, you can keep calling me Ms Egan.'

He caught the sides of her cheeks lifting into a smile as she turned back to face the wall.

'Do you think there's any chance at all that the kids will like this room just as it is?' she asked hopefully.

'Hmm,' Benjamin thought aloud, 'the nails protruding from the skirting board would be particularly fun for them to play with. I don't know,' he admitted. 'You're asking the wrong guy about kids. They're another species to me. We don't have a real close relationship.'

'Me neither,' Elizabeth muttered guiltily, thinking of her inability to connect with Luke like Edith did. Although after meeting Ivan she found herself spending more time with him. That morning in the field with Ivan and Luke had been a real milestone for her, yet when she was alone with Luke she still couldn't let herself go with him. It was Ivan that released the child in her.

Benjamin went down on his haunches, placing his hand on the dusty floor to steady himself. 'Well, I don't believe that for a second. You've got a son, don't you?'

'Oh, no, I haven't . . .' she started, then stopped. 'He's my nephew. I adopted him but the last thing in this world I understand is children.'

Everything was blurting out of her mouth today. She missed the Elizabeth who could have a conversation without revealing the tiniest part of herself but it seemed that lately the floodgates to her heart had been opened and things rushed out of it of their own accord.

'Well, you seem to have a pretty good idea what he wanted on Sunday morning,' Benjamin said softly, looking at her differently. 'I drove past you when you were dancing around that field.'

Elizabeth rolled her eyes and her dark skin pinked. 'You and the rest of the town, apparently. But that was Ivan's idea,' she said quickly.

Benjamin laughed. 'You give Ivan the credit for everything?'

Elizabeth thought about that but Benjamin didn't wait for the answer. 'I suppose in this case you just gotta sit here like you're doin' and put yourself in the position of the kids. Put that wild imagination of yours to use. If you were a kid what would you want to do in this room?'

'Other than get out and grow up quickly?'

Benjamin moved to get up.

'So how long do you plan on staying in the big smoke of Baile na gCroíthe?' Elizabeth asked quickly. She figured the longer he stayed, the more she could put off admitting to herself that for the first time in her life she had absolutely no idea of what to do with a room.

Benjamin, sensing her desire for a conversation, lowered himself to the dusty floor and Elizabeth had to ignore what she could imagine were millions of dust mites crawling all over him.

'I plan on leaving as soon as the last lick of paint is on the walls and the last nail has been hammered in.'

'You've obviously fallen head over heels in love with this place,' Elizabeth said sarcastically. 'Don't the stunning panoramic views of Kerry impress you?'

'Yeah, the views are nice but I've had six months of good views and now I could do with a decent cup of coffee, a choice of more than one shop to buy my clothes and to be able to walk around without everyone staring at me like I've escaped from a zoo.'

Elizabeth laughed.

Benjamin held his hands up. 'I don't mean to be offensive or anything – Ireland's great – but I'm just not a fan of small towns.'

'Me neither . . .' Elizabeth's smile faded at the thought. 'So where did you escape from then?'

'New York.'

Elizabeth shook her head. 'That is not a New York accent I hear.'

'No, you got me; I'm from a place called Haxtun in Colorado, which I'm sure you've probably heard of. It's well known for a great number of things.'

'Such as?'

He raised his eyebrows. 'Absolutely nothing. It's a small town in a big dust bowl, a good strong farming town with a population of one thousand.'

'You didn't like it there?'

'No I didn't like it,' he said firmly. 'You could say I suffered from claustrophobia,' he added with a smile.

'I know how that feels,' Elizabeth nodded. 'Sounds like here.'

'It's a bit like here.' Benjamin looked out the window. He relaxed then. 'Everyone waves at you as you pass. They haven't a damn clue who you are but they wave.'

Elizabeth hadn't realised it until now. She pictured her father in the field, cap on, covering his face, holding his arm up in an L shape to passing cars.

'They wave in fields and on the streets,' Benjamin continued, 'farmers, old ladies, kids, teens, newly born and serial killers. And I've studied this to a fine art.' His eyes twinkled at her. 'You even get the one-finger wave with the index finger raised off the steering wheel as you pass traffic. Man, you'd leave the place waving at cows if you're not careful.'

'And the cows would probably wave back.'

Benjamin laughed loudly. 'You ever think of leaving?'

'I did more than think about it.' Her smile faded. 'I went to New York too but I've commitments here,' she said, quickly looking away.

'Your nephew, right?'

'Yes,' she said softly.

'Well, there's one good thing about leaving a small town. They all miss you when you're gone. They all notice it.'

Their eyes locked on one another. 'I suppose you're right,' she said. 'It's ironic, though, that we both moved to a big city where we were surrounded by more people and more buildings than we'd ever known, just so we could feel more isolated.'

'Huh.' Benjamin stared at her, not blinking. She knew he wasn't seeing her face; he was lost in his own world. And he did look lost for a moment. 'Anyway,' he snapped out of his trance, 'it was a pleasure talking to you again, Ms Egan.'

She smiled at his address.

'I'd better go and let you stare at the wall some more.' He stopped and turned at the doorway. 'Oh, by the way,' she felt her stomach turn, 'without running the risk of making you uncomfortable, I mean this in the most innocent way possible, maybe you'd like to meet up outside of work sometime? It would be nice to have a conversation with a like-minded person for a change.'

'Sure.' She liked this casual invitation. No expectations.

'Maybe you'll know some of the good places to go. Six months ago, when I just arrived, I made the mistake of asking Joe where the nearest sushi bar was. I had to tell him it was raw fish before he directed me to a lake about an hour's drive away and told me to ask for a guy called Tom.'

Elizabeth burst out laughing, the sound, which was becoming more familiar to her these days, echoing around the room. 'That's his brother, the fisherman.'

'Anyway, I'll see you again.'

The room was empty once more and Elizabeth was faced with the same dilemma. She thought of what Benjamin had said about using her imagination and putting herself in the place of a child. She closed her eyes and imagined the sounds of children hollering, laughing, crying and fighting. The noisy clatter of toys, feet pounding on the floor as they ran around, the sound of bodies falling, a shocked silence and then wails. She pictured herself as a child sitting alone in a room, not knowing anyone, and it suddenly occurred to her what she would have wanted.

A friend.

She opened her eyes and spotted a card on the floor beside her, though the room was still empty and quiet. Someone must have crept in when she had her eyes closed and left it there. She picked up the card, which had a black thumb print on the side. She didn't even need to read it to know it was Benjamin's new business card.

Maybe imagining had worked after all. It looked like she'd just made a friend in the playroom.

Sliding the card into her back pocket, she forgot about Benjamin and continued staring at the four walls.

Nope. Still nothing.

Chapter 28

Elizabeth sat at the glass table in the spotless kitchen surrounded by gleaming granite worktops, polished walnut cupboards and shining marble tiles. She had just had a cleaning frenzy and her mind still wasn't clear. Every time the phone rang, she leaped at it, thinking it was Saoirse, but it was Edith checking up on Luke. Elizabeth still hadn't heard from her sister, her father was still waiting in her old bedroom for her mother; sitting, eating and sleeping in the same chair for almost two weeks now. He wouldn't speak to Elizabeth, wouldn't even let her come as far as the front door so she had arranged for a housekeeper to call round to cook him a meal a day, and tidy up now and then. Some days he let her in, others he didn't. The young man who worked with her father on his farm had taken over all the duties. This was costing Elizabeth money she couldn't afford, but there was nothing else she could do. She couldn't help the other two members of her family if they didn't want to be helped. And she wondered for the first time if she had something in common with them after all.

They had all lived together – the girls had grown up together – but separately, and still they stayed together in the same town. They hadn't much communication with one another but when somebody left . . . well, it mattered. They were tied by an old and fraying rope that ended up being the object of tug of war.

Elizabeth couldn't bring herself to tell Luke what was going on and, of course, he knew there was something. Ivan was right, children had a sixth sense for that kind of thing, but Luke was such a good child and as soon as he sensed Elizabeth's sadness he retreated into the playroom. Then she would hear the quiet clatter of building blocks. She couldn't bring herself to say more to him than to tell him to wash his hands, fix his speech and order him to stop dragging his feet.

She wasn't capable of holding her arms out to him, her lips couldn't form the words 'I love you', but she tried in her own ways to make him feel safe and wanted. But she knew what he really wanted. She had been in his position, knew what it was like to want to be held, cuddled, kissed on the forehead and rocked. To be made to feel safe for just a few minutes at least, to know that someone else is there looking out for you and that life just isn't in your own hands and you're stuck living it all alone in your head.

Ivan had provided her with a few of those moments over the past few weeks. He had kissed her on the forehead and rocked her to sleep, and she had fallen asleep not feeling alone, not feeling the urge to look out the window and search beyond for someone else. Ivan, sweet, sweet Ivan was shrouded in mystery. She had never known anyone have the ability to help her realise just exactly who she was, to help her find her feet, but she was struck by the irony that this man who jokingly spoke of invisibility actually did wear a cloak of invisibility. He was putting her on a map, showing her the way, yet he had no idea where he was going himself, where he came from, *who* he was. He liked to speak of her problems, help heal her, help fix her, and he never once spoke of his own. It was as though she was a distraction to him and she wondered what would happen when the distraction ended and the realisation dawned.

She got a sense that their time together was valuable, as though she needed to hold on to every minute as if it was their last. He was too good to be true, every moment spent with him magical, so much so that she presumed this couldn't last for ever. None of her good feelings had lasted; none of the people who lightened her life managed to stay. Going by her previous luck, from pure *fear* of not wanting to lose something so special, she was just waiting for the day he would leave. Whoever he was, he was healing her, he was teaching her to smile, teaching her to laugh, and she wondered what she could teach him. With Ivan, she feared that the sweet man with the soft eyes would reach a day when he would realise she had nothing to offer. That she had simply drained him of his resources and had none to give.

It had happened with Mark. She just couldn't give him any more of herself without taking away the care she had for her family. That's what he wanted her to do, of course – cut the strings that connected her to her family – but she couldn't do it, she would never do it. Saoirse and her father knew how to pull those strings and so she remained their puppet. As a result she was alone, raising a child she never wanted, with the love of her life living in America, a married man and a father of one. She hadn't heard from him or seen him for five years. A few months after Elizabeth had moved back to Ireland he visited her while on a trip home to see his family.

Those beginning months were the hardest. Elizabeth was intent on making Saoirse bring up the baby herself and as much as Saoirse protested and claimed she didn't care, Elizabeth wasn't about to let her sister throw away the opportunity of raising her son.

Elizabeth's dad couldn't hack it any more; he couldn't take the baby's screaming all night while Saoirse was out partying. Elizabeth supposed it reminded him too much of the years before when he was left holding the baby, the baby he subsequently passed on to his twelve-year-old daughter. Well, he did the same again. He threw Saoirse out of the bungalow, forcing her to arrive on Elizabeth's doorstep, cradle and all. The day that all happened was the day Mark decided to take the trip over to visit Elizabeth.

One look at the state of her life and she knew he was gone for ever. It wasn't long before Saoirse disappeared from Elizabeth's home, leaving the baby with her. She thought about giving Luke up for adoption, she really did. Every sleepless night and every stressful day she promised herself she would make that phone call. But she couldn't do it. Maybe it had something to do with her fear of giving in. She was obsessive in her strive for perfection and she couldn't give up on trying to help Saoirse. Also there was a part of her that was intent on proving she could raise a child, that it wasn't her fault for the way Saoirse turned out. She didn't want to get it all wrong with Luke. He deserved far better.

She cursed as she picked up another of her sketches, scrunched it in a ball and threw it across the room to the bin. It landed short of it and, not being able to cope with something out of place, Elizabeth walked across the room and delivered it to its rightful position.

The kitchen table was covered in paper, colouring pencils, children's books, cartoon characters. All she had succeeded in doing was drawing doodles all over the page. It wasn't enough for the playroom and it certainly wasn't the whole new world that she aspired to create. As usual, the same thing happened that always happened when she thought of Ivan: the doorbell rang and she knew it was him. She rushed to her feet, fixing her hair, her clothes, checking her reflection in the mirror. Gathering her colouring pencils and paper, she jogged on the spot in panic, trying to decide where to dump them. They slid from her hand; swearing, she dived down to pick them up. Her papers flew out of her hands and floated to the floor like leaves in an autumn breeze.

While on the floor, her eyes fell upon red Converse runners casually crossed one another at the doorway. Her body slumped, her cheeks pinked.

'Hi, Ivan,' she said, refusing to look at him.

'Hello, Elizabeth. Have you ants in your pants?' his amused voice asked.

'How good of Luke to let you in,' Elizabeth said sarcastically. 'Funny he never actually does that when I need him to.' She reached for the sheets of paper on the floor and got to her feet. 'You're wearing red,' she stated, studying his red cap, red T-shirt and red shoes.

'Yes I am,' he agreed. 'Wearing different colours is my favourite thing now. It makes me feel even happier.'

Elizabeth looked down at her black outfit and thought about that.

'So what have you got there?' he asked, breaking into her thoughts.

'Oh, nothing,' Elizabeth mumbled, folding the pages together.

'Let me see it.' He grabbed the sheets. 'What have we got here? Donald Duck, Mickey Mouse,' he flicked through the pages, 'Winnie-the-Pooh, a racing car – and what's this?' He twirled the page round to get a better view.

'It's nothing,' Elizabeth snapped, snatching the page from his hand.

'That's not nothing – nothing looks like this.' He stared at her blankly.

'What are you doing?' she asked after a few moments' silence.

'Nothing, see?' He held out his hands.

Elizabeth stepped away from him, rolling her eyes. 'Sometimes you are worse than Luke. I'm going to have a glass of wine, would you like anything? Beer, wine, brandy?'

'A ssalg of klim, please.'

'I wish you'd stop speaking backwards,' she snapped, handing him a glass of milk. 'For a change?' she asked irritatedly, throwing her pages into the bin.

'No, that's what I always have,' he said rather perkily, eyeing her suspiciously. 'Why is that cabi net locked?'

'Em . . .' she faltered, 'so Luke can't get at the alcohol.' She couldn't say it was to keep Saoirse out. Luke had taken to hiding the key in his room whenever he heard his mother coming.

'Oh. What are you doing on the twenty-ninth?' Ivan swung himself around on the tall bar stool at the breakfast table and watched Elizabeth rooting through the wine bottles, face twisted in concentration.

'When is the twenty-ninth?' She locked the cabinet and searched through the drawer for a corkscrew.

'It's on Saturday.'

Her cheeks pinked and she looked away, giving her full concentration to opening the wine bottle. 'I'm going out on Saturday.'

'Where to?'

'A restaurant.'

'With who?'

She felt like it was Luke firing questions at her. 'I'm meeting Benjamin West,' she said, still keeping her back turned. She just couldn't face turning round right at that moment but she didn't know why she felt so uncomfortable.

'Why are you meeting him on Saturday? You don't work on Saturdays,' Ivan stated.

'It's not about work, Ivan. He doesn't know anybody here and we're going to get something to eat.' She poured the red wine into a crystal glass.

'Eat?' he asked incredulously. 'You're going to eat with Benjamin?' His voice went up a few octaves.

Elizabeth's eyes widened and she spun round, glass in hand. 'Is that a problem?'

'He's dirty and he smells,' Ivan stated.

Elizabeth's mouth dropped open; she didn't know how to reply to that.

'He probably eats with his hands. Like an animal,' Ivan continued, 'or a caveman, half man half animal. He probably hunts for—'

'Stop it, Ivan,' Elizabeth started laughing.

He stopped.

'What's really wrong?' She raised an eyebrow at him and sipped her wine.

He stopped spinning on his chair and stared at her. She stared back. She saw him swallow, his Adam's apple moving down his throat. His childishness disappeared and he appeared to her as a man, big, strong, with such a presence. Her heart beat quickened. His eyes didn't move from her face and she couldn't look away, couldn't move.

'Nothing's *wrong*.'

'Ivan, if you've got anything to say to me, you should say it,' Elizabeth said firmly. 'We're big boys and girls now.' The corner of her lips twitched at that.

'Elizabeth, would you come out with me on Saturday?'

'Ivan, it would be rude of me to cancel the appointment at such short notice – can't we go out another night?'

'No,' he said firmly, stepping off the stool. 'It has to be July the twenty-ninth. You'll see why.'

'I can't—'

'You can,' he interrupted her firmly. He took her by her elbows. 'You can do whatever you want. Meet me at Cobh Cúin at 10 p.m. on Saturday.'

'Cobh Cúin? And why so late?'

'You'll see why,' he repeated, tipped his cap and disappeared as quickly as he had arrived.

Before I left the house I called in to Luke in the playroom.

'Hey there, stranger,' I said, collapsing on the beanbag.

'Hi, Ivan,' Luke said, watching TV.

'Have you missed me?'

'Nope,' Luke smiled.

'Wanna know where I've been?'

'Smooching with my aunt.' Luke closed his eyes and did fake kisses in the air before collapsing into hysterical laughter.

My mouth dropped open. 'Hey! What makes you say that?'

'You *love* her,' Luke laughed, and continued watching cartoons.

I thought about that for a while. 'Are you still my friend?'

'Yep,' Luke replied, 'but Sam is my *best* friend.'

I pretended to be shot in the heart.

Luke looked away from the television to face me with hopeful big blue eyes. 'Is my aunt your best friend now?'

I thought about that carefully. 'Do you want her to be?'

Luke nodded emphatically.

'Why?'

'She's much better fun, she doesn't give out to me as much and she lets me colour in the white room.'

'Jinny Joe day was fun, wasn't it?'

Luke nodded again. 'I've never seen her laugh so much.'

'Does she give you big hugs and play lots of games with you?'

Luke looked at me as if that was a ridiculous idea and I sighed, worried about the small part of me that felt relieved.

'Ivan?'

'Yes, Luke.'

'Remember you told me that you can't stay around all the time, that you have to go to help other friends and so I shouldn't feel sad.'

'Yes.' I swallowed hard. I dreaded that day.

'What will happen to you and Aunt Elizabeth when that happens?'

And then I worried about the part in the centre of my chest that pained when I thought about that.

I stepped into Opal's office, hands in my pockets and wearing my new red T-shirt and a new pair of black jeans. Red felt good on me today. I was angry. I didn't like the tone in Opal's voice when she called me.

'Ivan,' she said, putting down her feather pen and looking up at me. Gone was her beaming smile that once used to greet me. She looked tired, bags hung under her eyes and her dreadlocks were down around her face and not in one of her usual styles.

'Opal,' I imitated her tone, throwing one leg over the other as I sat before her.

'What are the things you teach your students about becoming a part of your new friend's life?'

'Assist don't hinder, support don't oppose, help and listen don't—'

'You can stop right there.' She raised her voice and cut in on my bored tones. 'Assist and don't hinder, Ivan.' She allowed those words to hang in the air. 'You made her cancel a dinner reservation with Benjamin West. She could have made a friend, Ivan.' She stared at me, her black eyes like coal. Any more anger and they would have gone on fire.

'Can I remind you that the last time Elizabeth Egan made any reservations with anyone for non-business purposes was five years ago. *Five* years ago, Ivan,' she stressed. 'Can you tell me why you undid all that?'

'Because he's dirty and he smells,' I laughed.

'Because he's dirty and he smells,' she repeated, making me feel stupid. 'Then let her figure that out for herself. Don't overstep your mark, Ivan.' With that she looked back down at her work and continued writing, the feather blowing as she scribbled furiously.

'What's going on, Opal?' I asked her. 'Tell me what's really going on.'

She looked up, anger and sadness in her eyes. 'We are incredibly busy, Ivan, and we need you to work as quickly as you can and move on instead of hanging around and undoing the good work you've already done. That's what's going on.'

Stunned by her chastising I silently left her office. I didn't believe her for one minute but whatever was happening in her life was her own business. She'd change her mind about Elizabeth cancelling her dinner with Benjamin as soon as she saw what I had planned for the twenty-ninth.

'Oh, and, Ivan,' Opal called out.

I stopped at her doorway and turned. She was still looking down and writing as she spoke. 'I'll need you to come in here next Monday to take over for a while.'

'Why?' I asked with disbelief.

'I'm not going to be here for a few days. I need you to cover for me.'

That had never happened before. 'But I'm still in the middle of a job.'

'Good to hear you're still calling it that,' she snapped. Then she sighed, put down her feathered pen and looked up. She looked as if she was going to cry. 'I'm sure Saturday will be such a success you won't need to be there next week, Ivan.'

Her voice was so soft and genuine that I forgot that I was angry at her and realised for the first time that if it was any other situation, she would be right.

Chapter 29

Ivan placed the finishing touches to the dinner table, snipped a stem of fuchsia that was growing wild and placed it in the small vase in the centre. He lit a candle and watched as the flame darted in the breeze, like a dog running around the garden yet chained to his kennel. Cobh Cúin was silent, just as the name, which literally meant silent cave, suggested, christened hundreds of years ago by the locals and untouched since then. The only sound was the water gently lapping, swishing back and forth, and tickling the sand. Ivan closed his eyes and swayed to the music. A small fishing boat tied to the pier bobbed up and down on the sea, occasionally bumping the side of the pier and adding a soft drumbeat.

The sky was blue and beginning to darken with a few stray wisps of teenage clouds lagging behind the older clouds of hours ago. The stars twinkled brightly and Ivan winked back at them; they too knew what was coming. Ivan had asked the head chef at the work canteen to help him out tonight. He was the same chef responsible for catering the tea parties in the back gardens of best friends but this time he went all out. He had created the most luscious spread Ivan could have imagined. For starter was foie gras and toast cut into neat little squares, followed by wild Irish salmon and asparagus cooked in garlic, followed by a white chocolate mousse with dribbles of raspberry sauce for dessert. The aromas were being lifted by the warm gulf wind and being carried past his nose, tickling his taste buds.

He played around with the cutlery nervously, fixing all that didn't need to be fixed, tightened his new blue silk tie, loosened it again, opened the button of his navy-blue suit jacket and decided to close it again. He had been so busy all day arranging the setup that he had barely taken time to think about the feelings that were stirring inside him. Glancing at his watch and at the darkening sky, he hoped Elizabeth would come.

Elizabeth drove down the narrow winding road slowly, barely able to see past the end of her nose in the thick blackness of the country-side. Wild flowers and hedge growth reached out to brush the sides of her car as she passed. Her full headlights startled moths, mosquitoes and bats as she drove in the direction of the sea. Suddenly the inky veil lifted as she reached a clearing and the whole world was spread out before her.

Ahead were thousands of miles of ebony sea glistening under the moonlight. Inside the small cove was a tiny fishing boat tied up beside the steps, the sand was a velvety brown, the edges being licked and teased by the approaching tide. But it wasn't the sea that took her breath away; it was the sight of Ivan standing in the sand, dressed in a smart new suit, beside a small beautifully set table for two, a candle flickering in the centre, casting shadows across his smiling face.

The sight was enough to bring a tear from a stone. It was an image her mother had stamped in her mind, an image she had whispered excitedly into her ear about moonlit dinners on the beach, so much so that her mother's dreams had become her own. And there Ivan was, standing in the picture Elizabeth and her mother had painted so vividly and that had remained etched in Elizabeth's mind. She understood the phrase of not knowing whether to laugh or cry and so she unashamedly did both.

Ivan stood proudly, blue eyes glistening in the moonlight. He ignored her tears, or rather, accepted them.

'My dear,' he bowed theatrically, 'your moonlit dinner awaits you.'

Wiping her eyes and smiling a smile so big Elizabeth felt she could light the entire world, she took his extended hand and stepped out of the car.

Ivan took a sharp intake of breath. 'Wow, Elizabeth, you look stunning.'

'Wearing red is my favourite thing to do now,' she imitated him, taking his arm and allowing him to lead her to the dinner table.

After much humming and hawing Elizabeth had purchased a red dress that accentuated her slender figure, giving her curves she never even knew she had. She had taken it on and off at least five times before she left the house, feeling too exposed in such a bright colour. To prevent herself from feeling like a traffic light she had brought a black pashmina to drape over her shoulders.

The white Irish table linen flapped in the light warm breeze and Elizabeth's hair tickled her cheek. The sand was cool and soft beneath her feet, like fluffy carpet, and was protected in the cove from the sharp wind. Ivan pulled out her chair for her and she sat. Then he reached for her serviette, which had been wrapped in a stem of fuchsia, and he laid it on her lap.

'Ivan, this is beautiful, thank you,' she whispered, not feeling able to lift her voice over the peaceful lapping water.

'Thank you for coming,' he smiled, pouring her a glass of red wine. 'Now for starters we have foie gras.' He reached under the table and retrieved two plates covered in silverware. 'I hope you like foie gras,' he said, frown lines appearing on his forehead.

'I love it,' Elizabeth smiled.

'Phew.' The muscles in his face relaxed. 'It doesn't really look like grass,' he said, examining his plate closely.

'It's goose liver, Ivan,' Elizabeth laughed, spreading some on her toast. 'What made you choose this cove?' she asked, wrapping the shawl tighter around her shoulders as the breeze began to chill.

'Because it's quiet and because it's a perfect location away from street-lights,' he explained, munching on his food.

Elizabeth thought it better not to ask any questions, knowing Ivan had his own peculiar way.

After dinner Ivan turned to look at Elizabeth, who had her hands wrapped around her wine glass and was staring wistfully out to the sea. 'Elizabeth,' his voice was soft, 'will you lie with me on the sand?'

Elizabeth's heartbeat quickened. 'Yes.' Her voice was husky. She couldn't think of a better way to end the evening with him. She was longing to touch him, for him to hold her. Elizabeth made her way to the water's edge and sat down on the cool sand. She felt Ivan padding behind her.

'You're going to have to lie on your back for this to work,' he said loudly, looking down at her.

Elizabeth's mouth dropped open. 'Excuse me?' She wrapped the shawl protectively around her shoulders.

'If you don't lie back, this just won't work,' he repeated, putting his hands on his hips. 'Look, like this.' He sat down beside her and lay back on the sand. 'You have to be flat on your back, Elizabeth. It's best this way.'

'Is it now?' Elizabeth stiffened and clambered to get to her feet. 'Was all this,' she gestured around the cove, 'just to get me flat on my back, as you so beautifully phrased it?' she asked, hurt.

Ivan stared up at her from the sand, eyes wide with a flabbergasted look on his face. 'Well . . .' he stalled, trying to think of an answer, 'actually, yes,' he squeaked. 'It's just that, it's better when it peaks, for you to be flat on your back,' he stuttered.

'Ha!' Elizabeth spat and, putting her shoes back on, she struggled through the sand to get back to her car.

'Elizabeth, look!' Ivan shouted with excitement. 'It's peaked! Look!'

'Uugh,' Elizabeth grunted, climbing the small sand dune to her car. 'You really are disgusting!'

'It's not disgusting!' Ivan said, panic in his voice.

'That's what they all say,' Elizabeth grumbled, fumbling in her bag for her car keys. Unable to see into her bag in the dark, she leaned it towards the moonlight and as she glanced up, her mouth dropped open. Above her, in the black cloudless sky, was a hive of activity. Stars glowed brighter than she had ever seen before, some darting across the sky.

Ivan lay on his back, staring up to the night sky.

'Oh,' Elizabeth said quietly, feeling foolish, glad that the darkness was hiding her skin absorbing the colour of her dress. She stumbled back down the sand dune, removed her shoes, allowed her feet to curl into the sand and took a few steps closer to Ivan. 'It's beautiful,' she whispered.

'Well, it would be a lot more beautiful if you lay flat on your back like I told you to,' Ivan huffed, crossing his arms across his chest and staring up to the sky.

Elizabeth covered her mouth with her hand and tried not to laugh out loud.

'I don't know what you're laughing at. No one accused you of being disgusting,' he said smartly.

'I thought you were talking about something else,' Elizabeth giggled, sitting down on the sand beside him.

'Why else would I be asking you to lie flat on your back?' Ivan asked in a dull tone and then he turned to her, his voice rising a few octaves, his eyes mocking. 'Oh,' he sang.

'Shut up,' Elizabeth said harshly, throwing her purse at him but letting her smile show. 'Oh, look,' she was distracted by a shooting star, 'what's going on up there tonight, I wonder.'

'It's the Delta Aquarids,' Ivan said as though that explained everything. Elizabeth's silence made him continue. 'They're meteors that come from the constellation Aquarius. The normal dates are the fifteenth of July to the twentieth of August but they peak on the twenty-ninth of July. That's why I had to take you out tonight, away from streetlights.' He turned to look at her. 'So yes, all of this was just to get you on your back.'

They studied each other's faces in comfortable silence until more action above diverted their attention.

'Why don't you make a wish?' Ivan asked her.

'No,' Elizabeth said softly, 'I'm still waiting for my Jinny Joes wish to come true.'

'Oh, I wouldn't worry about that,' Ivan said seriously. 'They just take a while to process. You won't be waiting long.'

Elizabeth laughed and stared hopefully up into the sky.

A few minutes later, sensing her sister would be on her mind, Ivan asked, 'Any word from Saoirse?'

Elizabeth gave a single shake of her head.

'She'll be home,' Ivan said positively.

'Yes, but in what condition?' Elizabeth said uncertainly. 'How is it other families manage to hold it together? And even when they've problems, how do they manage to keep it from the rest of the people in their neighbourhoods?' she asked in confusion, thinking about all the whispers she had been hearing over the past few days about her father's behaviour and her sister's disappearance. 'What's their secret?'

'See that cluster of stars right there?' Ivan asked, pointing upwards.

Elizabeth followed his hand, embarrassed to have bored him with talk of her family so much that he'd changed the subject. She nodded.

'Most meteors from a common meteor shower are parallel to one another. They appear to emerge from the same point in the sky called "the radiant" and they travel in all directions from this point.'

'Oh, I see,' Elizabeth said.

'No, you don't see.' Ivan turned on his side to face her. 'Stars are like people, Elizabeth. Just because they *appear* to emerge from the same point doesn't mean that they do. This is an illusion of perspective created by distance.' And as if Elizabeth hadn't quite understood the meaning he added, 'Not all families manage to hold it together, Elizabeth. Everyone moves in different directions. That we all emerge from the same point is a misconception; to travel in different directions is the very nature of every being and every existing thing.'

Elizabeth turned her head and faced the sky again, trying to see if what he said was true. 'Well, they could have fooled me,' she said quietly, watching more appear from the blackness every second.

She shivered and wrapped her shawl around her tighter; the sand was getting cooler with each passing hour.

'Are you cold?' Ivan asked with concern.

'A little,' she admitted.

'Right, well, the night isn't over yet,' he said, jumping to his feet. 'Time to warm up. Mind if I borrow the keys to your car?'

'Not unless you intend driving away,' she joked, handing them over.

He retrieved something from under the table once again and brought it to the car. Moments later music was softly drifting through its open door.

Ivan began to dance.

Elizabeth giggled nervously. 'Ivan, what are you doing?'

'Dancing!' he said, offended.

'What kind of dancing?' She took his extended hand and allowed herself to be pulled to her feet.

'It's the soft-shoe shuffle,' Ivan announced, dancing expertly in circles around her on the sand. 'Also called the sand dance, you'll be interested to know, which means that your mother wasn't so mad wanting to do the shuffle in the sand after all!'

Elizabeth's hands flew to her mouth, tears filled her eyes with happiness as she realised he was fulfilling yet another of her and her mother's intended activities.

'Why are you fulfilling all of my mother's dreams?' she asked, studying his face and searching for answers.

'So you don't run away like she did in search of them,' he replied, taking her hand. 'Come on, join in!'

'I don't know how!'

'Just copy me.' He turned his back and danced away from her, swinging his hips exaggeratedly.

Lifting her dress to above her knees, Elizabeth threw caution to the wind and joined in dancing the soft-shoe shuffle on the sand in the moonlight, laughing until her stomach was sore and she was out of breath.

'Oh, you make me smile so much, Ivan,' she gasped, collapsing on the sand later that evening.

'Just doin' my job,' he grinned back. As soon as the words had left his mouth his smile faded and Elizabeth detected a hint of sadness in those blue eyes.

Chapter 30

Elizabeth allowed her red dress to slide down her legs, gather at her ankles and then stepped out of it. She wrapped a warm bathrobe around her body, pinned her hair up and climbed onto her bed with a cup of coffee she had brought upstairs. She had wanted Ivan to come to bed with her tonight; despite her earlier protests she had wanted him to take her in his arms on the sand in the cove right there, but it seemed the more she felt drawn to him, the further he pulled himself away.

After they had watched the stars dancing in the sky, and then they had danced on the sand, Ivan had withdrawn into himself in the car on the journey home. He had asked her to let him out in the small town, from where he would make his own way home, wherever home was. He had yet to bring her there or introduce her to his friends and family. Elizabeth had never before been interested in meeting the others in her partners' lives. She felt as long as she enjoyed their company, whether or not she liked the company of those who surrounded him was irrelevant. But with Ivan she felt she needed to see another side to him. She needed to witness his relationships with other people so he could become a three-dimensional character to her. That was always the argument old partners had with Elizabeth and now she finally understood what it was they were searching for.

Elizabeth had watched Ivan in her mirror as she drove away; intrigued to know what direction he would walk in. He had looked left and right down the deserted streets that were empty at the late night hour, began to walk left in the direction of the mountains and the hotel. After a few steps he stopped, turned round and walked in the other direction. He crossed the road and strode confidently toward Killarney but halted suddenly, eventually folded his arms across his chest and sat down on the stone windowsill of the butcher's.

She didn't think he knew where home was, or if he did, he didn't know his way there. She knew how he felt.

On Monday afternoon Ivan stood at the doorway to Opal's office and chuckled as he listened to Oscar ranting to Opal for a steady ten minutes. As amusing as he was to listen to, they'd have to hurry their meeting along because Ivan was due to meet Elizabeth at 6 p.m. He had twenty minutes. He hadn't seen her since the Delta Aquarids viewing on Saturday night, the greatest night of his long, long life. He had tried to walk away from her after that. He had tried to leave Baile na gCroíthe, tried to move on to someone else who needed his help, but he couldn't. He didn't feel drawn to any other direction other than Elizabeth and it was stronger than any other pull he had experienced before. This time it wasn't just his mind that was pulling him, it was his heart too.

'Opal,' Oscar's serious tones floated out to the hallway, 'I desperately need more staff for next week.'

'Yes, I understand, Oscar, and we've already arranged for Suki to help you in the lab,' Opal explained gently yet firmly. 'There's nothing more we can do for now.'

'That's simply not good enough,' he fumed. 'On Saturday night millions of people viewed the Delta Aquarids, do you know how many wishes will come shooting in here over the next few weeks?' He didn't wait for an answer and Opal didn't offer one. 'It's a dangerous procedure, Opal, and I need more hands. While Suki is extremely efficient in the administration area, she is not qualified in wish analysis. Either I'm helped out by more staff or you'll have to find a new wish analyst,' he puffed. With that he stormed out of the office, past Ivan and down the hallway mumbling, 'After years of studying to be a meteorologist I get stuck doing *this*!'

'Ivan,' Opal called.

'How do you do that?' Ivan asked, entering the office. He was beginning to think she could see through walls.

She glanced up from the desk, smiled weakly, and Ivan took a quick intake of breath. She looked very tired, with dark circles under her bloodshot eyes. She looked as if she hadn't slept for weeks.

'You're late,' she said gently. 'You were supposed to be here at 9 a.m.'

'I was?' Ivan asked, confused. 'I only called in to ask you a quick question. I have to rush off in a minute,' he added quickly. *Elizabeth, Elizabeth, Elizabeth*, he sang in his head.

'We agreed you would cover for me today, remember?' Opal said firmly, standing up from her desk and walking round to the other side.

'Oh, no, no, no,' Ivan said quickly, backing towards the door. 'I'd love to help you, Opal, really I would. Helping is one of my favourite things to do but I can't now. I've made plans to meet my client. I can't miss it, you know how it is.'

Opal leaned against the desk, folded her arms and cocked her head to one side. She blinked and her eyes closed slowly and tiredly, taking an age to open again. 'So she's your *client* now, is she?' she said wearily. Dark colours surrounded her today. Ivan could see them spreading out from all around her body.

'Yes, she's my client,' he replied less confidently. 'And I really can't miss her this evening.'

'Sooner or later you're going to have to say goodbye to her, Ivan.'

She said it so coldly, without padding or frills, that it chilled him. He gulped and shifted his weight to his other foot.

'How do you feel about that?' she asked, when he didn't answer.

Ivan thought about it. His heart thudded in his chest and he felt as if it was going to move up through his throat and out of his mouth. His eyes filled. 'I don't want to,' he said quietly.

Opal's arms lowered slowly to her sides. 'Pardon?' she asked, a little gentler.

Ivan thought about his life without Elizabeth and he raised his voice more confidently. 'I don't want to say goodbye to her. I want to stay with her for ever, Opal. She makes me feel happier than I've ever felt before in my life and she tells me that I do the same for her. Surely it would be wrong to walk away from that?' He smiled widely, recalling the feeling of being with her.

Opal's hardened face softened. 'Oh, Ivan, I knew this would happen.' There was pity in her voice and he didn't like it. He would have preferred anger. 'But I thought you of all people would have made the right decision a long time ago.'

'What decision?' Ivan's face crumpled at the thought of his having made the wrong one. 'I asked you what I should do and you wouldn't tell me.' He began to panic.

'You should have left her a long time ago, Ivan,' she said sadly, 'but I couldn't tell you to do that. You had to realise it for yourself.'

'But I couldn't leave her.' Ivan sat down on the chair before her desk slowly as the sadness and shock crept through his body. 'She kept seeing me.' His voice was almost a whisper. 'I couldn't leave until she stopped seeing me.'

'You made her keep seeing you, Ivan,' Opal explained.

'No, I didn't.' He stood up and walked away from the desk, angry at the suggestion that anything about their relationship had been forced.

'You followed her, you watched her for days, you allowed the small connection you both had to blossom. You tapped into something extraordinary and made her realise it too.'

'You don't know what you're talking about,' he spat, pacing the room. 'You have no idea how either of us is feeling.' He stopped pacing, marched up to her and looked her directly in the eye, his chin lifted, his head steady. 'Today,' he spoke with perfect clarity, 'I am going to tell Elizabeth Egan that I love her and that I want to spend my days with her. I can still help people while I'm with her.'

Opal's hands went to her face. 'Oh, Ivan, you can't!'

'You taught me that there was nothing that I couldn't do,' he snarled between gritted teeth.

'No one else will see you but her!' Opal exclaimed. 'Elizabeth won't understand. It just won't work.' She was clearly distraught by this revelation.

'If what you said is true and I made Elizabeth see me, then I can make everyone else see me too. Elizabeth will understand. She understands me like nobody else has ever done. Do you have any idea what that feels like?' He was excited now by the prospect. Before it had only been a thought, but now, now it was a possibility. He could make it happen. He looked at his watch: 6.50 p.m. He had ten minutes. 'I have to go,' he said urgently. 'I have to tell her I love her.' He strode towards the doorway with confidence and determination.

Suddenly Opal's voice broke the silence. 'I do know how you feel, Ivan.'

He stopped in his tracks, turned and shook his head. 'You can't know how this feels, Opal, not unless you've lived through this. You can't even begin to imagine.'

'I have,' she said quietly and uncertainly.

'What?' He viewed her warily with narrowed eyes.

'I have,' she said with strength in her voice this time, and crossed her hands across her stomach, clasping her fingers together. 'I fell in love with a man who saw me more than I had ever been seen in my whole entire life.'

There was a silence in the room while Ivan tried to come to terms with this. 'So that should mean that you understand me all the more.' He stepped towards her, clearly thrilled by the revelation. 'Maybe it didn't end well for you, Opal, but for me,' he smiled widely, 'who knows?' He threw his hands up and shrugged. 'This could be it!'

Opal's tired eyes stared back at him sadly. 'No.' She shook her head and his smiled faded. 'Let me show you something, Ivan. Come with me this evening. Forget the office,' she waved her hand around the room dismissively. 'Come with me and let me give you your final lesson.' She tapped his chin fondly.

Ivan looked at his watch, 'But Eliz—'

'Forget Elizabeth for now,' she said softly. 'If you choose not to take my advice you'll have Elizabeth tomorrow, the next day and everyday for the rest of her life. Nothing ventured, nothing gained.' She held out her hand to him.

Reluctantly Ivan reached out to take it. Her skin was cold.

Chapter 31

Elizabeth sat on the end of the staircase and looked out the window to the front garden. The clock on the wall said 6.50 p.m. Ivan had never been late before and she hoped he was OK. However, her sense of anger was rather more active at that moment than her worry for him. His behaviour on Saturday night gave her reason to think that his absence was due more to cold feet rather than foul play. She had thought about Ivan all day yesterday, about not meeting his friends, his family or his work colleagues, the lack of sexual contact and, in the dead of the night, as she battled to find sleep, she had realised what it was that she had being trying to hide from herself. She felt she knew what the problem was: Ivan was either in a relationship already or unwilling to enter into one.

Any niggling feeling she had along the way she had ignored. It was unusual for Elizabeth not to plan, not to know exactly where a relationship was going. She wasn't comfortable with this big change. She liked stability and routine, everything Ivan lacked. Well, she was sure that now it could never work, as she sat on the stair waiting for a free spirit, just as her father was. And she never discussed her fears with Ivan – why? Because when she was with him, every little fear dissipated. He would just show up, take her by the hand and lead her into another exciting chapter in her life, and while she was reluctant to go with him at times, often apprehensive, *with* him she was never nervous. It was when she was without him, moments like now, that she questioned everything.

She decided immediately that she was going to distance herself from him. Tonight would be the night she would discuss it with him once and for all. They were like chalk and cheese; her life was full of conflict and, as far as she could see, Ivan ran so far so fast just to avoid it. As the seconds ticked on and it moved into his fifty-first minute of being late it looked as if she didn't need to have the conversation with him after all. She sat on the stair in her new cream casual trousers and shirt, colours she would never had worn before, and she felt foolish. Foolish for listening to him, believing him, for not reading the signs properly and, even worse, for falling for him.

Her anger was hiding her pain but the last thing she wanted to do was to stay home alone and allow it to surface. She was good at doing that.

She picked up the phone and dialled.

'Benjamin, it's Elizabeth,' she said rather quickly, speaking before she had a chance to backtrack. 'How would you like to get that sushi tonight?'

'Where are we?' Ivan asked, strolling down a darkly lit cobbled street in inner city Dublin. Puddles gathered in the uneven surfaces of an area that consisted mainly of warehouses and industrial estates. One red-brick house stood alone between them all.

'That house looks funny there, sitting all on its own,' Ivan remarked. 'A bit lonely and out of place,' he decided.

'That's where we're going,' Opal said. 'The owner of this house refused to sell his property to the surrounding businesses. He stayed here while they sprung up around him.'

Ivan eyed the small house. 'I bet they offered him a fair bit. He could probably have bought a mansion in the Hollywood Hills with what they would have paid him.' He looked down at the ground as his red Converse runner splashed into a puddle, 'I've decided cobblestones are my favourite.'

Opal smiled and laughed lightly. 'Oh, Ivan, you are so easy to love, you know that?' She walked on, not expecting an answer. Just as well, because Ivan wasn't sure.

'What are we doing?' he asked for the tenth time since they had left the office. They stood directly across the road from the house and Ivan watched Opal viewing it.

'Waiting,' Opal replied calmly. 'What time is it?'

Ivan checked his watch. 'Elizabeth will be so mad at me,' he sighed. 'It's just gone seven.'

Right on cue, the front door to the red-brick house opened. An old man leaned against the doorway, which appeared to act as a crutch. He stared outside and looked so far into the distance he appeared to be seeing the past.

'Come with me,' Opal said to Ivan, and she crossed the road and entered the house.

'Opal,' Ivan hissed, 'I can't just enter a stranger's house.' But Opal had already disappeared inside.

Ivan quickly skipped across the road and paused at the doorway, 'Em, hello, I'm Ivan.' He held out his hand.

The old man's hands remained clinging to the doorway; his watery eyes stared straight ahead.

'Right,' Ivan said awkwardly, moving his hand away. 'I'll just slide past you so, to Opal.' The man didn't blink and Ivan stepped inside. The house smelled old. It smelled as if an old person lived there with old furniture, a wireless and a grandfather clock. The clock's ticking was the loudest thing in the silent building. Time sounded and smelled to be the essence of the house, a long life lived listening to those ticks.

Ivan found Opal in the living room, looking around at all the framed photographs cluttering every surface of the room.

'This is almost as bad as your office,' he teased. 'Come on then, tell me what's going on.'

Opal turned to him and she smiled sadly. 'I told you earlier that I understand how you feel.'

'Yes.'

'I told you I knew how it felt to fall in love.'

Ivan nodded.

Opal sighed and clasped her hands together once again, almost like she was bracing herself for the news. 'Well, this is the home of the man I fell in love with.'

'Oh,' Ivan said softly.

'I still come here every day,' she explained, looking around the room. 'The old man doesn't mind us just barging in like this?'

Opal gave a small smile. 'He is the man I fell in love with, Ivan.'

Ivan's mouth dropped open. The front door closed. Footsteps slowly made their way towards them over creaking floorboards. 'No way!' Ivan hissed. 'The old man? But he's ancient – he must be at least eighty!' he whispered in shock.

The old man wandered into the room. A hacking cough stopped him in his tracks and his small frame shuddered. He winced from the pain and slowly, leaning his hands on the arms of the chair, he lowered himself into the seat.

Ivan looked from the old man to Opal and back, with a disgusted look that he tried unsuccessfully to hide from his face.

'He can't hear you or see you. We are invisible to him,' Opal said loudly. Her next sentence changed Ivan's life for good. Nineteen simple words he heard her say everyday but never in that order. She cleared her throat and there was a slight tremor in her voice as she said against the ticking of the clock, 'Remember, Ivan, forty years ago when he and I met, he wasn't ancient. He was as I am now.'

Opal watched as Ivan's face displayed many different emotions in a matter of seconds. He went from confusion, to shock, to disbelief, to pity, and then as soon as he had applied Opal's words to his own situation, to despair. His face crumpled, he paled and Opal rushed towards him to steady his swaying body. He held on to her tightly.

'That's what I was trying to tell you, Ivan,' she whispered. 'You and Elizabeth can live together perfectly happy in your own cocoon without anyone knowing but what you forget is that she will have a birthday every year and you won't.'

Ivan's body began to shake and Opal held on to him tighter. 'Oh, Ivan, I'm sorry,' she said, 'I'm so, so sorry.'

She rocked him as he cried. And cried.

'I met him in very similar circumstances to how you met Elizabeth,' Opal explained later that evening after his tears had subsided.

They both sat in armchairs in the living room of Opal's love, Geoffrey. He continued to sit in his chair by the window in silence, looking around the room and occasionally breaking into horrendous coughs that made Opal rush to his side protectively.

She twisted a tissue around in her hands, her eyes and cheeks were wet as she told her story and her dreadlocks fell around her face.

'I made every single mistake that you made,' she sniffed, and forced herself to smile, 'and I even made the one you were about to make tonight.'

Ivan swallowed hard.

'He was forty when I met him, Ivan, and we stayed together for twenty years until it became too difficult.'

Ivan's eyes widened and hope returned to his heart.

'No, Ivan,' Opal shook her head sadly and it was the weakness in her voice that convinced him. Had she spoken firmly he would have retaliated in the same manner but her voice displayed her pain. 'It couldn't work for you.' She didn't need to say any more.

'He seems to have travelled a lot,' Ivan remarked, looking around at the photos. Geoffrey in front of the Eiffel Tower, Geoffrey in front of the Leaning Tower of Pisa, Geoffrey lying on the golden sand on the shores of a faraway country, smiling and looking the picture of health, happiness at varying ages in every photo. 'At least he could move on in some way and manage to do those things alone,' he smiled encouragingly.

Opal looked at him in confusion. 'But I was there with him, Ivan.' Her forehead wrinkled.

'Oh, that's nice.' He was surprised. 'Did you take the photos?'

'No.' Her face fell. 'I'm in the photographs too, can't you see me?'

Ivan shook his head slowly.

'Oh . . .' She said studying them and seeing a different picture from Ivan.

'Why can't he see you any more?' Ivan asked, watching Geoffrey take a handful of prescribed pills and wash them down with water.

'Because I'm not who I once was, which is probably why you can't see me in the photographs. He's looking out for a different person; the connection we once had is gone,' she replied.

Geoffrey stood up from his chair, this time grabbing his cane, and made his way to the front door. He opened it and stood at the doorway.

'Come on, time to go,' Opal said, standing up from her chair and moving out to the hallway.

Ivan looked at her quizzically

'When we first started seeing each other I visited him from seven to nine every evening,' she explained, 'and seeing as I can't open doors, he used to be there waiting for me. He's been doing this every evening since we met. That's why he wouldn't sell the house. He thinks it's the only way I'll find him.'

Ivan watched his old frame wobbling on his feet as he stared out once again into the distance, perhaps thinking of that day when they had frolicked on the beach or the visit to the Eiffel Tower. Ivan didn't want that to be Elizabeth.

'Goodbye, my Opal,' his gravelly voice spoke quietly.

'Good night, my love.' Opal kissed him on the cheek and he closed his eyes softly. 'I'll see you tomorrow.'

Chapter 32

So it was clear in my mind. I knew what I had to do next. I needed to do what I was sent here to do – make Elizabeth's life as comfortable for her as possible. But now I had got so involved with her I would have to help heal old wounds *and* the new wounds that I'd foolishly caused. I was angry at myself for making a mess of everything, for getting caught up and taking my eye off the ball. My anger was overpowering the pain I felt and I was glad because, in order for me to help Elizabeth, I needed to ignore my own feelings and do what was best for her. Which was what I should have done from the start. But that's the thing about lessons: you always learn them when you don't expect them or want them. I'd have plenty of time in my life to deal with the pain of losing her.

I'd walked all night, thinking about the past few weeks and about my life. I'd never done that before – thought about *my* life. It never seemed relevant to my aim but it should always have been. I found myself back at Fuchsia Lane the next morning, sitting on the garden wall where I had first met Luke over a month ago. The fuchsia door still smiled at me and I waved back. At least that wasn't angry at me; I knew Elizabeth sure would be. She doesn't like people being late for business meetings, never mind dinner dates. I'd stood her up. Not intentionally. Not out of any malice but out of love. Imagine not meeting someone because you loved them so much. Imagine hurting someone, making them feel lonely, angry and unloved because you think it's the *best* for them. All these new rules – they were making me doubt my abilities as a best friend. They were beyond me, laws that I wasn't comfortable with at all. How could I teach Elizabeth about hope, happiness, laughter and love when I didn't know if I believed in any of those things any more? Oh, I knew they were possible, alright, but with possibility comes impossibility. A new word in my vocabulary.

At 6.00 a.m., the fuchsia door opened and I stood to attention as though a teacher had entered the classroom. Elizabeth stepped out, closed the door behind her, locked it and walked down the cobble-stoned drive. She was wearing her chocolate-brown tracksuit again, her only informal outfit in her wardrobe. Her hair was tied back messily, she had no make-up on and I don't think I'd ever seen her look so beautiful in my life. A hand reached into my heart and twisted it momentarily. It hurt.

She looked up and saw me and stalled. Her face didn't break into a smile like it usually did. The hand around my heart squeezed tighter. But at least she saw me and that was the main thing. Don't ever take for granted when people look in your eyes – you've no idea how lucky you are. Actually, forget about luck, you've no idea how *important* it is to be acknowledged, even if it is with an angry glare. It's when they ignore you, when they look right through you, that you should start worrying. Elizabeth usually ignores her problems; she usually looks right past them and never in the eye. But I was obviously a problem worth solving.

She walked towards me with her arms folded across her chest, her head held high, her eyes tired but determined.

'Are you alright, Ivan?'

Her question threw me. I expected her to be angry, to shout at me and not listen or believe my side of the story, like they do in the movies, but she didn't. She was calm, but with a temper bubbling beneath the surface, ready to erupt depending on my answer. She studied my face, searching for answers she would never believe.

I don't think I've ever been asked that question before. I was thinking about that as she was studying my face. No, it was as clear as day to me that I did not feel alright. I felt brittle, tired, angry, hungry, and there was a pain – not a hunger pain, but an ache that started in my chest and worked its way through my body and head. I felt that my views and philosophies had been changed overnight. The philosophies that I had gladly carved in stone, recited and danced upon. I felt as though the magician of life had cruelly revealed his hidden cards and it wasn't magic at all, just a mere trick of the mind. Or a lie.

'Ivan?' She looked concerned. Her face softened, her arms dropped from their folded position and she stepped forward and reached out to touch me.

I couldn't answer.

'Come on, walk with me.' She linked arms with me and we walked out of Fuchsia Lane.

They walked in silence deep into the heart of the countryside. The birds sang loudly in the early morning, the crisp air filled their lungs, rabbits bounded daringly across their path and butterflies danced through the air, waving through them as they strode along the woodlands. The sun shone down through the leaves of the dominant oaks, sprinkling light on their faces like gold dust. The sound of water trickled alongside them while the scent of eucalyptus refreshed the air. Eventually they reached an opening, where the trees held their branches out, making a grand and proud presentation of the lake. They crossed a wooden bridge, sat on a hard, carved bench and sat in silence, watching as the salmon jumped to the surface of the water to catch the flies in the warming sun.

Elizabeth was the first to speak. 'Ivan, in a complicated life, I try my best to make things as simple as possible. I know what to expect, I know what I'm going to do, where I'm going, who I'm going to meet *every single day*. In a life that is surrounded by complicated, un-predictable people, I need *stability*.' She looked away from the lake and met Ivan's eyes for the first time since they'd sat down. 'You,' she took a breath, 'you take the simplicity out of my life. You shake things around and turn them upside down. And sometimes I like it, Ivan. You make me laugh, you make me dance around streets and beaches like a lunatic and make me feel like someone I'm not.' Her smile faded. 'But last night you made me feel like someone I don't want to be. I *need* things to be simple, Ivan,' she repeated.

There was a silence between them.

Eventually Ivan spoke. 'I'm very sorry about last night, Elizabeth. You know me: it wasn't done out of any malice.' He stopped to try and figure out if and how he should explain the events of last night. He decided against it for now. 'You know, the more you try to simplify things, Elizabeth, the more you complicate them. You create rules, build walls, push people away, lie to yourself, and ignore true feelings. That is not simplifying things.'

Elizabeth ran a hand through her hair. 'I have a sister who is missing, a six-year-old nephew to mother, whom I know nothing about, a father that has not moved away from a window for weeks because he is waiting for his wife, who disappeared over twenty years ago, to return. I realised last night that I was just like him as I sat on the stairs staring out the window, waiting for a man with no surname who tells me he's from a place called Ekam Eveileb, a place that has been Googled, and searched in the damn atlas at least once a day and that I now know doesn't exist.' She took a breath. 'I care for you, Ivan, I really do, but one minute you're kissing me and the next you're standing me up. I don't know what is going on with us. I have enough worries and I have enough pain as it is and I am not volunteering myself for any more.' She rubbed her eyes tiredly.

They both watched the activities in the lake as the leaping salmon brought ripples to the surface, making soothing splashing sounds in the water. Across the lake a heron moved silently and skilfully on his stilt-like legs along the water's edge. He was a fisherman at work, watching and waiting patiently for the right moment to break the glassy surface of the water with his beak.

Ivan couldn't help but see the similarities in both their jobs at that moment.

When you drop a glass or a plate to the ground it makes a loud crashing sound. When a window shatters, a table leg breaks, or when a picture falls off the wall it makes a noise. But as for your heart, when that breaks, it's completely silent. You would think as it's so important it would make the loudest noise in the whole world, or even have some sort of ceremonious sound like the gong of a cymbal or the ringing of a bell. But it's silent and you almost wish there was a noise to distract you from the pain.

If there is a noise, it's internal. It screams and no one can hear it but you. It screams so loud your ears ring and your head aches. It thrashes around in your chest like a great white shark caught in the sea; it roars like a mother bear whose cub has been taken. That's what it looks like and that's what it sounds like, a thrashing, panicking, trapped great big beast, roaring like a prisoner to its own emotions. But that's the thing about love – no one is untouchable. It's as wild as that, as raw as an open flesh wound exposed to salty sea water, but when it actually breaks, it's silent. You're just screaming on the inside and no one can hear it.

But Elizabeth, she saw the heartbreak in me and I saw it in her, and without having to talk about it we both knew. It was time to stop walking with our heads in the clouds, and instead, keep our feet on the harder soil of ground level we should always have been rooted to.

Chapter 33

'We should get back to the house now,' Elizabeth said, jumping up from the bench.

'Why?'

'Because it's starting to rain.' She looked at him as though he had ten heads, and flinched as another droplet of rain landed on her face.

'What is it with you?' Ivan laughed, settling down into the bench as a sign he wasn't budging. 'Why is it you're always dashing in and out of cars and buildings when it rains?'

'Because I don't want to get wet. Come on!' She looked to the safety of the trees longingly.

'Why don't you like getting wet? All it does is dries.'

'Because.' She grabbed him by the hand and attempted to pull him off the bench. She stamped her foot in frustration when she couldn't move him, like a child who couldn't get her way.

'Because why?'

'I don't know.' She swallowed hard. 'I've just never liked rain. Do you have to know all the reasons for all my little problems?' She held her hands over her head to stop the feeling of the rain falling on her.

'There's a reason for everything, Elizabeth,' he said, holding out his hands and catching the raindrops in his palms.

'Well, my reason is simple. In keeping with our earlier conversation, rain complicates things. It makes your clothes wet, is uncomfortable and ultimately gives you a cold.'

Ivan made a game-show noise signalling a wrong answer. 'The rain doesn't give you a cold. The *cold* gives you a cold. This is a sun shower and it's warm.' He held back his head, opened his mouth and allowed the raindrops to fall in. 'Yep, warm and tasty. And you weren't telling me the truth, by the way.'

'What?' she shrilled.

'I read between the lines, hear between the words and know when a full stop is not a full stop but more like a but,' he sang.

Elizabeth groaned and stood with her arms wrapped round herself protectively and with her shoulders hunched as though gunge were being thrown over her.

'It's only rain, Elizabeth. Look around.' He waved his hands wildly. 'Do you see anybody else here running?'

'There *is* nobody else!'

'*Au contraire!* The lake, the trees, the heron and the salmon, all getting soaked.' He threw his head back and continued tasting the rain.

Before Elizabeth headed to the trees she gave one last lecture. 'Be careful of that rain, Ivan. It's not a good idea to drink it.'

'Why?'

'Because it could be dangerous. Do you know what effect carbon monoxide has on the air and the rain? It could be acidic.'

Ivan slid off the bench while holding his throat and pretended to choke. He crawled to the edge of the lake. Elizabeth's eyes followed him but she continued lecturing him.

He dipped his hand into the lake. 'Well, there's no fatal contaminations in this, is there?' He scooped out a handful of water and threw it at her.

Her mouth fell open and her eyes widened with shock as she stood there with water dripping from her nose. She held her arm out and pushed him roughly into the lake, laughing as he disappeared under the water.

She stopped laughing when he didn't reappear.

She began to get worried and stepped towards the edge. The only movement were the ripples caused by the heavy raindrops landing on the calm lake. The cold drops on her face no longer bothered her. A minute went by.

'Ivan?' Her voice was shaky. 'Ivan, stop playing. Come out now.' She leaned over further to see if she could see him.

She sang nervously to herself and counted to ten. Nobody could hold their breath for that long.

The glassy surface broke and a rocket shot out of the water. 'Water fight!' exploded from the water creature. It grabbed her by the hands and pulled her head-first into the lake. Elizabeth was so relieved not to have killed him she didn't even mind when the cool water hit her face and buried her.

'Good morning, Mr O'Callaghan; morning, Maureen; hello, Fidelma; hi, Connor; Father Murphy . . .' She nodded sternly to her neighbours as she walked through the sleepy town. Silent, stunned stares followed her as her runners squelched beneath her and her clothes dripped.

'That's a good look for you,' Benjamin laughed, holding up a cup of coffee to her while he stood beside a small crowd of tourists, who were dancing, laughing and sprinkling coffee on the pavement outside Joe's.

'Thank you, Benjamin,' she answered seriously, continuing on through the town, her eyes sparkling.

The sun shone over the town, which hadn't yet received any rain that morning, and its inhabitants watched, whispered and laughed as Elizabeth Egan walked with her head held high and her arms swinging by her side as a piece of seaweed clung to her tangled hair.

Elizabeth threw another colouring pencil down; crumpled up the sheet she had been working on and tossed it across the room. It missed the bin but she didn't care. It could stay there with the other ten crumpled balls. She made a face at her calendar. A red X, which had originally signalled the end date for Ivan, Luke's invisible friend, who had long since gone, now signalled the end of her career. Well, she was being melodramatic – September was the opening date for the hotel and everything was going according to plan. All the materials had arrived on time with only the minor disasters of a few wrong orders. Mrs Bracken had her team working long hours, making cushions, curtains and duvet covers, but unusually, it was Elizabeth who was slowing things down. She just couldn't find a design for the children's playroom and was beginning to detest herself for even mentioning the idea to Vincent. She was too distracted lately.

She sat at her favourite place at the kitchen table and laughed to herself at the memory of her earlier 'swim'.

Things between her and Ivan were more unusual than ever. Today she had effectively ended their relationship and it broke her heart to do it, yet here he was, still with her in her home, making her laugh as though nothing had happened. But something had happened, something huge, and she could feel the effect of it right under her chest. As the day wore on she realised that she had never backtracked so much in a relationship with a man and yet still felt satisfied to be in his company. Neither of them was ready for more, not yet anyway, but she wished so much that he was.

Dinner with Benjamin the previous night had been pleasant. She had battled with her dislike of going out to eat, her dislike of food and her dislike of unnecessary conversations, and while she managed to put up with those things with Ivan, sometimes even enjoy them, she still found it a task. Socialising wasn't enjoyable for her, however they had much in common. They had a nice chat and a nice meal, but Elizabeth wasn't upset when it was all over and time to go home. Her mind was hugely distracted, wondering about her future with Ivan. Not like when Ivan left her.

Luke's giggles brought her out of her daydream.

Ivan spoke. '*Bonjour, madame.*'

Elizabeth looked up to see both Ivan and Luke entering the conservatory from the garden. Each had a magnifying glass held up to his right eye, causing their eyes to appear gigantic. Across each of their upper lips a moustache had been drawn in black marker. She couldn't help but laugh.

'Ah, but zis is no laffing matter, madame. Zere 'az been a mur-dare,' Ivan said gravely, approaching the table.

'A murder,' Luke translated.

'What?' Elizabeth's eyes widened.

'We're looking for clues, madame,' Luke explained, his uneven moustache wobbling up and down as he spoke.

'A ghastly mur-dare 'az taken place in your jardin,' Ivan explained, running the magnifying glass along the surface of the kitchen table in search for clues.

'That's French for garden,' Luke explained.

Elizabeth nodded, trying not to laugh.

'Forgive us for just barging into your 'ome. Allow us to introduce ourselves. I am Mister Monsieur and zis iz my foolish sidekick, Monsieur Rotalsnart.'

Luke giggled. 'It's backwards for translator.'

'Oh,' Elizabeth nodded. 'Well, it's very nice to meet you both but I'm afraid I'm very busy here, so if you don't mind . . .' She widened her eyes at Ivan.

'Mind? Of course we mind. We are in ze middle of a very serious mur-dare investigay-c-on and you are what?' He looked around, his eyes fell upon the crumpled balls of paper by the bin. He picked one up and studied it with his magnifying glass. 'You are making snowballs, as far as I can see.'

Elizabeth made a face at him and Luke giggled.

'We must interrogate you. Have you any harsh lights we can shine in your face?' Ivan looked around the room and withdrew the question on glancing at Elizabeth's face. 'Very well, madame.'

'Who has been murdered?' Elizabeth asked.

'Ah, just as I suspected, Monsieur Rotalsnart.' They paced the floor in opposite directions with the magnifying glasses still over their eyes. 'She pretends to not know so we don't suspect her. Clever.'

'Do you think she did it?' Luke asked.

'We shall see. Madame, a worm was found squished to death earlier today on the path leading from your conservatory to the clothes line. His devastated family tell us he left home when the rain had stopped in order to cross the path to the other side of the garden. His reasons for wanting to go there are not known but it's what worms do.'

Luke and Elizabeth looked at one another and laughed.

'The rain stopped at 6.30 p.m., which is when the worm left his home to cross the path. Could you tell me your whereabouts, madame?'

'Am I a suspect?' Elizabeth laughed.

'At zis stage of the investigay-c-on, everyone is a suspect.'

'Well, I returned from work at 6.15 and put the dinner on. Then I went to the utility room and emptied the damp clothes from the washing machine into the basket.'

'Then what did you do?' Ivan thrust the magnifying glass in her face and moved it around, studying her. 'I am checking for clues,' he whispered to Luke.

'After that I waited for the rain to stop and then I hung the washing on the line.'

Ivan gasped dramatically. 'Monsieur Rotalsnart, did you hear that?'

Luke's giggling revealed his gums, from where yet another tooth had fallen.

'Well then, this means you are the mur-dare-air!'

'The murderer,' Luke translated.

They both turned to her with their magnifying glasses over their eyes.

Ivan spoke. 'As you tried to keep your birthday of next week a secret from me, your punishment will be to have a party in the back *jardin* in the memory of the recently deceased Monsieur Wriggles, the worm.'

Elizabeth groaned. 'No way.'

'I know, Elizabeth,' he changed to an upper-class British accent, 'having to socialise with the village folk is so terribly frightful.'

'What folk?' Elizabeth's eyes narrowed.

'Oh, just a few people we invited,' Ivan shrugged. 'Luke posted the invites this morning, isn't he great?' He nodded to a proud and beaming Luke. 'Next week you will be the host of a garden party. People you don't know very well will be stomping through your home, possibly making it dirty. Think you can handle that?'

Chapter 34

Elizabeth sat cross-legged on the white sheet covering the dusty cement floor of the building site, with her eyes closed.

'So this is where you disappear to every day.'

Elizabeth's eyes remained closed. 'How do you do it, Ivan?'

'Do what?'

'Just appear out of nowhere exactly when I'm thinking of you?'

She heard him laugh lightly but he didn't answer the question. 'Why is this room the only room that hasn't been finished? Or started, by the looks of it.' He stood behind her.

'Because I need help. I'm stuck.'

'Well, what do you know, Elizabeth Egan is asking for help.' There was a silence until Ivan started humming a familiar song, the song she hadn't been able to get out of her head for the past two months and the song that was making her almost broke, thanks to Poppy and Becca's pig in the office.

Her eyelids flew open. 'What are you humming?'

'The humming song.'

'Did Luke teach you that?'

'No, *I* taught *him*, thank you very much.'

'Oh, really,' Elizabeth grumbled. 'I thought his *invisible* friend made it up.' She laughed to herself and then looked up to him. He wasn't laughing.

Eventually he spoke. 'Why do you sound like you're speaking with socks in your mouth? What is that on your face? A muzzle?' he chortled.

Elizabeth flushed. 'It's not a muzzle,' she spat. 'You have no idea how much dust and bacteria this building has. Anyway, you should be wearing a hard hat,' she knocked on her own. 'God forbid this place should come down on us.'

'What else are you wearing?' He ignored her moodiness and looked her up and down. 'Gloves?'

'So my hands don't get dirty,' she pouted like a child.

'Oh, Elizabeth,' Ivan shook his head and strolled comically around her, 'all the things I've taught you and you're still worrying about being clean and tidy.' He picked up a paintbrush, which was sitting beside an open pot of paint and dipped it in.

'Ivan,' Elizabeth said nervously watching him, 'what are you going to do?'

'You said you wanted help,' he grinned.

Elizabeth rose slowly to her feet. 'Ye-es, help with painting the *wall*,' her voice warned.

'Well, unfortunately you didn't quite specify that when you asked, so I'm afraid that doesn't count.' He dipped the paintbrush into the red paint, held the bristles back in his hand and released them towards Elizabeth like a catapult. Paint splattered across her face. 'Ooh, too bad you weren't wearing protective clothing on the rest of your face,' he teased, watching her eyes widen in anger and shock. 'But it just goes to show, no matter how hard you try to wrap yourself in cotton wool, you can still hurt yourself.'

'Ivan,' there was venom in her voice, 'throwing me in the lake is *one* thing but this is *ludicrous*,' she squealed. 'This is my *work*. I'm serious, I want absolutely *nothing* more to do with you, Ivan, Ivan . . . I don't even know your surname,' she spluttered.

'It's Elbisivni,' he explained calmly.

'What are you, *Russian*?' she shouted almost hyperventilating. 'Is Ekam Eveileb Russian too or does it even *exist*?' She was screaming now, and breathless.

'I'm very sorry,' Ivan said seriously, his smile disappearing. 'I can sense that you're upset. I'll just put this back down.' He slowly lowered the paintbrush back to the pot and left it back at the perfect angle it had been placed, mirroring the others. 'That was over the top. I apologise.'

Elizabeth's anger began to subside.

'The red is perhaps too much of an angry colour for you,' he continued. 'I should have been more subtle.' Suddenly another paintbrush appeared before Elizabeth's face. Her eyes widened.

'White maybe?' he grinned, and splashed the paint down her top.

'Ivan!' Elizabeth half laughed and half shouted. 'Fine,' she dived towards the pots of paint, 'you wanna play? I can play. Wearing colours is your favourite thing to do now, you say?' she grumbled to herself. She dipped a paintbrush in the pot and chased Ivan round the room. 'Blue's your favourite colour, Mr Elbisivni?' She painted a strip of blue down his face and hair, and began laughing evilly.

'You thought that was funny?'

She nodded in hysterics.

'Good,' Ivan laughed, grabbing her by the waist and pushing her to the floor, pinning her down masterfully and painting her face while she squealed and struggled to get free. 'If you don't stop shouting, Elizabeth, you'll have a green tongue,' Ivan warned.

After they had both been covered head to toe in paint and Elizabeth was laughing so much she could no longer put up a fight, Ivan turned his attention to the wall. 'What this wall needs now is some paint.'

Elizabeth removed her mouth cover and tried to regain her breathing, revealing the only normal skin colour on her face.

'Well, at least that came in handy,' Ivan noted, and turned back to face the wall. 'A little birdie told me that you went on a date with Benjamin West,' Ivan said, dipping a fresh brush into the red paint pot.

'Dinner, yes. A date, no. And may I add that I went out with him the night you stood me up.'

He didn't reply. 'You like him?' he asked.

'He's a nice man.' She still didn't turn round.

'You want to spend more time with him?'

Elizabeth began to roll up the paint-splattered sheet from the floor. 'I'd like to spend more time with you.'

'What if you couldn't?'

Elizabeth froze. 'Then I'd ask you why.'

He avoided the question. 'What if I didn't exist and you'd never met me, would you want to spend more time with Benjamin then?'

Elizabeth swallowed hard, put her paper and pens into her bag and zipped it shut. She was tired of playing games with him and his talk was making her nervous. They needed to discuss this properly. She stood up and faced him. On the wall, Ivan had written 'Elizabeth ♥s Benjamin' in big red letters.

'Ivan!' Elizabeth giggled nervously. 'Don't be such a child. What if someone was to see that!' She went to grab the brush from him.

He wouldn't let go and their eyes locked. 'I can't give you what you want, Elizabeth,' he said softly.

A coughing from the doorway caused them both to jump.

'Hi, Elizabeth,' Benjamin looked at her with curious amusement. He glanced at the wall behind her and grinned. 'That's an interesting theme.'

There was a pregnant pause. Elizabeth looked to her right. 'It was Ivan.' Her voice came out childlike.

Benjamin chuckled slightly. 'Him again.'

She nodded and he looked to the paintbrush in her hand, dripping red onto her jeans. A red, blue, purple, green and white splashed face now turned crimson.

'Looks like it's *you* who's been caught painting the roses red,' Benjamin said, and went to take a step into the room.

'Benjamin!'

He paused mid-step, with a pained expression at the sound of Vincent's demanding voice. 'I'd better go,' he smiled. 'I'll talk to you later,' and he headed off in the direction of Vincent's shouts. 'Oh, by the way,' he called out, 'thanks for the party invitation.'

A fuming Elizabeth ignored Ivan, doubled over laughing and occasional snorting. She dipped her brush in the white pot and erased Ivan's words, trying to erase this embarrassing moment from her memory.

'Good afternoon, Mr O'Callaghan; hello, Maureen; hello, Fidelma; hi, Connor, Father Murphy,' she greeted her neighbours as she walked through the town to get to her office. Red paint dribbled down her arms, blue paint clung in strands around her hair and her jeans looked like Monet's palette. Silent, stunned stares followed her as her clothes continued to drip with paint, leaving a multi-coloured trail behind her.

'Why do you always do that?' Ivan asked, running alongside her to keep up as she marched through the town.

'Do what? Good afternoon, Sheila.'

'You always cross the road before you get to Flanagan's pub, walk on the opposite path and then cross again once you get to Joe's.'

'No I don't.' She smiled at another gawker.

'Talk about painting the town red, Elizabeth,' Joe called out to her, laughing as she left red footprints behind her as she ran across the road.

'Look, you just did it!' Ivan pointed out.

Elizabeth stopped and looked back on her track, visible by her footprints. True enough, she had crossed the road at Flanagan's, walked on the opposite path and crossed over once again to get to her office, instead of staying on the same path. She hadn't noticed that before. She looked back at Flanagan's pub. Mr Flanagan stood at the door having a cigarette. He nodded at her strangely, appearing surprised she held his stare. She frowned and swallowed the lump that had formed in her throat as she stared at the building.

'Everything OK, Elizabeth?' Ivan asked, cutting into her thoughts.

'Yes.' Her voice came out as a whisper. She cleared her throat, looked at Ivan in confusion and unconvincingly repeated, 'Yes, I'm fine.'

Chapter 35

Elizabeth passed a gobsmacked and disapproving Mrs Bracken, who was standing at the door with two other elderly women, all with pieces of fabric in their hands. They tutted as she trudged by, with paint in clumps in the ends of her hair, which was rubbing against her back and causing a beautiful multicoloured effect.

'Is she losing her marbles or what?' one of the women whispered loudly.

'No, quite the opposite.' Elizabeth could hear the smile in Mrs Bracken's voice. 'I'd say she's been on her hands and knees looking for them.'

The other women tutted and wandered away, muttering about Elizabeth not being the only one losing her marbles.

Elizabeth ignored the stare from Becca and the shout from Poppy, 'That's more like it!' and marched into her office, closing the door softly behind her. Shutting everything out. She leaned her back against the door and tried to figure out why her body was shaking so much. What had been stirred inside her? What monsters had awoken from their slumber and were bubbling away under her skin? She breathed in deeply through her nostrils and exhaled slowly, counting one, two, three times until her weak knees stopped trembling.

Everything had been fine, if not mildly embarrassing, as she walked through the town looking like she had dipped herself in a pot of rainbow-coloured paint. It had all been fine until Ivan said something. What did he say . . . ? He said . . . and then she remembered and a chill ran through her body.

Flanagan's pub. She always avoided Flanagan's pub, he said. She hadn't noticed until he brought it to her attention. Why did she do it? Because of Saoirse? No, Saoirse drank in the Camel's Hump, on the hill, down the road. She remained leaning against the door, thinking until her head was dizzy. The room spun her and she decided she needed to get home. Home to where she could control what went on, who could enter, who could leave, where things had their own place and where every memory was clear. She needed order.

*   *   *

'Where's your beanbag, Ivan?' Calendula asked, looking up at me from her yellow-painted wooden chair.

'Oh, I got tired of that,' I replied. 'Spinning is my new favourite thing now.'

'Nice,' she nodded with approval.

'Opal's really late,' Tommy said, wiping his runny nose along his arm.

Calendula looked away in disgust, straightened her pretty yellow dress, crossed her ankles and swung her white patent shoes and frilly socks while she hummed the humming song.

Olivia knitted in her rocking chair. 'She'll be here,' she rasped.

Jamie-Lynn reached out to the centre table to grab a chocolate Rice Krispie bun and a glass of milk, and as she coughed and spluttered, her glass of milk spilled all over her arm. She licked it off.

'Have you been playing in the doctor's waiting room again, Jamie-Lynn?' Olivia asked, glaring at her over the rim of her glasses.

Jamie-Lynn nodded, coughed again on her bun and took another bite.

Calendula wrinkled her nose in disgust and continued combing her Barbie's hair with a small comb.

'You know what Opal told you, Jamie-Lynn. Those places are full of bacteria. Those toys you like to play with are the cause of you being ill.'

'I know,' Jamie-Lynn said with food in her mouth, 'but someone's got to keep the kids company when they're waiting for the doc.'

Twenty minutes passed and eventually Opal showed. Everyone looked at each other with worry. It looked as though Opal's shadow had taken her place. She didn't float into the room like a fresh morning breeze as she usually did; it was as though every step she took she was laden down with heavy buckets of cement. The others all quietened down immediately, seeing the deep blue, almost black, colour that followed her in.

'Good afternoon, my friends.' Even Opal's voice was different, as though she was being muffled and held back in another dimension.

'Hello, Opal.' The replies were soft and hushed, as though more than a whisper would knock her to rubble.

She gave them a gentle smile, acknowledgeing their support. 'Somebody who has been a friend of mine for a great deal of time is sick. Very sick. He's going to die and I'm very sad to lose him,' she explained.

Everyone made soothing noises. Olivia stopped rocking in her chair, Bobby stopped rolling back and forth on his skateboard, Calendula's legs stopped kicking, Tommy even stopped sniffing the snot back up his nose and I stopped swinging on my chair. This was serious stuff, and the group talked about what it's like to lose people they love. Everyone understood. It happened to best friends all the time and each time it happened, the sadness was never less.

I couldn't contribute to the conversation. Every emotion I have ever felt for Elizabeth gathered and swelled in my throat like a pumping heart receiving more and more love every moment and growing bigger and prouder as a result. The lump in my throat prevented me from speaking just as my growing heart prevented me from stopping loving Elizabeth.

As the meeting was ending, Opal looked to me. 'Ivan, how are things with Elizabeth?'

Everyone looked at me and I found a tiny hole in that lump for my sound to seep through. 'I've left her until tomorrow to figure something out.' I thought of her face and my heart pumped quicker and grew, and that tiny hole in the lump in my throat closed.

And without anyone knowing my situation, they all understood it to mean 'not long now'. By the way Opal quickly picked up her files and fled the adjourned meeting, I figured it was the same case for her.

Elizabeth's feet pounded on the treadmill that faced the back garden in her home. She looked out at the hills, the lakes and mountains spread before her and ran even faster. Her hair blew behind her as she ran, her brow glistened, her arms moved with her legs and she imagined as she did every day that she was running over those hills, across the seas, far, far away. After thirty minutes of running and running yet staying in the same place she stopped, left the small gym panting and weak, and immediately began to clean, scrubbing furiously on surfaces that already sparkled.

As soon as she had cleaned the house from top to bottom, had wiped away all the cobwebs, cleared every darkened hidden corner, she began to do the same with her mind. All her life she had run from shedding light on those darkened corners of her mind. The cobwebs and dust had settled and now she was ready to start clearing them. Something was trying to crawl out of that darkness and now she was ready to help it. Enough running.

She sat at the kitchen table and stared out at the country spread before her, tumbling hills, valleys and lakes with fuchsia and montbretia lacing them all. The sky was darkening earlier now that August had arrived.

She thought long and hard about nothing and everything, allowing whatever was niggling her mind to have a chance to step out of the shadows and show itself. It was the same niggling feeling she ran from while she lay in bed trying to sleep, the feeling she fought while furiously cleaning. But now she sat at the table a surrendered woman, with her hands held high, stepping away from her weapon and allowing her thoughts to hold her under arrest. She had been like an escaped criminal on the run for so long.

'Why are you sitting in the dark?' a sweet voice called out to her.

She smiled lightly. 'I'm just thinking, Luke.'

'Can I sit with you?' he asked, and she hated herself for wanting to say no. 'I won't say anything or touch anything, I promise,' he added.

That twisted her heart – was she really that bad? Yes, she knew she was.

'Come over and sit down,' she smiled, pulling out the chair beside her.

They both sat in the darkened kitchen in silence until Elizabeth spoke. 'Luke, there are some things that I should talk to you about. Things I should have spoken to you before but . . .' She twisted her fingers, trying very carefully to decide how to word what she was saying. When she was a child, all she wanted was for people to explain what had happened, where her mother had gone and why. A simple explanation would have helped years and years of tortuous wondering.

He looked at her with big blue eyes from under long lashes, chubby cheeks that were rosy and a glistening upper lip from a runny nose. She laughed and ran a hand through his snow-white hair and left it resting on the back of his hot little neck.

'But,' she continued, 'I didn't know how to say them to you.'

'Is it about my mom?' Luke asked, his legs swinging below the glass table.

'Yes. She hasn't visited us in a while, as you've probably noticed.'

'She's gone on an adventure,' Luke said happily.

'Well, I don't know if you could call it that, Luke,' Elizabeth sighed. 'I don't know where she's gone, sweetheart. She didn't tell anyone before she left.'

'She told me,' he chirped.

'What?' Elizabeth's eyes widened, her heart quickened.

'She came to the house before she went away. She told me she was going away but she didn't know for how long. And I said that's kind of like an adventure and she laughed and said yes.'

'Did she say why?' Elizabeth whispered, surprised that Saoirse had the compassion to say goodbye to her son.

'Mm-hmm,' he nodded, kicking his feet faster now. 'She said because it was best for her and you and Granddad and me because she kept doing the wrong things and making everyone mad. She said she was doing what you always told her to do. She said she was flying away.'

Elizabeth held her breath lightly and remembered how she used to tell her baby sister to fly away when things were tough at home. She remembered how she watched her little six-year-old sister as she drove away to college and told her over and over again to fly away. All her emotions caught in her throat.

'What did you say?' Elizabeth managed to force out, running her hand through Luke's baby-soft hair and feeling and overwhelming urge to protect him more than anything for the first time in her life.

'I told her she was probably right,' Luke replied matter-of-factly. 'She said that I was a big boy now and it was my job to look after you and Granddad.'

Tears fell from her eyes. 'She did?' she sniffed.

Luke lifted his hand and delicately wiped her tear.

'Well, don't you worry,' she kissed his hand and reached out to hug him, 'because it's my job to look after you, OK?'

His reply was muffled as his head was pushed against her chest. She let go of him quickly to allow him to breathe.

'Edith will be home soon,' he said excitedly after he had taken a deep breath. 'Can't wait to see what she got me.'

Elizabeth smiled, tried quickly to compose herself and cleared her throat. 'We can introduce her to Ivan. Do you think she'll like him?'

Luke wrinkled up his face. 'I don't think she'll be able to see him.'

'We can't keep him to ourselves, you know, Luke,' Elizabeth laughed.

'Anyway, Ivan might not even be here when she gets back,' he added.

Elizabeth's heart thudded, 'What do you mean? Did he say something?'

Luke shook his head.

Elizabeth sighed. 'Oh, Luke, just because you're close to Ivan it doesn't mean he'll leave you, you know. I don't want you to be afraid of that happening. I used to be afraid like that. I used to think that everyone I loved would always go away.'

'*I* won't go away.' Luke looked at her caringly.

'And I promise you I won't go anywhere either.' She kissed him on the head, then cleared her throat. 'You know the things that you and Edith do together, like going to the zoo and the cinema, things like that?'

Luke nodded.

'Would you mind if I came along sometimes?'

Luke smiled happily. 'Yeah, that'd be cool.' He thought for a while. 'We're kind of the same now, aren't we? My mom leaving is kinda like what your mom did, isn't it?' he asked, breathing on the glass table and writing his name in the fog with his finger.

Elizabeth's body grew cold. 'No,' she snapped, 'it's nothing like that at all.' She stood up from the table, switched on the light and started wiping down the counter. 'They are totally different people, it's not the same at all.' Her voice trembled as she scrubbed furiously. Looking up to check on Luke she caught sight of her reflection in the glass of the conservatory and froze. Gone was the composure, gone were her emotions, she looked like a possessed woman hiding from the truth, running from the world.

And then she knew.

And the memories that lurked in the dark corners of her mind began to creep ever so slowly into the light.

Chapter 36

'Opal,' I called gently from her office doorway. She seemed so brittle and I was afraid that the slightest noise would shatter her.

'Ivan.' She smiled tiredly, pinning her dreadlocks back from her face.

I could see myself in her shining eyes as I entered the room. 'We're all worried about you – is there anything we, I can do to help?'

'Thank you, Ivan, but apart from keeping an eye on things around here, there's really nothing anyone can do to help. I'm just so tired. I've been spending the past few nights at the hospital and I haven't allowed myself to sleep. He's got only days left now; I don't want to miss it when he . . .' She looked away from Ivan and to the picture frame on her desk, and when she spoke again her voice was trembling. 'I just wish there was some way I could say goodbye to him, to let him know he's not alone, that I'm by his side.' Her tears fell.

I went to her side and comforted her, feeling helpless and knowing that for once there was absolutely nothing I could do to help this friend. Or was there?

'Hold on a minute, Opal. Maybe there is a way you can. I have an idea.' And with that I ran.

Elizabeth had made last-minute arrangements for Luke to sleep over at Sam's house. She knew she needed to be alone that night. She could feel a change within her; a chill had entered her body and wouldn't leave. She sat huddled up in her bed, wearing an oversized jumper covered by a blanket, desperate to keep warm.

The moon outside her window noticed something was wrong and guarded her protectively from the darkness. Her stomach cramped with anticipation. The things that Ivan and Luke had said today had turned a key in her mind and had unlocked a chest of memories so terrifying that Elizabeth was afraid to close her eyes.

She gazed out the window through the open curtains at the moon, then allowed herself to drift . . .

She was twelve years old. It was two weeks since her mother had brought her for a picnic in the field, two weeks since she had told her she was going away, two weeks of waiting for her to come back. Outside

Elizabeth's bedroom a screeching one-month-old Saoirse was held, hushed and comforted by her father.

'Hush now, baby, hush . . .' She could hear his gentle tones getting louder and then quietening as he paced the floor of the bungalow in the late night hour. Outside, the wind howled, squeezing itself through the windows and door locks with a whistling sound. It raced in and danced around the rooms, taunting, teasing and tickling Elizabeth as she lay in her bed, hands over her ears, tears falling down her cheeks.

Saoirse's cries got louder, Brendan's pleas got louder and Elizabeth covered her head with her pillow.

'Please, Saoirse, please stop crying,' her father begged, and attempted a song, a lullaby that Elizabeth's mother always sang to them. She clamped her hands over her ears harder but still could hear Saoirse's cries and her father's tuneless song. Elizabeth sat up in her bed, her eyes stinging from yet another night of tears and lack of sleep.

'You want your bottle?' her father asked gently over the roars. 'No? Ah, love, what is it?' he asked in a pained voice. 'I miss her too, love, I miss her too,' and he too began to cry. Saoirse, Brendan and Elizabeth all cried for Gráinne together, but all feeling alone, in their bungalow blown by the wind.

Suddenly headlights appeared at the end of the long road. Elizabeth leaped out of her covers and sat at the end of her bed with her stomach twisted in excitement. It was her mother – it had to be. Who else would be calling all the way down here at ten o'clock at night? Elizabeth bounced up and down at the end of her bed in delight.

The car pulled up outside the house, the car door opened and out stepped Kathleen, Gráinne's sister. Leaving the door open with the head-lights still on and the wipers moving violently across the windscreen, she marched to the gate, pushed it open causing it to creak, and banged on the door.

With a screaming Saoirse in his arms Brendan opened the door. Elizabeth rushed to the keyhole of her bedroom door and looked out into the hall at the action.

'Is she here?' Kathleen demanded, without a hello or a kind word.

'Sshh,' Brendan said, 'I don't want you waking Elizabeth.'

'As if she's not already awake with all that screaming. What have you done to the poor child?' she asked incredulously.

'The child wants her mother,' he raised his voice. 'Like us all,' he added in softer tones.

'Give her to me,' Kathleen said.

'You're wet,' Brendan stepped away from her and his arms tightened around the tiny bundle.

'Is she here?' Kathleen asked again, her voice still angry. She was still standing outside the front door. She hadn't asked to come in and she hadn't been invited.

'Of course she's not here.' Brendan bounced Saoirse around, trying to calm her. 'I thought you'd taken her to that magical place that would cure her for ever,' he said angrily.

'It was supposed to be the best place, Brendan – better than the other ones, anyhow. Anyway,' she mumbled the next few words, 'she's gone.'

'Gone? What do you mean, gone?'

'She was missing this morning from her room. Nobody's seen her.'

'Has a habit of disappearing in the night, does your mother,' Brendan said angrily, rocking Saoirse. 'Well, if she's not where you sent her, you don't need to look far from here. Sure won't she be in Flanagan's?'

Elizabeth's eyes widened and she gasped. Her mother was here in Baile na gCroíthe; she hadn't left her after all.

In between their bitter exchanges, Saoirse wailed.

'For Christsake, Brendan, can you not quieten her?' Kathleen complained. 'You know I can take the children. They can live with me and Alan in—'

'They're *my* children and you won't take them from me like you did Gráinne,' he bellowed. Saoirse's wails quietened.

There was a long silence.

'Be off with you.' Brendan spoke weakly as though his earlier boom had broken his voice.

The front door closed and Elizabeth watched from the window as Kathleen banged the gate shut and got into her car. It sped off, the lights disappearing into the distance along with Elizabeth's hopes of going with her to see her mother.

A glimmer of hope remained. Her father had mentioned Flanagan's. Elizabeth knew where that was – she passed it everyday going to school. She would pack her bag, find her mother and live with her away from her screaming little sister and father, and they would go on adventures every day.

The handle on the door shook and she dived into bed and pretended to be asleep. Squeezing her eyes tightly shut, she decided that as soon as her father had gone to bed, she would make her own way to Flanagan's.

She would sneak out into the night, just like her mother.

'Are you sure this is going to work?' Opal stood against the wall of the hospital ward, her hands trembling as they clasped and unclasped themselves against her anxiety-filled stomach.

Ivan looked at her with uncertain eyes. 'It's worth a try.'

Through the glass in the corridor they could see Geoffrey in his private room. He was hooked up to a ventilator, his mouth covered by the oxygen mask, and around him contraptions beeped while wires ran from his body into machines. In the centre of all this action, his body lay still and calm, his chest rising and falling rhythmically. They were surrounded by that eerie sound that only hospitals provided, the sound of everyone waiting, of being in between one timeless place and another.

As soon as the nurses who were tending to Geoffrey opened the door to leave, Opal and Ivan entered.

'Here she is,' Olivia spoke from beside Geoffrey's bed, as Opal entered.

His eyes shot open quickly and he began to look around wildly, searching the room.

'She's on your left-hand side, dear, she's holding your hand,' Olivia said gently.

Geoffrey attempted to speak, his sound coming out muffled from under the mask. Opal's hand flew to her mouth, her eyes filled and the lump in her throat was visible. It was a language that only Olivia could understand; the words of a dying man.

Olivia nodded as he made sounds; her eyes filled and when she spoke Ivan could no longer stay in the room.

'He said to tell you, that his heart has ached every moment you were apart, dear Opal.'

Ivan stepped out of the room through the open door and walked as quickly as he could down the hall and out of the hospital.

Chapter 37

Outside Elizabeth's bedroom window on Fuchsia Lane, the rain fell, hitting off the bedroom window like pebbles. The wind began warming its vocal chords for the night and Elizabeth, tucked up in bed, was transported back to the time she journeyed out in the late winter night to find her mother.

She had packed her schoolbag with only a few things – underwear, two jumpers and skirts, the book her mother gave her and her teddy. Her money box had revealed £4.42, and after wrapping her raincoat around her favourite floral dress and stepping into her red Wellington boots, she set out into the cold night. She climbed the small garden wall to avoid the sound of the gate alerting her father, who these days slept like the farmyard dog, with one ear pricked. She kept alongside the bushes so as not to be spotted walking up the straight road. The wind pushed and pulled the branches, scraping them against her face and legs, and wet kisses from soggy leaves brushed against her skin. The wind was vicious that night. It whipped her legs and stung her ears and cheeks, blowing against her face so hard it took her breath away. Within minutes of walking up the road, her fingers, nose and lips were numb and her body was freezing to the bone but the thought of seeing her mother that night kept her going. And on she journeyed.

Twenty minutes later she arrived at the bridge to Baile na gCroíthe. She had never seen the town at eleven o'clock at night; it was like a ghost town, dark, empty and silent, as if it were about to bear witness to something and never speak a word of it.

She walked towards Flanagan's with butterflies in her tummy, no longer feeling the lash of the cold, just pure excitement at the thrill of being reunited with her mother. She heard Flanagan's before she saw it; there, and the Camel's Hump, were the only buildings in the village with lights on. From an open window, out floated the sounds of a piano, fiddle, badhrán, and loud singing and laughter, occasional cheers and whoops. Elizabeth giggled to herself; it sounded like everyone was having such fun.

Outside, Aunt Kathleen's car was parked and Elizabeth's legs automatically moved faster. The front door was open and inside there was a small hallway, but the door to the pub, complete with stained glass, was closed. Elizabeth stood in the porch and shook the rain from her coat; hung it up alongside the umbrellas on the rack on the wall. Her black hair was soaking wet and her nose was red and running. The rain had found its way into the top of her boots, and her legs shook from the cold and her feet squelched in the ice-cold pools of water.

The piano stopped suddenly, and there was a loud roar from a crowd of men that made Elizabeth jump.

'Come on, Gráinne, sing us another one,' one man slurred, and they all cheered.

Elizabeth's heart leaped at the sound of her mother's name. She was inside! She was such a beautiful singer. She sang around the house all the time, composing lullabies and nursery rhymes all by herself, and in the mornings Elizabeth loved to lie in her bed and listen to her mother as she hummed around the rooms of the bungalow. But the voice that began in the silence, followed by the rowdy cheers of drunken men, was not the sweet voice of her mother that she knew so well.

In Fuchsia Lane, Elizabeth's eyes darted open and she sat upright in her bed. Outside, the wind howled like a wounded animal. Her heart was hammering in her chest; her mouth was dry and her body clammy. Throwing the covers off her, she grabbed her car keys from the bedside table, ran down the stairs, threw her raincoat around her shoulders and escaped the house to her car. The cold drops of rain hit her, and she remembered why she hated to feel the rain against her face: it reminded her of that night. She hurried to her car, shivering as the wind tossed her hair across her eyes and cheeks, and by the time she sat behind the wheel she was already drenched.

The windscreen wipers lashed across the window furiously as she drove down the dark roads to the town. Driving over the bridge she was faced with the ghost town. Everyone was locked safely inside, in the warmth of their houses and hostels. Apart from the Camel's Hump and Flanagan's there was no nightlife. Elizabeth parked her car and stood across the road from Flanagan's, standing in the cold rain staring across at the building, remembering. Remembering that night.

Elizabeth's ears hurt from the words of the song being sung by the woman. It was crude, the words disgusting, being sung in such crass and dirty tones. Every rude word Elizabeth was taught not to say by her father was winning the plaudits of a boozy, sozzled pack of beasts.

She stood on tiptoes to look through the red of the stained-glass windows to see what awful woman was croaking the awful tune. She was sure her mother would be sitting beside Kathleen, absolutely disgusted.

Elizabeth's heart jumped into her throat and for a moment she fought hard to breathe, for on top of the wooden piano sat her mother, opening her mouth and releasing all those awful words. A skirt she had never seen before was hitched up to her thighs and around her a handful of men taunted, teased and laughed as she threw shapes with her body Elizabeth had never seen any woman do before.

'Now, now, lads, calm down over there,' the young Mr Flanagan called from behind the bar.

The men ignored him, continuing to leer at Elizabeth's mother.

'Mummy,' Elizabeth whimpered.

Elizabeth walked slowly across the road towards Flanagan's pub, her heart beating at the memory so alive in her head. She held out her hand and pushed open the bar door. Mr Flanagan looked up from behind the counter and gave her a small smile, as though he expected to see her.

Young Elizabeth held out a trembling hand and pushed open the door to the bar. Her hair was wet and dripping around her face, her bottom lip out and trembling. Her big brown eyes looked around the room in panic as she saw a man reach out to touch her mother.

'Leave her alone!' Elizabeth shouted so loud the room was quietened. Her mother stopped singing and all heads turned to the little girl standing at the door.

Her mother's corner of the room erupted in such a loud laughter. Tears spilled from Elizabeth's terrified eyes.

'Boo hoo hoo,' her mother sang the loudest of them all. 'Let's all try to save Mummy, shall we?' she slurred. She set her eyes upon Elizabeth. They were bloodshot and dark, not the eyes Elizabeth remembered so well; they belonged to someone else.

'Shit,' Kathleen cursed, jumping up from the other side of the bar and rushing over to Elizabeth, 'What are you doing here?'

'I c-c-c-came t-t-t-to,' Elizabeth stammered in the quietened room, looking at her mother in bewilderment, 'I came to find my mum so I could live with her.'

'Well, she's not here,' her mother shrieked. 'Get out!' She pointed a finger at her accusingly. 'Drowned little rats aren't allowed in pubs,' she cackled, knocking back her glass, but she missed her mouth, causing most of the drink to land down her chest, where it glistened on her neck and replaced the smell of her sweet perfume with whiskey.

'But, Mummy . . .' Elizabeth whimpered.

'But Mummy,' Gráinne imitated and a few of the men laughed. 'I'm not your mummy,' she said harshly, stepping down onto the piano keys and causing a disturbing sound. 'Little drowned Lizzies don't deserve mummies. They should be poisoned, the whole lot of you,' she spat.

'Kathleen,' Mr Flanagan shouted, 'what are you doing? Get her out of here. She shouldn't be seeing this.'

'I can't,' Kathleen stayed rooted to the spot. 'I have to keep an eye on Gráinne, I have to bring her back with me.'

Mr Flanagan's mouth dropped open in shock at her. 'Would you look at the child?'

Elizabeth's brown skin had paled. Her lips were blue from the cold and her teeth were chattering, a soaking wet floral dress clung to her body and her legs shook in her Wellington boots.

Kathleen looked from Elizabeth to Gráinne, caught between the two. 'I can't, Tom,' she hissed.

Tom looked angry. 'I'll have the decency to bring her home myself.' He grabbed a set of keys from under the bar and started to come round the other side to Elizabeth.

'NO!' Elizabeth screamed. She took one look at her mother, who had already become bored by this scene and was lost in the arms of a strange man, turned to face the door and ran back out to the cold night.

Elizabeth stood at the door of the bar, her hair dripping, rain rolling down her forehead and off her nose, her teeth chattering and her fingers numb. The sounds of the room weren't the same. Inside there was no music, no cheers or whoops, no singing, just the sound of an occasional clinking glass and quiet chatter. There were no more than five people in the bar on the quiet Tuesday night.

An aged Tom continued to stare at her.

'My mother –' Elizabeth called out from the door. The sound of her childlike voice surprised her – 'she was an alcoholic.'

Tom nodded.

'She came in here a lot?'

He nodded again.

'But there were weeks,' she swallowed hard, 'weeks at a time when she wouldn't leave us.'

Tom's voice was soft. 'She was what you'd call a binge drinker.'

'And my father,' she paused, thinking of her poor father who waited and waited at home every night, 'he knew this.'

'The patience of a saint,' he replied.

She looked around the small bar, at the same old piano that stood in the corner. The only thing that had changed in the room was the age of all that was in it.

'That night,' Elizabeth said, her eyes filling with tears, 'thank you.'

Tom just nodded at her sadly.

'Have you seen her since?'

He shook his head.

'Do you . . . do you expect to?' she asked, her voice catching in her throat.

'Not in this lifetime, Elizabeth.' He confirmed for her what she had always felt deep down.

'Daddy . . .' Elizabeth whispered to herself and took off out of the bar back into the cold night.

Little Elizabeth ran from the pub, feeling every drop of rain lash against her body, feeling her chest hurt as she breathed in the cold air and the water splash up her legs as she pounded in the puddles. She was running home.

Elizabeth jumped into her car and sped off out of the town towards the mile-long road that led to her father's bungalow. Approaching headlights meant she had to reverse back the way she had come and wait for the car to pass before she could continue her journey.

Her father had known all this time and he had never told her. He had never wanted her to shatter her illusions of her mother and she had always held her up on a pedestal. She had thought her a free spirit and of her father as a suffocating force, as the butterfly catcher. She needed to get to him quickly, to apologise, to make things right.

She set off again down the road only to see a tractor slowly chugging before her, unusually at this late hour. She reversed the car back to the entrance of the road again. With her impatience rising she abandoned her car and began to run. She ran as fast as she could down the mile-long road that brought her home.

'Daddy,' little Elizabeth sobbed as she ran down the road towards the bungalow. She screamed his name louder, the wind helping her for the first time that night by lifting her words and carrying them for her towards the bungalow. A light went on, followed by another, and she could see the front door open.

'Daddy!' she cried even louder, and ran even faster.

Brendan sat at the window of the bedroom, looking out to the dark night, sipping a cup of tea, hoping among all hopes that the vision he was waiting for would appear. He had chased them all away, he had done exactly the opposite to what he wanted and it was all his fault. All he could do was wait. Wait for one of his three women to appear. One, he knew for certain, would and could never return.

A movement in the distance caught his eye and he sat to attention like a guard dog. A woman ran towards him, long black hair floating behind her, her image blurring as the rain hit against the window and streamed down the glass.

It was her.

He dropped his cup and saucer to the floor and stood up, knocking his chair backward.

'Gráinne,' he whispered.

He grabbed his cane and moved as quickly as his legs would take him to the front door. Pulling the door open, he strained his eyes in the stormy night to see his wife.

He heard the sound of distant panting as the woman ran.

'Daddy,' he heard her say. No she couldn't be saying that, his Gráinne wouldn't say that.

'Daddy,' he heard her sob again.

He was taken back over twenty years by the familiar sounds. It was his little girl, his little girl was running home in the rain again and she needed him.

'Daddy!' she called again.

'I'm here,' he called, quietly at first, and then he shouted louder, 'I'm here!'

He heard her crying, saw her opening the creaking gate, dripping wet, and just as he did over twenty years ago he held out his arms to her and welcomed her into his embrace.

'I'm here, don't you worry,' he soothed her, patting her head and rocking her from side to side. 'Daddy's here.'

Chapter 38

Elizabeth's garden on the day of her birthday was like the scene of the Mad Hatter's tea party in Wonderland. She had one long table set out in the middle of the garden decorated with a red and white tablecloth. Covering every inch of the table was a huge array of plates piled high with cocktail sausages, crisps, chips and dips, sandwiches, salads, cold meats and sweets. The garden had been pruned to within an inch of its life, new flowers had been planted and the air smelled of freshly cut grass mixed with the aroma of the barbecue in the corner. It was a hot day, the sky was an indigo colour with not a cloud in sight, the surrounding hills were a rich emerald green, the sheep upon them like snowflakes, and Ivan felt the pain of having to leave such a beautiful place and the people in it.

'Ivan, I'm so glad you're here.' Elizabeth came charging out of the kitchen.

'Thank you,' Ivan smiled, swirling round to greet her. 'Wow, look at you!' His mouth dropped open. Elizabeth was wearing a simple white linen summer dress that contrasted with her dark skin beautifully; her long hair was lightly curled and hung down past her shoulders. 'Give me a twirl,' Ivan said, still taken aback by her appearance. Her features had softened and everything about her seemed gentler.

'I gave up twirling for men when I was eight. Now stop gawking at me, there's work to be done,' she snapped.

Well, not *everything* about her was gentler.

She looked around the garden, hands on her hips as though she was on patrol.

'OK, let me show you what's happening here.' She grabbed Ivan by the arm and dragged him towards the table.

'When people arrive through the side gate, they come over here first. This is where they collect their napkins, knives, forks and plates, and then they go along here.' She moved on, still clutching his arm and speaking quickly. 'When they get here, *you* will be standing behind this barbecue where you will prepare whatever they choose from *this* selection.' She displayed a side table of meats. 'On the left is soya meat, on the right is regular. *Do not* confuse the two.'

Ivan opened his mouth to protest but she held a finger up and continued, 'Then after they take their burger buns, they move on to the salad *here*. Please note that the sauces for the burgers are *here*.'

Ivan picked up an olive and she slapped his hand, causing him to drop it back into the bowl. She continued, 'Desserts are over *here*, tea and coffee *here*, organic milk in the left jug, regular milk on the right, toilets through the door on the left *only*; I don't want them traipsing through the house, OK?'

Ivan nodded.

'Any questions?'

'Just one.' He grabbed an olive and popped it into his mouth before she had a chance to steal it from his grasp. 'Why are you telling me all this?'

Elizabeth rolled her eyes. 'Because,' she wiped her clammy hands in a napkin, 'I've never done this whole *hosting* thing before, and seeing as you got me into this mess, I need you to help me.'

Ivan laughed. 'Elizabeth, you will be fine but my barbecuing food will *clearly* not help.'

'Why, don't you have barbecues in Ekam Eveileb?' she asked sarcastically.

Ivan ignored her comment. 'Look, you don't need rules and schedules today. Just let people do what they like, roam the garden, mingle with everyone and choose their food themselves. Who cares if they start at the apple pie?'

Elizabeth looked horrified. 'Start at the apple pie?' she spluttered. 'But that's the wrong end of the table. No, Ivan, you need to tell them where the queue starts and ends. I won't have time.' She rushed towards the kitchen. 'Dad, I hope you're not eating all those cocktail sausages in there,' she called.

'Dad?' Ivan's eyes widened, 'He's here?'

'Yes.' She rolled her eyes but Ivan could tell she didn't mean it. 'It's just as well you weren't here the past few days because I've been up to my eyes in family secrets, tears, break-ups and make-ups. But we're getting there,' she relaxed for a moment and smiled at Ivan. The doorbell rang and she jumped, her face contorting into panic.

'Relax, Elizabeth!' Ivan laughed.

'Come around the side!' she called to the visitor.

'Before they get here I just want to give you a present,' Ivan said, removing his arm from where it had been hiding behind his back. He held out a large red umbrella towards her and her forehead crumpled in confusion.

'It's to protect you from the rain,' Ivan explained softly. 'You could have done with this the other night, I suppose.'

Elizabeth's forehead cleared as the realisation set in. 'That's so thoughtful of you, thank you.' She hugged him. Her head shot up suddenly. 'But how did you know about the other night?'

Benjamin appeared at the gate with a bouquet of flowers and a bottle of wine.

'Happy birthday, Elizabeth.'

She spun round and her cheeks pinked. She hadn't seen him since that day in the building site when Ivan had andrewsplattered her alleged love for him in large red letters across the wall.

'Thank you,' she replied, making her way to him.

He held the gifts towards her and she struggled to find a way to take them with the umbrella in her hand. Benjamin spotted the umbrella and laughed. 'I don't think you'll need that today.'

'Oh, this?' Elizabeth reddened even more. 'This was a gift from Ivan.'

Benjamin raised his eyebrows. 'Really? You give him a hard time, don't you? I'm beginning to think there's something going on with you two.'

Elizabeth didn't allow her smile to waver. She wished. 'Actually, he's somewhere around here – maybe I can finally get to introduce the two of you properly.' She scanned the garden, wondering why it was Benjamin found her so funny all the time.

'Ivan?' I could hear Elizabeth calling my name.

'Yes,' I replied, not looking up from helping Luke put on his party hat.

'Ivan?' she called again.

'Ye-es,' I said impatiently, standing to my feet and looking at her. Her eyes passed over me and she continued scanning the garden.

My heart stopped beating; I swear I felt it stop.

I took deep breaths and tried not to panic. 'Elizabeth,' I called, my voice so shaky and distant I barely recognised myself.

She didn't turn round. 'I don't know where he's disappeared to. He was here just a minute ago.' She sounded angry. 'He was supposed to get the barbecue ready.'

Benjamin laughed again. 'How appropriate. Well, that's a subtle way of asking me but I can do it, no problem.'

Elizabeth looked at him in confusion, lost in thought. 'OK, great, thanks.' She continued looking around. I watched as Benjamin put the apron on over his head and Elizabeth explained everything to him. I watched from the outside, no longer a part of the picture. People began to arrive and I felt dizzy as the garden filled, as the volume went up, voices and laughter grew louder, the smell of food became stronger. I watched as Elizabeth tried to force Joe to taste some of her flavoured coffee as everyone else looked on and laughed; I watched Elizabeth and Benjamin's heads close together as they shared a secret and then laughed; I watched as Elizabeth's father stood at the end of the garden, black-thorn cane in one hand, cup and saucer in the other as he stared out wistfully to the rolling hills and waited for another of his daughters to return; I watched as Mrs Bracken and her lady friends stood by the dessert table, sneakily taking another slice of cake when they thought that no one was looking.

But I saw them. I saw it all.

I was like a visitor in an art museum, standing in front of a busy painting, trying to make sense of it, loving it so much and wanting to jump in and become a part of it. I was pushed further and further to the back of the garden. My head spun and my knees were weak.

I watched as Luke carried out Elizabeth's birthday cake, helped by Poppy, and led everyone in singing 'Happy Birthday to You' as Elizabeth's face pinked in surprise and embarrassment. I watched as she looked around for me and couldn't find me, as she closed her eyes, made a wish and blew out the candles like the little girl that never had her twelfth birthday party and who was living it all now. It brought back to me what Opal had said about me never having a birthday, never ageing while Elizabeth did and would this day, every year. The local crowd smiled and cheered as she blew out the candles, but for me they represented the passing of time, and as she extinguished those dancing flames, she extinguished a tiny bit of hope that was left inside me. They represented why we couldn't be together, and that stabbed my heart. The cheery mass celebrated while I commiserated and I couldn't help but be more aware than ever that with every minute that ticked by she was getting older. Me, I just felt it.

'Ivan!' Elizabeth grabbed me from behind. 'Where have you been for the past hour? I've been looking all over for you!'

I was so shocked she acknowledged me I could barely speak. 'I've been here all day,' I said weakly, savouring every second her brown eyes were locked onto mine.

'No you haven't. I've been by this way at least five times and you weren't here. Are you OK?' she looked worried. 'You're very pale.' She felt my forehead. 'Have you eaten?'

I shook my head.

'I've just heated some pizza; let me get you some, OK? What kind do you want?'

'One with olives, please. Olives are by far my favourite.'

She narrowed her eyes and studied me curiously, looking me up and down. Slowly she said, 'OK, I'll go get it but don't go disappearing on me again. There are some people I want to introduce you to, OK?'

I nodded.

Moments later she came rushing out with a huge slice of pizza. It smelled so good, my tummy screamed out with joy and I hadn't even thought I was hungry. I held my hands up to take the luscious slice from her, but her brown eyes darkened, her face hardened and she pulled the plate away. 'Damn it, Ivan, where have you gone now?' she muttered, searching the garden with her eyes.

My knees were so weak now I couldn't keep my body up any more; I just collapsed onto the grass, back up against the wall of the house, leaning my elbows on my knees.

I heard a little whisper in my ear, felt the warm breath and smelled sweets on Luke's breath. 'It's happening, isn't it?'

All I could do was nod.

This is the part where the fun stops. This part is, by far, not my favourite.

Chapter 39

Feeling every mile with every step, every stone and pebble beneath the sole of my foot, and every second that ticked by, I eventually arrived at the hospital, exhausted and totally drained. There was still one friend that needed me.

Olivia and Opal must have seen it in my face when I entered the room; they must have seen the dark colours emanating from my body, the way my shoulders were slumped, the way the entire weight of everything in the atmosphere had suddenly decided to balance itself on my shoulders. I knew from the look in their tired eyes that they knew. Of course they knew – it was all a part of our job. At least twice a year we all met special people who consumed our days and nights and all of our thoughts, and each time with each person, we had to go through the process of losing them. Opal liked to teach us that it wasn't us *losing* them; it was a matter of them moving on. But I couldn't see how I wasn't losing Elizabeth. Without having any control, any ability to make her hold on to me, to still see me, she was slipping through my fingers. What did I win? What did I gain? Every time I left a friend I was as lonely as the day before I met them, and in Elizabeth's case, lonelier, because I knew that I was missing out on the possibility of so much more. And here's the sixty-four-million-dollar question, what do our friends get out of it?

A happy ending?

Would I call Elizabeth's current situation a happy ending? Mothering a six-year-old boy she never wanted, worrying about a missing sister, a mother who had deserted her and a complex father? Wasn't her life the exact same as when I arrived?

But I guess this wasn't Elizabeth's ending. *Remember the detail*, Opal always tells me. I suppose what had changed in Elizabeth's life was her mind, the way she was thinking. All I had done was plant the seed of hope; she alone could help it to grow. And because she was starting to lose sight of me, perhaps that seed was being cultivated.

I sat in the corner of the hospital room watching Opal clinging to Geoffrey's hands as if she was hanging off the edge of the cliff. Perhaps she was. You could see in her face that she was willing for everything to be as it once was; I bet she would have done a deal with a devil right then and there if it would have brought him back. She would have gone to hell and back, she would have faced every single one of her fears just for him, right then.

The things we do to go back in time.

The things we don't do the first time round.

Opal's words were being spoken through Olivia's lips; Geoffrey could no longer speak. Tears were falling from Opal's eyes and landing on his lifeless hands, her bottom lip was trembling. She wasn't ready to let go. She had never let go of him and now it was too late, he was leaving before she had a chance.

She was losing him.

Life seemed dreary to me right then. As depressing as the cracked blue paint on the walls built to hold up a building intended to heal.

Geoffrey slowly raised a hand; you could tell he was mustering all his strength. The movement surprised everyone as he hadn't spoken in days, hadn't reacted to anything at all. No one was more surprised than Opal, who suddenly felt the touch of his hand across her face, as he wiped away her tears. Contact after twenty years. He could finally see her. Opal kissed his large hand and allowed it to cradle her small face and comfort her through her shock, relief and regret.

Geoffrey gave one last gasp, his chest rose one final time and fell, his hand dropping to the bed.

She had lost him and I wondered if Opal was still telling herself that he had merely moved on.

I decided then and there that I needed to have control of my final moment. I needed to say goodbye to Elizabeth properly, tell her the truth about me one final time so she wouldn't think I had run off and deserted her. I didn't want her to spend years being bitter about the man she once loved who broke her heart. No, that would have been too easy for her; that would have given her an excuse to never love again. And she wanted to love again. I didn't want her, like Geoffrey, to wait for ever for my return and finally die a lonely old woman.

Olivia nodded to me encouragingly as I stood up, kissed Opal on the top of her head from where she sat face down on the bed, still grasping his hand and wailing so loudly I knew it was the sound of her heart breaking. I didn't notice until I got out into the chilly air that tears were streaming down my face.

I began to run.

Elizabeth was dreaming. She was in an empty white room and she was dancing around, sprinkling and splashing colours of paint all around her. She was singing the song she hadn't been able to get out of her head for the past two months and she was so happy and free as she leaped around the room, watching the thick pulpous paint land on the walls with a splish-splosh.

'Elizabeth,' a voice was whispering.

She continued to swirl around the room. No one else was there.

'Elizabeth,' the voice whispered, and her body started to rock slightly as she danced.

'Mmm?' she responded happily.

'Wake up, Elizabeth. I need to talk to you,' came the sweet voice.

She opened her eyes slightly, spotted Ivan's worried handsome face beside her, rubbed her hand over his face and for a moment they stared deeply into each other's eyes. She revelled in the look he gave her, tried to return it but lost the battle with sleep and allowed her eyelids to flutter closed again. She was dreaming, she knew that, but she couldn't keep her eyes open.

'Can you hear me?'

'Mmm,' she responded, twirling and twirling and twirling.

'Elizabeth, I came to tell you that I have to go.'

'Why?' she murmured sleepily. 'You just got here. Sleep.'

'I can't. I'd love to but I can't. I've got to go. Remember I told you this would happen?'

She felt his warm breath on her neck, smelled his skin; fresh and sweet as though he had bathed in blueberries.

'Mmm,' she replied, 'Ekam Eveileb,' she stated, painting blueberries across the wall, reaching her hand to the paint and tasting it as though it was freshly squeezed.

'Something like that. You don't need me any more, Elizabeth,' he said softly. 'You're going to stop seeing me now. Someone else will need me.'

She ran a hand across his jawline, felt his soft stubble-free skin. She ran the length of the room, running her hand along the red paint. This tasted like strawberries. She looked down to the can of paint in her hand and spotted them – fresh strawberries piled high.

'I've figured something out, Elizabeth. I've figured out what my life is all about and it's not that different to yours.'

'Mmm,' she smiled.

'Life is made up of meetings and partings. People come into your life everyday, you say good morning, you say good evening, some stay for a few minutes, some stay for a few months, some a year, others a whole lifetime. No matter who it is, you meet and then you part. I'm so glad I met you, Elizabeth Egan; I'll thank my lucky stars for that. I think I wished for you all of my life,' he whispered. 'But now it's time for us to part.'

'Mmm,' she murmured sleepily. 'Don't go.' He was with her now in the room, they were chasing each other, splashing each other, teasing one another. She didn't want him to go; she was having so much fun.

'I have to go,' his voice cracked. 'Please understand.'

The tone of his voice made her stop running. She dropped the paint brush. It fell to the floor, leaving a red smudge on the brand-new white carpet. She looked up at him; his face was crumpled in sadness.

'I loved you the moment I saw you and I will always love you, Elizabeth.'

She felt him kiss her below her left ear, so soft and sensual she didn't want him to stop.

'I love you too,' she said sleepily.

But he did stop. She looked around the paint-splattered room and he was gone.

Her eyes flew open at the sound of her voice. Had she just said 'I love you?' She leaned up on one elbow and groggily looked around the bedroom.

But the room was empty. She was alone. The sun was rising over the tips of the mountains, night had ended and it was the start of a new day. She closed her eyes and continued dreaming.

Chapter 40

One week on from that morning and Elizabeth found herself moping around the house in her pyjamas, dragging her slipper-clad feet from room to room early on a Sunday morning. She stood at the doorway of each room, gazed inside and searched for . . . something, although she didn't quite know what for. None of these rooms offered her any solution and so she wandered on. Warming her hands on a mug of coffee, she stood still in the hallway, trying to decide what to do. She didn't usually move so slowly and her mind had never felt so clouded before, but she was a lot of things now that she never used to be.

It wasn't as though she didn't have things to do; the house was due its bi-weekly scrub from top to bottom and there was still the problem of the children's room in the hotel to be completed. Never mind completing it, it wasn't even started. Vincent and Benjamin had been on her back all week, she was losing even more sleep than usual because she had simply no idea what to do and, being the perfectionist, she couldn't begin it unless it was completely clear in her mind. To pass this on to Poppy would be a failure on her part. She was a talented professional woman, but this month she had felt like a schoolgirl again, ignoring her pencils and pens and avoiding her laptop so she didn't have to do her homework. She was looking for a distraction, a decent excuse to drag her away for once from the mindless block she found herself in.

She hadn't seen Ivan since her party last week; she hadn't received a phone call, a letter, nothing. It was as though he had disappeared off the face of the earth, and as well as being angry, she felt lonely. She missed him.

It was seven o'clock in the morning and the playroom was alive with the sounds of cartoons. Elizabeth made her way down the hall and popped her head into the room.

'Mind if I join you?' *I promise I won't say anything*, she felt like adding.

Luke look surprised but shook his head. He sat on the floor, straining his neck up to see the television. It looked uncomfortable but she chose silence instead of criticising him. She collapsed on the beanbag beside him and tucked her legs close to her body.

'What are you watching?'

'*SpongeBob Squarepants.*'

'*Sponge* what?' she laughed.

'*SpongeBob Squarepants,*' he repeated, not taking his eyes away from the television.

'What's it about?'

'A sponge called Bob who wears square pants,' he giggled.

'Any good?'

'Mm-hmm,' he nodded. 'Seen it before twice, though.' He spooned Rice Krispies into his mouth messily, spilling milk down his chin.

'Why are you watching it again? Why don't you go out into the fresh air and play with Sam? You've been inside all weekend.'

She was greeted with silence.

'Actually, where is Sam? Is he away?'

'We're not friends any more,' Luke said sadly.

'Why not?' she asked in surprise, sitting up and placing her coffee cup on the floor.

Luke shrugged.

'Did you have a fight?' Elizabeth asked gently.

Luke shook his head.

'Did he say something to make you sad?' she probed.

He shook his head again.

'Did you make him mad?'

Another shake of the head.

'Well, what happened?'

'Nothing,' Luke explained. 'He just told me one day he didn't want to be my friend any more.'

'Well, that's not very nice,' Elizabeth said gently. 'Do you want me to talk to him for you, see what's wrong?'

Luke shrugged. There was a silence between them as he continued staring at the screen, lost in thought.

'You know, I know what it's like to miss a friend, Luke. You know my friend Ivan?'

'He was my friend too.'

'Yes,' she smiled. 'Well, I miss him. I haven't seen him all week either.'

'Yeah, he's gone now. He told me so; he has to help someone else now.'

Elizabeth's eyes widened and anger welled inside her. He hadn't even the decency to say goodbye to her. 'When did he say goodbye to you? What did he say?' From the startled look on Luke's face she immediately stopped firing questions so aggressively. She needed to keep reminding herself that he was only six.

'He said goodbye to me the same day as he said goodbye to you.' His

voice went up a pitch as though she was crazy. His face crumpled up
and he looked at her as though she'd ten heads, and if she hadn't been
so confused she would have laughed at the sight of him.

But inside she wasn't laughing. She paused and thought for a moment
and then exploded. 'What! What are you talking about?'

'After the party in the garden, he came to the house and he told me
that his job with us was finished, that he was going to be invisible again
like he used to be but he would still be around and that meant that we
were OK.' He spoke chirpily turning his attention back to the television.

'Invisible,' Elizabeth said the word like it had a bad taste.

'Yep,' Luke chirped. 'Well, people don't call him imaginary for no
reason, doh!' He hit himself on the head and fell over onto the ground.

'What is he putting into your head?' she grumbled angrily, wondering
if she was wrong to introduce a person like Ivan into Luke's life. 'When
is he coming back?'

Luke lowered the volume on the TV and turned to her with that
crazy look on his face again. 'He's not. He told you that already.'

'He didn't . . .' Her voice failed her.

'He did, in your bedroom. I saw him go in; I heard him talking.'

Elizabeth cast her mind back to that night and to the dream she had,
the dream she had been thinking about all week, the dream that had
been *bothering* her and suddenly realised with a sinking feeling in her
heart that it hadn't been a dream at all.

She had lost him. In her dreams and in real life, she had lost Ivan.

Chapter 41

'Hello, Elizabeth.' Sam's mother opened her front door wider and welcomed her in.

'Hi, Fiona,' Elizabeth said, stepping in. Fiona had been taking Elizabeth's relationship with Ivan so well during the past few weeks. They hadn't discussed it directly but Fiona was being as polite as she always was. Elizabeth was thankful there was no awkwardness between them. Unfortunately, she was worried Sam hadn't taken it as well. 'I came round to have a chat with Sam, if that's OK. Luke is so upset without him.'

Fiona looked at her sadly. 'I know, I've been trying to talk to him all week about it. Maybe you can do a better job than me.'

'Has he told you what their falling-out is about?'

Fiona tried to hide a smile and nodded.

'Is it about Ivan?' Elizabeth asked, worried. She had always been anxious that Sam would be jealous of the amount of time Ivan was spending with her and Luke, and so she had invited him over to the house and included him in Ivan's activities as much as possible.

'Yes,' Fiona confirmed with a broad smile. 'Children can be funny at that age, can't they?' Elizabeth relaxed at finally learning Fiona hadn't a problem with the time she and Luke spent with Ivan, and was putting it down to Sam's behaviour.

'I'll let him tell you in his own words,' she continued, leading Elizabeth through her home.

Elizabeth had to fight the urge to look round to see if Ivan was there. As much as she was here to help Luke she was also trying to help herself. Finding and returning two best friends was better than one and she ached to be with Ivan so much.

Fiona pushed open the playroom door and Elizabeth entered. 'Sam, honey, Luke's mom is here to talk to you,' Fiona said gently, and for the first time, Elizabeth experienced a warm glow when she heard those words.

Sam paused the PlayStation and looked up at her with sad brown eyes. Elizabeth bit on her lip and fought the urge to smile. Fiona left them alone to talk.

'Hi, Sam,' she said gently. 'Mind if I sit down?'

He shook his head and she balanced herself on the edge of the couch.

'Luke tells me you don't want to be his friend any more, is that right?'

Unashamedly, he nodded his head.

'Do you want to tell me why?'

He took a moment to ponder that and then nodded. 'I don't like to play the same games as him.'

'Did you tell him this?'

He nodded.

'And what did he say?'

Sam looked confused and shrugged his shoulders. 'He is weird.'

A lump formed in Elizabeth's throat and she was immediately defensive. 'What do you mean, weird?'

'At first it was funny but then it just got boring and I didn't want to play any more but Luke wouldn't stop.'

'What game is that?'

'The games with his *invisible friend*.' He put on a bored voice and made a face.

Elizabeth's hands grew clammy. 'But his invisible friend was only around for a few days, and that was months ago, Sam.'

Sam gave her a funny look. 'But you played with him too.'

Elizabeth's eyes widened. 'Excuse me?'

'Ivan whatshisface,' he grumbled, 'boring old Ivan who just wants to spin on chairs all day, or have mud fights or play chasing. Every single day it was Ivan, Ivan, Ivan and,' his already squeaky voice raised a pitch, 'I couldn't even see him!'

'What?' Elizabeth was confused. 'You couldn't see him? What do you mean?'

Sam thought hard about how he could explain that. 'I mean, I couldn't see him,' he said simply, shrugging his shoulders.

'But you played with him all the time.' She ran her clammy fingers through her hair.

'Yeah, because Luke was, but I got sick of pretending and Luke wouldn't stop. He kept saying he was *real*.' He rolled his eyes.

Elizabeth placed her fingers on the bridge of her nose. 'I don't know what you mean, Sam. Ivan is your mum's friend, is he not?'

Sam's eyes widened. He had a startled expression. 'Eh, nope.'

'No?'

'No,' he confirmed.

'But Ivan minded you and Luke. He collected you and brought you home,' Elizabeth stammered.

Sam looked worried. 'I'm allowed to walk home by myself, Ms Egan.'

'But the, eh, the, em . . .' Elizabeth suddenly snapped to attention, remembering something. She clicked her fingers, making Sam jump. 'The water fight – what about the water fight in the back garden? It was you, me, Luke and Ivan, remember that?' she probed. 'Remember, Sam?'

His face paled. 'There was only three of us.'

'What?' she shouted louder than she meant to.

Sam's face crumpled up and he began to cry silently.

'Oh, no,' she panicked, 'please don't cry, Sam, I didn't mean to.' She held her hands out to him but he ran towards the door, shouting for his mother. 'Oh, I'm sorry, Sam. Please stop. Ssshhh,' she said quietly. 'Oh God,' she groaned, listening as Fiona hushed him.

Fiona entered the room.

'I'm sorry, Fiona,' Elizabeth apologised.

'It's OK.' Fiona looked a little worried. 'He's a bit sensitive about it.'

'I understand,' Elizabeth gulped. 'About Ivan,' she swallowed again and stood to her feet, 'you know him, don't you?'

Fiona's brow wrinkled. 'What do you mean by "know him"?'

Elizabeth's heart raced. 'I mean, he's been around here before?'

'Oh, yes,' Fiona smiled, 'he was here many times with Luke. We even had him over for dinner,' she winked.

Elizabeth relaxed but was unsure of how to interpret the wink. She placed her hand on her heart and it began to slow down. 'Phew, Fiona, thank God,' she laughed with relief. 'For a minute there, I thought *I* was going mad.'

'Oh, don't be silly,' Fiona placed a hand on her arm. 'We all do it, you know. When Sam was two years old, he went through the exact same thing. Rooster, he called his little friend,' she beamed. 'So, believe me, I know exactly what you're going through, opening car doors, cooking extra dinners and setting an extra place at the table. Don't worry, I understand. You were right to play along.'

Elizabeth's head was beginning to spin but Fiona's voice kept going on and on.

'When you think about it, it's *such* a waste of food really, isn't it? It just sits there through the entire meal completely untouched and, *believe* me, I know, I was keeping an eye on it. I'll have no spooky invisible men in this house, thank you very much!'

Moisture was rising to Elizabeth's throat. She grabbed the corner of the chair to steady herself.

'But like I said earlier, that's six-year-olds for you. I'm sure this so-called Ivan will disappear in time; they say they don't last for more than two months really. He should be gone soon, don't you worry.' She finally stopped talking but moved her face quizzically towards Elizabeth, 'Are you OK?'

'Air,' Elizabeth gasped. 'I just need to get some air.'

'Of course,' Fiona said hurriedly, leading her towards the front door. Elizabeth charged outside, taking in big gulps of air.

'Can I get you a glass of water?' Fiona asked worriedly, rubbing her back as Elizabeth leaned over facing the ground, with her hands resting on her knees.

'No, thanks,' she said quietly, standing up. 'I'll be OK.' She wandered unsteadily down the path without a goodbye, leaving Fiona staring after her nervously.

Once back in her own house, Elizabeth slammed the front door behind her and slid down to the floor with her head in her hands.

'Elizabeth, what's wrong?' Luke asked worriedly, still in his pyjamas and barefoot as he stood before her.

She couldn't answer. She could do nothing but go through the past few months over and over in her mind – all her special memories and moments with Ivan, all their conversations together. Who was there with them, who had seen them, spoken to him. They had been in crowded places, people had seen them together, Benjamin had seen them, and Joe had seen them. She kept on thinking back over everything, trying to remember moments when Ivan had conversations with all of these people. She couldn't be imagining all this. She was a sane, responsible woman.

Her face was pale as she finally looked up to face Luke.

'Ekam Eveileb,' was all she could say.

'Yep,' Luke giggled. 'It's backwards language. Cool, isn't it?'

It took Elizabeth seconds to work it out.

Make Believe.

Chapter 42

'Come *on*,' Elizabeth shouted, pounding on her horn, to the two coaches inching by each other slowly on the main street of Baile na gCroíthe. It was September and the last of the tourists were passing through the town. After this the busy place would return to its usual silence, like a banquet hall the morning after a party, leaving the locals to tidy up and remember the events and people that came through. The students would be heading back to college in the neighbouring counties and towns and the locals would once again be alone to struggle with their businesses.

Elizabeth held her hand down on her horn and blasted it at the coach before her. A sea of foreign faces turned around in the back of the bus to glare at her. Beside her, the locals spilled out of the church after attending morning Mass. Taking advantage of the glorious sunny day they gathered around in groups on the street, chatting and catching up on the week's events. They too turned to stare at the source of the angry beeping but Elizabeth didn't care. She was following no rules today; she was desperate to get to Joe's as she knew Joe at least could admit to seeing Ivan and her together, putting an end to this cruel and bizarre joke.

Too impatient to wait for the coaches to pass one other, leaving the car in traffic, she jumped out and ran across the road to the café.

'Joe!' she called, charging in through the door. She couldn't keep the panic out of her voice.

'Ah, there ye are, just the woman I was lookin' for.' Joe stepped out from the kitchen. 'I want to show ye my new fancy machine. It's—'

'I don't care,' she butted in, breathlessly, 'I've no time. Just please answer me this question. You remember me being in here with a man a few times, don't you?'

Joe looked up to the ceiling in thought, feeling important.

Elizabeth held her breath.

'Aye, I do.'

Elizabeth breathed a sigh of relief. 'Thank *God*,' she laughed, a little too hysterically.

'Now could you pay attention to me new device,' he said proudly. 'It's a brand-new coffee-makin' machine. Makes these espressos and cap'chinos and all.' He picked up an espresso cup. 'Sure that would only hold a drip. Brings a whole new meanin' to the phrase "hot drop".'

Elizabeth laughed, so happy about the news about Ivan and the coffee she could have jumped over the counter and kissed him.

'So where is this man?' Joe asked, trying to figure out how to make Elizabeth an espresso.

Elizabeth's smile faded. 'Oh, I don't know.'

'Gone back to America, is he? Sure, doesn't he live there in New York? The Big Apple, don't they call it? I've seen it on the telly and if you ask me it looks nothin' like an apple at all.'

Elizabeth's heart pounded in her chest. 'No, Joe, *not Benjamin*. You're thinking of Benjamin.'

'The fella you had drinks with in here a few times,' Joe confirmed.

'No,' Elizabeth's anger rose. 'Well, yes, I did. But I'm talking about the other man who was with me here. *Ivan* is his name. I-v-a-n,' she repeated slowly.

Joe made a face and shook his head. 'Don't know an Ivan.'

'Yes you do,' she said rather forcefully.

'Listen here,' Joe took off his reading glasses and put down the manual, 'I know just about everyone in this town and I don't know an Ivan nor have I ever heard of one.'

'But, Joe,' Elizabeth pleaded, 'please think back.' Then she remembered. 'The day we splashed coffee all around outside – that was Ivan.'

'Oh.' Joe understood now. 'Part of the German crowd, was he?'

'No!' Elizabeth shouted in frustration.

'Well, where's he from?' Joe asked, trying to calm her.

'I don't know,' she said angrily.

'Well, what's his surname then?'

Elizabeth swallowed hard. 'I-I-I don't know that either.'

'Sure then how can I help you at all if you don't know his surname or where he's from? It doesn't sound much like you know him either. As far as I remember you were dancin' around out there on your own like a mad woman. Don't know what got into you that day, at all.'

Elizabeth suddenly had an idea, grabbed her car keys from the counter and ran out the door.

'But what about your hot drop?' he called as she banged the door behind her.

'Benjamin,' Elizabeth called out, banging her car door shut and running across the gravel to him. He was standing among a group of builders hunched over documents, which were spread across a table. They all looked up at her.

'Can I talk to you for a minute?' She was breathless and her hair danced around her face from the strength of the wind at the top of the hill.

'Sure,' he said, stepping away from the silent group and leading her to a quieter area. 'Is everything OK?'

'Yes,' she nodded uncertainly, 'I just want to ask you a question, is that OK?'

He braced himself.

'You've met my friend Ivan, right?' She cracked her knuckles and shuffled from foot to foot, in anticipation of his answer.

He adjusted his hard hat, studied her face and waited for her to laugh or tell him she was joking but no smile hid behind those dark and worried eyes. 'Is this a joke?'

She shook her head and chewed nervously on the inside of her cheek, brow furrowed.

He cleared his throat. 'Elizabeth, I don't really know what you want me to say.'

'The truth,' she said quickly, 'I want you to tell me the truth. Well, I want you to tell me you've seen him, but I want that to be the truth, you see.' She swallowed.

Benjamin studied her face some more and eventually shook his head slowly.

'No?' she asked quietly.

He shook his head again.

Her eyes filled and she looked away quickly.

'Are you OK?' He reached out to touch her arm but she swayed her body away. 'I assumed you were joking about him,' Benjamin said gently, slightly confused.

'You didn't see him at the meeting with Vincent?'

He shook his head.

'At the barbecue last week?'

Another shake.

'Walking through the town with me? In the playroom that day when that, that . . . *thing* was written on the wall?' she asked hopefully, her voice full of emotion.

'No, I'm sorry,' Benjamin said kindly, trying to hide his confusion as best he could.

She looked away again, turned her back on him to face out towards the view. From this point she could see the sea, the mountains and the neat little village tucked away in the bosom of the hills.

Finally she spoke. 'He was so real, Benjamin.'

He didn't know what to say so he remained silent.

'You know when you can feel someone with you? And even though not everyone believes in that person, you know they're there?'

Benjamin thought about it and nodded understandingly even though she couldn't see him. 'My granddad died and we were close.' He kicked at the gravel self-consciously. 'My family never agreed on much – they never believed much in anything – but I knew he was there with me at times. You knew Ivan well?'

'He knew me better,' she laughed lightly.

Benjamin heard her sniff and she wiped her eyes.

'So was he a real person? Did he pass away?' Benjamin asked, feeling confused.

'I just believed so much . . .' she trailed off. 'He's really helped me over the past few months.' She looked around at the view for another moment in silence. 'I used to hate this town, Benjamin,' a tear rolled down her cheek. 'I used to hate every single blade of grass on every hill, but he taught me so much. He taught me that it's not the job of this town to make me feel happy. It's not Baile na gCroíthe's fault that I don't feel I fit in. It doesn't matter where you are in the world because it's about where you are up here,' she touched the side of her head lightly. 'It's about the other world I inhabit. The world of dreams, hope, imagination and memories. I'm happy up here,' she tapped her temple again and smiled, 'and because of that I'm happy up here too.' She held out her arms and displayed the countryside around her. She closed her eyes and allowed the wind to dry her tears. Her face was softer when she turned to Benjamin. 'I just thought it was important for you of all people to know that.' Quietly and slowly she headed back to her car.

Leaning against the old tower Benjamin watched her walk away. He hadn't known Elizabeth as well as he'd have liked but he had an idea she'd let him in her life more than she'd let others. Likewise, he had done the same. They'd had enough conversations for him to see how similar they really were. He'd seen her grow and change and now his unsettled friend had settled. He stared out to the view Elizabeth had been looking at for so long, and for the first time in the year he'd been here he opened his eyes and saw it.

In the early hours of the morning Elizabeth sat up in her bed, wide awake. She looked around the room – saw the time, 3.45 – and when she spoke aloud to herself, her voice was firm and confident.

'To hell with you all. I *do* believe.'

She threw off the covers and jumped out of bed, imagining the sound of Ivan howling with laughter in celebration.

Chapter 43

'Where's Elizabeth?' Vincent Taylor hissed angrily at Benjamin, out of earshot of the crowd that had gathered for the opening of the new hotel.

'She's still in the kids' room,' Benjamin sighed, feeling the cement of the building wall of pressure from the last week finally dry and lay heavy on his aching shoulders.

'*Still?*' Vincent shouted, and a few people turned round from paying attention to the speech being made at the top of the room. The local politician from Baile na gCroíthe had come to open the hotel officially, and a few speeches were being made beside the original tower in the hotel grounds that had stood at the top of the mountain for thousands of years. Soon the crowd would be trampling through the hotel, looking in each room to admire the work, and the two men still didn't know what Elizabeth was up to in the playroom. The last time either of them had seen it was four days ago and it had still been a blank canvas.

Elizabeth literally hadn't come out of that room for the past few days. Benjamin had brought her some drinks and food from a vending machine and she had hastily grabbed it from him at the door and slammed it shut again. He had no idea what the interior was like and his life had been hellish all week, trying to deal with a panicking Vincent. The novelty of Elizabeth speaking to an invisible person had long since worn off on Vincent. He had never had rooms being worked on during the very moment the building was being opened, it was a ridiculous and extremely unprofessional situation.

The speeches finally finished, there was polite clapping and the crowd filed inside where they inspected the new furniture, everyone inhaling the smell of fresh paint as they were led round.

Vincent swore loudly over and over again, receiving angry glances from parents. Room by room, they got closer to the playroom. Benjamin could barely take the suspense and paced the floor behind the crowd. He recognised Elizabeth's father, looking bored while leaning on his blackthorn cane, and her nephew with his nanny, among the crowd and he hoped to God she wouldn't let them all down. Judging by their last conversation on top of the hill, he believed she would come through for them. At least he hoped so. He was due to fly back to his home-town in Colorado next week and he couldn't take having to deal with any delays on site. For once, his personal life would come before his work.

'OK, boys and girls,' the guide spoke as if she were in an episode of *Barney*, 'this next room is especially for *you* so, moms and dads, you'll have to take a few steps back to allow them through because this is a very *special* room.'

There were oohs and aahs, excited giggles and whispers as the children let go of their parents' hands, some shyly, some daringly racing to the front. The guide turned the handle on the door. It didn't open.

'Jesus Christ,' Vincent muttered, placing his hand over his eyes, 'we're ruined.'

'Eh, just a minute, girls and boys.' The guide looked questioningly at Benjamin.

He just shrugged and shook his head hopelessly.

The guide tried the door again but to no avail.

'Maybe you should knock,' one child shouted out, and the parents laughed.

'You know what, that's a very good idea.' The guide played along, not knowing what else to do.

She knocked once on the door and suddenly it was pulled open from the other side. The children slowly shuffled forward.

There was complete silence and Benjamin covered his face in his hands. They were in big trouble.

Suddenly one child let out a 'Wow!' and one by one, the hushed and stunned children gradually began calling excitedly to one another: 'Look at that!', 'Look over there!'

The children looked around the room in awe. The parents followed them in and Vincent and Benjamin looked at each other in surprise as they heard similar whispers of approval. Poppy stood at the doorway, her eyes darting about, her mouth open wide in total shock.

'Let me see this,' Vincent said rudely, pushing his way through the crowd. Benjamin followed and what he saw inside took his breath away.

The walls of the large room were covered with enormous murals of splendid bursts of colour, each wall with a different scene. One wall in particular was a familiar sight to him: three people happily jumping in a field of long grass, their arms held upward, bright smiles on their face, their hair blowing in the wind as they reached up to catch –

'Jinny Joes!' Luke exploded with excitement, his eyes popping along with those of the other children in the room. They were mostly silent as they all stood alone, looking at the detail on each wall. 'Look, it's *Ivan* in the picture!' he shouted to Elizabeth.

Stunned, Benjamin looked at Elizabeth, who was standing in the corner in scruffy denim overalls, splattered in paint, with dark circles under her eyes. But despite her apparent tiredness, she was beaming, her face alight from the visitors' reaction to the room. The pride in her shining eyes was evident as everyone pointed to each painting.

'Elizabeth!' Edith whispered, her hands flying to her mouth in shock. '*You* did all this?' She looked at her employer with both confusion and pride.

Another scene was of a little girl in a field watching a pink balloon floating up to the sky; in another a crowd of children were having a water fight, splattering paint and dancing on the sand on a beach, a little girl sat in a green field having a picnic with a cow who wore a straw hat, a group of young boys and girls climbed trees and hung from its branches, and on the ceiling Elizabeth had painted it a deep blue with shooting stars, comets and distant planets. On the far wall she had painted a man and a boy with magnifying glasses held up to their eyes and black moustaches, leaning over and studying a set of black footprints that led from the wall, all the way across the floor and up the wall on the other side. She had created a new world, a wonderland of escapism, fun and adventure but it was the attention to detail, the looks of glee on the characters' faces, the happy smiles of pure childish enjoyment, that jumped out at Benjamin. Such a face he had seen on Elizabeth when he had caught her dancing in the field and traipsing through the village with seaweed in her hair. It was the face of someone who had let go and was truly happy.

Elizabeth looked down at the floor, to a toddler who was playing with one of the many toys scattered throughout the room. She was about to bend down to talk to the little girl when she noticed that the girl was speaking to herself. Carrying out a very serious conversation, in fact, she was introducing herself to mid-air.

Elizabeth looked around the room, breathed in deeply, and tried to smell that familiar Ivan smell. 'Thank you,' she whispered, closing her eyes and imagining him with her.

The little girl continued babbling away all by herself, looking to her right as she spoke and listening before speaking again. And then she began to hum, that familiar song that Elizabeth hadn't been able to get out of her head.

Elizabeth threw her head back and laughed.

*   *   *

I stood at the back wall of the playroom in the new hotel with tears in my eyes and a lump so huge in my throat I didn't think I'd ever be able to speak again. I couldn't stop looking around at the walls, at the photo album of all I had done with Elizabeth and Luke over the past few months. It was as though someone had sat in the distance and painted a perfect vision of us.

Looking at the walls, at the colour and at the eyes of the characters, I knew that she had realised and I knew that I would be remembered. Beside me, standing in a line at the back of the room, my friends joined me for moral support on this special day.

Opal placed a hand on my arm and gave me an encouraging squeeze.

'I'm very proud of you, Ivan,' she whispered, and planted a kiss on my cheek, no doubt leaving a purple lipstick stain on my skin. 'We're all here for you, you know. We will always have each other.'

'Thank you, Opal. I know that,' I said, feeling very emotional and looking to Calendula, who was on my right, Olivia, who was beside her, Tommy, who was looking around the walls in fascination, Jamie-Lynn, who had bent down to play with a toddler on the ground and Bobby, who pointed and giggled at each of the scenes before him. They all gave me the thumbs-up and I knew that I would never be truly alone as I was in the company of real friends.

Imaginary friend, invisible friend – call us what you like. Maybe you believe in us, maybe you don't. The point is, it's not important. Like most people who do truly great work, we don't exist to be talked about and praised; we exist only to serve the needs of those who need us. Maybe we don't exist at all; maybe we're just a figment of people's imaginations; maybe it's just pure coincidence that children of two, who can barely speak, all decide to start making friends with people only adults can't see. Maybe all those doctors and psychotherapists are right to suggest that they are merely developing their imagination.

Or humour me for a second. Is there possibly another explanation that you haven't thought about for the entirety of my story?

The possibility that we do exist. That we're here to help and assist those who need us, who believe in believing and who can therefore see us.

I always look on the positive side of things. I always say that with every cloud there's a silver lining but, the truth be told – and I'm a firm believer of the truth – for a while I was struggling with my experience with Elizabeth. I couldn't figure out what I had won, all I could see was that my losing her was one big black stormy cloud. But then I realised that, as every day went by and I thought about her every second and smiled, I knew that meeting her, knowing her and above all loving her, was the biggest silver lining of all.

She was better than pizza, better than olives, better than Fridays and better than spinning and even these days when she is no longer with us – and I'm not supposed to say this – of all my friends, Elizabeth Egan was *by far* my favourite.

Keep up to date with Cecelia!

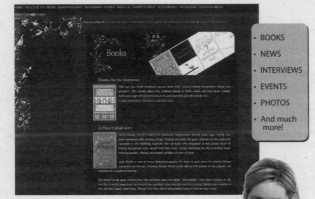

- BOOKS
- NEWS
- INTERVIEWS
- EVENTS
- PHOTOS
- And much more!

Log on to www.cecelia-ahern.com
for the latest Cecelia news,
photographs and interviews.

You'll also find details on all Cecelia's
books and short stories, as well as the
film adaptation of *PS I Love You*, and
information on *Samantha Who?*, a hit
US comedy co-created by Cecelia.

There are details of forthcoming events,
plus links to other Cecelia websites.

And why not sign up for the exclusive
HarperCollins Cecelia Ahern
newsletter while you're there?